no one you know

no one you know

a novel

Emma Tourtelot

SHE WRITES PRESS

Published in 2026 by
She Writes Press, an imprint of The Stable Book Group

32 Court Street, Suite 2109
Brooklyn, NY 11201
https://shewritespress.com

Library of Congress Control Number: 2025915421
Print ISBN: 979-8-89636-048-3
eISBN: 979-8-89636-049-0

Interior designer: Katherine Lloyd, The DESK

Printed in the United States

For Muz

Life is short,
though I keep this from my children.
—Maggie Smith

prologue

I pull onto the Taconic State Parkway, past the poorly situated WRONG WAY sign that I know is meant for drivers coming from the opposite direction, but that stops my heart every time nonetheless. This is how it begins, I think. This is what it looks like when a mother loses her teen daughter. Not the way you lose a toddler, in a supermarket or at the county fair or some other place where an intercom announcement brings her back to you, the damage no more than a stranger's disapproving glance—and, seriously, fuck them for that, like they never misplaced an inquisitive child?—but lost in the world.

I hate this road. The undivided parkway curves like a speedway, and I feel my car drift out of its too-narrow lane, guided by centrifugal force and a retaining wall so close I could run my fingers along it. The Taconic is famously "scenic," which means an abundance of trees and shrubbery—hickory, oak, ash, mountain laurel, even rhododendron—for state troopers and deer to hide behind. The frequent yellow and black DEER CROSSING signs along the route once suggested to me a sight either majestic or sweet: a buck leaping after a doe in mating season; a family of deer in single file, Bambi in the rear. *Crepuscular*, I remember Ethan telling me when we first moved upstate. The word for animals that are active at dawn and dusk. It seemed so magical back then, a creature that favored twilight, but this was before I learned how deer could emerge from the woods without warning, and how, when this happens, I shouldn't swerve, because I might hit humans instead.

I am supposed to drive straight into the deer, the country living experts say, as if this were a completely reasonable suggestion.

It is near dusk now, prime deer time, and I am flying down the left lane, a steady eighty-two—twenty miles faster than the country living experts recommend. They don't know everything, though. They don't know where my daughter is.

I can't travel this route without remembering the mother who drove her minivan the wrong way on the Taconic for two miles before crashing head-on into an SUV. She killed her two-year-old daughter and her three nieces, and everyone in the other car, too—a news story that was surprising only to people who had never driven the Taconic before.

Indie was two when it happened. The woman was going eighty-five, I remember, and that, more than anything—more than the broken Absolut bottle on the driver's side or the lack of car seats in the back of the minivan—convinced me she was at fault. Eighty-five on the Taconic in *any* direction, I could tell you how that story ends. A bad mother, everyone said, although this seemed a bit of a leap to me, all those hours and days measured against two wrong miles.

When I drove along Main Street on my way out of town today, businesses were already hanging flyers: Indie's eighth-grade yearbook photo and the plea, HAVE YOU SEEN THIS GIRL? I press the gas pedal, nudge the car to eighty-five. I tell myself I am closing the distance between us.

chapter one Indie

Six months earlier

Maddy and I officially met in second grade, the first time we had the same classroom teacher.

"India's a country," she said, wrinkling her nose. "On the map."

"It can be a person, too," I said.

"Okay," Maddy said. "Can I call you Indie?"

And that was that. We traded snack items and compared blisters from the monkey bars. We agreed on everything. When the new boy shared during Morning Meeting that he was seven and a half but had a "Lego age" of sixteen, I knew exactly what Maddy was thinking. "You're not supposed to say things like that," she whispered to me. I put a hand over my mouth and whispered back, "It's called bragging." Best friends, we said, until we die or get married, because both felt like endings, and we didn't know any grown-ups who had a BFF. *Indivisible*, I thought, each morning that I recited the Pledge of Allegiance.

When we started middle school, I stopped saying the Pledge and took a knee instead, and so Maddy did too, although she didn't want her name on the editorial I wrote about this for the school newspaper. I'd offered her a joint byline the same way I used to share my snack every morning. She said my parents would get it, and she was right: Dad's a high school social studies teacher who hasn't said the Pledge in years, and he turned our Sunday brunch that weekend into a First Amendment workshop. Mom, meanwhile, asked if she could share my article with the fifty thousand strangers who subscribe to her online thing, *If You Lived Here.* (No thanks.) It was like they were trying to one-up each other with their support, actually, because that's my parents' style: competitive meets petty. *Com-petty-tive*, Maddy would have said. She loved word mashups.

Maddy knew her own parents would be "disappointed" in her—a consequence that doesn't seem like a big deal when you're a kid, but then one day they say it and you think, *roasted*. She also suspected they'd make her explain the protest to her grandfather (Navy), uncle (Marines), and cousin (Army). I think she didn't want to break her patriot dad's heart over *my* pet cause—that she was waiting for something she truly believed in. Who knows what that something would have been? There is too much about Maddy I'll never know.

chapter two Kate

We give names to assign permanence, to trick ourselves into thinking we can't lose something if it's properly labeled. Think of the millions of sparrows and trillions of ants that die each year without a name. We want to believe *our* time on this planet means a little more.

What surprises me is how many of us—most of us, in fact—agree to name and love something we know we can't keep. Every day we get up and we brush our teeth and toast a bagel and check our email as if we're okay with this. There are so many conceivable ways to lose a child. How are parents not in a permanent state of panic? How are we not making daily sacrifices to the gods, whether or not we believe in them?

It's a bargain we strike without even realizing we're doing it: *I will love this child, but don't let me outlive her.* As with the rising seas that will destroy cities (but only after we're gone), we go on with our days because we won't be around for the unimaginable. We understand our child will die in the same way we understand the sun will one day extinguish the Earth.

When Ethan and I first moved to the Hudson Valley, we bought a small wooden coop and six baby chicks from MyPetChicken.com. All Buff Orpingtons, because the website advertised the breed as cold-hardy, friendly, and "wonderful mothers"—a golden retriever in chicken form. We raised the chicks under a heat lamp in the laundry room and, like true cid-iots, we named every bird: Pio Pio, Goldie, Madonna, Big Bird,

Dixie, Nugget. As the years went on, we lost enough chickens—to raccoons, hawks, foxes, neighborhood dogs, cold weather, hot weather—that we stopped naming them. We stopped raising them from chicks, too, and instead bought teenage pullet chickens, ready to lay, from a local farm. "Chickens are the potato chip of the animal kingdom," one of Ethan's teacher friends told him. "Everyone loves them, and they can't eat just one."

Still, though, we humans agonize over our children's names, as if we have any say in how they will turn out. In the nature vs. nurture debate, a baby name is an opening salvo. *This is who you are*, it says, with a confidence that is both touching and a little psycho. The daughter we name must wait until she is eighteen to mark her body with a tattoo, but we are encouraged to label her ourselves before she's even born. Once she is a person in the world, it's actually against the law *not* to name her.

My father has been a widower for almost a year now, and he has spent most of that time in his tool shed, a place he obsessively organizes, categorizes, and labels. His tools hang on an annotated pegboard, and every variety of screw or washer has its own labeled jar, including my favorite jar of all, the one labeled *bits of wire too small to use*. I was charmed by the whimsy of this the first time I saw the jar, although my father does not mean to be charming. His shed, his rules: Everything gets a label, and everything has a place. He can find anything he wants, and he loses nothing he needs. He doesn't even lose the things he has no use for.

And perhaps this is why we agonize over baby names: Like the bits of wire too small to use, we name the child to give her a place in the world, because we think we know where she belongs. Because we want to keep her from becoming lost.

When I first suggested our daughter's name, Ethan was unsure. He said, "Aren't we limiting her prospects? What if she wants to go into finance?" If only it were so easy to ensure she would never desire a job on Wall Street. Also, what should you name your daughter if you were *hoping* for her to thrive in the world of big money?

As it turns out, her name isn't even that unusual. How is it that a name you are *sure* you came up with—you can so clearly remember the day you turned to your husband at brunch and suggested it—ends up on a Hipster Baby Name list right after your child is born? What strange osmosis causes couples in progressive cities across the country to simultaneously imagine they are rediscovering names like Holden and Finn?

I read somewhere that a liberal mother is fifty percent more likely than a conservative mother to give her daughter an uncommon name. And yet a name is an aspiration, no matter where you fall on the political spectrum—even if the aspiration is for your child to fit in. To not be the "weird" one.

My daughter befriended Maddy in second grade, except back then she referred to her as *Maddy W.* The first time I met her, I thought, this is not a name to anger the gods. This is not the kind of name you give a child to mark her as special. So foolish, I see now, to believe it is possible to trick the gods into thinking: *Nothing to see here.* The gods—or fate, or cancer, or school shooters, or riptides, or drunk drivers—could care less what we mere mortals name our children. We can mark them as special, or we can give them a name that fits right in, but either way, we may lose them.

chapter three ⸙ Indie

"Which Maddy?" Mom said when I first told her about my new best friend. "There are so many in your grade."

"You are such a snob," Dad said amiably.

"Shut up," Mom said, laughing. "I like the name Maddy. It's refreshing when people don't try so hard to be different. Plus, it reminds me of my childhood, all those Tiffanys and Tinas. What did Zach and Lizzy call their second kid again?"

"Keats," Dad said.

"Keats!" Mom repeated, like she'd just served an ace. Then she started typing something into her phone, which usually means that whatever she just said will end up on *If You Lived Here*. Her "platform," she calls it. Her "creative outlet," Dad says, like she's an Instant Pot that needs venting.

This is why the conversation stuck in my head: I hadn't known a person's name was something you should have opinions about.

My parents have never been to India, although everyone assumes they have because of my name, and also because Mom does a lot of yoga. But I wasn't named for the country, I was named after a character in a novel, *Mrs. Bridge*. Mom was sitting on a barstool reading this book, the story goes, when Dad showed up five minutes early for their blind date. After Mom got woke, she used to tell this story *all the time*, because god forbid anyone think the name India was some kind of cultural appropriation.

I once asked Maddy how her parents met.

"How they *met*?" she said, as if I'd used the wrong word.

"Like, when did they start dating?"

"Oh," she said. "Prom, I think."

Her parents don't have a meet-cute story, and when I was in elementary school, I found this disappointing. I also thought it might explain why my parents held hands and shared in-jokes, and why my dad said things like, "Look at your beautiful mother." I rolled my eyes when they were like this, hamming it up like a kid actor on the Disney Channel, but secretly I thought they made a pretty cute couple: My mom the introverted writer-slash-realtor, and my dad the self-professed resident cool guy at the local high school. (No joke, Dad has a tattoo of Benjamin Franklin's "Join, or Die" snake on his forearm, which he uses as a lesson hook when he teaches the Revolutionary War.)

Maddy's mom and dad, meanwhile, seemed to parent in shifts, tagging in and out like professional wrestlers. Later, I realized they did this because they have two jobs each, on top of their volunteer work at the firehouse. And they don't have a meet-cute story because people who are from this town never really *meet*. Instead they grow up together and gradually develop an awareness of each other. It would be like me marrying Wyatt or Noah from preschool: We met at the button-sorting table, or maybe it was the sensory bin. Maddy's parents didn't need to bond over some ancient novel that's so highbrow it can't be bothered with a plot.

Halfway through my parents' blind date, Dad suggested they walk to the Strand Bookstore on Broadway, where he bought a used paperback copy of *Mrs. Bridge*. He finished it before their second date, the following evening. "Love at first sight isn't real," Mom likes to say, whenever she has a chance to tell the story. "But at the end of that date, I did know that as far ahead as I could see, as far ahead as I could *imagine*, he was right there beside me."

I'm sure she means this to sound both romantic and rational, like a recipe for modern love. I'm even more sure she posted something about it online, which probably made other people feel bad about their own relationships. But I've started to notice things lately. The way Mom rolls her eyes when she thinks Dad isn't looking. The way Dad picks up his phone when Mom is in the middle of a sentence. The way Dad talks about something he read online and Mom pretends to listen, when really she's just waiting for her turn to speak. *This* version of modern love looks more like two customer service chatbots stuck in an infinite conversation loop, spitting out canned responses and calling it a relationship.

And so now, when I think about Mom telling me how far she could see, I picture a winding road that goes all the way to the horizon, and my parents, marching stiff as Lego people, not equipped to make a turn.

chapter four ❦ Kate

I pull into the circular driveway in front of a Georgian brick manor and make a mental note to point out the mature boxwoods at the property's edge. My clients park behind me, and I can see Oona, their adorable three-year-old daughter, gesticulating wildly in the back seat. (A pretty impressive feat, given that her dad buckled the car seat like he was prepping her for shock therapy.) They've seen four properties already today, plus five yesterday, and I guarantee they won't be able to distinguish among them when they get back to the city tonight. The wife will ask whether the chandelier she liked was in the renovated barn or the parsonage in need of renovation, and the husband will not recall whether the babbling brook belonged to the modern farmhouse or the recently modernized eyebrow colonial. Oona, meanwhile, like Goldilocks in a fairy tale of her own imagining, will be able to tell them precisely which house had the couch that was too squishy, and which one felt just right.

Hi Bean, I text Indie. I haven't called her this in years, but today is the first time I've been apart from her since Maddy died. Seven long nights I've slept in her bed and held her while she cried. *I'll be home soon.*

Ethan returns to work tomorrow, and it was his idea for me to start back this weekend. He said Indie needs to see us both doing things that are familiar to her, that this will help her find a way back to her own life. Of all the familiar things, this is the one he settled on: Weekends when I have to work and he and Indie stay home.

Oona gets out of the car and shuffles her feet in the gravel driveway like it's a pile of fall leaves.

"This one is safe!" Oona announces, tilting her head back dramatically. She grabs a handful of Goldfish crackers from the bag she's holding and pops them in her mouth without taking her eyes off the house.

"This whole town is safe," Oona's mother replies. She's done her research.

"*No*," Oona says, frustrated. "Watch." She puffs her cheeks and blows toward the brick house, orange crumbs flying through the air. "Huff and puff and can't blow it down! It's made of bricks!"

When Indie was Oona's age, she dropped wisdom like Yoda. She had no idea she was doing this, it was just the way she saw the world. I guess all kids do this, but, being human, I found my own daughter's truisms to be particularly endearing. I started posting her quotes online, because at the time it seemed I might never have an original thought again. It wasn't writing, exactly, but it was something. If this was to be my new normal, at least I could take some kind of Darwinian pride in my daughter's brain. At least I could get some followers out of it, my family would say, although that wasn't always the plan. *If You Lived Here* began simply as a way to bookmark a moment in time. It was me stating something—our life—for the record. I liked watching my subscriber count go up, of course I did. But this was mostly because the readers made me feel less alone, and even more so after Indie's quotes became a kind of writing prompt, helping me find my own voice. Still, the audience grew, and the only explanation I can come up with is this: I made *them* feel less alone. Ethan and Indie tell me it's probably just bots in China subscribing and commenting, but they don't actually read *If You Lived Here*. Algorithms can't fake human connection.

I watch my client smooth her daughter's bangs in a gesture I recognize on a primal level: The way I used to soothe Indie and tidy her hair, the way the two actions were indistinguishable.

"Mommy," Indie said to me when she was four, "where was I before I was born?" The question didn't scare her; she was genuinely curious. While I tried to think how to describe this terrifying blankness—to my daughter, and also to my readers—Indie raised a finger in the air to show me she had another thought. A character in one of her picture books did this, and she'd adopted the gesture immediately. "I was extinct!" Indie exclaimed. "Like the dinosaurs!" I nodded and smiled, as if I were perfectly okay discussing the extinction of my only child. "But when will I be *little* again?" Indie asked, her bottom lip now quivering, and I hugged her tight. "You'll always be little to me," I said, which was a lie. Her mind was wide open right then, big enough to encompass the entire universe and the history of time.

I punch the code into the lockbox and let the clients walk in ahead of me, so they'll know: *It's already yours*. They think they're looking for square footage, acreage, ceiling height, but what they're really seeking is a feeling. It's surprisingly touching, when I get to witness this moment, because so often it takes them by surprise. Suddenly their eyes are shiny because they see not just a house but a home, and after that, it doesn't matter if the master bathroom has a purple tub or the kitchen has a stenciled wall border or the back porch is sagging with termite rot—they're in.

"This room would be great with pocket doors," I tell the young couple, as I guide them through the final property of the weekend. I am helping them conjure a home. "Isn't this the coziest breakfast nook?"

"How high are the ceilings in here?"

They ask this at the same time and then laugh at themselves, pretending to be embarrassed by how cute they are.

My colleague Sara is convinced my slight "chilliness" in person—she means my tendency to stick to small talk, and not too much of that—makes clients want to please me by buying something expensive. "It's the ultimate subscriber upgrade," she joked once. "They think if they buy a house, you'll be their friend." Sara is a city expat, too, although ten years ahead of me. "You're like those waitresses in the East Village," she said. "7A, remember that place? The more flat affect a waitress was, the more I tipped her. The more I wanted her to like me." I think Sara is wrong, though. I just know when to shut up, because it is in the pauses that clients start telling themselves stories about their new life.

The woman slips her hand into her husband's and whispers something in his ear. *Pocket doors*, I'm guessing. There are no pocket doors in this house, not yet, but they won't remember this later.

I feel a sudden, ugly urge to tell this couple the truth: Picture breakfast in this cozy nook every morning for the next fifty years, sixty if you're "lucky." Watch your partner's face grow slack with age and disinterest. See him scroll through his phone at breakfast. Check his scalp for ticks, check his hairy back, too, and remember how you used to joke that this was what passed for foreplay in the Hudson Valley. Ask him if he called the electrician yet, just to see how much he resents you for the reminder, even though he'll never do it unless you prompt him, and if he would just do something when you asked, you wouldn't have to nag him in the first place. Notice how it's only called "nagging" when *you* say it.

How do you like your cozy breakfast nook now?

Parenthood is the opposite, although I don't think Oona's parents see this yet—how a child becomes less known to you with each passing year. The more familiar Ethan and I become to each other, the more my daughter is a stranger to me, and the easier it is to find wonder in her face.

I mean, of course I loved Indie from the beginning. That's the rule. Love is the word you use when all the other things you're feeling are too frightening to say out loud. But when Indie was a newborn, she rarely left my chest. She nursed there and she slept there, and because of this, I experienced her more as bodily weight than a face to gaze upon. When I looked down, I would see her pulsing fontanelle, and what love felt like back then was a need, both pressing and vague, to protect that soft spot in her skull. (Protect it from what, I think now. Was the sky falling in heavy chunks?) She was such an extension of my own body that love felt a lot like narcissism.

After I stopped nursing, though, I could *see* my daughter. Propped up in a turquoise foam Bumbo chair on our kitchen island, she had four limbs and a pudgy nose. Her feet were soft and rounded, like tiny dinner loaves. I'd gotten so used to the top of her head that this physicality surprised me—she had become a person, distinct from me. Her first week in the Bumbo, I actually introduced myself: "Hi Bean, I'm Mommy." That's the moment when I felt like I'd be able to lift a car off her body to save her, and yes, I realize this is an urban legend, but what matters is that I felt it to be true.

Later still, each time Indie used her words to tell me what she needed, to tell me she wanted someone other than me, to ask for "alone time," to find fault with my politics or make fun of my clothes or beg me not to sing along with the radio, I loved her a little more. *This*, I thought. *This is what it feels like to be a mother.*

"Mommy!" Oona calls out. "What shape is this room?"

Oona is standing in a hexagonal sunroom that looks out onto the Hudson River. I follow her into the room and crack a window, because I know a lilac bush is planted right outside and I want the scent to fill this space. I love showing houses in late spring. I crouch down next to Oona, her brown eyes serious beneath her Amélie bangs.

"Count the walls," I tell her. "How many can you count?"

Her parents enter the room and I catch it, the moment.

"The light in here," the woman says dreamily. "It's—"

"ELEVEN!" Oona yells, holding up seven fingers. "I counted!"

"Let's try again," I say softly, holding out my hands. "Why don't you count on my fingers?"

Oona squeezes each of my fingertips, gazing at me like I'm a fairy godmother.

"You look pretty," she says, fingering the silky fabric of my blouse.

"I like the flowers on your skirt," I say. Mini Boden, of course. "Do you like to read?" I add, instinctively correcting myself. *Ask her more*, that was the hashtag.

Oona's mom smiles vaguely in our direction. She doesn't see me, she sees her future. She sees her best self, drinking a latte in this sunroom and sharing the *Times* with her husband. She sees their children—because of course there will be more, she doesn't see miscarriages or secondary infertility—and these children are miraculously occupied with BPA-free, battery-free toys. The wooden kind that make a pleasant clunking sound to let you know the kids are still playing in the next room, that they haven't accidentally twisted a pull cord around their necks.

"Sometimes," Oona says, leaning forward and whispering right into my ear, "when I'm wearing really pretty clothes, I feel like I'm magic."

I assume some women see their children as distinct people the moment they give birth, and maybe these women experience that car-heaving love from day one. Did Laura see her newborn daughter Maddy this way? I've always imagined that she did. She doesn't seem like someone who ever questioned her maternal instinct, who got hung up on what love is supposed to *feel* like. Perhaps she loved Maddy from the first kick in the womb.

At a college reunion a few years back, my old roommate told me how she picked out two baby names as soon as her pregnancy test was positive: one for a boy, one for a girl. Later, as she held her newborn daughter for the first time, she turned to her husband and said, "She's *so* not a Ruby. Let's call her Olivia." Really, though? Our daughter was purple and cone-headed and hungry and *mad*. She didn't look like a Ruby or an Olivia or an Edie or a Harper, she looked like need. Also kind of like Newt Gingrich, once her cone head became round again.

"This is the one!" Oona's dad says to me, his arm around his wife's shoulders. "We'd like to make an offer today." They glance at each other briefly and then back at me, like newlyweds on a honeymoon cruise still enamored with the pronoun *we*. "We're thinking cash offer, three percent above asking?"

I remember the day Ethan and I fell in love with our house. The realtor was rambling on about the best farm shares in the area—she liked the CSA with fresh flowers, but there was a different one with fresh yogurt and milk, and she wished there were one that offered both—when I grabbed Ethan by the arm and steered him into the pantry. On the wall behind him, penciled lines recorded the heights and ages of the kids who used to live there, and the shelves were dotted with Pokemon stickers that someone had made a half-hearted effort to remove. I looked at my husband, wondering if he could read my mind. Tears filled my eyes, and I swiped them away, embarrassed at the sudden emotion. Ethan grinned and pulled me in for a hug. "I think we just found our new home," he said. "Either that or you're *really* invested in our realtor's farm share dilemma."

"Six!" Oona shouts triumphantly, spinning in a circle. "Six walls!"

"It's called a hexagon," I tell her. "You get to live in a house with a hexagonal room!"

"And no wolves!" Oona stretches her fingers to the ceiling like a ballerina and spins until she stumbles, dizzy. Her parents laugh and scoop her up and I click my phone on to put the process in motion.

"Is that your daughter?" Oona's mother asks me, catching sight of my phone's lock screen. "She's so cute."

It's a photo of Indie at four, dressed in head-to-toe rainbow stripes, arms spread triumphantly at the top of Burger Hill. She had not yet learned to hold up her hand like a tiny stop sign whenever I pointed my phone in her direction.

"That was ten years ago," I say, and the way the woman smiles, I can tell she pities me. I remember when Indie was Oona's age, how kids even a year older seemed ungainly and lacking in charm. I once found an abandoned Minecraft hoodie at the playground and it was just so *big*, compared to the adorably tiny socks and shirts I pulled out of the dryer each week. "Indie's a great babysitter," I offer up now, as if this redeemed her hulking presence in the world, and the woman nods as if this were true, because: *A babysitter!* I am just the realtor today, and as far as the clients are concerned, my daughter is just a babysitter; she exists only in relation to them.

I don't tell this woman about Indie's Grecian nose or olive skin, I don't tell her that Indie is taller than me and sharply funny, that she can play Liszt piano sonatas but prefers to come up with her own Radiohead arrangements, that she reads Virginia Woolf and Joan Didion but not Hemingway or Fitzgerald or Salinger. These things are all true, but they feel like fiction today, when Indie's cheeks are pale and her voice is ragged from crying and she hasn't left her room in the seven days and nights since her best friend died. Even if I had the words to talk about Indie, Oona's parents wouldn't want to hear how this town lost a child, how even a brick house is not enough to protect your daughter from the world. They still believe this is the kind of place where a child never gets lost because she's already home. And who could blame them? I created an entire brand out of the illusion.

IF YOU LIVED HERE—SOLD! 5BR/4.5BA BEAUTIFULLY RENOVATED 1920s GEORGIAN MANOR

Sometimes all it takes to sell a house is a funny-shaped room. (An Insta-ready hexagonal sunroom, in the case of today's listing.) I mean, on top of the river views, eleven-foot ceilings, and state-of-the-art kitchen, of course. Shopping for a new home is kind of like online dating in this way: We have all these criteria in mind as we browse profiles—a person's height or hairline, their career stability and value system, whether or not they want children—and while some of these things are important, ultimately what we fall for is the quirky detail. Call it the hexagonal sunroom of the soul. For me, it was my future husband's narration of a pigeon's inner monologue as it crossed the sidewalk in front of us. Don't ask me to explain why it was funny—I just knew in that moment that he would crack me up for the rest of our life together.

I googled *hexagon room why* on my phone while my clients toured the house today, and it turns out nature can't get enough of the shape: honeycombs, snowflakes, crystals, plant cells, turtle shells, the compound eye of an insect. Also sound engineers (for the acoustics), architects who have something against right angles, and witchy women who think the hexagon represents wisdom, spirituality, and celestial power. "Apparently the hexagon has good feng shui," I told my clients, although I didn't tell them I'd learned this fact on a website that sells bed linens. And that's how the sausage is made, folks.

Speaking of sausage-making: A new reader (hi Jen!) recently commented that the way I open posts with real estate listings makes me seem "smug and elitist." So, you know, *ouch*, and also, let me explain myself. The listings certainly lack the guileless charm of my toddler daughter's pearls of wisdom, which I used to post instead, but guess what? Toddler daughters grow into laconic teens. I know, I know, my heart is breaking, too. (Side note: No one prepared me for the feeling of having my entire range of facial expressions critiqued by a person I once applauded for pooping on the potty.)

Listen, I'm not a #girlboss or anything. Truthfully? I began the practice as a kind of mantra. It wouldn't be an exaggeration to say that my entire career in real estate has been a form of atonement. I know this sounds grandiose (possibly even "smug and elitist"), but hear me out.

I'd been living upstate for maybe a week when I first felt the urge to raise the drawbridge. "Shhh," I said to my husband. "Now that we're here, let's not tell *anyone* about this magical place." Our new hometown was perfect, I thought, and I didn't want it overrun by "newcomers." Ditto the weekenders, the leaf-peepers, the pushy new parents from Park Slope. This feeling only intensified as my daughter grew out of her stroller, as she graduated from kindergarten, and then aged out of bedtime stories. Who *were* all these assholes bulldozing their high-end strollers down Main Street like they belonged here? Well, they were us, of course: Couples who wanted to grow vegetables in raised beds, despite being unclear what a raised bed actually was. Families who were sick of living in apartments more cramped than a Spirit Airlines flight. And every single one of us thought about pulling up the drawbridge the moment we arrived.

But what I finally came to understand is this: The *real* reason those high-end strollers piss me off is that they remind me of a time in my life I will never get back. I resent the newcomers for everything they have yet to experience: first Tooth Fairy note, first pumpkin carving, first school concert. The parenting milestones I didn't appreciate enough at the time—even that goddamn fourth grade recorder recital. Seriously, I would cheer so hard for a recorder recital right now. It seems inevitable, in fact, that I will one day approach complete strangers in the supermarket and insist that they *treasure this time* with their toddler and newborn, because *it goes by so fast*. (By the way, if anyone ever dares say this to you, let me confirm your worst suspicions: Yes, they are attempting to make you the receptacle for all their regret and longing. And you, who are too tired to treasure anything except nap time, should feel free to tell them where to go.)

The way I see it, I have two choices: I can be the troll under the drawbridge, or I can stand on top of the bridge with a welcoming smile on my face and a stack of business cards in my pocket. I can resent the women who have so many more moments to treasure, or I can help them find a home with a little breathing room in it. A place for the kids to play. A room for the mother-in-law to stay, because even though she drives you nuts, she's a pretty good babysitter.

I know some of you (hi again, Jen) will say I've simply found a way to cash in, and, sure, real estate pays the bills. But I prefer to think of it as my version of the Stoics' *memento mori*—remember you will die. We're all here on a temporary basis, the locals and the cidiots alike. None of us own the maple trees on Main Street, no matter how personally offended we feel when the power companies carelessly hack off tree limbs and call it "pruning." In other words, come on in! The drawbridge is down. I swear I'm happy to see you.

xok

---

ann-no-e: *THIS. What is UP with those people who act like it's their god-given right to tell me to treasure the moments with my kids?! One woman tapped me on the shoulder in the checkout line because I was scrolling on my phone instead of talking to my kid. She was like, "When you get to be my age, you'll regret all the times you chose your phone." And it's only women who do this, have you noticed? Like, it's just one more unrealistic expectation that we place on each other.*

i_live_here: *Totally, Ann! Why can't we cut each other some slack? Motherhood sometimes feels like a version of the*

Hunger Games designed by momfluencers. This week's challenge: Embrace slime as a crafting activity and don't you dare stress about how much mess it makes! But also, have an immaculate playroom with labeled storage buckets at child height, and teach your kids how to use these buckets without yelling at them. And don't forget to treasure the moment! xok

really_jen: *Wait, aren't you a momfluencer? Also, hi.*

i_live_here: *Not according to advertisers, Jen. Maybe I don't go on enough barefoot meadow walks? Also, most of those tradwives live in Tennessee or Utah or one of those other states where home-schooling is cool but abortion is not. xok*

ann-no-e: *Oh my god, the moms who brag about their playroom storage systems! They're always wearing peasant dresses, too, and I don't know why this annoys me so much, but it does. Also, I'm convinced slime was invented to torture women. I mean, it showed up right after the epidural went mainstream, making pain-free childbirth available to us all. Coincidence? I don't think so.*

i_live_here: *Motherhood = refusing to make slime with the same tiny human you'd throw yourself in front of a moving car for. #MomsAgainstSlime xok*

go-ask-your-dad: *#MomsAgainstPeasantDresses*

mazel-tough: *Those moms make me feel hella old—they're pushing out kid #3 when most people their age are still trying to pick a major. I could be grandmother to their "little rays of sunshine."*

ann-no-e: *Can I just say on behalf of all your readers, THANK YOU for never posting something like, "I hope my daughter's childhood feels as magical to her as it does to me." No shit, I read that caption under a photo yesterday. VOMIT.*

i_live_here: *Maybe if you're monetizing your toddler, it's a little easier to feel those treasured moments slipping through your fingers?! I know, I know—pot, kettle, black, etc. xok*

ann-no-e: *Pretty sure you never posed pregnant on the beach in a white string bikini, so all is forgiven.*

mazel-tough: *Or in a meadow.*

f-bomb-mom: *Or a cornfield.*

f-bomb-mom: *It's like there's a fucking manual telling them exactly how to pose: hand on belly, toddler on hip, adoring aryan husband attached at the lips. Whatever happened to being a fuck-up in your twenties??*

i_live_here: *Now I kinda want to recreate those classic momfluencer poses, except with my frizzy brown hair, forehead furrows, and the sensible one-piece bathing suit I wear to swim laps. xok*

ann-no-e: *DO IT.*

really_jen: *Geez, guys, why don't you pick on someone your own size? Not everyone went to a fancy East Coast Ivy League school, you know.*

ann-no-e: *Jen, I don't think those moms give a shit what we think. Have you seen their houses? Six thousand square feet of natural light and white furniture, and not a ketchup stain in sight. They're raking it in, even if half of us are hate-following them. No wonder they all feel #blessed.*

f-bomb-mom: *Parenting in the age of the smartphone is the best. Now I get to rewatch all those moments I didn't treasure because I was stretched so thin and exhausted all the time and spending approximately 36 hours a day in the school pickup line. THAT'S how I treasure the moments. So fuck off when Mommy's on her phone.*

go-ask-your-dad: *LOL, same.*

i_live_here: *Goodnight, ladies! In this fucked-up battle royale we call motherhood, you're all winners to me. #MomsAgainst UnrealisticExpectations #ParticipationTrophiesForEveryone xok*

chapter five Indie

I always assumed that if I was going to lose a friend, it would be in a school shooting. Not like I morbidly obsessed over this, it just seemed like a thing that was possible. We drill for it often enough. But then I get to Maddy's funeral, which is on the same day the town pool opens for the season, three weeks before the end of eighth grade, and I realize it's all possible: Every awful thing you can imagine, and also the things so awful you can't drill for them or even begin to imagine them.

The worst part about Maddy's funeral is that Maddy isn't here. I mean, yeah, of course, that's why we're all so fucking sad. But it's more than that. Maddy was how I experienced the world. She would understand my mortification at the dress Mom is wearing. Puff sleeves? Really, Mom? For a funeral? When I make a face, Mom insists that everything is puff sleeved right now, as if this were a red carpet issue. How hard is it to know the difference between a funeral dress and a not-funeral dress? Puff sleeves are for bridesmaids and beauty queens, they're sewn out of sugar and spice and unequal pay for equal work. Puff sleeves are desperate to be liked.

If Maddy were at this funeral, she would text me from inside her pocket to tell me how cute Asher looks in a tie. Her undercover texting skills were legendary. She would notice Asher arriving early to get a good seat. And she would catch my eye when Violet snort-cries in the middle of the homily, right when the minister notes what a loyal friend Maddy was. This is the same Violet, by the way, who called Maddy "Ms. Frizzle," and who asked, one particularly humid day, if she could "pet" Maddy's curly red hair. Today Violet is sitting in a pew with her actual friends—June, Mackenzie, and Other Mackenzie—and they are clutching each other's hands as if their plane were going down. The Minkles, Maddy and I called them: her word mashup for mean girls. The Minkles turn every minor incident into an OMG. *Did you hear what he said? Did you see what she wore? Omigod this is the cutest thing ever. Oh my god this is the saddest thing ever.*

The Minkles shared photos online of their school locker memorials: the metal doors adorned with black ribbons, pictures of Maddy they found online, and cheesy quotes about friendship from Buzzfeed. *Rest in peace, Maddy*, they write. *You were loved.* They don't have their own photos of Maddy because, oh yeah, *they never hung out*. Not since fourth grade, anyway, and even back then it was only because the rule was, if you wanted the teacher to hand out your party invites, you had to include every kid in the class.

If I were being kind, I might say that Violet, June, Mackenzie, and Other Mackenzie do actually feel like their plane is going down. Maybe Maddy's sudden death caused them to ponder their own mortality. But you know what's worse than feeling mortal? Being dead. So shut up and wipe your noses, bitches.

chapter six ✎ Kate

What do you wear to the funeral of your teenage daughter's best friend? That's a trick question. The universe stopped working the way it was supposed to, and nothing you do or say—or wear—will change that.

But doing nothing, of course, is not an option. This is what it means to be a parent, to oscillate between self-flagellation and hubris—between the belief that nothing you're doing is right, and the certainty that if you just tried a little harder, you could fix everything. Parenthood wouldn't be bearable if you didn't occasionally believe it was in your power to make your child happy.

"Indie," I say softly, reaching into the back seat for her hand. I rub her knuckles like rosary beads.

"I'm not hungry." Indie pulls her hand away and shoves it under her thigh.

We rarely drive places as a family anymore; I'm not used to seeing my daughter in the back seat. She looks so vulnerable back there, a little girl again, and yet somehow also too big for the space, as if she had folded herself in half. She reminds me of a newborn calf we saw at the county fair one year, still slimy from birth and yet stumbling to its feet. That calf got stuck on its way out of the birth canal, I remember now, and two farmers attached heavy chains to its front legs to deliver it.

"I wasn't going to make you eat," I say, although I do have a bag of almonds in my purse, just in case. I don't know what else to offer her.

This morning I woke at 4 a.m., and when I couldn't fall back asleep, I grabbed my phone from the nightstand and googled "how to comfort a grieving teen." The internet told me it's helpful to prepare teenagers for a funeral. "Normalize the range of emotions grievers may experience," one article recommended. "Give her permission to laugh if someone tells a funny story."

"We don't have to go to the reception," I say now. "If you want to go home, we can go home. You made it through the funeral, that's enough."

Indie didn't cry at the funeral, and she is dry-eyed now, too. Her stoicism hurts my heart, and I want to take her home, where the only grief she has to consider is her own.

"Of course we have to go to the reception," Indie says, her gaze fixed out the window.

"She's right," Ethan adds. "We should go."

So this is how *we* parent our grieving teen: I offer snacks, and my husband takes Indie's side, even when there should be no side to take. *Same team*, I want to say, like Indie's first soccer coach used to yell, back when she was in kindergarten and the players would swarm after the ball like bees.

"Okay," I say, turning my body to face the back seat again. "If you want to go, we go. But I need you to know that people might tell funny stories about Maddy at the reception. They might laugh, and that's okay. It's okay if you want to laugh, too."

Indie pulls her gaze from the window and stares at me with a weary contempt that chills me. I am used to disappointing her, but this is different: It's as if I were behaving exactly as she expected me to. She doesn't say a word, but I know what she's thinking: *Why would I* laugh *at my best friend's funeral?* She is right and I am getting this wrong wrong wrong.

I face forward and wrap my arms around myself, around my ridiculous puff sleeves. She was right about my outfit, too. This is not a sad dress.

I look at Ethan, willing him to say something to Indie or to me, to reach out for her hand or mine. I glance at the speedometer to confirm he isn't driving over the speed limit, then back at my daughter one more time, to triple-check she is wearing her seatbelt. I open my mouth to ask if she needs more AC in the back, then close it again without saying a word.

Two weeks ago, I was driving Indie to the orthodontist when I hit the brakes too hard at a stop sign. As the car lurched forward, I reached in front of Indie with my arm, like a barrier at a tollbooth—a useless instinct to save her. Force equals mass times acceleration, no matter how much you love her.

When we get home, I leave a journal on Indie's nightstand. I read online that she might share her feelings on paper before she's ready to open up to me. A psychology professor at Northwestern even studied this—the way we create narrative arcs when we write down what happens to us, and how the right arc can propel us forward through trauma. But when I'm changing into pajamas for bed, I notice the journal has been returned to my nightstand, still blank. I stare at the mint green, soft leather cover. It was the most expensive journal in our town's overpriced paper goods store, and I genuinely believed, for a dumb moment, that all my daughter needed was the right narrative arc. I place the journal in my nightstand drawer.

Indie's right: I'm the one who writes my way through hard times. I have no idea what her thing might be. Or maybe she never had a thing, because she had Maddy.

I open my laptop and start a new post.

IF YOU LIVED HERE—NEW LISTING! 5BR/4BA VICTORIAN PARSONAGE

Raise your hand if you walked to school as a kid. Remember when that was a thing? Breaking news, people: It still is. My new listing, a Victorian parsonage, is five blocks from the elementary school. And I'm not talking five city blocks. It's five *country* blocks, with wide sidewalks and friendly neighbors and, honest to god, a crossing guard with a hand-held stop sign. Yep, crossing guards are still a thing, too, it turns out. What's *not* a thing is creepy men in white vans, no matter how many unsubstantiated rumors your friends repost online. Statistically, you'd have to leave your daughter unattended on a street corner for 446,760 hours before a stranger would show up to kidnap her. I had two thoughts upon reading this statistic online. My first thought was that the specificity of the number makes it sound like how-to advice. Like, *Hang in there, parents! Don't give up after the first ten thousand hours!* And my second thought was this: While everyone considers their own offspring to be adorably, irresistibly precious, the men in white vans apparently find them entirely resistible. The only people stalking children, in fact, are helicopter parents convinced their kids will forget to look both ways before crossing.

I've never been a helicopter parent myself (at least, I do my best not to be). Nor am I a snowplow parent or a bulldozer parent or whatever other insult gets thrown at women—only women, notice that?—who coddle their children, from birth through an Ivy League education. One of my favorite things about living upstate is that parenthood doesn't feel like a competitive sport here: There's only one school, and if you live in the district, your kid gets to go. (It's a good school, too, in case you were wondering, which I know you were.) If you're not within walking distance of the school, a yellow bus will stop at the end of your driveway. That's it, end of story. No need for character references just to get into preschool.

Here's the kind of parent I *am*, though: When given the choice between concealing something from my daughter and explaining it, I've always chosen the latter. Questionable song lyrics, political scandals, sex, sexism, racism, all the other 'isms, the pain of childbirth, class warfare in our small town, the child labor that went into the cheap hoodie she bought at the Poughkeepsie mall—we've explored it all together. (I'm sure there's a dismissive term for *this* style of parenting, too; I'm even more sure one of you will let me know what it is.) I've never shielded my daughter from the ugliness of the world because I want her to appreciate its beauty. I also want her to be angry enough about the ugliness to fight it when she grows up.

Just, you know, after she graduates magna cum laude from Princeton. *Kidding*. (Sort of.)

xok

---

really_jen: *I don't know about a cutesy nickname for what you're doing. That sounds like straight-up woke parenting to me.*

i_live_here: *And there it is. Knew I could count on you, Jen! xok*

ann-no-e: *I was just reading about "free range parenting" the other day, and I thought, wait, didn't that just used to be called childhood?! Our house is a 15-minute walk from school, but I'd never let my kids do it alone, I'm too worried some Karen would call CPS.*

go-ask-your-dad: *Is it still helicopter parenting if you are ONE HUNDRED PERCENT SURE your 11 y.o. son will not look both ways before crossing? Asking for a friend.*

i_live_here: *Tell your "friend" she's doing great. Self-reliance is cool, but making it safely to the other side of the road—literally AND metaphorically—is even cooler. xo*

I cross the hall to Indie's room. It's already dark and she is sprawled diagonally across the bed.

"Hi Bean," I say, nudging her body gently so I can slide in next to her.

"Can you sleep in your own room tonight?" she says into her pillow. "I sleep better like this."

Maybe I got it all wrong. Now, I want to go Tipper Gore on this world. I want to slap warning labels on everything that might hurt my daughter. I want to clear every path and then hover above to keep her safe. I want speed bumps and helmet laws and knee and elbow pads. I want front airbags, side airbags, inflatable seatbelts. I want to give her more mattresses than the Princess and the Pea. I want to do penance for that one time I showed my five-year-old daughter the unedited video of her own birth, causing her to break out in sobs and declare, "I don't like what happened to you! I don't ever want a baby!"

What if I could rewind her childhood and be the kind of parent who'd shielded her from ugliness and disappointment, hurt and pain? Had I been that parent more often, maybe Indie would let me hold her right now. Maybe she'd even believe, if only for as long as she was in my arms, that I could make things okay again.

Ethan's nightstand light is already off and his body is turned away from me, sleep mask on. He takes a rigorously scientific approach to a good night's sleep, snapping off bright overhead lights after 9 p.m. like they're radioactive. "What are you, a gremlin?" Indie said once, flipping her overhead light back on. I ask Ethan if he minds my reading for a while, if it will keep him up. He doesn't respond, and I realize he's wearing earbuds, listening to something on his phone.

We used to fall asleep together to podcasts. "Terry Gross is basically our post-coital cigarette," Ethan joked once, as the Fresh Air host's warm, rich voice drifted across our bed before his erection had even subsided. Despite being the one with insomnia, Ethan always let me choose the podcast we listened to in bed. I vetoed all shows about health and wellness, plus any podcast with multiple male hosts (too much work distinguishing among voices).

The first time I noticed Ethan sleeping in earbuds was a couple of months after my mom died. I was still getting knocked sideways by grief, still floored by the indifference of strangers who wanted to know when we planned on returning my mom's wheelchair. (We'd lost track of it when she went into hospice care, not understanding it was a rental from a separate company. "She died," I said to one man who called, thinking he may have misunderstood the situation. "Yes, ma'am," he said.) I told Ethan there was nothing he could do when I woke at 2 a.m. crying, that I didn't expect him to stay up and hold me. "I just need to cry," I said. "You should get some sleep." The truth was, when he held me, I felt like a stopwatch was running. Even so, I didn't expect the earbuds.

I read on my phone until I am so tired it hurts to close my eyes, a hundred earnest articles about how to reach your child. They tell me to keep trying, to try every route possible to connect. They tell me to *stop* trying, to wait for my daughter to reach out to me, like a plant edging its way through dark soil toward the light. They tell me to "Keep Calm and Parent On," and even offer a discounted magnet featuring this message.

I pull up *If You Lived Here* and skim the latest comments from my readers, irritated at their lack of concern for Indie and me. They're arguing about mothers who join in with their kids' pretend play, and whether this expands a child's imagination or limits it. Also whether it's bad for the feminist cause to play with your kids. One woman asks, *Remember when it was okay to just watch your children play?* Another responds, *Remember when it was okay to boil meat in water for dinner? Not everything about the fifties was awesome.* My resentment is preposterous, of course. My readers couldn't possibly know what we're going through, because I haven't told them—I promised Ethan I wouldn't do that to Indie. Still, I can't shake the feeling: These people have no idea.

I tiptoe into the hallway with my laptop and sit on the floor, my back to the wall and my eyes on Indie's bedroom door. What the hell, I think: They don't need to know anything to be there for me. No matter the time, day or night, someone is always *there.* I just need to remind them I'm here. I open my laptop and compose another post.

IF YOU LIVED HERE—NEW LISTING! 4BR/2.5BA MAIN STREET BROWNSTONE

Hey cidiot, brownstones aren't just a Brooklyn thing! Although plenty of you act like you own the concept of living in one. It's actually just *overpriced* brownstones that are a city thing. We have brownstones here, too. And I don't mean mass-market, suburban reproductions for the Panera crowd.

Look, I get it, some of you like having neighbors in close proximity. Shared-wall proximity, even (which I guess disincentivizes screaming at your kids and spouse?). Readers often tell me they could never give up the city like I did, that their happy place is a four-story townhouse a block from their favorite coffee shop.

Hi [waves], may I show you my new listing? This brownstone is a block and a half from the locally roasted, fair trade, woman-owned coffee shop. (Not everyone here drinks K-cup coffee, it turns out.) It's even walkable to the co-op, in case you like your milk raw and your yogurt unpasteurized and you want to pretend like you still live in Park Slope.

I won't be fighting you for the brownstone, though, because my family and I prefer neighbors of the bovine variety. When my daughter was little, she used to say *all done* if she didn't like something. *All done, broccoli*, at dinner. *All done, fireworks*, every July 4th at the riverfront. And once, on a crowded Manhattan street when we were visiting for the day, *All done, all the people*. That was the moment I realized we had raised a human being who considered green space a birthright. A child who understood that being jostled by strangers was a choice, and an odd one at that. Who ranked crowds right up there with *broccoli* in terms of nuisance factor. My first thought was, *Who is this child?* My second thought was, *We are never moving back*. Seeing the city through my daughter's eyes, I understood that we had found our forever home. So, while I will never be considered a true local myself—I still get my hair cut in the city, for a start—I am willing to stake our claim as the parents of a country mouse: She is our very own anchor baby. *All done, all the people*.

xok

---

ann-no-e: *Hey, just a heads up, pretty sure the term "anchor baby" is considered racist, so you might wanna fix that. I know you're not using it that way, but still, figured you'd want us to tell you! It just landed a bit off for this reader.*

i_live_here: *THANK YOU Ann, just deleted it. Total brain fog moment. That's what I get for posting after midnight. xok*

really_jen: *"The Panera crowd"?? That'd be me, I guess. Sorry I'm not as cool as your other readers. Believe it or not, K-cup is considered bougie where I live.*

i_live_here: *Jen! I'm so sorry! My daughter and I totally love to get Panera take-out and sneak it into the multiplex movie theater across the river. I think that snarky comment was just my former downtown-hipster-self judging my current upstate-soccer-mom-self. Does anyone else get mean texts from their former selves? Twenty-something me can be a total biatch sometimes. #BreadBowlsForever xok*

really_jen: *"Across the river," huh? That's where you slum it?*

ann-no-e: *Come on, Jen, play nice. You know what she means.*

go-ask-your-dad: *Is anyone else craving broccoli cheddar soup right now?*

f-bomb-mom: *YES.*

ann-no-e: *YES.*

i_live_here: *YES. xok*

I remember a road trip when Indie was seven or eight. We were driving to Cape Cod to visit Ethan's parents at their Chatham beach house, and we stopped for dinner at one of those mid-range chain restaurants where every dish is either Cajun-season or blackened, and the word "smothered" appears on the menu an alarming number of times. Indie was captivated by the touch screen system built into the table, and she immediately took over the ordering process. "This place is *awesome*," she declared, when she discovered the touch screen also had a trivia game. "How come we never ate here before?" Usually we waited to eat dinner at the family-owned lobster shack on the outskirts of Cape Cod, but on this occasion, we'd left home too late and got stuck in traffic. I don't recall what I ate that night, although I'm sure it was smothered in something. I do know that by the end of the meal, Ethan and I had promised Indie we would stop there every time we visited her grandparents. We kept our word; on one occasion we did so well at trivia that we got to enter our team name on the high score table. "Mommy and Daddy really like to win things," Ethan explained to Indie, when our over-zealous high-five scattered nachos across the table. Later, as Indie snoozed in the back seat of the car, Ethan whispered, "I need to tell you something." He took a deep breath, as if steeling himself for a confession. "I actually look forward to the loaded potato skins."

I hold these images in my head like a talisman, or a piece of evidence: We were good once, the three of us. We worked. I try to imagine Indie, a decade or more from now, walking into one of these restaurants somewhere in the country and being flooded with sense memories. It wouldn't matter what city or state, because wherever she went, the menu and the novelty sports signs and the dark wood banquettes would be identical. And she would remember a time when things were good.

The next morning, I find my daughter lying on the couch in the living room, staring at the TV, which is not on. I watch her back rise and fall and I feel a familiar loosening in my chest: She is breathing. How many nights did I check her crib for the same thing? Sometimes it would be a few seconds until I heard the sigh of her breath or felt her back move beneath my hand, and as I waited, I felt time stop.

I perch on the edge of the couch next to Indie's legs and place a palm on her back. So long as my hand is here, she cannot leave me. My hand is an umbilical cord: I breathe, she breathes. I start to tell Indie how it undid me to lose my mother, how the grief broke me open and changed me, how it hasn't gone away but, almost a year on, I'm learning to live with it. She does not say a word and so I keep talking, my words a faucet streaming forth, like she is five again with a scraped knee and I am washing the gravel from her wound.

"Hundreds of years ago, these artisans in Japan figured out a way to mend shattered pottery," I tell her. I am staring at the blank TV, too, my hand still resting on her back, the lifeblood flowing from my body to hers. "They glued the shards back together and dusted the seams with gold powder. They made the scars beautiful."

This was the last article I found on my phone before falling asleep last night, and it rang so true, I could almost believe I was summoning each sentence into existence as I scrolled down the page. When I read how this ceramics process is called *kintsugi*, the word felt instantly familiar, like a faded photograph in an old family album. *I* wanted to be a clay pot, mended and precious, able to be filled up again.

"Grandma was old," Indie says suddenly, her voice flat.

This is what Ethan said to me the day my mom died, although he used different words. *Your mom lived a good life*, he said. Unlike his brother, he meant.

My mom was sixty-five when she died. She never got to be old, but I don't say this because Indie is right: Measured against Maddy's short life, my mom was ancient. She lived a thousand lives. Besides, I don't want *kintsugi* for my daughter. I don't want her to have beautiful scars, I want her unblemished. She is fourteen. She should shimmer at the edges, gloriously uncertain about who she will grow up to be. She is too young to be glued back together, calcified by loss.

Indie stands and sways a little as she moves across the room. She catches herself in the doorframe, and I wonder when she last ate.

"Can I make you eggs?" I say. "Or waffles? Or both? Or maybe just a piece of toast with honey? I could run out to the bakery and pick up that special breakfast bread you like."

"PLEASE STOP," Indie says loudly—a staccato plea, as if she were dictating a telegram.

She closes her eyes and this feels so final, a door slammed shut between us. I can almost hear her tiny voice: *All done, all the words*. As she walks out of the room, it is like limbs being torn from my body. But her grief is all she has left of Maddy, and she is not willing to share this with me.

I would like to write a letter to the editor of the internet. I want to tell the authors of every article I read: You got it wrong. She is not a shattered pot, she is my daughter, grieving down to the marrow. I want a refund, I want my time back, I want you to publish a correction. Most of all, though, I want a real answer to my question: How does a parent fix the world?

chapter seven **Indie**

Sometimes I lie on my bed, sometimes I sit at my desk or in my beanbag chair, sometimes I stand at the window, but always with my back to the miniature Polaroids of me and Maddy that are clipped to a string of lights above my headboard. This room is where I will wait for the world to make sense again.

I am lightheaded with hunger, but I cannot eat. My whole body feels off, and nothing about my physical being, or my physical presence in the world, feels right to me. Mom brings me meals on a tray, and I return them to the hallway, untouched. Mac and cheese from a box, grilled cheese on white bread, mini pizza bagels. Every single processed food item she has denied me my entire life. The grease lingers in the air, clinging to my bed sheets, and I want to gag. The idea of food decomposing inside me is just too awful—I don't want intestinal sludge moving through my body. Dad brings me granola bars in the afternoon, when he gets home from school and Mom goes out to work, and these I nibble on slowly, one a day. I can see it in my parents' eyes: If I eat any less than this, they will drag me out of my room. They will take me to the pediatrician who still talks to me like I'm ten, and she will diagnose me with body dysmorphia, then some other doctor will pump sustenance through my system. As if the real problem is that I want to be thin.

I don't have any stake in my body, though, and my weight is no more than a gravitational force. I just want everything to stop for a little while. If there was a cosmic pause button, I would press it. I actually google this repeatedly—*how to stop thinking*—not because I'm expecting an answer but because I need to tell someone: Make it stop. The internet says I should doodle, crochet, knit, sew, scrapbook, take up origami. Really, *crafting* is meant to stop the dark thoughts? Apparently the internet thinks I live in a retirement community.

But then one evening, exactly a week after my best friend's funeral, *how to stop thinking* brings me to a video of a Buddhist monk meditating in a fire pit. He's literally sitting in a giant hot pot, suspended over flames while he meditates, and I know that this must be something different, because I've never seen someone scrapbook while their ass is on fire. Whatever superpower the monk has, I want it.

I watch the next video recommended to me, and the next, and the next. *So* many people want to tell me how to meditate. I mean, isn't meditation just sitting there with your eyes closed? It's not like making choux pastry. (Which, for the record, Maddy and I totally nailed—thank you internet.)

One video says that meditation done wrong is thinking with your eyes closed—it's a classic rookie mistake, I guess. Well, duh, then tell me how to *stop* thinking. Another video says I shouldn't wish for something when I meditate, and I wonder if wishing for nothing counts as a wish. Still another says I'm not supposed to judge myself when I do it. Also, don't sit too long, but don't stop too soon, either. Apparently we're all getting this wrong, which is why the Buddhist monk can sit in a fire pit while he meditates and the rest of us can't even ignore an itch on our nose. Except, nobody really explains how to do it *right*. Not in a way that makes sense to me, anyway. I sit cross-legged on the floor and touch the tips of my index fingers to my thumbs and turn my palms upward, resting my wrists on my thighs. Now I *look* like I'm meditating, but it feels like pretend play. Meditation is like opening your eyes and opening them again, I read. It's like letting go of a hot frying pan. It's the mirror but not the reflection. It's the ocean but not the wave. It's Clark Kent taking off his glasses. I'm supposed to be a metaphor, I guess? But what do I do with my thoughts, I want to know. How do I make them stop?

I don't know how to be in this room without Maddy, and I don't know how to be still without her beside me. I don't know how to do *anything* without my best friend—I'm like one of those science experiments where they sever the left hemisphere of the brain from the right, and all my neurons are firing into blank space. I've known Maddy for so long that I have no real memories before her. Sure, I could tell you who my teacher was in first grade (Mrs. Yarnell), and what I did for my birthday party that year (the bounce house at the mall), but I have no idea how it *felt* to be me back then. How am I supposed to be me without her? I have this strange notion that if I ever speak again, it will have to be in a new language.

And then I remember something. I turn on my phone and open my text thread with Maddy. I scroll up quickly because I don't want to see how it ends. Not because our last exchange was meaningful, but because I'm sure it wasn't. I want to be in the middle of everything, when we were just two teenage girls who didn't weigh our words, who made a joke of clogging our thread with emojis that meant nothing at all: How many waffle emojis could we text each other in a day? How many avocados? It didn't mean anything but it meant everything, too, each message the tick of a metronome, back and forth, marking time. Me, then you, then me again. As I scroll up, past the emojis, past the videos, past the selfies, past the good morning and goodnight texts, past the I'm-on-the-bus texts, past the Asher-is-wearing-a-Dwight-hoodie texts, I imagine I am watching a movie in reverse, the dialogue a Chipmunk-style babble. If I asked Siri to read this thread backwards, would I hear a secret message? *Worship Satan. Kill yourself. Drink Ovaltine.* Eventually, I find the video I'm looking for, the one I sent Maddy a week before she died. I put in my earbuds and press Play.

chapter eight Kate

I sit in the hallway outside Indie's room, picking at her untouched meal. When she was little, I rarely made myself breakfast or lunch, subsisting instead on what she rejected. Back then, vegetables were the only problem in her life, and I know this because she told me so frequently: "My life would be perfect if you didn't make me eat green things." I could have made her life perfect at that point, but I chose not to.

What if I placed a hand on her closed bedroom door, would I find any clues in its surface? This is what firefighters tell you to do, if you're trapped in a room and smell smoke in the house: Feel the temperature of the door with the back of your hand. If it's hot, you exit through a window instead. Would Indie break her silence and call out to me if the house were on fire? I can't say for sure.

I pick up my phone. One of the other moms from Indie's grade just shared an article about how therapy dogs can help in the aftermath of a death, which feels like a performative post to remind us all that her daughter knew Maddy. It's been up for twenty minutes, and already more than two hundred people have reacted with the crying face emoji. There's a glittering darkness to tragedy, and everyone wants a part of it—house fire, mom of three with cancer, dead teenager. The women in this town, we organize meal trains and launch GoFundMe campaigns to make our rubbernecking look like concern. The real concern, though, is for our own houses, our own bodies, our own children. We draw close to the train wreck as if we could inoculate ourselves against tragedy. We are placating fate.

I know exactly what my own mom would have said about therapy dogs, because she grew up on a farm and didn't much care for animals inside the house. Also, she believed this was God's job, to walk humans through the valley of the shadow of death; she would have rolled her eyes at the idea that a dog could do better. Even after my mother stopped recognizing her own children, she never forgot that she had God on speed-dial. Funny how easy it is to hear her voice when I know she would disapprove of something. In the rare moments when I imagine she might be pleased with me, I can conjure nothing.

Indie was distraught when my mom lost her battle with early-onset Alzheimer's. Theirs was an uncomplicated, cozy love; my daughter brought out a side of my mother I'd never known myself. "Just tell the poor kid Grandma's in heaven," my brother said at the funeral. "You know that's what Mom would have wanted." Even in death, apparently, I was disappointing my mother.

But I was grieving and lonely and mad at the world, enraged that I had a mother-in-law but no mother, furious at my husband for still having a mother, furious at *anyone*, including my brother, who'd had a mother who loved them without reserve. People said to me, thinking this was a kindness, "It still must be hard losing her, even though you had a difficult relationship." As if my grief were of a lesser kind.

Not just people. My own husband said this.

Most of all, I was heartbroken that the story of me and my mom was over. She'd never soften with age and tell me she'd been proud of me all along but just didn't know how to show it. We'd never have that heart-to-heart I'd fantasized about since I was a teenager. She'd never acknowledge that she could have been a different kind of mother. She'd never *be* a different kind of mother. And so I told my daughter nothing except, *I know it hurts*. I didn't even get her a puppy.

I click away from the woman's post about therapy dogs and type up something of my own.

IF YOU LIVED HERE—SOLD! 5BR/4.5BA HILLTOP CONTEMPORARY

Earlier this week, while touring an old farmhouse that had been sitting empty for a while, a client couple came across a dead mouse in the master bedroom. The wife shuddered and said, "Can we see some houses that were built this *decade*?" Hence the whitewashed hilltop contemporary I just sold, all shiny and new. Because sometimes the clincher is a funny-shaped room, and sometimes it's the (false) promise of a clean slate.

The thing is, lady, death is everywhere when you live in the country: dead spiders and dead mice in the house; dead birds in the car's grille and dead bunnies wrapped around the tires; dead possums, flattened, on the side of the road. I actually read somewhere that new houses might attract *more* mice than old ones, because they're built in areas that were recently cleared, disturbing all the brush and trees where creatures had been living. Confession: I did not say any of this to my clients.

Living where we do, E. and I taught our daughter early that death is an integral part of life. That old people have to die to make room on the planet for new babies. That we each get one shot, and *that's* what makes life beautiful—not an afterlife of teacup puppies and rainbow sherbet sundaes.

The coldest winter I remember, one of our hens froze to death when the rest of the flock exiled her from the coop. (Total mafia move, right?) "Chickens being chickens," E. said gently, when our daughter's eyes filled with tears. "This one reached the end of its life cycle, that's all."

It wasn't always an easy position to defend. The year our daughter turned seven, she discovered a cardinal nest in a tree just outside her bedroom window. She checked in each day until—magically, it seemed to her—the baby cardinals hatched. She watched as the male cardinal continued to bring the chicks food each day, long after the female had departed to build another nest. (Side note: Male cardinals are the feminist superheroes of the avian world.) And then one afternoon, as my daughter looked on in horror, frantically banging the glass of her bedroom window, a blue jay picked off two baby cardinals from the nest.

Oh man, I wanted to believe in bird heaven that day. But we had already committed to the path of blunt truth, and so we told our daughter how nature only seems cruel when you pick a side.*

Of course, our approach isn't a requirement for upstate living. If you prefer warm and fuzzy belief systems, this town is lousy with churches, and some of the nicest people I know attend them on the regular. I like to think that, in the end, we all want the same thing: to make sense of this world and our place in it.

xok

*But if I *had* to pick a side? I'm team cardinals all the way. Fuck those blue jays.

---

ann-no-e: *I love that you did this. We lied and told our daughter we were using catch-and-release mouse traps, then she busted us when she was looking for slime supplies under the kitchen sink. I feel like she'll be talking about that dead mouse in therapy ten years from now. Also, I'll say it again: FUCK SLIME.*

i_live_here: *Apparently it's not enough to keep our children safe, now we're expected to look after all the rodents, too? Ann, maybe in this case, inventing mouse heaven could be seen as a feminist reclamation of our mental resources. #GoCardinals xok*

go-ask-your-dad: *Nature's only cruel when you pick a side—so true! I learned this from watching nature documentaries. I never knew I could care so much about an iguana until I saw one desperately fleeing a swarm of snakes. #GoCardinals*

really_jen: *"Lousy with churches"?! You make it sound like religion is an infestation.*

f-bomb-mom: *It kind of is, really_jen.*

i_live_here: *Apologies, Jen, I forget that not everyone here knows I grew up in the church. Real save-yourself-for-Jesus stuff. I guess maybe I'm still unpacking some of that—hence the unintentional allusion to pests. xok*

really_jen: *Did you also tell your daughter Santa isn't real?! Paging the Mother of the Year award committee!*

i_live_here: *I'm not a monster, Jen—of course my daughter believed in Santa! I think I actually worked harder than my own mom to keep up the Santa ruse. Have you noticed how Christians can be pretty dismissive of the lesser magical beings? xok*

really_jen: *Well, we do make a distinction between the actual creator of this universe and tiny garden fairies, if that's what you mean. By the way, birds and mice don't go to heaven, but people do. SOME people do, anyway, because God's only "warm and fuzzy" if you believe in him. #WWJD*

i_live_here: *Jen, my mom said the same thing about dogs and heaven. Not even puppies, she said! Although this may have had more to do with her low opinion of pets than any biblical reference point. xok*

really_jen: *Seems like you gave yourself more freedom to make up your own mind about this stuff than you give your own daughter.*

ann-no-e: *Read the room, really_jen.*

The God my mom believed in was never warm and fuzzy—that wasn't the point. God was there in times of adversity, she said, but you shouldn't bother him with the small stuff. And because my life was an endless stream of small stuff back then, giving up on God wasn't a tortured decision: I brushed off organized religion as carelessly as I'd once abandoned gymnastics. When I was twelve, I finally accepted that I was never going to nail a backflip like Nadia Comaneci, and when I was a college freshman, I finally had to admit: There was no genial man in the sky, clad in a linen robe, and the stars were not, in fact, tiny pinholes in the floor of heaven—even an English major could see that. There was nothing but clouds in the sky.

What I don't tell my readers is that tragedy comes for us all in the end, no matter what we believe about the stars. Parents die, pets get run over by cars, spouses stop loving us. Of course we want to believe there's a soft landing at the end. And so now I sit outside Indie's bedroom in a silent vigil, wishing I could go back in time, unscramble the egg, get a do-over. I want to give my grieving daughter God. I want to give her Saint Peter at the gates of heaven and the leprechaun at the end of the rainbow. I want to give her Santa, the Tooth Fairy, the Buddha, the Easter Bunny. I want to give her whatever it would take to stop her pain.

I click back to the therapy dog post and select the crying face emoji to react to it, because what if someone notices that I didn't? Then I text Ethan and ask him to pick up chocolate milk for Indie on his way home.

Don't tell the haters, I add.

I once ignited a flame war in a local parenting group when I posted something about how maybe we shouldn't serve chocolate milk in the school cafeteria. "Because sugar," I wrote, which, looking back, was perhaps a mistake of tone. Still, you would've thought I'd suggested taking away their guns.

Ha, Ethan responds. *Will do.*

Finally, I swipe out of the text thread so I can look up the website for a local animal rescue organization. I start searching for the puppy who will save us.

chapter nine ❦ **Indie**

It's easy to avoid food. It's easy to stop talking, stop showering, stop changing my clothes. What's hard is to stop noticing the world. I sit cross-legged on the floor in my room and try to empty my mind of all thought. I try to imagine I am waiting for nothing instead of waiting for something. But every time I pick up my phone to watch a guided meditation video, I find myself drawn to other people's feeds, and I can never decide which is worse: when they're posting about Maddy, or when they're not. I follow Maddy's sisters online, and her younger sister Kaitlynn's posts are blowing up. Everyone wants to tell her they're sorry, she is loved, she is in their prayers. They shower her with hashtags and hearts, and she responds with even more images: her bare feet in the cemetery grass; a TBT shot from an old family vacation; Maddy's bed, still unmade. *#gonetoosoon #foreveryoung #untilwemeetagain #footprintsinthesand #anotherangelinheaven*

When I was in fourth grade, I asked my parents if we could go to Maddy's church.

"We're not really church people," Dad said. "We're more like brunch and farmer's market people."

"Maybe *I'm* a church person," I said.

Maddy had shown me her new Easter dress that came with a matching headband and purse, and I wanted to go someplace with a dress code. Brunch never required a purse.

"We can go at Christmas," Mom said, though we never did. The first time I was in Maddy's church was for her funeral.

Maddy told me I was lucky my parents didn't make me go to church, but I never quite believed her. Not that she was lying to me. I think she meant it in the day-to-day sense, that she disliked spending Sunday mornings in a wooden pew, listening to a rambling sermon about sin and salvation. But I suspected she worried about my soul in a long-term sense. Because that's how her parents treated church—like a habit that would eventually, given enough time, lead to belief. They made their children attend church every Sunday the way other parents set aside money for their kids' college funds, a kind of savings account for when the girls really needed God. It never occurred to any of us that the afterlife might be more of an immediate concern.

Last year, on our way to Grandma's funeral, I asked Dad again how he was so sure we weren't church people. He said that history teachers like him know nothing is permanent—not national borders, not cultures, and certainly not religion. In Dad's view, there isn't a single thing that's always been here. Not even quarks and electrons—although this, Dad said, is above his pay grade. As if he didn't nerd out on a million white-guy podcasts about things that aren't in the high school social studies curriculum.

On the drive back from the funeral that day, Mom asked Dad to tell us something interesting. "It doesn't matter what," she said, pressing the heels of her hands into her eyes. "I just want to pretend we're on our way home from brunch."

So Dad told us about the Prince Philip Movement, a religious sect on a tiny island in the South Pacific. The people there believed Prince Philip was a messiah, and they used to pray to him for sun or rain or a bountiful harvest. I was sure Dad was pranking us until he told me to search YouTube on my phone for a documentary about the whole thing. "Why didn't anyone tell the islanders he was just some racist dude who married the queen?" I asked. "Didn't they *know*?" Dad smiled at me in the rear-view mirror and made a ding-ding sound like I'd just nailed the answer in a game show. I made a WTF face back at him. Sometimes he forgets that he's not grading me on this stuff. "Think about it," he said. "Why is *that* any more absurd than believing in Jesus? It's just more recent, that's all."

That settled it. No way was I letting Dad anywhere near Maddy's church.

"Humans have a capacity for awe," he went on. "But so do chimps—just ask Jane Goodall. People mistake awe for a religious experience, but what they really mean is that nature sure is pretty sometimes."

Mom sniffled a little and then smiled.

"It sure is," she said, looking out her window as we passed an apple orchard. "Why do you think we moved here?"

Is this what Kaitlynn sees when she points her phone's camera at the pink and orange poppies growing at the edge of the cemetery where her sister is buried? Because I've seen some nice sunsets over the Hudson River, and I've seen more forsythia than I care to remember—thanks to my mom pointing it out *every single time* we pass it, as if it didn't grow like a weed in our town each spring—but I've never seen God.

What if it's not enough, the amount of church Maddy's parents saved up? What if Maddy's family runs out of God feelings? And what happens if they find out they're just chimps like the rest of us, dazzled by pretty things?

chapter ten **Kate**

I slip into the back pew right before the Sunday service starts, not wanting anyone to notice me. Wherever I go, I am certain people can see it in my face, the relief that it wasn't my daughter. The naked, selfish gratitude that she was the one to be spared. I can't be the only person who feels this way. Parents all over town must be haunted by the number of times their own children walked home after dark, unharmed. But none of them could be thinking my ugliest thought, which is this: Maddy's parents still have two daughters. They lost something, but they didn't lose everything. I only have Indie. If it had to be one of them, it couldn't have been her.

"Welcome," the minister says to the congregation, his voice loud but his eyes soft and kind. I heard somewhere that this minister is gay, and out, and fully supported by his congregation, although I could be thinking of one of the other churches in town—this doesn't seem like that kind of place. Church is not one of the things my clients typically ask about, so my knowledge of the local religious scene is cursory at best.

One of the last times my mom still recognized me, she said she hoped she would see me in heaven. "Of course," I said, mustering a sincere tone, and I told myself this was a form of grace. The truth was, I was touched she wanted me to join her in the afterlife. I hadn't thought she'd care.

Most days I'm glad I helped my mom die with her faith intact—that in the end, I chose to corroborate the story of her life. That I read aloud to her from a book of devotions I found in her nightstand. That I closed my eyes when she asked me to and pretended to pray. But then I'll remember a hurt, like the way she confided in me one afternoon, thinking I was one of her nurses, "I did my best, but my daughter was so difficult to love." And in those moments, I fantasize that I told her the terrifying truth instead—that none of us know. That maybe, in the end, we're just worm food.

"We are *so glad* you're here with us today," the minister says, and he genuinely seems to mean it. Up there in the pulpit, he radiates a bartender's alpha energy: A man who has access to what we crave. "Please rise for the first hymn."

As I stand, I glimpse Maddy's sisters near the front of the church, one on either side of their mother. My breath catches at the sight of Kaitlynn's hair, scraped into two neat French braids, the part between them a perfect straight line. I think of Laura waking up this morning to a world where she still has to braid hair. How does she make sense of that, how the world goes on without Maddy, how the rules don't change? It's been almost a month, although perhaps she still marks the time in smaller increments—days, hours, minutes—the way mothers do at the start of a child's life.

There's a dairy farm near our house, and once a year the cows bellow when they are separated from their newborn calves. If our windows are open, we hear the mournful sound for days, and then, suddenly, it is quiet again. And every year I wonder: If the cows know to cry, what makes them stop?

I flip to the right page in the hymnal out of habit; I have no intention of singing. I once learned that if you mouth the word *cauliflower* over and over, everyone will think you know the words to any song you sing. This piece of trivia lodged in my brain as confirmed fact, although the source was an eleven-year-old kid on the school playground. I move my lips to form the word: *cauliflower*. It makes about as much sense to me as anything else in the hymnal.

Still, though I haven't been a churchgoer in decades, there is a familiarity here I hadn't expected. I mumble along with the call and response of the opening prayer, and while I have forgotten the words, the cadence is comforting. It feels good to let my voice blend in with the others, the words rising to the ceiling in unison like, well, like a prayer. Ethan says this aspect of religion reminds him of Orwellian groupthink, but he didn't grow up in the church. (Also, he says the same thing about flash mobs.) In high school I had a French pen pal, and she didn't understand peanut butter and jelly sandwiches—I guess it's only comfort food if you were raised on it. And perhaps this is why people return to church: It's a peanut butter and jelly sandwich. You can count on it.

Halfway through the second hymn, I sense someone slide into my pew. I glance sideways and realize it's Maddy's dad. His name is Kevin, although everyone calls him Chief, because he's the local fire chief. I've only ever seen him in a firehouse job shirt, or in his dress uniform at the Memorial Day parade, but this morning he's wearing dark slacks and a blue button-down. He nods his head in my direction, eyes glazed and unfocused. He's never struck me as a man who is late to anything, especially not church.

As the sermon begins, I focus my attention on Maddy's mom and sisters, on the back of their heads. I notice they saved a seat in the pew for Kevin. Or perhaps this was unintentional, an unconscious gesture by a family used to taking up more space. Still, it looks safer where they're sitting, up front and surrounded by friends, as if the three of them are being guided home. We, the congregation, are a lighthouse in the fog, and this is what I wanted to see today, I realize now: how they are being held close. I wanted to be part of this, however peripherally—to do something other than bake a stupid casserole.

As the final hymn starts up, Kevin slips out as quietly as he slipped in. This had been my plan, too; instead, I wait until the last verse to make my exit, to give him some privacy. Walking through the parking lot to my car, however, I see him sitting in his pickup truck, and I feel my pits get clammy. I don't know how to talk to someone who is this sad. It's one thing to take part in a ritual, voices in unison, reciting a familiar prayer from the back row. But I have no words of my own for what happened.

Kevin looks up and sees me and now I have to stop. Now I have to find the words. I tap gently on the driver's side window and he holds up a hand in apology, *just a second*, as he turns the key in the ignition and lowers his window.

"Sorry," I say. "I didn't mean to startle you."

He shakes his head no. Kevin is a firefighter who wears a pager on his belt all day and probably sleeps next to it at night; he can't be a man who startles easily.

"I have to pick up donuts," he says, as if I'd asked him for an explanation, as if this explained anything. "I promised the girls."

"Is there anything I can do to help?" I say, because this is how humans respond to grief when left to our own devices. I cringe at the dumb platitude. What could I possibly do to *help* him right now—carry a donut box? Someone loses a child and we are so ill-equipped, we have so little to offer, that we insist on running unnecessary errands.

"Actually, there is," Kevin says. He moves his two-way radio from the passenger seat and unlocks the door. "You have a few minutes?"

I climb into the truck and feel dizzy as I sit, being this close to Kevin. His sadness is so big, so incomprehensible, and the cab of this truck too small. I don't trust my voice and so I sit in silence. We could drive from here to California and still I would not find the words. My chest feels tight and I have a fleeting premonition that Kevin plans to swerve his truck into oncoming traffic. I wouldn't blame him.

He doesn't speak to me again until we have exited the Dunkin' Donuts drive-thru.

"I need to sell my parents' house," he says suddenly.

I remember Maddy telling me they had to move her grandmother into a memory care center a few months back, less than a year after her grandfather died. She must have told Kevin about my mom. I should have reached out to him sooner, when this was still the worst thing that had ever happened to him, but I never really had that kind of relationship with Maddy's family.

"Do you mind taking a look at it?" Kevin says.

Right. This has nothing to do with my mom. I'm here because I'm a realtor.

"Now?" I say dumbly, because of course not now. Now is coffee and donuts after church with his family. Now is being with people who aren't afraid of his grief, who can bear witness to it.

"If you don't mind," he says, already hitting the indicator on his truck and making the turn.

Because of course now. *Now* is the moment that needs filling, now is all that exists, because the past contains Maddy and the future does not and these are equally agonizing impossibilities. *Now*, you get up and you make breakfast and you braid hair and you go to church and you pick up donuts and coffee. You get things done and then you find more things that need doing. You pass hours that add up to days, and you keep busy until, eventually, you can bear to be still. How unbelievably thoughtless of the rest of us, to deplete this family's to-do list because we want to *help*.

"I'd love to see it," I say.

We pull up in the driveway of a ranch-style house, the light blue paint mottled and cracked. There is a haphazard, blocky addition in the rear, and an old-fashioned sliding patio door in front, the rubber seal peeling off. The lawn, though, is buzz-cut short, and the flower beds are freshly mulched. I glance over at Kevin's hands on the steering wheel, notice the dirt under his fingernails. I think of Maggie Smith's poem.

Any decent realtor,
walking you through a real shithole, chirps on
about good bones: This place could be beautiful,
right? You could make this place beautiful.

"It's charming," I say.

"No it's not," Kevin says, folding up the cuffs of his shirt.

I once told Ethan that his forearms were my favorite part of his body—any man's body, really, although I did not mention this part—and I immediately regretted the confession. After I told him, it felt forced when Ethan folded his cuffs, like he was trying to turn me on. It stopped being sexy the moment I said it was. I reach down for my bag and let myself out of the truck.

Kevin leads me through the house, past the family photographs that fill a wall and the ceramic angels that fill a bookcase. As we enter each room, Kevin tells me things a realtor can't see: the window he and his brothers crouched under to slingshot squirrels; the wall his dad patched up after his brother, heartbroken and drunk, punched a hole in it; the nook where his mom kept her sewing machine and puzzle table, because she needed natural light for both. In the master bedroom, he points out a basket of knitting needles and yarn and tells me his mom's favorite item to knit was socks, until she forgot how.

"See?" he says, hitching up his pant leg to reveal a wool sock.

Half a sock in the same shade of navy is still attached to one of the needles in the basket. I should be used to this by now, the incomplete projects the dead leave behind when they will a house to a grown child, but the optimism of that half-knit sock just about breaks my heart. How then, to even contemplate the death of a girl?

"I'm so sorry about Maddy," I say, and these words feel grotesquely inadequate, but the same would be true of every word that's ever been uttered, and the inadequacy of language is no excuse for saying nothing. "I don't even know what to—"

"My mom didn't throw anything out," Kevin says, gesturing to a framed puzzle on the wall. It's one of those fake Venice scenes, gas-lit lamps and gondolas rendered in saturated hues. "Drove my dad nuts."

"My mom was the same," I say, although she wasn't. She hated clutter.

Fitting, then, that in the end her brain was the ultimate de-clutterer, erasing every face she'd ever known, including mine.

"I'm really sorry about your mom," he says. "Indie told me."

"It was a year ago," I say, as if time healed everything, as if I would ever stop being a woman who lost her mother too soon. As if Kevin would ever be anything other than a man who lost his child.

He walks into the kitchen and gestures toward the well-stocked pantry, tells me how he helped his dad build the floor-to-ceiling shelves the summer after he graduated high school. I run my hand along a shelf to show my appreciation, then quickly pull it back in case Kevin thinks I'm checking for dust. It really is nice work.

"My mom believed in dry goods," Kevin says. "I guess her parents talked about the Depression a lot? All I know is, she *really* liked to buy in bulk, and it got worse after my dad died. I never had the heart to tell her she was buying more food than she had time left to eat. I mean, how much pasta—"

He turns away, shaking his head, and walks into the dining room.

"You did the right thing," I say, walking behind him.

"Thanks," he says. "Alzheimer's is a bitch. Excuse my language, but it is."

We have words for this, I realize. This is the natural order of things. Parents get sick, parents die, and it's shitty, but we expect it. We don't turn away from this sort of grief because we have always known it would come, ever since the first time we asked our parents, "How old will you be when I'm a hundred?"

"She called me by my dad's name the last time I visited," Kevin says. "Then she noticed Laura in the doorway and she lost it. She thought I was cheating on her."

"Jesus," I say, and immediately regret that this is my default curse word, a habit I picked up from Ethan. *Christ on a bike* is another of his favorites. My husband may be an atheist, but when it comes to expletives, he is squarely in the Anglican tradition. "I'm so sorry."

"Yeah," he says.

"I always felt like the nurses were judging me for watching TV in my mom's room," I say. "But I never knew what to talk about. Sometimes I'd literally read my shopping list out loud, or I'd look up a recipe on my phone, and I'd read that. My whole life, I was so used to her interrupting me or criticizing me, I didn't know what to say when she went quiet. She was a narcissist, I think, so listening wasn't exactly her strong suit."

Kevin smiles a little, and I want to kick the wall until my toes break. *Listen to yourself*, I think, my body pulsing with shame. This man lost his child—his *child*—and I am bathing in his polite acknowledgment that I lost something, too. I used to think it was proof I wasn't a narcissist, how often I feared that I might turn out to be one. But what if the exact opposite were true?

"You showed up," Kevin says gently, and his essential goodness makes me feel both better and worse. "That's everything. How'd you do it for so long?"

I'm not sure Ethan ever asked me this question.

I think about the way my mom cursed out the nursing aides whenever she misplaced an item of clothing, accusing them of stealing from her and selling her things on eBay—my mom, who'd only ever allowed herself the occasional *phooey* in her former life. Also, how did she know about eBay? She didn't even have email. I think about how the mom I knew gradually receded, until she was a blank page and I could project onto her any kind of mother

I wanted. I think about how this was when our relationship was at its most tender, neither of us disappointed in the other.

And then I think about Maddy, how she will never grow old enough to care for her own mother. The day of my mom's funeral, Indie offered to blow out my hair, even though she's always telling me to leave it curly. As she combed argan oil through my hair with her fingers, raking her nails across my scalp, I closed my eyes and saw the past blur into the future—generations of grown daughters tending to their own mothers. It was like that photo app that ages your face: Indie showed it to me once, and I'll never forget the revulsion I experienced, watching my beloved teen daughter's face morph into wrinkles and crags. And yet I couldn't look away.

None of this is an answer to Kevin's question.

He comes to stand at my side. We are in the front room now, facing the patio window. The wall-to-wall cream carpeting is spotless; if his mom were here, I'm certain she would ask us to remove our shoes. Or perhaps she let Kevin keep his work boots on because he was Chief, like his father and grandfather before him, and always on call.

"We loved Maddy so much," I say eventually, because everything that's not Maddy feels beside the point. "We—"

I catch myself and pause. I lost four pregnancies in the years after Indie was born—the last at twenty-two weeks—and every single one was devastating, but I don't want Kevin to think I'm comparing my loss to his. Even using the word *loss* to describe both things is abhorrent, as if they existed on the same scale. What Kevin lost cannot be measured on any scale.

"We always wanted a sibling for Indie, but that wasn't in the cards for us," I say. "Then we met Maddy, and she was better than a sister, she was a kindred spirit. I told the girls their friendship reminded me of Anne Shirley and Diana in *Anne of Green Gables*—she was the friend Indie had been waiting for her whole life. Maddy was more than any of us could have hoped for."

I force myself to turn and look at Kevin. He is stricken, I can see it in his eyes; but his jaw is tight. He is not going to cry in front of me, a near stranger.

Kevin's whole being is one word right now, *Maddy*, and I just let her name slip off my tongue so casually. My own thoughtlessness apparently knows no bounds. *Like a daughter*, I almost told him. *We loved her like a daughter.* As if this were something that happened to me, too. I am no better than the rubbernecking do-gooders in town, hoping to ward off tragedy with meal trains and teardrop emojis. I, too, am standing where the lightning has already struck, as if the odds will save me.

"So, what do you think?" Kevin asks eventually, glancing around the room. "We need to sell the house as soon as possible to pay for the nursing home. Can you do it?"

"For sure," I say, but the phrase comes out chipper and fake, Valley Girl style. *Fer sherr.* "It's got good bones," I add, although it doesn't. "And the market's pretty hot right now, especially after that piece in the *Times*. I bet we can convince some cidiot to pay through the nose for it."

So many meaningless words piling on top of each other, like misspelled subject lines in a junk email folder.

"My parents could never afford to buy a house here today," Kevin says. "Most of my friends can't, either. Just this year, five guys from the firehouse had to move out of the district. One guy, he's been renting here for twenty-seven years, and the landlord just raised his rent by eight hundred bucks. Where's he going to find eight hundred a month? I walk down Main Street now, I don't recognize anyone."

I say nothing, because I know he's right. I picture Kevin in town, sharing the sidewalk with people who casually drop eight hundred dollars on a *jacket*, brandishing their high-end logos like Boy Scout patches. Strangers who never knew Maddy, who never even heard of her, who showed up only because they read about this place in the real estate section of the *Times*. My cheeks burn as I think of my own quote in the article. "This place radiates small-town charm," I gushed to the reporter. "It's like a Hallmark Christmas movie come to life." The online version of the piece included pictures from my feed. "*If You Lived Here* might be country living porn, but it's not necessarily an unreachable fantasy," the reporter wrote. "Because Kate Campbell wants you to join her here. She'll even sell you the house, if you have a million and change to spare."

"How many cidiots you think volunteer at the firehouse?" Kevin asks me. "I'll tell you how many: zero. Who's gonna be left when one of their fancy renovated houses catches fire? Who's gonna show up when one of their kids—"

He stops himself. He can't say it.

But I know exactly what would happen. No matter how much they take from him—how much *we* take from him, I correct myself—Kevin will still point a firehose at their burning homes. He'll still show up in the ambulance for their kids. Every guy in the firehouse will do the same, because that's what they signed up for.

When we first moved upstate, we woke one Sunday morning to an ice-cold house, and Ethan immediately called a guy to come fix the boiler. It turned out the oil tank was just empty; as renters in city apartments, it had never occurred to us to wonder where heat came from. *Cidiots*, I could see it in the guy's face as he waved off my attempt to pay him for the unnecessary weekend visit. There was kindness in his gesture, but there was something beneath the kindness, too, something we weren't allowed access to.

I turn to Kevin, see a muscle twitch in his jaw. I want to say something real.

"I wish I could have met your mom before all this," I say gently. "I think I would have liked her."

"Yeah?" Kevin says, and he turns to face me, a slight smile in his eyes. "Well, she would have hated you. No offense."

"None taken," I say lightly, because this is something I can do: I can be a stand-in for everything Kevin lost before he lost Maddy. "I get it, I'm the one helping the cidiots move in."

"Everyone talks about how this town is *charming*," Kevin says, his eyes hard now. "If it's that freakin' charming, why do they try so hard to change it once they get here?"

We drive back to the church so I can pick up my car. The parking lot is empty now, the church closed up, and despite everything, the realtor in me can't help but think, *what a waste*. All this space, all this beauty, for just a few hours a week.

"See you in church," Kevin says as I climb out of his truck.

"Of course," I reply, just as I once reassured my mother: Of course I'll see you in heaven. Because show me a human being on the planet who would dare undermine this man's faith right now, who would tell this father, *I don't know. Cauliflower.*

chapter eleven Indie

Dad was right, brunch *is* our version of a sacred ritual. At least, it used to be. But then Mom started to work weekends, and Dad said Sunday was the only time he could "squeeze in" a fifty-mile bike ride, and now I can't remember the last time we went. For years, though, my parents treated Sunday brunch like a pilgrimage, occasionally even crossing multiple county lines to try someplace new. Yes, for eggs.

If the word *brunch* makes you think of pancake mix from a box and high fructose corn syrup on the side, then let me explain how our denomination does things: Brunch in my family means going out to restaurants that serve entrées in miniature cast iron pans, usually with charred kale or house-made garlic aioli on the side. (Mom loves the way those cast iron pans look in her posts.) Pour-over coffee is our holy communion, except I'm not allowed any because apparently it prevents my brain from forming neural connections. Maddy got to take her first communion when she was eight, which is considered the age of reason in church, she said. Try telling my parents that. I'm not allowed to check my phone during brunch—I'm not even allowed to bring homework. Instead we have to talk about the news, as if my parents' over-caffeinated take on current events had the same nutritional value as charred kale. Maddy's parents volunteer at the firehouse, and *mine* act like getting all worked up over the news is a legit contribution to the planet. Like the families living in a war zone or stranded in refugee camps feel a little cheerier this morning, because my parents care. Often they get so mad about the state of the world, it sounds like an argument, no matter that they're on the same side.

I never hated brunch, though, I guess in the same way Maddy didn't hate church. We each understood that our parents were trying to impart something. And my parents didn't *only* talk about the news. We also shared our thorns and roses, we did the *New York Times* crossword together, and sometimes we'd play a made-up family game called Cidiot vs. Teenager: Mom would nominate her most oblivious client of the week, Dad would tell a story about one of the basic boys in high school, and we'd all vote on which one was less likely to survive an apocalypse. Cidiots are clueless, we all agreed, but Dad's a good storyteller, so usually the teenagers would win. Also, cidiots don't fail gym because they refuse to wear anything but Crocs or slides to school, even when it snows, and cidiots don't film themselves shotgunning seltzer, either. "I can't believe we live in a town where the teenagers chug pink grapefruit seltzer," Mom said, and for some reason this cracked them both up. "Knuckleheads," Dad said.

I wonder, do they think they've already passed on everything I need to know, is that why we don't do brunch anymore?

On the one-month anniversary of Maddy's death, Kaitlynn posts a photo of Maddy's roadside memorial. Some of the real flowers have wilted, which makes the plastic bouquets look extra fake. The stuffed animals look a little weathered, too, as if they'd been sitting there for years already, soaking up rain and pollen and exhaust fumes from the trucks that barrel past on their way to the slate quarry.

No one asked me to participate in the memorial. From the comments on Kaitlynn's post, it seems like the Minkles started the shrine. Of course it was the Minkles. I bet they talked about how "aesthetic" it looked, various shades of lavender on dark green—at least until "randoms" started contributing their own off-brand memorabilia. I'd like to swipe up and pretend the shrine doesn't exist, but I can't unsee all those purple teddy bears sitting around a cross. Even the cross is painted lavender. These people have no idea who Maddy really was. Come on, a teddy bear picnic? It's like they believe Maddy froze in time after they stopped inviting her to their birthday parties. Also, she hated purple. That was *my* favorite color, not hers.

I step out of my bedroom into the hallway and almost trip over Mom, who is sitting on the floor, working on her laptop. She's wearing her clunky phone headset that makes her look like an air traffic controller and she has a pile of papers stacked next to her on the floor. Apparently this is her new home office. She stands suddenly, kicking over her mug of coffee.

"You're up!" Mom says, as if I'm Sleeping Beauty, as if I'm some average teenager sleeping 'til noon because it's the first day of summer break and, *oh, you know how teenagers are.*

I stare at the coffee puddling on the floor, soaking into Mom's papers, but she doesn't follow my gaze. She is standing in the middle of the hallway, her legs planted wide like a bouncer at a nightclub, and I realize that if I want to get by her, I'm going to have to talk.

I can't remember the last time I spoke. It's not like a vow of silence or anything, I just don't see the point in words. I try to think of the right thing to say now, but all I can come up with is a secret password: *Rumpelstiltskin.* There are other words swirling around inside my brain, but I can't make them stay still long enough to read them.

"Can I get you something?" Mom says. "Something to eat? Or drink?"

I shake my head.

"Do you want to go for a walk?"

I nod.

"Can I come?"

I shake my head.

"Take a water bottle, please," she says. "It's hot out there today."

And just like that, she lets me past. See? Who needs words? All Mom wanted to know was that I'd be getting fresh air. Every time she delivers a meal, she opens my window, and every time she leaves, I close it again and crank the AC. I like it icy in my room. But Mom believes in fresh air; she says it makes the house smell like something, while AC makes it smell like nothing. It drives Dad crazy, the way she insists on opening windows when the AC is on.

I ride my bike over to Maddy's house. It's so hot that every inch of my body is sweating, even my eyelids. When I drop my bike on Maddy's front lawn, the handlebars gliding out of my sweaty palms, I realize I have no memory of the twenty-minute ride over, of signaling left or right with my arm, of looking both ways before crossing a road. Yet somehow I found my way here, like a horse who's thrown its rider. I stand on the front lawn, unsure of what to do next. As I start walking toward the house, Maddy's sister Kaitlynn opens the front door.

Even back in second grade, when I still believed in the Easter Bunny—not just a magical bunny, but a bunny who *laid eggs*—I never entertained the fantasy that people might mistake me and Maddy for sisters. I have straight, dark brown hair that I've worn in a pixie cut for years, while Maddy and her sisters have curly hair that frizzes like a halo on hot summer days. Maddy's funeral was open casket, and as I stood in front of her body, it seemed impossible to believe her wild red curls had stopped growing. I realize that, officially, *everyone's* hair is dead, but this gross fact never seemed true of Maddy.

Maddy shared a small room with Kaitlynn, but she rarely complained about this. I know for a fact that Kaitlynn annoyed the shit out of her, so I guess Maddy was doing this for my benefit, assuming that I envied her surplus of siblings. One time she said,

"Your room is *huge*!" and then looked at me quickly, as if she'd blurted out something hurtful or inappropriate. She was wrong about that, though. Why would I want a sister when I had Maddy?

"Hi," I say to Kaitlynn. *Is Maddy home?* That's what I'm supposed to say next, because that's what I've said a million other times on this doorstep.

"Hi," Kaitlynn says, and she steps aside, as if I have an appointment.

She's supposed to call out, *MADDY! INDIE'S HERE.* She never turned her head into the house when she did this, she just yelled it right in my face, like some psycho drill sergeant. She knew my arrival meant Maddy was about to kick her out of their bedroom.

I step inside the house and see that the kitchen is full of Maddy's extended family. This is not unusual—her cousins and aunts and uncles are always stopping by—except today everyone is talking in soft, low voices, like they're in a theater waiting for a play to start. Kaitlynn disappears and I stand in the hallway, unsure of what to do next. I cross my arms, uncross them, cross them again. I wonder if Mom would have let me go if she'd known my destination.

And then Maddy's mom finds me and envelops me in a hug, crossed arms and all. She holds me so tightly, I imagine I am sinking into the folds of her soft, warm body, like I'd been falling from a great height and she caught me. I want her to tell me, *You just missed her, honey, Maddy's at a church youth group meeting.* But she says nothing, she just cries and strokes my hair. Her head barely reaches my shoulder. When did that happen? I am a month older than I was when Maddy died, and this seems like something I should apologize for. Standing here in Maddy's house, in her mom's arms, I want to stay fourteen forever.

When she finally releases me from the embrace, I tell her there's a roadside memorial and I'd like to contribute something from Maddy's room. My voice comes out scratchy from underuse, and my throat hurts, like the time I had strep. I swallow hard. There was probably something else I should have said first, something nice. I clear my throat as if that was just the warm-up.

"Obviously I wouldn't take anything big," I say. "Nothing you'll miss."

Maddy's mom makes a strangled noise and I scrape my fingernails across my arms. I should have stayed home. I have so much of Maddy in my own room, I didn't need to come here for the memorial. But our house is too quiet. My parents act like I'm a convalescing patient who's been prescribed minimal stimulation. They've even found a way to argue in monotone, their voices permeating my room like a soft hum. *She has to eat. She can eat later. She has to talk. She can talk later. She has to leave her room. She feels safe there. She has to sign up for summer school. Please don't tell me you're actually worried about her GPA right now.*

The Alexa speaker in our kitchen used to play the local NPR affiliate dawn to dusk, and because my bedroom is right above the kitchen and our ancient house is poorly insulated, I learned about the passage of time from each show's theme music—All Things Considered, Northeast Report, Marketplace, Fresh Air. But Alexa is silent now. I kind of miss Kai Ryssdal's voice, actually.

I wanted just a few minutes with Maddy's loud, chaotic family. I wanted her sisters to bicker over the family iPad, and I wanted her dad to tease me about the slogan on my shirt or the latest button on my backpack. I wanted to watch Maddy's mom make dinner while she sang along to Kiss FM. I wanted to ask if she needed help folding laundry, because there's always a mountain of clean clothes on top of the machine. Stupid, so stupid, to imagine they would be the same.

Maddy's mom walks up the stairs and I follow her into the room that Kaitlynn no longer has to share. I see Kaitlynn in the corner, and she is wearing Maddy's denim jacket now, her hands in the pockets, clutching it around her body like she's bracing against a high wind. Kaitlynn knows this is what I wanted to take for the memorial: Maddy's favorite jacket, decorated with buttons we collected together. I have the twin of each button on my backpack.

Maddy's mom kneels in front of a wooden trunk in the closet and opens the lid. She grips the edge of the trunk with both hands as if she's seasick, and she makes that sound again, like something is lodged in her throat and she can't breathe. I put a hand to my own neck.

I watch her sort through the collection of stuffed animals that Maddy evicted from her bed when we started middle school. Maddy's mom holds each one up for inspection, and occasionally she hesitates, as if considering whether she could let this one go. Each time, though, she returns the stuffed animal to its home in the trunk. How could I ask her to give up anything? Each one holds a story inside.

"Here," she says eventually, just when I am ready to leave, to say never mind, to tell her it all belongs right here, in Maddy's room.

She hands me a pale blue stuffed animal—a giant narwhal that Maddy used to sleep on like a pillow back in elementary school. *Unicorn of the sea*, I think. When Maddy and I were in our narwhal period, Mom asked us, "Doesn't it blow your minds that narwhals are real?" But, no, it didn't, because we were eight and had not yet learned to expect so little of the real world.

"Thank you," I say. "It's perfect."

And it is, I realize, because why would I want to share the Maddy I knew with anyone else? It was always us against the world, and we liked it that way. Not even *against* the world, because that makes it sound like we were misunderstood. We didn't need anyone else to get us, because we got each other.

"She went to the mall with you and your mom and spent all her birthday money on this," Maddy's mom says. "I was so mad at her, remember? I thought it was way too much to spend on a stuffed animal."

Of course I remember. Mom gave Maddy some money to make up the total—*that* was the real reason her mom got so mad. And this is why she can let the narwhal go, I realize: It's a story she doesn't need.

"I bet she's looking down right now and laughing at what we picked," Maddy's mom says, and her eyes are bright and urgent, as if she's willing me to see it, too.

I wish I could see it, I really do, but wishing seems like a weak offering right now.

"Maddy's in heaven," Kaitlynn announces firmly, as if I might have forgotten. I turn toward her, surprised to find her still in the room. It's like she's informing me that Maddy is at another friend's house and can't hang out with me right now.

Just smile and nod. Pretend you agree.

But then something moves through me like an understanding, and it all comes together in this one moment, in the middle of Maddy's bedroom, next to her still-unmade bed, her pillow still molded to the shape of her head: I know in my bones that my best friend isn't here, and it feels like a betrayal to pretend she is—a far worse betrayal than some stupid memorial that misses the entire point of who she was. Saying nothing now feels like lying through my teeth, and how can *that* be right?

"She's not in heaven," I blurt out. "Souls aren't real."

Maddy's mom's face goes slack and I can't tell if she's about to scream or throw up, but I need to help her understand: Her daughter is not trapped up there in the sky, forced to watch us all suffer like this. One of the meditation videos I watched said that every breath you take includes at least one molecule from Julius Caesar's last breath. It's not heaven, but it's real, which has to make it better.

"Maddy was an arrangement of particles," I say. "The same particles that make up everything we can see and touch. Her atoms will always be here, even after you make her bed and clean her sheets. Even a thousand years from now."

I'm a little breathless, rushing through the words while I still feel brave enough to say them. I have to tell her the most important part.

"And it's okay!" I say, my voice trembling. "It's better than okay, actually, because particles can't be sad or scared or lonely, can they? Particles can't miss us."

We may not be okay, but isn't it good news that Maddy no longer feels a thing? When her skull smashed into the county road, there was no soul in there, no essence of Maddy that leaked out. The real Maddy isn't buried underground and she isn't looking down on me from above, and she's definitely not giggling about a stupid narwhal stuffy. My best friend is not a rotting body, and she's not my guardian angel. *Maddy* was just the name we gave to a temporary arrangement of particles. I clutch the narwhal to my chest and look at Maddy's mom, and now I'm the one silently pleading with her to understand.

What I really want, though, is to smash open my own skull and show her how empty it is. *Do you see it now?* I would say. *Do you see how, when you break the atoms apart, there's nothing left, not a single thought?*

And *that's* how you empty your mind, I think.

"Do you need anything else?" Maddy's mom asks, as if I hadn't said anything about heaven or souls or particles, as if it was all just an embarrassing burp she's choosing to ignore.

I shake my head no, and Maddy's mom walks over to her youngest daughter, cups a hand around Kaitlynn's cheek, and whispers something in her ear. Then she walks out and I am standing there in Kaitlynn's room, a place that will never again be Maddy's, and Kaitlynn is looking at me, waiting for me to leave.

I'm not surprised when Mom tells me she heard about my visit. The only surprising thing is that it was Maddy's dad who made the call.

"I talked to Kevin," Mom says, handing me a glass of water. "He told me you were there, he told me you spoke."

"*Kevin*?" I say. "No one calls him that. Only Maddy's mom."

Mom gasps at the sound of my voice, a gentle *oh* sound, and now her eyes are glassy with tears. She reaches out and rubs her thumb across my cheek, like she's checking to see if I'm real.

"I'm so happy it helped you to go over there," she says eventually, dropping her hand from my face. "I really am. I'm so happy you're talking again, you have no idea. But Maddy's parents are worried about you. Kevin—the Chief—he said the things you were saying—"

"It's fine," I say. "I won't bring it up again, you don't have to worry."

"He said you told Laura that Maddy doesn't have a soul," Mom says. "Why would you *say* something like that to them?"

"Not just Maddy," I say, because I want her to understand: It was the opposite of personal. "I told her no one does."

I should have known it wouldn't comfort Maddy's family to hear this.

"But I still don't—" Mom says, then pauses, like a glitched video.

"She told me Maddy is *watching* me," I say, and I think I might be yelling now, though it's hard to tell because my ears fill with this rushing sound like we're in a tunnel with the car windows down. "Why would *she* say something like *that*?"

Mom nods, teary again. She pulls me toward her and presses her lips to the top of my head.

"He said maybe it's better if you don't visit them for a while," she says softly, into my hair. "He asked if you could maybe—not forever, just for now—give his family some space."

I wonder, though, if Maddy's dad really used the word *space*, because there were five people living in that house and now there are four. Maddy's absence must make the place feel cavernous. I imagine every sound bouncing off the walls like in the school gym, and maybe that's why they were all speaking so softly when I visited. If I lived in that house, I would want to shrink it down until I had to duck my head like Alice in Wonderland to get through the door. I would make the house so tiny that it would be impossible to imagine there had ever been enough room for five.

"Okay," I say.

"I've missed the sound of your voice," Mom says, like everything is fine now. Like I'm fixed. "I wasn't sure when I'd hear it again."

So what, I think. I ate a couple of granola bars, I left my room, I pedaled a bike, I spoke. My t-shirt is soaked through with sweat and my lips taste salty and now I'm thirsty. This proves I have pores and vocal cords and a digestive system that produces enzymes. This proves I have a body that is growing, decaying, holding on. I am flesh and bone. So what?

A few days later, Mom asks if I want to go to Maddy's church. She's unloading the dishwasher like she's mad at the bowls and plates for being clean, and Dad is pretending not to notice. I guess maybe they both think it's the other person's turn? I don't know, adults can be so weird sometimes. Dad is assembling a green smoothie at the other end of the kitchen, and I swear he's feeding weeds into the blender.

"I know I told you to give them space," Mom says. "But Kevin said they'd be okay with you going to their church."

"Just a little casual brainwashing, huh?" Dad says. "Since when are we okay with that?"

Then he turns on the blender so Mom can't respond right away. Such a douche move.

When I was little, Dad used to ask me if I wanted to hear a secret—where the treasure was buried in the backyard, or what Santa really looked like. Then he'd turn on the blender and pretend to clue me in, mouthing words I couldn't hear. As soon as he'd flicked the blender off again, he'd say, in a conspiratorial whisper, "*Don't tell anyone!*"

"It feels nice at their church," Mom says, when the kitchen is quiet again. "The vibe, the people, the music. I thought Indie might like it, too."

"The *vibe*?" Dad says, incredulous. His green drink is the size of a Big Gulp and the kitchen smells like freshly cut grass. "We agreed on no religion for Indie, remember?"

"I'm just taking her to church," Mom says. "It's hardly indoctrination."

"Um, yes, that's exactly what it is. Especially right now, when she's so vulnerable."

"It's a *community*," Mom says. "It's people taking care of each other."

"That's how they get you," he retorts, which is verbatim what he says about car rental companies' hidden fees and any kind of free trial period. It's a dad thing, I guess.

"Oh, come on, they're not Scientologists," Mom says. "I just think it would mean a lot to Maddy's family to see Indie in church."

"Don't put that burden on her," Dad says. "It's too much."

I'm waiting for either of them to notice I'm still in the room, to ask me how *I* feel about going to church. If they did ask, I might say that I find it hard to believe her family would consider this a fair trade: Maddy's life for one soul saved. As if her entire existence was just a hand-me-down sweater that will fit me just fine.

"I'm going for a walk," Dad announces suddenly. He pours his green drink into a travel cup, then turns to me and squeezes my hand. "Want to come?"

I don't reply because I don't want any part of this annoying land grab over my emotional and spiritual state.

"I didn't mean you should do it for *them*," Mom says to me after the door closes behind Dad.

She's standing at the kitchen island now, making a shopping list from the open cookbook in front of her. I bet this is one of those "sneaky" parenting tips Mom likes to share with her readers: *So your monosyllabic teen won't open up? Take eye contact out of the equation!*

"I thought it might be comforting for *you*," Mom continues, still not looking up. "Maddy grew up in that church, she was baptized there. They're grieving for her, too."

Her voice is so calm and normal, it's like she's asking me to join 4H or some other dumb after-school club that might look impressive on my college application.

"You're actually serious about this?" I say. "I always thought you were supposed to *lose* your faith when bad shit happens to good people. But you've decided this is the perfect time to get on board with God's plan for my life?"

I imagine sitting in church, listening to the minister explain how Maddy is in a "better place." I picture the pews full of people who think they have it all figured out, who look up to the fucking *ceiling* when they say Maddy's name, who are so sure that "God never gives you more than you can handle." They'd throw around identical platitudes if a hundred-year-old woman died gently in her sleep, and how is that even close to the same thing?

"Indie," Mom says. She looks up at me now, but she still has a finger in the cookbook, marking her place. "I know it hurts."

"No," I say, slamming the cookbook shut on her finger. "You don't know. You're meal planning right now. You think you know exactly how next week will go. You think I'm going to be here for Meatless Monday and Taco Tuesday. You don't know anything."

"You're right," Mom says. "You're so right. We have to treasure every moment."

"*Treasure every moment?!*" I yell, and I watch her flinch. I bet she wishes I hadn't started talking again after all. "I can't believe that's your takeaway. None of this matters, don't you get it? It doesn't matter how many lists you make or how many teddy bears you leave on the side of the road. It for sure doesn't matter how many stupid stories you make up about guardian angels in the sky. None of it changes anything. So go ahead and treasure your stupid moments if you want, post them online or whatever, but don't think that makes your life special."

I run to my room and slam the door behind me. I sit cross-legged on the floor and squeeze my eyes shut, but this only makes the thoughts louder. I can feel my heartbeat in my belly, in my temples, in my fingertips and toes, it's like there's a hamster trapped in my body, searching for a way out. *Transcend the body*, the meditation experts say, but they don't mention the hamster. I feel this urge to unzip my skin and leave the whole stupid thing behind.

An hour later I hear Dad return from his walk. My parents are arguing again, and I'm sure Dad thinks he won this round, because I said no to church. But what I didn't tell either of them, what I don't realize myself until I'm alone, is that a small part of me is secretly glad Mom's going to church, and glad she wants me to go, too. It's like Maddy's death has made her fear for my soul, even though she doesn't believe I have one. In her desire to protect me, she plans to leave no stone unturned. She'll even go to *church*, because it's more important to enlist every safety net than to be right, no matter what she thinks about the patriarchy. Lying on my bedroom floor as my mom meal-plans below me, this thought is the only thing that comes close to making me feel safe.

chapter twelve ❦ Kate

I sit in the back pew again, but this time Kevin sits with his family, up front. I cannot take my eyes off them, this family of five-now-four, standing dutifully for each prayer and hymn. Today Kaitlynn's braid is threaded through with a pale blue ribbon, and for some reason this makes me wonder how Laura would have reacted if Indie had been the one to die. I find it hard to picture her allowing Maddy to cocoon in her room, to stop speaking, to skip the last month of middle school. She would have forced her daughter outside, into the world. She would have made Maddy do homework and go to church and practice piano and eat dinner with the family. This makes me feel like a failure, but also—irrationally, and only for a moment—this makes me angry at Maddy's mom.

The service concludes with "How Great Thou Art," and I am riveted to the pew, unable to slip out early, even though the old lady playing the organ is at least a measure ahead of the choir. The last time I heard this hymn was at my mom's funeral. I used to think it was proof of my faith, the way this hymn gives me chills—the way the soaring refrain frog-marches me toward some kind of euphoria. Adele ballads do the same thing, I've discovered.

As I exit the church in a stream of people dressed in their Sunday best, all of them greeting each other warmly as they wait their turn to thank the minister, I smile and nod without making eye contact with anyone. This feels like middle school all over again. And then I sense Maddy's family behind me. Is there a collective intake of breath in the bustling vestibule, or a sudden shift in volume? Something changes, and I know. The crowd parts for them as they walk toward the exit, Laura first, Kyleigh and Kaitlynn next, and then Kevin passes me and I feel his hand cup my elbow for a brief moment before they are gone. The door closes behind Maddy's family and the room settles again, like sloshing water righting itself.

My hands are shaking so hard, it takes me three tries to get the key in the ignition of my car. I thought Kevin and I were done, that we would return to being near-strangers, that I would sell his mom's house and hand over a check and he would find solace with family and old friends. But there was a connection in that simple gesture: For whatever reason, he needs me still.

As I pull into our driveway, my phone buzzes in the center console, and I know before looking that it's him. *Do you need to take pictures of the house?* Kevin texts. *Meet there in an hour?* He already showed me where his mom kept the spare key, under an empty flowerpot in the shed, but I do not remind him of this. *Someone else takes the photos*, I text back. *But we should stage the house first. See you there.*

Kevin is wearing a fire department t-shirt tucked into navy work pants, and he is kneeling on the floor, assembling cardboard boxes. It's sweltering out today, but I'm guessing he's old school about shorts. My dad's the same, maintaining that shorts are for the gym or the beach—not that he frequents either place.

A pager is attached to Kevin's belt, and I think of how this pager is never off, how he must have heard the call come through that night and how there must have been whole minutes when he knew it had happened but did not yet know it had happened to her. There is sadness in the abstract, there is what it means to be a grieving parent, and then there is this human being in front of me: six-foot-three, at a guess, maybe two hundred pounds, his dark gray hair buzzed short and his firefighter mustache bushy but neat. And this man is not keening or wailing or prone on the floor—although this feels inevitable and terrifying—he is handing me a trash bag and asking me where we should start.

I look around the front room, at the accumulation of vacation trinkets, grandchildren's artwork, family portraits. Maddy is everywhere; how will they ever take another photograph? She will always be missing.

"Is the basement dry?" I ask, and Kevin nods.

"Let's pack up everything except the furniture," I say. "You can keep the boxes in your basement until—"

I pause. I was going to say, *until you're ready*, as if there would ever be a time when he'd know what to do with a framed photograph of Maddy's kindergarten graduation—a duplicate of the one in his own house, I'm sure, but no matter.

We start working our way through each room, and before long we are caked in dust and soaked with sweat.

"My mom didn't believe in air-conditioning," Kevin says apologetically, turning on a standing fan in the corner of the dining room. The blades become a blur of motion, wafting the dust on the fan's wire frame. I wonder if Kevin realizes he's already speaking of his mom in the past tense; I remember catching myself doing the same thing. I walk toward the fan until I am so close I worry my hair will get sucked into the blades, and only then can I feel the air move.

"You don't have to be here," he says when I sneeze.

I think of what Indie said about Maddy's funeral reception: *Of course we have to go*. I bend my knees to pick up a stack of old newspapers, and Kevin reaches out to lighten my load.

"I'm good," I say, turning away from him so I can push open the door with my back.

We fill trash bag after trash bag, box after box, and in this way we fill the hours, too. At times we talk, and at times we are quiet, but when we talk, it's always about the before times. Before Maddy, although we never say her name. I sort through talking points in my head, and when I speak, my words are slow and deliberate, my hand on the emergency brake. Everything could be about Maddy. Everything *is* about Maddy. Still, we circle the topic, her death a sinkhole between us.

Kevin tells me about his brother's HVAC business, and I tell him about my brother's string of way-too-young girlfriends, each of them convinced she'll be the one to domesticate him. Kevin tells me how his dad lost half a finger on a table saw, and I tell him about my dad's tool shed. He tells me about his work as a contractor, and I tell him about my failed attempts to monetize *If You Lived Here*, although of course I don't use the word *monetize*, nor do I tell him how Ethan rolls his eyes whenever I bring this up. (My husband is making fun of the *racket*, he insists—the whole idea of making money from a dramatized reenactment of your own life—as if this were any less of a slight.)

When we come across his mom's King James Bible, heavily annotated in her elegant cursive, I tell Kevin about attending sleep-away Bible camp, and he tells me about the capital campaign to fix his church's leaky roof—the same roof his parents were married under, and his grandparents before them. He does not ask why God lets children die, and I think maybe Kevin believes in God the same way he believes in the New York Giants and American-made trucks—not as a leap of faith, but as a matter of course.

Late afternoon, I text Ethan that I'll pick up Thai for dinner on my way home. He gives the message a thumbs-up. I put my phone back in my pocket and then take it out again. *How's Indie?* I type. Another thumbs-up. I resist the urge to tell him, *You're using it wrong. Please answer in a complete sentence.*

As we pack up the framed photographs crowding every surface in the house, Kevin shares the story behind each one: his nephew just back from Afghanistan; his mom holding her twelfth grandchild; his dad celebrating fifty years in the firehouse, almost every guy in the picture sporting a mustache. "It's a firefighter thing," Kevin tells me when I laughingly point this out. I'd forgotten he has one, too. "If you're on air, you can't get a proper seal on the mask with a beard, but a mustache is okay." I nod and smile. Listening is harder to get wrong than talking. There are generations of firefighters in Kevin's family, all male, and I find myself wondering if he ever wished for a son. How could he not? And yet, I don't know how a father could wish for anything besides his own children.

On a bedroom dresser is a picture of Maddy learning to knit, her tongue poking out in concentration and her grandmother leaning in to help. This, Kevin places gently in a box without a word.

When I go to pick up a trash bag he has filled, Kevin takes each of my forearms in his hands and turns them over. I feel a jolt at the intimacy of this act, and immediately hate myself. *This is Maddy's father*, I think, but still my body thrums. It has been so long since any man besides Ethan touched me like this. I watch Kevin read the tattooed quote that begins on my inner right arm and ends on my left: *the world was hers / for the reading*. He nods, releasing my arms unceremoniously.

"I always wondered what that said."

The repulsive vanity, to imagine he might be flirting with me. To have *wanted* him to do that.

"It's from a book," I begin, and then I find I can't say more.

Usually I tell people about the first time I read *A Tree Grows in Brooklyn*, how I was in my twenties and just figuring out that I could lose myself in books but find myself there, too. (In books I could also find other daughters who were loved less than sons, and other mothers who couldn't help it; this part I never shared with anyone except Ethan.) Today, though, my tattoo's origin story feels callous—all the books in the world that Indie can still find herself in. How anything at all could be hers for the taking. *God willing*, I hear my mom say. She used this phrase like punctuation, and now I think I understand why: It's a tiny offering to the sky, a vow to take nothing for granted.

"It's nice work," Kevin says. "I like the typewriter letters."

When we are done, we stand in the front yard, surrounded by trash bags, looking up at his parents' house.

"In five years, who'll even remember that she lived here?" Kevin says. "They'll probably just tear it down and build something new."

I wonder if he's thinking of the picture of Maddy, how she learned to knit in this house.

"You'll remember," I say.

Kevin doesn't own a passport—no one in his family does, Indie told me once, back when she was still too young to understand why—but he has an internal map of this town that goes back decades, generations of history and ownership layered like coats of paint on a wall.

"What's next?" he says.

"I'll bring a lawn sign over," I say. "And we should talk about how much we're going to list it for."

Kevin is silent for a moment, and I understand then what he really wants to know: *Tell me how to go home again.* I want to right this imbalance—how much he lost, how much I didn't. I feel an urge to do something huge, to make a grand gesture. How do you write it in the sky, how sorry you are?

"We could paint the bedrooms," I say. "The other rooms, too—it would really freshen things up. I could help you."

It's a meagre offering, but I have nothing else to give. If this were a Bible story, I would render him my child.

"Okay," Kevin says, and then his pager goes off and he taps something into his phone and he is gone.

chapter thirteen Indie

A few weeks before Maddy died, I watched a video about how we don't control our own thoughts, we only *feel* that we do. I sent the link to Maddy, because I sent everything to Maddy, and that's how I find the video again today, scrolling through our text thread. It feels like a gift from her: *HERE is how to stop thinking.* It was there all along, waiting for me. Of course the answer would come from Maddy. I press Play.

"Thoughts just pop up," the old guy in the video says. "The brain is basically a glorified auto-complete system." He looks like Professor Dumbledore, and I remember how this brought out my inner straight-A student the first time I watched the video: I wanted to ace his test. Our thoughts, Dumbledore goes on to explain, are actually generated by a kind of committee—a committee that's made up of our experiences, our genes, and our environment. And apparently no one's in charge of this committee, it just runs itself, which makes it sound a little like the health food co-op in town. ("I'm not sure I need my groceries to be self-governing," Dad said once, when no one in the store could tell him where the tahini was located, or if they even sold it.)

Anyway, I guess most of us are pretty attached to the idea of being the boss of our own minds, and so, after our thoughts "pop up," we're like, *Yeah, I decided to think that.* But we're not in charge of our own thoughts, any more than we control the sound of a bird chirping, or the feel of the ocean breeze on our skin. It's all just shit happening to us. Dumbledore does not use the word *shit*, though. I added that part myself.

What this means is that there's no "me" inside my head—that's just an illusion. And it's an illusion that can disappear if I take the right steps, Dumbledore says. He even guides viewers through a step-by-step process for erasing their "me."

The first time I watched the video, I remember thinking, *cool*, and when I sent it to Maddy, she did, too, although neither of us really got it. Mostly, it seemed like a lot of work. Who wanted to sit there doing nothing when there was so much Netflix to stream?

But today, when I find the video in my Maddy thread and watch it over and over again, I think, *yes*. If I can unbelieve in the self, then I can unbelieve in Maddy, too. It's the answer I've been looking for, to a question I didn't know to ask.

It takes practice and patience, Dumbledore says, if I want to feel the self fall away. But every time I get close, I remember something about my best friend: her denim jacket, that narwhal stuffy, the way she always made me check her teeth for food after lunch. These memories anchor me to a world I no longer believe in. It feels like I'm a scuba diver trapped by kelp on the ocean floor, and I cannot breathe down here. I need to get to the surface. I tell myself it's impossible to miss someone who was never really here, who was only ever an illusion, but it turns out I'm a slow study when it comes to reality. And failing this test is unbearable, because failing means I miss Maddy. Every single day I discover the absence of something new.

Today what I miss is the feeling of being bored with my best friend. During the long, hot days of late August each year, when summer break became a thing we took for granted, when the sun had lost its shine but not its oppressive heat, when our texts were some variation on *what's up / nuthin*, Maddy and I turned boredom into an art form. How long could we make a single ice pop last? What was the ultimate chip to guac ratio in a perfect bite?

Did ice cream taste better from a tiny spoon? What if we put the spoon in the freezer first? One August we even tried practicing witchcraft, after we read a thing online about how to cast spells. Time stretched like putty then, and like putty it snapped back into place the moment school started up.

Now it is summer again, and again the days are long and hot. But I'm not bored. "Only boring people get bored," Dad likes to say, as if boredom were a character defect brought on by too much screen time. He's wrong about that, though. Only carefree people get bored. The real reason kids bore easily is that most of them haven't yet experienced true loss.

One of the first times I remember going over to Maddy's house, I arrived to find the sisters playing a game I'd never heard of: Kaitlynn was holding an imaginary mango in her hand, Maddy pretended she had grapes, and Kyleigh had a fake clementine. "You have a kiwi," Kyleigh informed me. I didn't understand the rules, but I found the game surprisingly fun until Maddy decided not to share her grapes with Kaitlynn. The screaming! The slapping! The hair-pulling! The inevitable time-outs. As an only child, it had never occurred to me it was possible to brawl over imaginary fruit.

Which is why Maddy and I spent so much time at my quiet house, in my quiet room. How many hours did we spend this way, drawing pictures we didn't bother to keep, because we knew we'd create more? Each hour that I forget is an hour in Maddy's life that is erased, because we were the only two people in that room. This is how you lose someone. Or, this is how you grasp that she was never really here in the first place. I don't understand how her parents can believe that Maddy is still here, still watching over us, when an hour or a day in her short life is so easy to lose track of.

I keep my focus. *I cannot miss someone who was never here, I cannot miss someone who was never here, I cannot miss someone who was never here.* And yet, somehow, I do.

chapter fourteen Kate

I'm in the checkout line at the grocery store with nothing but cans of seltzer in my cart, because I drove here on autopilot after work and now I can't think of a single thing we need. I've already stocked our shelves with Indie's childhood favorites, and none of it helps. I text Ethan, *At the store, need anything?* He doesn't respond. My gaze lands on a stack of brown paper bags at the end of the conveyor belt, and I find myself thinking: *Gone are the days of hoarding plastic bags under the kitchen sink.* This is a good thing, obviously. I'm happy for the sea turtles, *obviously.* I was one of the cidiots who pushed for the single-use plastic ban in the first place. And yet, there's that unmistakable grip of nostalgia, like a tightness in my chest.

Nostalgia is an unruly beast. I understand the nostalgia I feel for my first apartment in the East Village, even though the bathtub was in the kitchen and the cockroaches were the size of my MetroCard. It was my first apartment—the place where I learned to think for myself. And I get it when I feel nostalgia for my daughter's babyhood, even though she woke every forty-five minutes to nurse, and would nap only when in motion. She was my child—the person who allowed me to *stop* thinking about myself. But nostalgia for the *plastic bag*? Apparently I've now reached the point where I feel nostalgia for things I never liked in the first place.

The only explanation I can come up with is this: Most days, time passes without us noticing. It slides by, another hour, another month, another year. But occasionally we snag on a single moment, like, well, a plastic grocery bag caught on a tree branch. And in this moment we are, for a second or two, intensely aware of the passage of time. Of how the future becomes the present becomes the past in the blink of an eye.

It's possible, of course, to manufacture these moments—to allow ourselves to be snagged on that tree branch. It's why we celebrate wedding anniversaries and birthdays. It's why, after Indie's piano recital last year—I can still picture her hands flying over the keys like barn swallows skimming a pond—Ethan texted me a video of one-year-old Indie smashing birthday cake into her ear. And it's why I insist on first-day-of-school photos every fall, even though Indie made me ditch the vintage chalkboard sign years ago. Her clenched fists in the image from kindergarten still slay me; she literally white-knuckled her way through that first day. Every first day until she met Maddy, actually.

A few months ago, Indie would have rolled her eyes at my eco-unfriendly nostalgia. Last summer she and Maddy returned from a trip to the mall with matching stainless steel water bottles and a selection of stickers to decorate them. (One of Indie's stickers was the word *anxious* in glittery purple script, which confused me but also warmed my heart.) "We'd rather go thirsty for a few hours than drink from a single-use plastic bottle," Indie announced proudly. The two girls used to stop by the firehouse after every company meeting to separate the recyclables, donning rubber gloves to sort through the trash by hand. There was a recycling bin right next to the trash can, but no one ever used it. Maybe it was a hard habit for the firefighters to break, or maybe the recycling bin felt like one more symbol of enemy occupation. Indie and Maddy never complained about this task, though, most likely because they never expected adults to do better. They identified with this planet—its rivers and oceans, its trees and its air—in a deeply personal way that has never come naturally to me.

How much has Indie lost, in disentangling herself from a dead girl? I'd like to believe the rivers and oceans still move her, but it doesn't feel like enough.

I pull out my phone and type a few notes for a post. When I get home, I sit at the kitchen island and write.

IF YOU LIVED HERE—NEW LISTING! 2BR/1.5BA VILLAGE CHARMER

Listen, I'm all for the tiny house movement, but I do wonder how many tiny house enthusiasts are familiar with toddlers—or teenagers, for that matter. Also, when the standards are set so impossibly high, it's tempting to just throw up your hands and move into a McMansion. So, how about a small house instead? With my new listing, you can feel good about your carbon footprint while also maintaining the ability to poop in private.

Because here's the thing about tiny houses: Even my snarky, environmentally conscious teenage daughter wants a fully air-conditioned room of her own. And this is a girl who takes the future of this planet to heart. She chides me if I complain about bees spoiling a cookout ("You do know the planet needs bees more than it needs us, right?"), or if her dad dares to enjoy an unseasonably warm winter's day ("It's not a *good* thing, Dad, it's climate change."). She once told me that the Post-It notes I used to slip into her lunchbox each day were "kind of bad for the environment," even though her own room is littered with them. (Proving once again that teenage daughters are the original mean girls.)

I'll be honest, sometimes I miss the ignorance of my youth, back when a plastic bag was just a thing to carry other things in, and the planet was just a place to live. When a tiny house was something kids built in a fairy garden. But the olden days are nothing to pine for, my daughter tells me—unless, of course, you miss acid rain and flip phones—and also, this planet is screwed, so don't pin your hopes on the future, either. In other words, the only moment you can count on is the one you're in. No wonder her generation loves SnapChat so much.

xok

---

mazel-tough: *On the level, I kinda miss flip phones.*

i_live_here: *Yeah, I kinda do, too. xok*

ann-no-e: *My snarky, environmentally conscious TEN year old chides me in the same way! The other day he caught me throwing out a Ziploc bag and he looked at me like I'd just dropkicked the Easter Bunny. I swear I usually wash and reuse Ziplocs, but I'd used this one to marinate chicken thighs, and, you know… [weighs future of this planet vs. raw chicken juice]*

i_live_here: *Raw chicken juice definitely violates the undue burden standard. xok*

really_jen: *Humble brag much, ann-no-e?*

f-bomb-mom: *Our house is tiny and I'm just going to pretend it's because we care deeply about the planet.*

really_jen: *YES f-bomb-mom. Am I supposed to be grateful for all these rich people who are downsizing to the same size house I spent decades saving up for?? Thank you for your service to Planet Earth, Matthew McConaughey, but if you really care that much about global warming, how about we just trade places? I'll live in your Mediterranean-style mansion and you can live in my split-level stucco.*

i_live_here: *Jen, trust me, I'm not handing out trophies to the tiny house dwellers, either! It's my daughter's generation I feel grateful for. (No pressure, kids.) xok*

chapter fifteen Indie

My parents think this all started because my best friend was hit by a drunk driver on her fourteenth birthday, but that wasn't the beginning. I can understand the confusion. Maddy's body flew six feet in the air when the car struck, and I was walking right behind her. Usually we linked arms when we walked together at night, but the footpath was too narrow on the curve. We were on our way home from the ice cream stand, singing some dumb song that had been stuck in our heads for most of eighth grade, because if a song was stuck in Maddy's head, then it was stuck in mine, too.

I could have told this story at her funeral, how she died with a song on her lips, but everyone would have wanted to know what song, and I have no answer for them. Everyone wants to know everything: her last words; whether she died instantly; if she'd been drinking or vaping; what she meant by that final post; what her body looked like on the asphalt, as the metallic blue Honda Accord skidded away. They never ask me these questions, but I stalk my classmates online, so I know.

The thing is, I remember the first fireflies of the season in the trees that night as we walked. I remember how the May air was so perfectly warm and still, I couldn't tell where my body ended and the world began. But I have no idea what song Maddy and I were singing when she died. It's like my brain deleted the file.

What I do remember is how everything began: How I started to see the world for what it really is.

If you ask my dad, I'm just grieving, because he thinks he

knows what that looks like. And if you ask my mom, although I don't recommend this, I'm apparently experiencing a case of *dissociation*, which I'm guessing is the first Google result you get if you look up my "symptoms."

But this thing didn't start with grief or death, and Maddy was there in the beginning, just as she was there for every other important moment in my life: first crush, first frenemy, first zit, first period, first protest march, first time I didn't make the honor roll (only one marking period in sixth grade, but still: pretty traumatic at the time). Maddy was my Day One. So, yes, it began with Maddy, and it also began with a cute boy named Asher, who was so far out of our league, it never occurred to either of us to call dibs on him. What would have been the point?

It was a few weeks before the hit and run, and Mrs. Cincotta was giving an overview of our persuasive writing unit. When she paused for questions, Asher raised his hand and said he'd seen a video online about how the Apollo 11 moon landing could have been faked, and would that be a good topic?

"It's just a theory," Asher said, shrugging. "I thought it was interesting. And we're supposed to take charge of our own learning with this project, right?"

Asher is a new-ish arrival from Park Slope. He's one of those overconfident Brooklyn-bred boys who still says "we" about people who live in the city, and who assumes he's smarter and more worldly than his small-town teachers. Dude, it's the Hudson Valley, not Hicksville, Mississippi. My desire to show him up was matched only by my desire to impress him.

"Let's see," Mrs. Cincotta said slowly. "That's a *conspiracy* theory, which is not quite the same thing as a theory. Class, what do I mean when I say something is a conspiracy theory?"

Nobody raised their hand, because it was first period, and nobody except Asher ever did.

"Hunter?" Mrs. Cincotta said. "How about you?"

“Wait,” Hunter said, drawing out the word like he was stoned, which maybe he was. He brought a fist to his mouth as if he was covering a burp, and I knew this meant he was teeing up a joke for the other gym rats. “It’s, like, girls who say something is—”

The bell rang, mercifully saving us from his genius.

“Extra credit tomorrow for anyone who brings in a paragraph responding to Asher’s conspiracy theory,” Mrs. Cincotta shouted over the din of scraping chairs. “You need three reliable sources. And remember, folks, Google is a search engine, not a source.”

Asher raised his hand again, even as he was crossing the room toward the door, and I swear Mrs. Cincotta sighed. I like her. She used to come over for Dad’s monthly poker nights, but she quit the game after she and one of the other players got into an online feud over whether or not teachers should be armed. According to Dad, pretty much everyone at school took her side, the gist of which was: Most teachers can barely handle a laminator, let alone a firearm. But the guy on the other side of the argument didn’t offer to quit the poker group. Mom said this was some patriarchal bullshit, although Mrs. Cincotta seems like a badass to me. She dresses as Rosie the Riveter every Halloween, and she’s the only teacher who ever asked us for our pronouns. Maybe she was just over being the token female at poker night.

“Do we still get the extra credit if we prove the theory right?” Asher asked.

“Three *reliable* sources,” Mrs. Cincotta said, holding up her fingers like a Boy Scout. “Let’s leave it at that.”

And so Maddy and I went online after school, looking for evidence to refute the cute boy’s claim.

“I can’t believe we’re seriously fact-checking the moon landing right now,” I said, and Maddy snorted.

We read about the lack of stars in Neil and Buzz’s moon vacay pics (which, hello, is not the same thing as a lack of stars in the *sky*, because everything was #nofilter back then). We read about multiple-angle shadows and Stanley Kubrick and radiation in the Van Allen Belt. Pretty soon we were tumbling down a conspiramania rabbit hole, and we forgot all about the extra credit. Squeezed into my beanbag chair together, we watched hours of videos on my phone, each one more oddly compelling than the last. It was like we'd accidentally stumbled on the password for the tin foil hats' secret fort. At one point my dad stuck his head in my room to see if we needed anything—parent code for checking up on us—and when he saw what we were watching, he frowned.

"Mrs. Cincotta really told you to look up this stuff?"

We nodded. It was sort of true.

"I know these guys seem like bozos," Dad said, stepping into my room. "But they can suck you in, even if you think you're too smart for that."

Yep, my dad uses the word *bozo* on a regular basis, and always without a trace of irony.

"Sometimes the truth is boring," he went on. "But it's still the truth, no matter how many hashtags the conspiracy theory gets."

"I think you mean *likes*," I said.

"Sure," Dad said, gesturing toward my phone. "Whatever. You know what I mean. Just be careful, okay?"

"Got it, Dad," I said, shooing him away. "Don't be a bozo."

As soon as he left, we returned to the video we'd been watching: a conspiracy bozo whose stringy black hair hung over his forehead like bangs he'd cut himself after a bad breakup.

"When something weird happens that you can't explain, most people forget about it and move on," the guy said. "I don't. I *can't*. If that makes me a conspiracy theorist, well then, guilty as charged."

"He has a point," Maddy said, pausing the video. "Remember our neighbor who broke her leg skiing, and it turned out her twin sister in California felt a pain in her own leg at the exact same time? Totally weird, right?"

"Identical twins *are* creepy," I said. "But I still think we landed on the moon."

"I guess," Maddy said, laughing as she held the phone out of my reach. She grabbed the Magic Eight Ball from my desk and shook it. "*All signs point to yes*," she read. "But who planted those signs that point to yes? Who made the Magic Eight Ball? I can see how someone would start to ask questions, that's all."

"You just have a lady boner for Asher," I said. "*That* is all."

We dove deeper into the rabbit hole, past crop circles and Bigfoot and a whole bunch of stuff about 5G. ("They should move here," Maddy said. "They think 5G is so bad, let them see what it's like when your phone only ever has one bar.") We were introduced to flat Earthers and Obama birthers, Holocaust deniers and anti-vaxxers. We pored over diagrams of JFK's assassination and grainy photos from Area 51. We learned about the "incel" community, and immediately wished we could unlearn it. We discovered the 9/11 truthers, and we moved on quickly, because my parents actually saw the second plane hit, and Maddy's dad drove down to the city to help out at Ground Zero. We learned about Sandy Hook skeptics and we moved on even faster, because we've been drilling for school shootings since kindergarten—we grew up with this country's "thoughts and prayers." And at the center of this fucked-up Venn diagram of deniers, we discovered, of course, the straight white men pining for America's good old days.

We clicked on a video posted by a twenty-something guy with floppy, sun-bleached hair. He was a pleasant surprise after three hours of pasty basement dwellers. This guy looked like he was sitting outside a hunting cabin, and he was cute in a wholesome, country boy kind of way. He jerked his head to flick the hair out of his face while he whittled a stick with a hunting knife.

"I love my country," he said. "Let me say that again, because y'all don't hear it often enough: *I love my country*. It's the greatest nation in world history. Remember when that wasn't up for debate? What happened?" The guy held up the stick he'd been whittling to show off his progress. It looked like an arrowhead. "I'll tell you what happened. Someone invited Satan to the party. And when you invite Satan to the party, shit gets real. Shit gets fucked up. Babies kidnapped for their blood, kids turned into sex slaves. The liberals keep attacking me like *I'm* the crazy one, but all I'm trying to do is save some fucking children."

"That's it," Maddy said, tossing the phone aside and rolling onto her back. "I draw the line at babies' blood."

"There's a plot to destroy this country," the guy continued, his video still playing from across the room. "And if we don't do something, we'll end up living in a godless nation. We'll be a third-world dictatorship with a bunch of Marxist misfits in charge! And when this country is—"

"Dude, what a fucking redneck," I said as I quit out of the video. "There's no way he even knows what Marxism is. How much you wanna bet he's dating his cousin?"

"God," Maddy said, "Could you be any more condescending? You sound just like Asher."

I was stunned into silence. Maddy never spoke to me like this.

"You don't know anything about that guy," she went on. She yanked the claw clip out of her hair and tossed it into her open bag. "You don't know what his life is like."

"I didn't mean—You don't think he's actually—" I stumbled over my words. "I just meant—"

"It doesn't matter," Maddy said, getting to her feet. As she stood, she pulled her backpack on, although my mom had already invited her to stay for dinner. "You wouldn't get it."

I knew what Maddy was doing: She was drawing a line. *This close and no further*. We had always known how much our parents would disagree on everything, if they ever talked about anything, which they never did—most likely because my mom is the kind of person who googles people's bumper stickers and lawn signs. (She was pleased to discover that the "I Brake for Brown Signs" sticker on my principal's car referred to national parks and historical landmarks. "You just never can tell," she said.)

When Maddy and I were kids, the imaginary arguments our parents had were easy to dismiss. They were about chocolate milk in the school cafeteria or crop spraying at the local farm or the price of a breakfast sandwich at the new bakery in town. Stuff we could care less about. But more recently, it's snowflakes vs. patriots, blue vs. black, red-white-and-blue vs. all the colors of the rainbow. It's more like a civil war than a town planning meeting. Still, I'd always assumed Maddy and I would end up on the same side.

"I have to go," Maddy said. "I just remembered my parents need me to watch Kaitlynn."

Maddy's sister Kaitlynn is twelve; no one has "watched" her for years. But Maddy stood in my doorway defiantly, typing out a text. A few seconds later her phone dinged with a response.

"I guess I can stay after all," she said, shrugging off her backpack irritably. "My mom will pick me up later."

Maddy pulled a folder out of her backpack and started on her math homework, but I was stuck on her reaction. Did the guy in the video look like one of her cousins? And then it hit me: He reminded Maddy of her dad. Not how he looked, but the way he loved this country, and how he sat in the yard whittling. Maddy's dad always has a knife in his pocket. I basically called the Chief a redneck. I used to forget, sometimes, that Maddy had a life separate from me—that she had conversations and hobbies and entire relationships that did not include me. She spent so much time at my house and with my parents, the reverse did not feel true.

"Check out this video," I said to Maddy a while later, passing her my phone. She gave me a suspicious look. "No babies' blood," I added quickly. "It's Jim Carrey losing his mind on live TV."

Because this is how the internet works: You spend a few years watching anime online, and then you spend a few hours researching deep state conspiracy theories, and suddenly you're served up a video about how Jim Carrey thinks "there is no me." *Jim Carrey!*

"I mean," Maddy said, as we watched the actor's manic interview. "He's not *wrong* about how meaningless all that red carpet shit is."

"He's actually sort of making sense," I said, looking over to see how Maddy would react to this. "Crazy eyes, though."

"I know, right?" Maddy said.

And so we made up, like we always did, because it's hard to storm out and slam the door when you're too young to drive yourself home and your mom can't pick you up for another two hours.

Later, alone in my bedroom, with a browser history that made the internet think I was ready to believe anything—or, at least, ready to believe *something*—I clicked my phone on again and gave into the tide of recommendations. It felt like bobbing along in a lazy river. With each video I watched, I got a little closer to figuring it out. I wasn't sure what *it* was, I just had a sense I was homing in on something true. I sent links to Maddy as I went, like breadcrumbs in a forest, because whatever this was that I was moving towards, I wanted her to come along.

I didn't know I was leaving the breadcrumb trail for myself. Some days I forget I'm just retracing my own steps. Some days I can actually convince myself it's Maddy, two steps ahead of me, leading the way.

And *that's* how it all began, Mom.

chapter sixteen ❦ **Kate**

Ethan is chopping onions at the kitchen island, listening to one of those podcasts where a bunch of guys interrupt each other.

"Smells amazing in here," I say, turning down the volume on the speaker.

"The raw onions?" Ethan says. "I haven't started cooking yet."

I smile.

"The *idea* of you cooking dinner smells amazing," I say.

I take a seat at the island across from him.

"Can I read you my latest post while you prep?" I say. "You're in this one."

Ethan isn't among my fifty thousand subscribers—he says he'd rather hear it all firsthand—but I'm applying the universal standard of vacation photographs and dreams here: No one's interested in yours unless they're in them.

"Alexa, pause," Ethan says, a flicker of irritation passing across his face.

I start reading.

IF YOU LIVED HERE—NEW LISTING! 3BR/3BA MID-CENTURY CRAFTSMAN

I stood on the back deck of this hilltop craftsman cottage this morning, looking for details that would make the listing sing. I noted a pond and a willow tree and, beyond that, two acres of woodland. *An owl*, I thought. The seller mentioned seeing owls from his deck—I could include that. And then I remembered that I'm a realtor, not a poet, and—good god, how did I end up here? I don't mean to dis on real estate, it's just, I'm not even particularly good at *this*. As my daughter would say, I low-key hate talking to strangers.

My husband's the one who should be the realtor in our family (except for the fact that he picked a profession that actually qualifies as a "calling"). He has a special talent for connecting with strangers. Not just a talent—a genuine *interest* in strangers, which is a whole lot rarer, I think. Uber drivers, car mechanics, train conductors, the UPS guy, even those customer service reps based out of India. One of the first times E. and I took a cab back to his place, the driver gifted my future husband a VHS tape from his recent trip to Egypt. "I have copies," the driver said, pressing the home video into E.'s hands. "I want you to see how beautiful my country is." (We had to take his word for it, as neither of us had owned a VCR since college.)

This afternoon, I arrived home to find a plumber in our house, installing a new water filter. I've known him for more than ten years—he's the only plumber I've ever called—but we've never exchanged more than pleasantries. My husband was sitting at the kitchen island while the plumber had his head under our sink. "Mother's Day must have been rough this year," E. was saying. "Yeah," the plumber responded. "All those firsts. I'm dreading Thanksgiving without my mom, that was always her favorite holiday."

This is how humans are meant to live, I thought. Not stacked twenty stories high and hiding behind triple-locked doors, but in a community. Where every stranger is a potential friend, if you can just look up from your phone for long enough.

"I'm so sorry," I called over to the plumber. "I just lost my mom, too, it's really hard."

The plumber scooted out from under the sink.

"It's Kate, right? I'm sorry for your loss," he said.

I liked that he wanted to make eye contact when he said this. I liked, too, that he wanted to get my name right before saying it.

"It was a year ago," E. clarified, maybe for me, maybe for the plumber, I wasn't sure.

He's right, I've already been through all those firsts, and let me tell you, it was a lonely fucking year. I should have talked to more strangers, I guess—plumbers, electricians, bank tellers, maybe even the dentist. That's not a joke: My husband claims he has in-depth conversations with our dentist, which confuses me to no end. Don't you have, like, stuff in your mouth? But maybe if I'd tried a little harder—if I'd perfected the art of talking with a saliva ejector and dental mirror in my mouth—maybe then someone besides my husband would have said to me, "Mother's Day must be rough." Because perhaps *this* is how humans are meant to live: Showing up for each other when a spouse doesn't get the memo. Think how different this world might look if we lowered our expectations of lovers a little, and at the same time raised our expectations of neighbors (not to mention dentists). If we each aspired to *be* that kind of neighbor.

So, hey, move here! My husband will be your friendly neighbor. He can recommend an excellent dentist. I'll be the awkward one in the corner, taking notes.

xok

Ethan is stirring onions at the stove by the time I'm done reading. I watch him squeeze cloves of garlic into the pan.

"That's the end," I say lamely.

"Cool," he says to the onions.

"Is it okay that I wrote about that?" I say.

"It's your blog," he says, shrugging.

I don't bother pointing out that no one's *blogged* since 2004.

"But what do you think?" I say to his back, cringing at the neediness in my voice. "I'm just curious."

Ethan sighs and turns to face me.

"I mean, you make me sound like kind of a dick," he says. "But, like I said, your blog."

Ethan turns back to the stove and tells Alexa to start up the podcast again. I'd hoped he would see the hurt in my post; I'd hoped he would apologize for all the times he didn't ask how I was doing. I'd even hoped this might be the day we would finally connect with each other over the loneliness of grief. *Hope is the thing with feathers*, Emily Dickinson wrote, although I'm guessing she composed that poem before she learned how too much hope can also crush you.

I scroll down to my reader comments.

> **anne-no-e:** *The second year is worse, because the second year, NOBODY thinks to ask if you're okay on Mother's Day. Not even the dentist. My mom died five years ago and Mother's Day still sucks. Thanks a lot, Hallmark! Also, I'll ask it: Are you okay?*

My eyes fill with tears.

"Next week will be a year," I say, but Ethan doesn't hear me over the podcast.

I try again.

"THE ANNIVERSARY IS NEXT WEEK," I shout, and it feels good, actually, to state this with such urgency. It feels appropriate.

Ethan pauses Alexa again.

"My mom's death," I say. "Tuesday will be one year."

"I know," Ethan says. "A year, that's what I said."

"I wasn't being pedantic," I say. "I just thought you'd want to know the actual date. I didn't expect you to have it memorized or anything."

"It's in my calendar," he says, picking up his phone as if to prove this to me. "Of course I know the date."

And then I notice Ethan's expression change, and I realize a text message just popped up on his screen.

Ethan is still in regular contact with his friends from high school. And I don't mean he clicks the Like button when they post online. (Ethan "abstains" from social media—his term, as if it were right up there with conscious objection and sobriety.) Instead, he texts multiple times a day with his closest friends. They share dumb videos of skateboard wipeouts; they riff on the news; they discuss the best health supplements for middle-aged men; and then, almost as an afterthought, they talk about their personal lives. "So, kind of like Facebook then?" I said once, my tone teasing. "No," Ethan said. "Kind of like being friends." But I couldn't let it go. "It walks like a duck, though, you have to admit." Ethan took a deep breath. "Maybe it looks trivial to you," he said. "But I've been through a lot with these guys." This sort of glancing mention, often but not always intended to shut me out, is the closest Ethan ever gets to talking about his brother.

When we were first dating, Ethan told me Luke died, and I always figured he'd share more when he was ready, but that time never came. I only know it was Ethan who found Luke because his mom told me. She's the one who told me it was an overdose, too, and that it happened while Ethan was home for Thanksgiving, his sophomore year of college. Luke was a high school senior, and he'd gotten hooked on opioids after a football injury.

I asked Ethan's mom once how I could be there for him if he never talked about his brother. It was Thanksgiving, I'd had a few glasses of wine, and we were doing the dishes together while Ethan and his dad watched the game. (I disliked football more than I disliked the old-school division of labor. Also, I liked Ethan's mom, and I wanted her to like me.) "He talks about everything," I said to her. "*We* talk about everything. But not this." I wanted her to tell me he was the same with everyone, the same with her, but I also hoped to hear the opposite, that there was at least *someone* Ethan could talk to about his brother. "Then that's your answer," she said, her voice kind but firm. "When he can't put words to something, it's probably about Luke. That's when you listen for the thing he's asking for, even if he's not saying it with words."

Basically, she was saying I was married to the Marlboro Man, except my rugged cowboy preferred pot gummies to filtered cigarettes, and he was loquacious when the conversation turned to processed sugar or the failure of globalization. Only when I tried to talk about loss did he shut down.

My mother-in-law's approach worked so well that it took me years to realize it was also pretty shitty marriage advice. It was how I intuited that Ethan's road bike was about more than exercise, and it was also why I never questioned how long he rode for, even when Indie was tiny, even when everything in me wanted to text him in all caps, WHERE THE FUCK ARE YOU??? *He's not saying it with words*, I reminded myself each time. I never blamed Ethan's mom, though. She just wanted someone to take care of her boy.

Here's the worst thing Ethan never said with words: *Your mom's death counts for less than my brother's.*

He said it in the way he went back to work the day after my mom died, although I know for a fact the school gives teachers five bereavement days for any death in the family—even a mother-in-law you didn't like all that much. He said it in the way he stopped asking how I was doing after a week. A *week*! And he said it in the way he went on a guys' trip two weeks after the funeral and then checked in via text just once, to see how *Indie* was doing. Ethan had offered to skip the weekend away, but it was his oldest friend's forty-fifth birthday and he hadn't seen these guys in forever. I told him I wanted him to go, and I did. But I had at least thought he would call me from the road. I thought he might say *thank you, this is a big deal, are you okay?* He never did.

chapter seventeen ❦ **Indie**

A few days after Maddy and I tumbled down the conspiracy theory rabbit hole, Mom ambushed me with a road trip. She *claimed* the falling-down barns she kept stopping to photograph just happened to be on the way to the outlet mall, but I didn't believe her for a second. Halfway through the afternoon, I checked the maps app and informed her that the drive now officially qualified as a "journey," which meant I was allowed to wear earbuds. (Mom ruled against earbuds during short "trips" in the car, like to the supermarket or the orthodontist.)

So while Mom scoured the entire Hudson Valley in search of the perfect shot for *If You Lived Here*, I listened to a podcast called "Make Me One with Everything." This phrase, I would learn later, is a classic punchline among people who sit around discussing the "hard problem of consciousness" for fun. It's like a Buddhist dad joke, I guess. Who knew consciousness was even a problem to be solved? Not me. Apparently, material science has no explanation for consciousness, and that's a really big deal. Like, if everything from a coffee table to a human being is made up of the same ingredients, at a particle level, what turns the light on inside for humans but not for the coffee table? *That's* the hard problem.

If you believe this podcaster, then humans aren't some mysterious exception. Instead, we're on a continuum, and *everything* that's made of *something* is experiencing what it's like to be that thing. Everything has some kind of inner life. This theory is known as *panpsychism*, which is some epically bad branding if you ask me, but whatever. According to the theory, there's the experience of being a person in the world, and that's my consciousness, but there's also the experience of being a bat, which must be pretty fucking cool, now that I think about it. I mean, echolocation? So awesome. Maddy and I saw a video once about a blind kid who learned echolocation so he could ride a bike. He made these clicking sounds with his mouth and called himself Bat Boy.

Anyway, if you keep going with this idea, there's also the experience of being a fish, or a worm, or . . . a coffee table, I guess? Except, these aren't really *individual* experiences, it's more like one big, shared experience. Like we're all in the same Minecraft Realm, but some things are able to mine a deeper vein of consciousness than others.

Later that day, when I got home, I FaceTimed Maddy and tried to explain panpsychism, but she just laughed. "Does a cucumber feel pain when you slice it?" she said. And then: "Wait, if the cucumber is psychic, does that mean it can tell me my fortune?" It was Maddy's favorite after-school snack to eat at my house: salted cucumber slices. I'm not sure her own mom even knew she liked cucumbers.

I wanted to explain to Maddy how the idea made me feel connected to something bigger for the first time in my life, but I couldn't find the words. "Is that why we have coasters for hot drinks?" Maddy went on, cracking herself up. "So we don't hurt the coffee table's feelings?" She was acting hyper and fake-dumb, which made me think Kaitlynn was probably listening in. "Wait, I've got it: The cucumber has locked-in syndrome!" The podcaster's argument had seemed so solid when he made it, but it felt wobbly as it passed from him, through me, to Maddy, like one of those water-filled snake toys that turns in on itself.

"I'm sending you a link to the podcast," I told her, typing out a text. "He explains it way better."

Dad would have gotten it, but that's why I didn't share it with him at dinner that night. ("Indie listened to top secret hipster music in the car today," Mom told Dad, and I didn't correct her.) He would have immediately understood the whole thing better than I did, even if, *especially* if, he didn't believe it. Back when I first told him Maddy's broken leg twin story, he took the opportunity to lecture me on coincidence. He told me the human brain has "an innate need to create order out of chaos," and to "ascribe meaning to random events," especially when that meaning provides comfort. Sometimes my dad is the human equivalent of a sad trombone sound. I felt dumb and deflated that day, but I also learned my lesson: Don't hand my father anything fragile and new.

chapter eighteen ❦ **Kate**

I let myself out of the house quietly, not wanting to wake my husband and daughter. *Heading out early*, I text from the car. *Leftovers in the fridge*. This is my way of letting Ethan know he's on Indie duty without appearing to nag him, because apparently men find it emasculating to be reminded about things. That's what the momfluencers say, anyway. "Going on a girls' weekend? Don't leave a list, just bounce! He'll thank you for it later."

I never left lists because I never really left. I left the *room*, sometimes, when Indie was a baby, but even then I always let Ethan know when I'd be back: *Taking a five-minute shower. Grabbing kale from the garden. Folding laundry in the basement.* All just different ways of saying, *Heads up, you're on duty, don't let her die. Also, if you can't locate the sprouts at the back of the fridge while I'm gone, you'll have to find a way to move forward with your morning, sprout-free.* I don't remember Ethan ever alerting me in the same way. We parented as a team, sure, that's what we told everyone, and it's true that we share household responsibilities as equitably as any couple I know, which is to say, it feels like a fifty-fifty split to Ethan. But someone has to be the default parent. The one who buys school supplies and birthday presents, the one who books dentist appointments and flu shots, the one who sends in orange cupcakes for the Halloween class party and pink ones on Valentine's Day.

I'm not sure Ethan even realized there was such a thing as a default parent, and I never pointed this out. Back then I still believed that a good marriage depended on me thanking him for what he did, rather than pointing out what he didn't do.

And maybe I was right, maybe that's *exactly* what a happy marriage looks like. Maybe I just stopped noticing the things I had to be thankful for, and started bearing grudges instead. Because when I look back on those years, yes, I remember taking thirty-second showers with my eyes open so I could pull goofy faces at Indie, who was strapped into her bouncy seat on the bathmat—and Ethan, meanwhile, was out on some kind of Ironman bike ride. But also, I remember the year Ethan let Indie teach him every single viral dance on the internet, and the hours of writing time that afforded me. I remember how, when there was a chore Indie hated, Ethan would compose a dumb song about it on the ukulele and sing until she was laughing too hard to whine. (For seriously entrenched problems, like dental hygiene or eating green things, the songs would expand with each performance, gaining verses, bridges, and even calls for audience participation.) I remember the way Ethan looked at me when he stood in the doorway of Indie's room and watched me read her a bedtime story. How he'd hand me a glass of wine, kiss us each on the forehead, and ask what I wanted for dinner.

As I pull out of the driveway, Kevin texts me that he's running an hour late. Instead of turning back, I drive to the coffee shop in town and write a new post.

IF YOU LIVED HERE—SOLD! 4BR/2.5BA 1850s CARPENTER GOTHIC #TBT

My Photos app just reminded me that E. and I closed on this house twenty years ago today. It's not like we saw the small-town real estate boom coming, we just really liked the wraparound porch and the old-school diner down the road. NOT A HUMBLE BRAG! Or a straight-up brag, either. (Really, Jen.) I mean, sure, we could sell our house and make a tidy sum, but then where would we go? This is home.

Emma Tourtelot

When we first toured the house with our realtor, it was empty except for an inflatable mattress and sleeping bag in the master bedroom. There was a small digital alarm clock plugged into the wall, the cord stretched halfway across the room, and an open suitcase in the closet, overflowing with unfolded clothes. I could almost believe someone was squatting there, but the truth was much sadder: These were the belongings of a man who used to make his kids waffles in the kitchen. Who used to watch *CSI* in the den with his wife.

At the closing, the sellers each came with a separate lawyer and sat on opposite ends of a conference room table that was big as a swimming pool. The ex-husband didn't make eye contact with anyone, and I had the distinct feeling he hated us. The ex-wife smiled sadly and said, "The soil is amazing in the yard. You can grow anything there." I had the distinct feeling she hated us, too. (I mean, wouldn't you? It wasn't like we held hands at the closing, we weren't *that* insensitive, but we were in love with the idea of our new life together, and that's hard to hide.)

That afternoon, we let ourselves into our new home. As we walked in, I called out, "Hello?" just in case, or maybe because I still couldn't believe it was ours. I think I half-expected to find the ex-husband still squatting in the master suite. All we found, though, was a small vintage dish under the kitchen sink. The shallow kind you might keep on the windowsill, a place to put your rings while you roll meatballs in your hands. It had a quote in French, which I initially misread as, *Le mariage est un duo et un duel*. Marriage is a duet and a duel. "We should keep this," I told my husband, handing him the dish. "As a reminder not to turn into those people." I liked the idea of creating a marriage with enough wiggle room to do battle occasionally, and I assumed that the former owners of our house had failed at this task. (I know, I know: Newlyweds can be such arrogant pricks.)

"A little on the nose, don't you think?" E. joked. He turned the dish over and pointed out that it was actually made in China, not France. I could see then that it was tacky and mass-produced, not vintage and hand-painted. "Even better," I said, and laughed, although my heart hurt a little for this estranged couple that never even made it to Paris.

It was years before I caught my misreading: The dish actually says, *Le mariage est un duo ou un duel*. Marriage is a duet *or* a duel. You're supposed to pick just one, I guess?

I still have the dish, though. I like to think the secret to a good marriage lies somewhere between my first reading and my second. Or maybe the secret is not to take marriage advice from fake souvenirs made in China?

xok

---

really_jen: *I'm sorry, but that was SO a humble brag. Always appreciate the shout-outs, though.*

ann-no-e: *I feel like houses can be haunted by bad divorce energy. You know how realtors are supposed to tell you if a murder happened in a house? (At least, this seems like something they should do.) I think maybe they should also tell you if a messy divorce happened there.*

i_live_here: *Wait, you mean I'm supposed to tell my clients about the local serial killer who scouts for victims at the honor system farm stand? OOPS. xok*

i_live_here: *KIDDING, in case that wasn't clear. We had a "crime spree" here a few years back, it lasted maybe three days. Some teens from the next town over stole cash from a handful of unlocked homes. The police posted a description online and someone's aunt snitched within hours. xok*

mazel-tough: *Screw the crime rate, I want to know the local divorce rate! Not sure I believe in bad juju, Ann, but I do think divorce can be contagious.*

really_jen: *Totally, Mazel. Being an asswipe husband is definitely contagious. Turns out all those guys' nights out were just a way for him to plan his escape route.*

really_jen: *Huh. I guess I just said that out loud.*

mazel-tough: *Oof. Sorry, Jen.*

i_live_here: *Hugs, Jen. If I hear of a town with a Be-a-Better-Man Beer and Wings Night, you'll be the first to know. xok*

mazel-tough: *Golf for Good Guys*

ann-no-e: *Bowling with Integrity*

really_jen: *Principled Poker Night*

i_live_here: *We could save mankind if only they'd let us. xok*

Kevin is sitting in his truck when I pull up to his parents' house. While I park, he gets out and reaches into the back of his truck for two cans of paint and a brown paper bag from the hardware store. I follow him into the house without a word.

When he gets to one of the bedrooms, he finally turns to face me.

"Should we start in here?" Kevin says. "I got white paint for now, I wasn't sure about colors."

"Great," I say, pushing up my sleeves.

I've never painted a room myself. Ethan and I hired some local guys to paint our house while we were out of town a few years back.

"Painting is usually Ethan's thing," I lie, because this is something Kevin will understand. "So I'll just follow your lead."

We cover the carpeted floor with a plastic drop cloth, then Kevin hands me a roller and tray and shows me how to apply just the right amount of paint. We work on opposite walls of the room, silent except for my occasional questions about technique, and his assurances that I'm doing just fine.

"Do you guys have family around here?" Kevin asks eventually. "Is that why you moved here?"

I turn to see him bent over the second can of paint, levering it open with a screwdriver.

"No," I say. "Ethan and I both come from small families, and none of them live close by. The first time Indie met Maddy's cousins, she got so mad at us. It was as if we'd failed her somehow."

Jesus Christ, why would I bring up Maddy? Why would I say *anything* that suggests Maddy had it better?

"Sorry," I say under my breath. "I wasn't thinking."

Kevin gives me a quizzical look, and I finally understand what I've been missing. Nothing I say could possibly make things worse for him. It's not in my power to hurt him, and it's not in my power to help him, either.

"I'm blabbing," I add, as if this explained everything, as if I were just some realtor who talked too much on the job.

We go back to painting in silence. When we're done, we stand in the doorway to admire our work.

"This used to be my room," Kevin says. "Me and Kyle's. My dad built these bunk beds."

"I love the fireman's pole," I say.

"Maddy did too," Kevin says. "She loved to sleep over here."

It's the first time I've heard him use Maddy's name since she died. Kevin presses a fist to his chest, as if it hurt, physically, to say her name out loud. Before I can respond, Kevin walks to the center of the room and starts packing up. When he pulls the masking tape from the drop cloth, I grab the other end to help him fold it.

"I saw my mom yesterday," Kevin says, walking toward me as we fold the sheet of plastic.

"How is she?"

We step back and then toward each other again as we fold, like we're at a square dance.

"I'm not sure," he says, taking the folded drop cloth from me. "Sometimes she seems happy, but she's lost everything—her husband, her house, her memories. So it doesn't seem like it's *her* in those moments, you know? If she really understood what was going on, I don't think she'd be happy."

I nod. I remember.

"My dad's hands made her happy," Kevin says. "She even loved his missing finger. He was hanging a picture one time, and she turned to me and said, 'Don't his hands look so strong and rugged?' They'd been together fifty years at this point, but it was like she was a teenager again."

I try to imagine feeling this way about Ethan after half a century together. Twenty years in, even the way he opens the fridge to look for a snack grates on my nerves—the way he sighs irritably when he finds nothing to his liking, as if it were anyone's fault but his own. And then I can't help it, my eyes go to Kevin's hands. I think about him holding my forearms, how I felt like a delicate and rare object he was trying to understand.

"I don't think she even remembers she had kids," Kevin says.

I wait for him to say what he really fears: That his mom doesn't remember her grandchildren. That she doesn't remember Maddy.

"Tell her stories," I say when he doesn't go on. "One of my mom's nurses suggested that. Even if she doesn't realize the stories are about her own life, there's a lingering familiarity that can be comforting, that's what the nurse said."

If Kevin asks, I will tell him every Maddy story I remember—every joke she cracked at the dinner table, every macaron she and Indie baked in our kitchen until they'd perfected the recipe, every cut and scrape I found a Band-Aid for. Because this, I think, is why Kevin needs me: I remember. If there are things about Maddy he can still learn, however small, she is not completely gone, not yet.

"Did you tell your mom stories?" he says.

"Sometimes," I lie.

The truth is that my mom would get this vexed look on her face whenever I tried to talk about Indie, and even though she didn't have the words to explain, I understood: She wanted to know why I was going on about some kid she was convinced she'd never met. As a general rule, my mom was not interested in children. Indie had always been the exception.

"She got agitated if I lowered the volume on her TV," I say, because this part is true. "So mostly we watched a lot of cable news together."

"That's sweet," Kevin says, and then he winks. "Especially if you let her watch Fox News."

While we sat together, I would snip the labels out of my mom's clothes, like I used to do with Indie's pajamas and shirts when she was little. Because a thought had occurred to me in the middle of the night: If my mom found a clothing tag irritating, she wouldn't have a way of letting me know. She might not even realize what was bothering her, only that something in her world wasn't right. I couldn't give back what she'd lost to a fogged up brain—her beloved granddaughter, the one girl she'd been able to love decisively, instinctively—but I could remove small irritants from her day. I could keep a pair of sharp nail scissors in my bag.

"Today's the anniversary of my mom's death," I say to Kevin.

"Shit," he says, and looks around the room, flustered. "Why'd you let me drag you out here?"

"It's fine," I say. "I suggested today, remember?"

I hadn't meant to tell Kevin about the anniversary. I chose today because I wanted the distraction, and also because I was afraid Ethan would say the wrong thing—or, worse, say nothing at all. Kevin is silent for a moment, nodding slowly as if he's listening to me explain myself. As if he gets it.

"I'm not going to tell my mom about Maddy," he says eventually. "I'm going to let her forget."

He holds my gaze as if daring me to contradict him—or perhaps urging me to understand—and I take this to mean Laura does not agree with his decision.

"That's okay," I say, and I look away, because this does not feel like my permission to give.

"It is?" Kevin says, and I have to look at him again. I notice his hands are clenched in fists, and they remind me of pill bugs, how they curl into balls when you touch them. I nod, trying to reassure him. As he relaxes his fists, silent tears roll down his face.

My own eyes fill with tears in response, and instinctively I cross the room to hug him. When I clasp my arms around Kevin's body, I feel his posture slacken, as if I released something that was holding him up, and suddenly he is sobbing into my shoulder. It's like nothing I've ever heard before, and here, at last, is the unimaginable: the sound of a man who has lost his child. I rub his back in circles, like I used to do when Indie couldn't sleep.

I don't know how long we stand like that—maybe a minute, maybe ten—but eventually his breathing slows. I take a step back, my hands still on his shoulders, and look at his face. His eyes are red and glassy and I don't want him to feel any shame about this. I smile a little. *Good job*, I want him to know. *It's okay.*

But then his face is closer and he's leaning in and he puts a hand on either side of my face and he kisses me. And I kiss him back, this country handsome man who has my face in his strong hands. I kiss him like we're twenty and standing outside a bar in the city, responsible to no one and too young to have lost anyone.

Except, I am responsible for everyone in this moment, including him. I push against his chest so hard, he stumbles back into the wall.

"Oh my god," I say. "Sorry, I'm so sorry, I didn't mean, I don't—"

My entire body is trembling.

"Fuck," he says, sinking to the floor. "Fuck, fuck, fuck, fuck, *fuck*. You can go. Please, just go."

Down on the carpeted floor, in a whitewashed room empty of his parents' belongings, the walls still wet to the touch, Kevin looks broken, and it is too much, he is too naked and I shouldn't be here.

"I'm sorry," I say again. "I'm so sorry."

I want to scream, I want to leave, I want to tear down this house and pretend I was never here. But Kevin is rocking back and forth now, his body heaving and shaking with grief, and I am paralyzed by the display. How can I leave him like this?

"If I stand over here," I say eventually, walking backwards until I reach the opposite wall, the one I painted, "is it okay with you if I stay for a few minutes?"

He doesn't respond. I don't know if he hears me, I don't know if he even remembers I'm in the room, or that I ever was. I see paint sample cards that spilled out of the bag of supplies from the hardware store, a confusing selection of bright colors that Kevin must have grabbed at random. There is no way he wants to paint his parents' walls fuchsia or cobalt blue. I scoop up the cards and put them in the back pocket of my overalls.

"I think just white for every room," I say, soft and slow, like I'm telling him a bedtime story. "But not too bright," I add. "Not a blue-white. There's a Benjamin Moore eggshell white, it's called Swiss Coffee, it's easily as good as the Farrow and Ball whites and it's incredibly affordable, too. Or any interior white, really, the light in here is so lovely you can't go wrong."

Kevin doesn't ask me to leave, he doesn't ask me to stop, and so I go on. I keep my voice lullaby soft as I tell him the same inane things I've said to a hundred other clients who actually care about Farrow and Ball. People who don't think it's immoral to spend a hundred dollars a *gallon* on white paint—who don't even consider this embarrassing. I will stand here all night and watch over him, if he needs me. I will tell him stories about Wolf stoves and subway tiles, about pocket doors and raised ceilings and everything else my clients want that has nothing to do with making a house a home.

Eventually, Kevin is quiet again. He wipes his face with his palms and gets to his feet. He turns toward me and nods once, brisk and business-like.

"Thanks for all your help," he says, his voice steady and neutral, and I can tell we're done here.

"Anytime," I say. "It was nothing, really."

It feels like the truest thing I've said all day.

chapter nineteen Indie

I'm stuck on Planet Earth on a Saturday night, watching an ancient Tom Cruise movie with my parents, because I am a fourteen-year-old nobody who lost her only friend, and the best way to stop my parents obsessively checking up on me is to sit where they can see me. Also, "watching a movie" basically means the three of us sit in the same general area of the house, each on our own personal device.

I can't remember when my parents started being okay with this setup. Mom used to insist that all devices be stowed in the entryway charging station after 7 p.m., although she broke this rule more than any of us. I'd catch her standing at the charging station, her phone plugged in like it was a landline. Still, she was big on everything being "device-free," and I guarantee she bragged about this online. Device-free dinners, device-free hikes, device-free bedrooms. A few months back I made a snide comment about her "device-free texting," and she said I was ready to take responsibility for my own screen time. Apparently it's important for me to learn to set my own limits. Which sounds a lot like an excuse for her phone to be in her back pocket at all times. Dad's more into his iPad than his phone—because he has clumsy thumbs, he says—but he's just as attached as she is. Sometimes he even tucks the iPad into the back of his pants, like a waiter's order pad, except way nerdier.

No one is talking about the fact that it's summer break and I should have started my internship with our district's congressman this week. No one's talking at all. I'm sure my parents argued over whether or not I should show up, but they never bothered to loop me in on that conversation. Probably they decided I'm too sad to make phone calls or write letters to constituents or whatever other meaningless crap an unpaid intern is expected to do.

What I *will* be doing this summer is rewatching a lot of eighties movies, because Mom claims American cinema peaked in 1988, despite the fact that pretty much every movie made that decade fails the Bechdel test. And Mom's the one who told me about the Bechdel test! Her feminism has convenient blind spots.

Maddy and I became friends the same year Mom first introduced me to eighties movies, so she was indoctrinated right along with me. Collateral damage, Dad joked, not that he ever complained about spending his Saturday evenings rewatching *The Breakfast Club*. I guess marriage is a form of Stockholm Syndrome? Mostly, though, this lockup looked pretty benign to me. It looked like Dad quoting *Dirty Dancing* whenever Mom came back from the farmer's market with a watermelon. God, parents are such dorks.

Mom even made popcorn tonight. She keeps jumping up to offer the popcorn bowl to me and Dad, or running back to the kitchen for more nutritional yeast to sprinkle on top. It's as if she wants it to *look* like a cozy family movie night, in case anyone walks in. Dad is next to me on the couch, reading old people websites on his iPad, and when I glance over, I see an ad for men's "active sandals." Every site he clicks on, there are those ugly-ass Keens again. (Who thought dad toes needed more air time?) Across the room, Mom is responding to reader comments on *If You Lived Here*, and when she puts down her laptop to offer us more popcorn, I see an ad for baggy overalls made in Japan, enough fabric in them to sail a ship. What I'm saying is, the internet knows who we are. That's not a conspiracy theory, it's just plain data tracking. Ask Zuckerberg.

Here's why I bring up those billowy overalls and those ridiculous dad sandals: Back in 1600 BCE, Babylonians used algorithms to find square roots. Hundreds of years later, a Persian scientist invented algebra, and when his books were translated into Latin, his Latinized name, *Algorithmi*, was given to the modern algorithm. Even more years later, but still during the Stone Age of the internet, some coder in Palo Alto figured out that AI algorithms can help companies understand human preferences. (Ironic, I guess, that I learned all this on a YouTube video that was suggested to me.) And I don't just mean the internet knows what we like to wear. It knows what pisses us off, and it knows what gets us all up in our feelings, too. It probably knows before *we* do. Forget prayer—here's your higher power: Hang out on Google long enough and the internet will give you what you need. How do I know? Because this is exactly how I discovered a series of videos that finally helped me understand what my parents refuse to believe: That I am nobody at all.

chapter twenty **Kate**

IF YOU LIVED HERE—SOLD! 5BR/3BA FARM ESCAPE

My mom would have been horrified at the way I titled this listing: *farm escape*. She grew up on a farm, and to hear her tell it, tilling the land and tending to livestock was a slog. It certainly wasn't a place to "get away from it all." Of course, the proud new owners of today's listing—a gay couple in fashion and finance, respectively—aren't planning on a lot of animal husbandry, unless you count designer chickens. What they *are* planning on is using the farmhouse as a kind of weekend recharging station, to better equip themselves for life in the city. Here's where it helps to be a realtor with impostor syndrome: It's a breeze for me to act like I'm okay with my entire life being a backdrop for someone else's pastoral fantasy. It's almost a relief, in fact, because backdrops aren't expected to make small talk.

Anyway, while I was meeting with these newly minted weekenders in my office, a woman from my yoga class knocked on the storefront window and waved as she walked past. One of the guys asked me, "Don't you ever miss the anonymity of the city?" As if being anonymous were as endemic to city life as experimental theater or decent sushi.

But really, there are so many ways for a woman of my age to be invisible. There is the way, for example, that she is no longer commanded to smile when she passes a construction site. (To be fair, this could also be a small-town thing: The construction worker might accidentally catcall his buddy's wife. Or his buddy's *daughter*.) Even in a small town, though, there's the way the cute twenty-something guy who works at the health food store asks if she'd like to sign up for a customer loyalty card, even though she's been a regular for years. There's the way school aides mistake her for another mom who also has dark curly hair—a woman who is pounds heavier and dresses exclusively in L.L. Bean.

Back when we were first married and E. was going through a phase of reading the Stoic philosophers, he once yelled across the house, practicing gratitude, "Thank you for existing!" Talk about being seen. But a woman can be invisible in her own home, too. Sometimes I fantasize about my early death, not because I'm depressed or anything, but just because I imagine E. finally discovering all the invisible things I do: How gross a dish towel gets if you never swap it out. How socks don't magically get turned right side out when you wash them.

Here's the good news, though: The invisible woman can see *herself* in a small town, and when she looks in the mirror, she might even like what she sees. (So long as she avoids shopping at the shoe store on Main Street, which specializes in "comfort shoes" in an impressively broad range of browns and maroons.) I mean, who *doesn't* feel old and uncool in Soho? It's like the entire city is one giant funhouse mirror, the concave surface screwing with our heads. The last time I was in the city, even the shape of my arms seemed frumpy.

Meanwhile, I saw a sixty-something woman grocery shopping in overalls and a tank top this morning, her wavy gray hair tied back with a paisley bandana, and she looked like a fucking rockstar. She sauntered through the aisles like she knew it, too.

I think maybe it has something to do with the pace of life here, how it dials down your resting heart rate. An old friend of E.'s, visiting from the city, once teased the two of us about how we even *talked* more slowly than we used to. The friend laughed and we did, too, each of us thinking we had it better. One of my yoga teachers said she changed her entire practice when she moved upstate, because she could finally slow her breath. In the city, I guess, even the yogis are in a hurry, moving aerobically from one pose to the next like it's a Jane Fonda workout tape.

Upstate, though, time slows, and it's not cryogenic freezing or Botox or any of the ridiculously expensive anti-aging products I buy online after spending too much time in the city—it's something better: It's breathing out. It's breathing in. It's watching the sky turn pink over an apple orchard and thinking not of rush hour traffic or the unstoppable marching of time, but of apple pie. Of how the neighborhood apple butter party is coming up.

So, no, I don't miss the anonymity of the city. Also, the only "comfort shoes" you'll ever catch me in are my beat-up Converse high-tops.

xok

---

ann-no-e: *Moms in Converse high-tops, unite!*

go-ask-your-dad: *Been there. I feel bad about my frumpy arms, too.*

mazel-tough: *LOL, Jane Fonda workout tapes. There is NOTHING relaxing about doing yoga in Brooklyn.*

really_jen: *So now you've got something against L.L. Bean?! Also, way to fat-shame another mom. This post was just straight-up mean.*

ann-no-e: *No one's forcing you to read these posts, really_jen. Plenty of other places on the internet where you can troll people, if that's your thing. This here is just a bunch of moms trying to lift each other up a little. Is that really who you want to take down?*

really_jen: *So how come I never feel uplifted when I'm here?*

i_live_here: *Jen, please stick around! I count on you to keep my inner Regina George in check. For the record, I was a total loser all the way through middle and high school, so the last thing I want to be now is a mean mom. xok*

go-ask-your-dad: *I know some mean moms (thanks to five years serving on the PTSA), and trust me, you don't come close. Also, what's up with the Regina George reference? I can't believe you passed up a chance to quote Heathers.*

i_live_here: *I guess I had a brain tumor for breakfast. #Heathers xok*

ann-no-e: *If you were happy every day of your life, you wouldn't be a human. You'd be a game show host. #Heathers*

go-ask-your-dad: *I say we just grow up, be adults, and die. #Heathers*

f-bomb-mom: *Fuck me gently with a chainsaw. #Heathers (One of us had to go there.)*

i_live_here: *I'm serious, you guys, y'all need to move here. xok*

My phone vibrates in my back pocket while I'm making dinner, but I don't answer it. I don't even look at it, because what if Ethan or Indie walks in? I don't trust my own face. I texted Kevin earlier, asking him to call me, and my plan is to give him a choice: I can sell the house if he still wants my help, or I can drop out of the deal and he can work with my colleague Sara instead. I want to give him space to mention the kiss, or to pretend it never happened. Most of all, I want him to know he did nothing wrong. That there is no story here, except the story of a man who lost his child.

We did nothing wrong, I tell myself. Although, if this is true, where did that *we* come from? And why does my skin now prickle every time I think about Kevin, no matter how unhinged I know this to be?

After I slide the tray of chicken and leeks into the oven, I call out to the rest of the house: "I'm running to the corner store for milk. Anyone need anything?" No one answers. I don't know why I even bothered with a cover story.

I suppose I should be grateful that my mere existence is no longer something for Ethan to marvel at. Dissembling is a whole lot easier when you're both on your phones. Except, the longer I say nothing, the guiltier I feel. The guiltier I *am*. Maybe the kiss wasn't wrong, but hiding it feels like crossing a line.

I climb into my car and take out my phone. The missed call was not from Kevin; it was a robocall from Indie's school, reminding me to register her for a fall sport. I drive to the corner store anyway, and buy milk we don't need. From a hundred feet above, I think, this sure looks like the routine of a guilty woman.

I try to convince myself that I'm protecting Kevin, that keeping this secret is the least I can do for him, after everything he's been through. Really, though, I'm too chickenshit to tell. After all, when's the last time Ethan gave me the benefit of the doubt in anything?

Twenty years ago, he found a way to understand me: a woman testing the limits of something she was scared to trust. A girlfriend afraid of seeming too "needy," because everyone from her mother to her last boyfriend had said this was a problem area for her. Pragmatic to his core, Ethan was able to weigh my one, stupid, drunken mistake against our potential future together. That was the moment I knew I'd marry him. Not because he'd always forgive me, but because he could see right through me—and still he stayed.

And how insignificant my one-night stand seemed after we moved here and brought Indie into the world—Indie expanding our universe and making everything else seem so distant and small. It was inconceivable then that we, the three of us, almost didn't happen.

But I know how the conversation would go this time around: Ethan would be incapable of hearing the facts—that it just happened, that no one is to blame, that grief is messy and human connection messier. Instead, he would see all the ways I fell short. My husband is closer to knowing the truth, then, if I simply keep my mouth shut.

Ethan is the most rational person I know, inherently suspicious of both whimsy and gut instinct, and so, when I met him and he began to talk about our future together, it already seemed like established fact. *Okay*, I said to myself, halfway through our first date, because that was how soon I felt it start to happen. *Here we go*. I fell in love with Ethan's certainty—about the way the world worked, about his place in it, about what it all meant, or didn't mean. Most of all, I loved the feeling of being one of these things he was so sure about. It was as if he had pinpointed my location on a map I didn't even know existed.

"You're so stubborn," he said once, and it was clear he meant this as a compliment. He said it the way someone else might say, *You're a badass*, or, *You mean business*. I'd never thought of myself as particularly stubborn before, but when Ethan said it, I felt that he was right. I liked this idea of myself, and I liked that he was the only one to see it.

During a road trip before we were married—a romantic weekend getaway to the town we would ultimately call home—he said I made him feel like a motormouth. "You only talk when you have something worth saying," he said, his eyes flitting over to me and then back to the road ahead. "You're not one of those people who says something trivial just to stay in the conversation."

We sat in silence for a few minutes, and the silence was companionable but also—how could I be the first to speak after that?

"And look at your seltzer bottle!" Ethan motioned to the center console of our rental car. "You screw the cap back on after each sip. You're so deliberate about everything." I smiled as I picked up my lime-flavored Poland Spring (this was before East Coast liberals discovered LaCroix). "What are you talking about? Everyone does that." Ethan laughed and showed me his empty bottle. "Nope," he said. "Just you."

In that moment and in many others, he redefined me. I wasn't timid; I simply weighed every word with care. I didn't lack charisma; I was *serene*, with the inner calm of a Zen monk. I hadn't lost my way; I was seeking my own path. I was *cool*, he said, after I taught his younger cousins poker at a family wedding (no matter that I was taking a break from talking to adults I didn't know). I was *stoic*, he said, after I lost yet another pregnancy. I felt myself expand in response to these characterizations, swept up in his certainty—and in this way his ideas about me felt generous, as if he'd elevated me to something worth believing in. He was more sure of me than I'd ever felt myself.

"You're gorgeous," Ethan said to me on our second date. "You know that, right?"

Except the way he said it, it was clear he knew I didn't. I smiled at him and said nothing, because I understood that he was accepting this responsibility, to be the one to tell me. In that moment, my appearance and his appreciation of it became the same thing. Only later would I see how Ethan's characterizations were a chalk outline of my body, establishing, for the record, his impression of me: That I was the listener in our relationship. That he gave the compliments and I received them. That he had the answers and I was still looking for them.

And then my mom died, and the way I grieved didn't fit Ethan's idea of me. The way I am *still* grieving, although he refuses to see it. He never said any of this out loud, but I can tell what he's thinking: I've been too sad for too long. I cry in the middle of dinner, sometimes when Ethan or Indie are trying to tell a funny story about their day. I sigh heavily while reading the news, or whenever something reminds me of her. I talk too much, working over my relationship with my mom out loud. This, I think, is when Ethan discovered the flip side of the characterizations he'd bestowed on me in the first place.

During a stupidly clichéd fight about where to spend Christmas last year—I said my dad was lonely and his parents had each other; he said my dad had two children while his parents had just him—Ethan told me I wasn't a Zen monk after all; I was a robot, deficient in warmth and empathy. And when my mom's early death led me to question whether I might be squandering something in my own life—time, intellect, creative potential—Ethan huffed irritably, as if we'd had this conversation a thousand times before. "You need to stop obsessing over what you're meant to *be*," he said. "We're apes. We do shit and then we die."

As I pull into the driveway, I check my phone one more time. There's no message from Kevin, only a notification that my text to him has been read. I turn off the engine and take a deep breath. I pull back my shoulders and imagine contorting myself into that chalk outline, adjusting my pose until I fit just so. I am a wife. I am a mother. I am home.

chapter twenty-one **Indie**

I climb into the passenger seat of Mom's car in the CVS parking lot. She thinks it's some big feminist deal to make me go into CVS to buy my own tampons. She's been doing this since I first got my period: She just hands me her credit card and waits in the car. Apparently, even though I was allowed to skip the last month of middle school because of Maddy, this menstruation errand is carved in stone.

"I saw Maddy's dad in there," I say as I buckle my seatbelt.

"You saw Kevin?" Mom says, and her voice gets all high when she says his name. Seriously, no one calls him Kevin. "What did he say? How did he seem?"

"Nothing," I say. "He didn't see me."

He didn't see me because I hid in the seasonal display aisle until he was gone.

"Probably for the best," I add. "I don't know, it might really hurt his feelings if he saw me buying tampons."

This doesn't make any sense—Maddy got her period years before she died, and also, if her dad felt anything seeing me with a box of o.b. tampons, it would be embarrassment—but Mom nods like I've said something important. She cranes her neck toward the CVS entrance.

"He's gone," I say. "Can we please leave?"

I don't tell Mom how much I'd actually wanted to talk to the Chief. I don't say that this feels against the rules now, like I'm not part of their family anymore. I gave up that privilege when I told them Maddy's not in heaven. Besides, why should I get the Chief when Maddy doesn't?

Watching Maddy's dad from my hiding spot in CVS, overwhelmed by the familiar scent of inflatable pool toys—toxic off-gassing, I remind myself, nothing to get misty-eyed about—I imagined he was struggling to move his limbs through the salty water of the ocean. How could we possibly have a conversation underwater? Maddy and I used to go to the town pool every summer, and when we were little, we would sit cross-legged on the bottom of the pool and mime out a tea party. We tried to share secrets, too, our mouths releasing bubbles that rose to the surface and popped, the secrets gone forever.

"What was he buying?" Mom says.

We're at the only stoplight in town, and it feels strange to be around so many humans, even from the distance of a car.

"Hm?" I say. "What?"

I'm looking out the passenger window, thinking how none of the people walking by look real. I squint and now they're all moving through water, bubbles coming out of their mouths like thought bubbles in a comic. I can almost believe that if I opened the car window, water would gush in.

"Kevin. What was he buying?"

"I don't know, Mom. He was on the other side of the store, and also, I think it's rude to check out the contents of other people's shopping baskets at CVS. Why do you even care?"

"I just wonder who he has to talk to," she says. "Everyone expects him to be so strong. He's the *Chief*, you know?"

"You don't even know him," I say. "Besides, what difference would it make to anything if you knew he preferred Crest to Colgate? You'd probably just make fun of him for buying toothpaste with artificial sweetener."

Maddy's dad is the kind of patriot who doffs his hat for the national anthem, even when it's on TV and he's alone in the den.

Last year he started a whole thing against a proposed law that would have banned American flags on fire trucks. According to the liberals on the town board, the flags are big as bedsheets, making them a potential safety hazard.

My parents told me they hung an American flag outside our house when they first moved here, but it's in the basement now, and has been for years. Dad says the flag doesn't mean the same thing it used to, although I think they just stopped trying to fit in.

At some point, my parents decided to fly their true colors, literally: pink lawn signs for Planned Parenthood, black for BLM, and blue for every Democratic candidate in a hundred-mile radius. I don't understand local elections; it seems like someone is always running for something, and they all know our lawn is fair game. After my parents outed themselves as the neighborhood's bleeding-heart liberals, Dad warned me to give wide berth to a nearby house that flies the Confederate flag (not the only Dixie flag in town, by the way). That family has since added a huge FUCK YOUR FEELINGS banner to their racist lawn exhibit. Welcome to our town! Population: five thousand white people.

Back when I used to play in soccer tournaments on the weekends, both my parents would show up to cheer me on. It's an only-child thing; most girls on the team had to carpool because of multiple siblings playing different sports. Anyway, at one of these tournaments, Mom commented under her breath, "There are more one-armed men here than people of color right now." (Both an assistant coach and a player's dad happened to be born this way, go figure.) Neither Dad nor I responded, though, because it sounded more like Mom was workshopping a joke for *If You Lived Here* than actually talking to us. *The Kate Kate Show*, Dad and I call her online thing, or sometimes *Kate Expectations*, or *Better Kate Than Never*. During a hike last summer—Mom couldn't come because she was working—Dad and I made a list of Kate puns, and we got all the way to fifteen before deciding this was mean.

Mom once told me she'd feel more comfortable if I didn't read her posts. Though, why would I? It's not like this is the secret diary of an international spy. It's Mom, who tells us what she thinks over dinner every single night. When you're the only child of a feminist realtor "momfluencer" (ew) and a history teacher who reads the news obsessively, dinner table conversations are basically Socratic seminars. I was raised on nerdy historical factoids and strategies for fighting my inner gender bias. The only difference is, I can't unsubscribe from family dinners.

"Tell me about him," Mom says, as we pull away from the light.

Bye bye fake fish people, I think.

"Tell you about who?"

"*Kevin*," she says. "The Chief. You're right, I don't know Maddy's dad, and I feel awful about that. So, tell me: What was he like?"

What *was* he like, she wants to know. Because he stopped being like anything after Maddy died.

"I just can't with this right now," I say. "Why don't you stalk him online or something?"

Maddy's dad doesn't think much of my parents, and I'm sure Mom knows this. Whenever he used to complain about the invasion of "cidiots," which was often, he would shrug apologetically in my direction, as if he was sorry I'd been born into such a family. He claimed the town was being overrun by vegans and man buns, although Maddy would point out that he didn't know any vegans personally, and he'd never seen a man bun in the wild. The Chief did see a lot of grown men carrying designer backpacks, and this he found equal parts baffling and irritating. "They look like children," he said. "Do their moms still label their clothes, too?"

Nor could he understand why liberals made such a big deal about the questionably "historic" but definitely racist carved wood art hanging in one of the family-owned restaurants in town. "They don't even eat there," he said, which was mostly true, except *someone* saw it. "What's next, they gonna cancel God because he's a cis white man?" When Maddy shot him one of her looks to let him know he'd gone too far, he looked more sad than mad. "I love this town," he said. "I just wish it wasn't so divided."

I believed him, too; Maddy's neighbors had a COLD BEER MATTERS sign in their front yard, and her dad disliked it as much as we did. Standing up for what you believed was serious business in his book. None of this was funny to him.

"Indie," he liked to say to me. "You stick around here long enough, we'll make a local out of you yet." When I pointed out that I was actually born at the same hospital as Maddy, he swatted the air with his hand as if this were irrelevant.

The Chief liked to use air quotes when he asked about Dad's "hobbies," as if there was something unmanly about leisure time. "What's next?" he said once. "Bees or llamas?" When I told him how Dad was doing a deep dive on mushrooms, totally geeking out on mycelium—and making way too many dad jokes about fungi—I thought the Chief was going to lose his shit.

Despite all this, Dad is convinced he could pass as a local, which makes me think I should probably tell him to ditch the Herschel backpack. Maddy's dad mostly left Mom alone, although I think this had more to do with old-school chivalry than a lack of material to work with. I mean, she makes her own kale chips and then arranges them artfully on an enamel tray so she can document the achievement online. And she drives a *Subaru.* "No one in a Subaru ever gets out of our way," Maddy's dad said once. "It's like they think the lights and sirens don't apply to them."

Maddy's family is from our town in a way I never will be. Her grandfather was the Chief before her father, her uncles and cousins volunteer for fire departments throughout the county, and her mom and aunts run soup and bake sales for the Ladies Auxiliary. Mom once called Maddy's parents the firehouse power couple.

When we were little, the Chief would let Maddy ride up front in the fire truck for the Memorial Day parade. She threw candy to all the kids waving from the sidewalks, and I think she wore a tiara, too. Though perhaps I'm just imagining the tiara thing because of how much she seemed like royalty in that moment. I wanted to be her. Turns out, history teachers and realtors-with-a-platform don't get a parade, no matter how many nice things they say about immigrants and people of color. Even after Maddy got too old to ride in the truck, after we were all too cool to wave flags and scramble after candy in the street, the two of us still went to the parade to wave at her dad, and he still saved us a bag of candy for when we met him back at the firehouse after.

I skipped the parade this year, but this is a small town: I'm always going to be bumping into Maddy's extended family. They're waitresses and school aides, they're landlords and small business owners, they're nurses and mechanics, they build houses and mow lawns, and one of her cousins is even the disembodied voice at the Dunkin' Donuts drive-thru attached to CVS—though I know this only because Maddy told me. Mom never took me there once, not even as a reward for buying my own tampons.

Mom pulls into our driveway and turns off the car. When I don't move, she leans over and unbuckles my seatbelt, which gives me déjà vu. Maybe she used to do that for Grandma when we would pick her up from the nursing home and take her out for lunch.

"Indie," she says. "We're home."

I don't open the car door, and neither does she.

"You can tell me anything," she says. "You know that, right? That's the deal: You get to say anything, and I'm still your mom. I might have a little panic attack on the inside, but I'm not going anywhere."

"You don't want to hear it," I say. "You've already made that perfectly clear."

"I said Maddy's parents were worried about you," Mom says. "That's not the same thing."

"It kind of is, though."

"Just tell me what you're thinking," she says. "I worry more when you say nothing."

"*Fine*," I say. "I'm thinking about how Grandma is kind of like a star that exploded and died. They're both just particles that have disbanded. It *seems* like Grandma's more real, but that's just an idea in your head."

Mom swallows loudly, and I can tell she's trying not to cry.

"See?" I say. "You don't want to hear it."

Mom is silent for a while, except for the annoyingly loud way she's exhaling, like she's blowing out candles on a cake. I guess she's thinking about Grandma.

"I read that most of the stars we can see in the sky have already died," she says eventually. "It's just that their light takes so long to reach us. But they're still beautiful, right? They still light up the night sky."

"Actually, that's not true," I say. "Maddy and I watched a thing about it, and it's just a myth. According to astronomers, all visible stars are still alive."

Mom takes my hand and holds it to her wrist.

"Can you feel my pulse?" Mom says. "Can you feel that I'm real?"

"I feel a pulse," I say, shrugging. "But it doesn't *belong* to you, that's the part you're imagining."

"Tell me more about that," she says, still holding my hand.

I think of all the subreddits I've followed, all the podcasts I've binged in the middle of the night. I think of the new videos I've found, and how lonely it feels—and how wrong—to keep learning without Maddy. And so I decide to tell Mom the truth. I tell her there's no senior manager in her head, typing up her thoughts and hitting Send. Thoughts are more like butterflies, I explain, touching down briefly and moving on. We don't own our thoughts and we don't control them either.

Mom smiles like I've said something cute.

"What?"

"It's just the phrase you used," Mom says. "*Senior manager*. I'm imagining some tiny corporate drone in my head, monitoring my thoughts and feelings like the TPS reports in *Office Space*."

"There *is* no manager," I say huffily. "That's the whole point."

"Got it," Mom says, like I'm being cute again. "No TPS reports."

I reach into the center console for my phone, then pull my hand back quickly, like I'd touched something hot. I was going to text Maddy and tell her how annoying Mom's being. This must be what it feels like to have a phantom limb.

For the seven years Maddy and I were best friends, we existed on our own planet. Our moms and their inability to see us as actual human beings, our dads and their dad jokes, our parents and their politics, all the man buns and Herschel backpacks, the FUCK YOUR FEELINGS lawn signs, the backyard bees, the cidiots, the flags (both American and Confederate), even the "All Lives Matter" protest that went right through the center of our town—these things were simply orbiting objects. Like a comet or a supernova you only think about because someone on TikTok reminds you to check out the night sky.

Maddy and I used to watch the Perseid meteor shower together every August, lying on our backs in the grass. We always slept out in a tent in my yard. In fifth grade, we even set an alarm for 3 a.m. to catch the peak. That was the year Maddy decided she wanted to be an astrophysicist, and so it felt important to do it right—like staying up past midnight on New Year's Eve. It was the year she carried a Neil deGrasse Tyson book everywhere and lived in a tee that declared, *Forget Princess, I Want to Be an Astrophysicist*. We both had those glow-in-the-dark stars on our ceilings, but only Maddy's were arranged in actual constellations.

Sometime during middle school, Maddy stopped talking about the stars, and she seemed embarrassed whenever I brought it up, as if wanting to be an astrophysicist was the same thing as wanting to drive a train or work in a candy store—the kind of job only little kids wished for. When I asked her what she wanted to be instead, she said, *happy*. "That's it?" I asked. "Nothing else?" She laughed and said, "Best friends with you, of course."

I turn back to Mom.

"I'll tell you the really cool part," I say. "The self isn't real. There's no you, there's no me. *That's* what I meant about no senior manager. We're all just bags of chemicals when you get down to it."

"And you think that's *cool*?" Mom says.

I feel this to be true, deep in my being. I can feel how I am not separate from the world, but I guess Mom isn't ready to hear it. She still thinks I'm something special. She believes I came *into* this world, like a messiah or an alien, when really I came *out* of it, like a tomato sprouting from one of the vines in Dad's vegetable garden. What she thinks of as "me" is just nature doing its nature thing.

"I didn't finish," I say. "If there's no self, then death isn't really a thing, either. It's just atoms rearranging themselves. Someone dying—*Grandma* dying—that's no different from a fallen leaf turning into mulch."

Boom, I think. Nothing cute about that.

chapter twenty-two **Kate**

"I've been thinking," I say to Indie. "What you said about Grandma."

Indie is sitting across from me at the kitchen island, eating Grape-Nuts out of a tiny ramekin that reminds me of the pretend breakfasts she used to make for her Big Bird stuffed animal. She doesn't respond. I reach forward and wave a hand in front of her face, and when she looks up, I point at her earbuds. She tugs one out, already annoyed at me.

"*What*?"

I take a deep breath.

"There weren't any clean bowls," she says, gesturing at the ramekin. "I'm not anorexic, so you can skip that lecture."

"The dishwasher's clean," I say, somehow dragged into the argument she assumed I wanted to start.

Indie goes to put her earbud back in.

"Wait!" I say, loud and frantic, as if she were running to catch a train.

Indie sighs.

"That thing about Grandma not being real," I say. "I was thinking how I haven't taken you to see her grave, not since the funeral. You never even got to see the headstone."

The cemetery is a ninety-minute drive on windy roads and Indie gets carsick, but that's not the only reason I visit when she and Ethan are at school.

"I'm sorry I haven't taken you," I say. "I've been so focused on how I lost my mom, I forgot that you lost your Grandma, too. Maybe we could visit her together sometime."

Indie stares at me.

"Grandma's not there," she says. "You do realize that, right?"

"You know what I mean," I say. "We could visit her grave. It's beautiful there, and so quiet. It helps me remember her."

"You mean you don't go on your phone while you're there?" Indie says.

I bite my lip. She's right. I always leave my phone in the car.

"It can be quiet anywhere," Indie says, picking up her earbud again. "If you just stop talking."

This stings, but I press on, before I lose her attention for good.

"We could go to Maddy's grave," I say. "I could come with you. Or I could just wait in the car. It's nice to have a place to go."

I brace myself, assuming Indie will lash out, tell me I don't get it, tell me she's not ready, tell me a grave is just a rock in a field.

"No, thank you," she says instead, as if I were a waitress offering the pepper grinder. As if I were a complete stranger. As if Maddy's death had nothing whatsoever to do with either one of us.

Indie used to ask me why we didn't vacation with Maddy's family, or at least invite her parents over for dinner. "We're not that close," I would say, to which she would respond, "That's because you've never tried. You could *get* close." She was so sure Laura and I would be BFFs, if only we made the time. That was how much faith Indie had in her own friendship; she believed that any relationship in its wake would be imbued with the same magic.

I think of Kevin, how he would wave from the driveway, where he was always either washing his truck or working on it. For years, I smiled politely in his direction when I picked up Indie, seeing only his buzz cut and the oversized decal, NEVER FORGET, on the back windshield of the truck. He was an archetype—Local Hero—and it never occurred to me that he might have something interesting to say. I rarely even got out of my car. Mostly I just texted Indie, *here*, and she would come right out.

And now it's too late. If I'd been more like Ethan, if I'd seen Kevin as someone worth even ten minutes of my attention, maybe I would have had more to offer when he collapsed in front of me. Instead, he kissed me, because I am no one to him. He still hasn't called, and I'm not sure he ever will.

At some point, Indie stopped asking me to invite Maddy's family over. Perhaps this was because she finally understood it wasn't going to happen. More likely, she simply stopped caring. She and Maddy no longer needed their moms to be friends, just like they didn't need us to arrange playdates, either. They took on sole responsibility for the relationship.

One night at dinner last year, a month or so into eighth grade, Indie announced: "Mom, do you realize I spend more time with Maddy than I do with you?" I opened my mouth to argue the point before realizing, (a) Indie wasn't trying to start something, she was just stating a fact that was interesting to her, and (b) she was right.

"I suppose so," I said. "Middle school is basically a full-time job, isn't it?"

The same statistic was true of Indie and Ethan, although she did not feel the need to point this out to him.

"It's not just school," Indie said. "Most of the photos on my phone are of me and Maddy, too."

I looked across the table at Ethan and he shrugged.

"I've been eating lunch with the same guys for ten years," he said. "During the school year, I probably spend more time with them than I do with you."

I mostly eat lunch in my car between appointments, if I eat at all.

"Huh," I said, the word coming out more bitter than I'd intended. I'd been aiming for wry bemusement.

Ethan turned to me, as if an idea had just occurred to him.

"Maybe you need a hobby where you meet actual people," he suggested. "Not just followers. People you could meet for lunch."

A *hobby*. Ethan has never considered my online presence a legitimate accomplishment.

"Too bad there's no Buddy Bench for grown-ups," Indie said, cracking herself up. "Like, right outside the coffee shop or something."

"I have friends!" I insisted, my voice now squeaky and defensive. "I'm just really busy. I'm not sure if anyone told you this, but moms don't get lunch breaks."

Indie dominated family dinners with her thoughts on the world back then, holding the floor like a nightly filibuster. "Is she going to take a breath?" I murmured to Ethan on more than one occasion. But I let this happen because I knew Indie had years ahead of her when the world would tell her all the ways in which she was *less than* as a girl. Mothers like me, we want to raise girls who'll run the world, and so we pass the mic. "No offense, Mom," our daughters say before each withering remark, and we train ourselves to not take offense. We do this for the greater good, or perhaps because our daughters' success is easier to imagine than our own.

Where are all those words now, I wonder? They seemed so integral to Indie's sense of self, and yet how easily she let them go.

Last spring, Indie and Maddy created "How Well Do You Know Me?" quizzes for each other online. I insisted on taking Indie's quiz, because I was sure I would do at least as well as her BFF, and also because middle school girls have a knack for making their middle-aged mothers feel and act thirteen again. Maddy got ten out of ten, while I scored a measly six. But here's the kicker: After my D-minus humiliation, I made Ethan take the quiz, figuring I would at least do better than him. He got eight and a half—a solid B.

"It's okay," Indie said to me, when she saw the look on my face. "You're always working on your thing, that's all. Dad and I watch more shows together."

My *thing*. It was like middle school gaslighting: I chose the internet over family bonding, and now I had the failing quiz grade to prove it. I wasn't a realtor scrabbling for writing time at the edges of my day, I was a distracted and disinterested parent who didn't care to watch *The Office* with her daughter. Unlike Ethan, of course (all nine seasons, three times over).

"Your mom works hard," Ethan insisted to Indie, as if this made us even. "We're really lucky, do you realize that?"

There's an ice-breaker game Ethan sometimes plays with his students in the fall. Two people go back and forth, grilling each other on their identities: "Who are you?"—"I'm a girl."—"Who are you?"—"I'm a student."—"Who are you?"—"I'm a friend." You keep going until you get to the heart of who you *really* are—or, at least, until you've said all you're willing to say in public. I imagine playing this game with Indie now. Who are you? I'm mulch on the ground. Who are you? I'm an arrangement of atoms and the space between them. Who are you? I'm no one.

chapter twenty-three ❦ **Indie**

It's Sunday morning, which means my mom is drinking coffee and swiping through her camera roll, in search of material for *If You Lived Here*, and my dad is approximately two hours into a five-hour bike ride. (It can't be healthy for a grown man to spend that much of his day in Lycra.) I'm sitting in bed, watching videos on my phone, which is what I do every morning, not just Sundays. For weeks, I rewatched the videos Maddy and I found together, but then I ran out of thread: I had scrolled back to before we started thinking about this stuff, and it didn't feel like time travel, it felt like losing her all over again.

I put in my earbuds and watch a new video, start to finish, then I refresh and listen from the beginning. Over and over I click Play, until the philosopher's ideas start to make sense, until his words feel like something I would say. Until the knowledge feels so familiar, so deeply implanted in my brain, that it's impossible to believe I never shared this video with Maddy.

Mom checks in on me at one point. She leans in to look at my phone, and the smell of coffee on her breath makes me shrink away from her.

"What's that?" Mom says.

"I'm studying the hard problem of consciousness," I say snidely, turning my phone over so she can't see the screen. "Heard of it?"

She gives me a strange look and shakes her head.

"You feeling okay today?" Mom says, running a hand through my hair.

"Sure," I say, brushing off her hand.

She takes a seat on the edge of my bed.

"Can I watch with you?" Mom says.

Then she puts on this dumb brave smile like she deserves a parenting medal. It's the same look she wears when she's trying to understand my math homework.

"You wouldn't get it," I say.

She'll *never* get it. How the world is pretty unbearable lately, and how this helps. How consciousness doesn't belong to us, and it doesn't begin and end with us either. It's a stream that came before anything and runs through everything, and each life is just a whirlpool in that stream.

I imagine looking into that stream and seeing Maddy's reflection gazing back at me, her face rippling with the motion of water. I imagine the whirlpool gradually unspooling, like a ball of yarn being tugged by a cat, the circles widening and loosening, until all I can see is a stream, and my own face staring back at me. I am Maddy and she is me and we are both the stream.

There was a YouTube video Maddy and I used to watch obsessively, back when she still dreamed of being an astrophysicist. It was a time-lapse simulation of the future, spanning trillions and trillions of years. We watched in awe as the sun burned hotter until the oceans dried up and all plant life died out, as Earth was destroyed by the dying sun, as the sun became a white dwarf and then faded and died, as every last sun in the universe died and starlight itself came to an end. And still the numbers at the bottom of the video kept ticking up, like a slot machine after a big win—I didn't think of these numbers as *dates*, they were too big for that—until all remaining matter and energy was sucked into a giant black hole.

When I showed the video to Mom, she said it caused a lurch in her stomach, like she was in an elevator that was plunging to the ground, except the lurch stayed for days. But Maddy and I didn't experience it that way. We were twelve, and our feelings were so *big* back then, it felt like we were expanding along with the universe. Imagining humanity as a cosmic blip was just another big feeling, and we contained within us all the feelings.

"Don't take it so personally," I told Mom.

Now, I think of these numbers ticking up as I pull on my clothes each morning. I think of how time spins like a slot machine and consciousness burns through every atom—atoms that come together and break apart and come together again, in endless combinations, for trillions of years, until the protons begin to decay and the atoms are gone and time, at last, becomes meaningless. Nothing personal.

chapter twenty-four ❦ Kate

"We need to talk about Indie," I say.

Ethan is scanning news headlines on his phone while he eats breakfast. He's still wearing the ratty t-shirt he slept in because it's summer break and he can shower whenever he feels like it—probably after he's gone for a bike ride, checked in on his vegetable garden, and had a leisurely lunch with a teacher friend.

"Did something happen?" Ethan says. He looks around the kitchen, as if he might find a clue. "Is she okay?"

I'm not sure how to respond to this. Is it not enough, what's already happened to our daughter?

"Well, her best friend died," I say eventually. "Pretty sure you heard about that."

Ethan nods and picks up his phone again.

"Really? I say. "Is it too much to ask for your undivided attention right now?"

"She's *sad*," Ethan says, and he actually sounds irritated. "She's going to be sad for a really long time. There's no parenting hack here. It's not some school project you can take over to make sure she gets an A."

Ethan is fully aware that I have never been this kind of mother, although I did once make Indie stay up way past her bedtime because I knew *she* could do better on her Native American longhouse model. I take a deep breath. I *put a pin in it*, as the podcast dudes like to say, because that's how marriage works sometimes.

"I realize you have more experience with this than I do," I venture, and then I pause, to be sure Ethan sees what I'm doing.

It feels like the marital version of a copyright acknowledgment. If Ethan needs me to say that my experience with loss is a faded Xerox copy, and his the original, the starkest form of grief—if that's the only way he can hear me today, I will do it. I will relegate my mom to the status of a distant relative whose demise was sad but not tragic, early but not untimely.

"It's just—she's given up everything she used to love," I say. "Have you noticed? She hasn't touched the piano since Maddy died. She doesn't draw, she doesn't read, she doesn't even watch TV. She barely speaks. She's so *flat* all the time, and it's freaking me out."

I'm standing, my work bag already on my shoulder. This is how I talk to Ethan these days, with a prop on hand that suggests I'm just passing through. *Can't really chat, gotta go.* He's always been able to read me. He says my voice gets high when I give a compliment I don't mean, and apparently I open conversations with the word *um* when I'm about to suggest something I know he won't like. I'm convinced that if Ethan looked at me directly now, he would detect something—a hesitant smile, darting eyes—and he would know I'm keeping a secret: *I kissed the Chief.* And so I am careful to hover at the outskirts of his attention.

Except, I need to know if he sees it too, what's happening to Indie.

"I'm sorry our daughter's behavior is *freaking you out*," Ethan says. "But Indie's working through this in her own way."

"Jesus Christ, Ethan," I say. "You know that's not what I meant. I'm worried about her. She's acting like Maddy's death doesn't mean anything. She never cries. It's not—" I struggle for the right word. I don't want to say *normal*, I've never wanted anything close to normal for Indie, but that's what I mean. "The things she's saying," I settle on finally. "They're just—a little *off*."

"*Kate*," Ethan says, exasperated now. "She lost her best friend. She's destroyed. Her grief isn't supposed to make sense to you. Maybe *she* doesn't think piano practice will help her right now."

"I don't mean she should *practice*," I say weakly, because I'm no longer sure what I do mean.

Indie used to hate it when Ethan and I made eye contact while she was playing something gorgeous on the piano. "Stop being so *proud* all the time," she said once. "It's so annoying. Can you please just go find your own thing to do?" After that, whenever she played a new piece, Ethan would text me from across the room instead, pretending to be absorbed in an article on his iPad. *We made this*, he wrote once.

"I realize she's not acting like all your internet friends say she should," Ethan says now. "But she's not a blog post, she's our daughter, and this is how *she's* grieving."

This must be what it's like to be married to a veteran. To be a bystander who hates the war, too, but isn't allowed to say so, because she hasn't earned her opinion in blood.

"I know she's grieving," I say. "But what if she does something stupid? What if she—"

I cut myself off. I can't say it.

"I just think she could use someone to talk to," I say.

I once asked Ethan's mom if he saw a therapist after Luke died, and she said she wasn't sure, the first weeks were a blur and then he went back to college. "He found his own way," she said smoothly, as if he had any choice in the matter, although maybe he did. Maybe absconding with his grief was the only way he could think to lighten his parents' load.

"She talks to me," Ethan says. "You act like this household can't function without you, but the two of us manage to scrape by."

What does she say? I want to ask him. *Is she herself? Does she smile? Does she eat? What does she need?*

"That's good," I say instead, and I try to mean it. "But—what if she feels like she has to act a certain way around us?"

Act a certain way around *you*, I mean.

"Maybe it would be a relief for her," I add. "To talk to a stranger."

How many years did I dread the idea of our daughter talking to a stranger at the county fair? Now a stranger feels like our last best hope.

"I'll ask the school counselor if she sees students over summer break," Ethan says, and he picks up his phone and starts tapping at the screen. "She's a friend."

How lightly he says that word, *friend*, as if it were an unremarkable thing to find and keep one. And then he half-smiles to himself as he reads something on his screen. I learned long ago that this is not a prompt for me to ask him what's so funny.

"I'll be back around seven," I say, but only out of habit. He's not listening. "Please make sure Indie eats lunch."

When I get to the office, I ask Sara if she wants to split the Orchard Street deal with me.

"I'll do all the paperwork," I say. "But I think it'd be better if you did the in-person stuff with the clients."

"The *clients*?" Sara says, giving me a strange look. "You mean Maddy's parents?"

"I just think it would be easier for him," I say. "For them, I mean. Not to see me."

Laura seems like the kind of wife who casually reads her husband's texts, not because she's nosy or suspicious but simply because you can't rely on a man to relay the necessary household logistics—not with three kids, four jobs, and a huge extended family between them. So I assume I am addressing my message to the two of them. *I think we should start showing the house this week*, I text. *Okay? My colleague Sara will be helping out.* I feel a flutter of panic in my chest, imagining Laura seeing this text, reading between the lines. What if she *is* the suspicious kind of wife, after all?

Two kids between them, I remind myself. Four jobs and *two* kids, not three.

When I get home, I go straight to Indie's room and knock on her door.

"No," she calls out.

"I didn't ask you anything," I say through the closed door.

"The answer is still no."

Downstairs, I sit at the kitchen island and scroll mindlessly through the contacts on my phone. Except, it's not really mindless. After a few minutes I realize what I'm secretly hoping for: That somehow, miraculously, I will come across a childhood friend I forgot about. A best friend I could tell everything to, because she has nobody's back but my own.

The thing is, in a town this small, everyone has skin in the game. The friends I've made here exist within the structure of the life Ethan and I have built together—they're married to Ethan's friends, they're mothers to Indie and Maddy's classmates, they volunteer for the PTSA with Laura. If their house catches fire or their husband has a heart attack, it's Kevin who gets the call on his pager. Nobody gets to be an island here, and this social contract is lovely, it really is, until you accidentally kiss the Chief and have no friend to confide in.

I always thought that the kind of woman who clung to her childhood friends was the kind of woman who didn't like her current life all that much. She was the kind of woman who wanted to reminiscence with people she used to hang out with, back when every choice was still ahead of her. The kind of woman who wanted a home team advantage when she bitched about her husband. (I never thought the same of men, I suppose because I assumed close male friendship in middle age was a rarer thing, and not to be taken for granted.) I was *all in* when it came to our new life, that's what I told myself. I was good with the choices I'd made. Sure, Ethan could be exasperating sometimes, but I didn't need to bore anyone else with the details.

I didn't know I was supposed to save an old friend for a time like this. *In case of emergency, break glass.* That kind of a friend.

There's a handful of former colleagues from the city I'm still in touch with, plus a college roommate and a couple of high school friends, but these relationships consist almost entirely of superficial exchanges on social media: *Miss you so much, catch up SOON!* (We won't.) Everyone else I've ever known exists now as information: Their updates appear in my feed, and sometimes I read them, and perhaps they skim mine, too. How deranged I would seem—and how pathetically lonely—if I actually called one of these people to "catch up."

I've never understood how Ethan has the energy to maintain his old friendships while forming new ones. Nor would Ethan understand my confusion, I suppose, because connecting is just what he does. It never feels like work to him. I let friends go; that's what I do, and sometimes this feels like a factory defect that surfaced years after I could do anything about it. I used to think it was because I'd morphed so much over the years, unlike the women who move back to their hometown right after college, into a house just like the one they grew up in. Or perhaps I'm more of a day-to-day shape-shifter, unwilling to be truly known. Either of these explanations is easier to stomach than the one I find myself returning to: I'm just not the kind of old friend that people keep. I'm the holdover friend, the new-in-town friend, the geographically convenient friend.

I think about my mother in the nursing home, visited by just one friend she'd known for a handful of years. They were in a Bible study together, and maybe once or twice they went for coffee after. Even that friend stopped visiting once she realized my mom didn't know her name, as if the point were to receive credit.

I used to hope my brother and I would age into friendship when he married and had kids. Our offspring would be more than blood relations; they would be a common interest, too, and his cool, smart wife a bridge between us. Instead, he remains the unattached perpetual teenager my mother adored—the brother who never could understand what my problem with her was. He actually brought a *date* to our mom's funeral.

Through the kitchen window, I can see Ethan's car in the driveway, but I don't hear him anywhere in the house. *Home*, I text him, and he gives the message a thumbs-up but doesn't respond further. I glance around the kitchen. He doesn't appear to have a plan for dinner—no open cookbook, no chicken thighs defrosting on the counter.

Movie night? I text Indie. *Sneaky TV dinner?* I once swore we would never be the kind of family who texted each other under the same roof, and Indie loves to catch me in a moment of hypocrisy. At least, she used to. I wonder if it's too soon to tease her. Is she rolling her eyes at Ethan's dad jokes when I'm gone? I text her some more: *[Cue horror movie soundtrack and creepy voice-over]: The call is coming from inside the house!*

n, Indie writes back.

You can pick the movie, I text. *Congratulations, you've officially graduated from eighties movie school!*

Indie tells me only old people text in complete sentences. "It's not *email*, Mom," she likes to say, and the way she says the word *email*, it's like she's talking about the Pony Express. She says a lot of things about old people, though her sample size seems to be limited to a population of two: me and Ethan. Or, more often, just me.

Old people are so quick to forgive eighties movies their sins, Indie says. She's right, of course. (I mean, date rape passed off as a favor to a geek? Really, *Sixteen Candles*?) But the friendships in eighties movies are pure of heart, and that's why I bear no grudge. Maverick and Goose. Ferris and Cameron. Elliot and

E.T. *The Goonies. The Breakfast Club.* Gordie and the gang in *Stand By Me*. The kids in *Stranger Things*, because obviously that show gets grandfathered in. And who walked off into the sunset with Tom Hanks at the end of *Big*? Not Elizabeth Perkins—because that would be pedophilia, oops—but his best friend Billy. I keep returning to the last line of *Stand By Me*, and every single time, I think my heart might split open in two: "I never had any friends later on like the ones I had when I was twelve. Jesus, does anyone?"

I didn't really believe this kind of friendship existed, not until my daughter showed me what it looked like. I was relieved when Indie found Maddy—relieved that she took after her father and not me—and a little jealous, too. Mothers want more for their daughters than they themselves had, but also, they want to know what it feels like to have more. To have a lifelong friend who rests her head in your lap while you watch a movie together.

I once asked Indie what made her and Maddy such good friends. "I know it's hard to explain," I said, when she didn't respond immediately. "I'm just curious." She gave me an exasperated look. "It's not *hard* to explain," she said, her voice peevish. "It's impossible. It's a billion different things that all add up."

Watching Indie and Maddy in their first intense weeks together, I thought about how friendships progress on a different timescale for the young, or maybe they're on no timescale at all. A kid can make and lose a best friend in a single day, while adult friendships plod along, dutifully checking off each step along the way: conversations in the school pickup line; meetups at the playground; coffee dates or yoga classes or happy hour wine; and eventually, maybe, a book club. We're expected to put in real work before an acquaintance becomes a friend. But why should a relationship mean less just because it's forged in a single day?

One August, after Indie and Maddy had spent every day together for a two-week stretch, I said, "Why don't you spend today apart?" I tried to explain how they might tire of each other, or run out of things to say. I knew Indie depended on the friendship, and this gave me a kind of low-grade panic: She should preserve it.

That's exactly how little I understood of best friendship. I imagined it to be like a bar of soap, something that would wear with use. My daughter, of course, looked at me like I knew nothing, then picked up the landline to call her best friend. The relationship never felt tenuous to her. It was a simple fact, as incontestable as if they'd been blood-related. They were friends in the way that the ocean meets the beach, the way heads is the opposite of tails.

This is the strongest argument I can make to Indie, when she tells me the self is not real: Do arrangements of particles form bosom friendships? For seven years, Indie was soul to soul with another human being, someone not related by blood. She had a friend who saw her through line—from the pig-tailed girl in second grade who literally stomped her right foot when she got mad, to the eighth grader in a pixie cut who joined protest marches to change the world. I glimpse this in Ethan's friendships, too, and I try not to resent him for it: His friends remind him of who he is, at the core—the part of his inner self that is unchanging and truly *him*. His closest friends have known him for almost forty years—talk about a through line. There have been many chapters to his life, and he has friends who know the whole story, beginning to end.

But I suppose the opposite argument could also be true: The loss of Maddy so undid my daughter—on a metaphysical level—*because* she was an inmost-soul friend who saw Indie, start to finish. This kind of friend can reassure you, in a billion different ways, that you exist. But who are you when she's no longer there to look?

Some people claim that a spouse can be your through line—the same sort of people, I suppose, who brag that they married their best friend. Except, when a marriage fails, we often say that the couple "grew apart," as if marriage weren't meant to sustain outsized individual growth. In the twenty-first century, we're supposed to enter marriage with a solid sense of self. No wonder, then, that so many of us spend decades with spouses who bore us: We know only one version of each other. A single chapter, containing neither story arc nor plot twist.

So now here I find myself, an overgrown teenager pining for the best friend I never had, while my husband replies to yet another text. I pick up my phone again. I scroll through my reader comments, replying to each one in turn, taking particular care with the names I am most familiar with. I keep my tone light and airy, because—as Ethan likes to remind me—these people are not my old friends. Not the graduated-kindergarten-together kind. I post peppy quips and self-deprecating anecdotes. I imagine I am sticking a finger down my throat, vomiting up exclamation points and LOLs. I pretend that someone out there is holding back my hair.

chapter twenty-five **Indie**

The school counselor tells me to look for small moments of grace in the world. She claims that if I observe, and especially if I journal, eventually these small moments will add up to a world I recognize. A world I want to return to.

"Like random acts of kindness?" I say. "You want me to catch people returning their shopping carts to the right place or something?"

"Not necessarily people," Mrs. G says. "Maybe it's a tree in your yard, maybe you notice how it looks each day—what changes, what stays the same. There's grace to be found everywhere."

"We covered the seasons in kindergarten," I say. "My mom has all the artwork to prove it, so."

The counselor smiles.

"So, draw the same tree," she says. "You still like to draw, right? Draw the same tree every day."

Clearly Dad already told Mrs. G everything she needs to know. I'm not sure why I even need to be here.

"I like to watch starlings," she says, her gaze drifting to the wall, even though she's in one of those depressing pod offices with no windows. "In the fields near my house at twilight, flocks of starlings swoop and dive like one being. It's breathtaking, how they know exactly what to do and where to go."

People only think nature is meaningful when it moves them. It's like this entire planet is just a Netflix menu for them to swipe through.

"I'm not a birder," I say. "Nature's not really my thing. Plus, my dad says starlings are an invasive species."

He also told me it's called a *murmuration* when starlings swoop like that. He said it has something to do with physics, how each bird follows the movements of its neighbors, but when he first taught me the word, I imagined the birds literally murmuring to themselves, reciting the moves under their breath like novice dancers counting the beat.

"It doesn't have to be nature, either," Mrs. G says, crossing her legs. She's wearing a wrap dress made of flax, and I know this because there's a clothing store in town that's had a FLAX IS HERE! sign in the window for years. "Maybe it's the smell of a Pumpkin Spice Latte from Starbucks."

"Seriously?"

"Yes," she says. I wonder if that's a therapist thing, answering rhetorical questions. "But you're right, what I see when I look at a tree or a bird is not what you see. I can't tell you what to look for."

Everything in here is laminated. The inspirational quotes in "fun" fonts, the building map, the bell schedule, the growth mindset chart, the list of phone extensions, and did I mention the inspirational quotes? *Mistakes are proof that you're trying. Sprinkle kindness like glitter. Success begins with believing you can. What would you do if you knew you couldn't fail?* I guess this counselor's moments of grace all come in laminated form.

"Think of it like going to the dentist," Mom said last night. "Just an emotional checkup, that's all." I think we were both surprised by how quickly I agreed to come here. I guess maybe I was a little curious, because, what if the counselor actually got it?

"Fine," I say now. "The world is full of grace. Trees moving in the wind, flowers that only open in moonlight, cute baby butts, birds that dance like synchronized swimmers. That doesn't make any of it real, though."

"What *is* real?"

Mrs. G says this room is a safe space, and she won't share anything with my parents unless she has my permission, or has reason to think I might hurt myself. I'm not entirely sure I believe her, though. I mean, my dad's classroom is literally down the hall.

"It depends on what you mean by real," I say.

"*I* think all those things are real," Mrs. G says. "Trees, flowers, babies, Starbucks. But I'm interested in what feels real to you."

"If what feels real to you is different from what feels real to me, how can we be sure *any* of it's real?" I say. "It's like we're all playing the same video game but seeing different things."

The counselor rolls her chair a few inches closer to me and then tucks her feet under her butt. I see what she's doing. She wants me to know that *now* is when we get real. Now is when it's okay to cry and tell her how sad I am that Maddy's dead. I wonder if my parents told her I don't cry anymore. How *psyched* would this counselor be if she got me to bawl my eyes out right now?

"What do you see in the video game? Do you see Maddy?"

"No," I say. "I don't see Maddy. Maddy's dead."

Mrs. G can't help me, I realize, because she works for the school district, and they just want to make sure I graduate on time without shooting up my classroom. They want me to be normal again, to un-know what I know.

Last night I told Dad that free will doesn't exist, and he looked at me like he wanted to check my temperature. I said I was feeling fine, that I just wanted him to hear me out: Free will is a made-up idea, I explained. It was Christians who first invented free will, to let God off the hook for all the bad shit that happens in this world. And I guess the idea stuck around, because these days even atheists like him want to feel like their decisions matter. But nobody *decides* to be good or bad, I told Dad. Nobody decides anything we're all just a configuration of atoms reacting to stuff. I expected Dad to be a little more open-minded on this topic. I mean, he's the one who first told me that humans made up the idea of God. But neither of my parents can get past their idea of *me*. I'm a sad kid, that's all they see, and everything I do or say is just a symptom to be cured.

I don't know why I bothered. I mean, yeah, Dad told me people invented God, but he's also a history teacher who likes timelines and artifacts and other evidence that humans are exceptional. Not to mention, in his spare time, he listens to podcasting bros like Tim Ferriss for tips on how to "optimize" his life. (Mostly cold showers and kettlebell workouts, from what I can tell.) As for Mom, where do I start? She's a shallow, insecure fake who obsesses over how many people comment on her posts. She once used Portrait Mode to capture a head of lettuce at the farmer's market. My parents are both way too invested in this world to see through it.

When I retrace the path that led me from a classroom debate about the moon landing to this counselor and her laminated deep thoughts, I see a crowd of people asking the wrong questions. They're thinking too small. Because the real question is not whether we landed on the moon or built the pyramids or are ruled by a deep state conspiracy, but whether we're here at all.

You want a conspiracy theory? Here's the ultimate con: This thing we call life is one giant illusion. The human brain cannot perceive anything beyond space and time, and so we insist that space and time are universally true, rather than just the view from our window. Our brains are simple: We have this idea of things *happening*, one after the other, of things *changing*, of one thing *causing* another, because that's the way we see things. It's like we're watching a movie, and because we can see only one frame at a time, we assume that only one frame *exists* at a time, and that one frame must *cause* the next. Our brains superimpose this arrow onto everything, tricking us into thinking that time is moving in one direction. As each frame passes, we imagine it's gone. Poof! In the past. But every frame already exists—always has, always will—and we are no more real than the collection of pixels that assemble themselves to represent each character on the screen. The only reality is this: Most people spend their entire lives with not one fucking clue about any of it.

"Tell me what you're thinking," Mrs. G says.

"Puppies," I say. "Puppies are real. Puppies are cute. Puppies are real cute!"

chapter twenty-six Kate

I text Ethan, who is somewhere upstairs: *Okay if I go to yoga tonight? It's been a while.*

Ethan: *y*

Me: *You sure? I don't have to go.*

Ethan: *You don't need a permission slip.*

This might have been a gentle tease if he'd added a smiley face. I cringe at the thought that it's come to this: I'm no longer hoping he'll reach for me in tenderness, just that he'll end one of his texts with an emoji. No wonder the simple fact of Kevin's hands threw me off-balance.

Me: *I couldn't get much out of Indie today, maybe check in on her?*

Ethan: *already w her*

Ethan once asked what I got out of yoga. (This was before he learned on a podcast that the practice increases neuroplasticity.) "It's just a workout," I told him. "Easy on my knees, good for the core."

I was lying though. The simplest answer to Ethan's question is that we live in a town of stressed out yoga moms, and I'm just trying to fit in. A significant portion of these moms are so invested in yoga that they become stressed out yoga instructors, until eventually, I suppose, the instructors will outnumber the students in this town. The rest of us become realtors who do a lot of yoga, because real estate is a career that can accommodate snow days and sick days and oh-crap-my-kid-has-head-lice days.

None of us, so far as I know, become poets.

After I met Ethan, I started writing poetry again for the first time since college, but I only ever showed him one stanza. He was so supportive, I didn't want to disappoint him. What if he realized his encouragement had been misplaced, that he'd been wrong to get my hopes up? It was easier just to let him imagine how gifted I was, and eventually, it was easier just to let myself imagine the same thing. Now, I help hedge fund managers and their first wives find second homes, which means I am at least partially responsible for introducing the G-Wagon to this town.

At the yoga studio, we *om* and we press our hands to our hearts and we watch our breaths and we stretch our muscles like tight smiles. We try to let things go, despite being wedged in between someone whose kid didn't invite our daughter to a birthday party and someone else who railed against critical race theory at the school board meeting. I'd like to see Sadhguru rock a cobra pose while simultaneously wondering why the woman two mats over went with a different realtor. But when we do manage, against all these odds, to let things go, it feels like a superpower.

And when we move, as one, into savasana, we close our eyes and for a few minutes we don't miss the women we imagined we'd grow up to be. The gong sound from the Tibetan singing bowl fills the room, like bells at the end of a church service, and in this moment, we are not grocery shopping or cooking or driving or working. We are not even working out. We are not wives or mothers, and we are not concerned that maybe we are failing at both. We're just lying there, like it's Sunday at noon and we're thinking about getting up for brunch. *That's* why I do yoga, Ethan.

As I'm rolling up my mat, I feel someone tap my shoulder. Not a rude tap like she's asking me to turn off my phone at the movies. More of a yoga thing, where she gently rests her hand on me to connect.

"Hey," the woman says when I look up. Ellen, I think, or maybe Elle. Ella? Her daughter must be in Indie's grade, because I recognize her from the elementary school birthday party circuit. "How's Indie doing?"

She's smiling. She seems nice. There's a possibility she really cares how Indie's doing, that she's not just looking for an inside scoop on what happened to Maddy. Her hand is still on my shoulder, and I don't know if I'm supposed to stay seated. It feels rude to stand up, like I'm shrugging her off, but it also feels awkwardly deferential to be at her feet.

"Indie's okay," I say, and I return the woman's smile. "It's hard, but she's doing okay, given everything."

Elle or Ella nods like she knows exactly what I'm talking about.

"Same with Mackenzie," she says. "She has good days and bad, you know?"

Her tone is light and casual, as if we were discussing the homework load in Algebra II. As if Indie's pain were nothing special. She pulls her hand from my shoulder and I realize the exchange is over. Her friend is waiting for her at the door.

"Actually," I say, and the woman turns back to me, a question on her face, like I'm going to tell her she forgot her yoga blanket. "Indie's not okay, she's heartbroken. She's a mess. I don't know how to help her. But she should be a mess, right? She shouldn't be okay yet?"

"Tell her to call Mackenzie," Elle or Ella says. "They should connect."

I seem to recall there are two Mackenzies in Indie's grade, but now doesn't feel like the right time to ask which one is hers.

"Nice seeing you," I say as she leaves.

She doesn't see Indie's pain as special, I realize, because everyone in town has claimed this tragedy as their own. Only Indie was there, only Indie lost her best friend, but anyone's daughter *could* have been there, *could* have lost a friend. Maybe their daughters would have been invited to Maddy's next birthday party, and how sad is it that now they never will?

In my car, I compose and then delete a text to Sara. Sara is a work friend: Sometimes we go for drinks straight from the office, but that's not the same thing as a spontaneous plan to meet after nine on a weeknight. That's best friend, emergency contact stuff. Sara would probably tell me she's already in her pajamas because she's old and boring. This is something else the moms in this town do, we pretend it's embarrassing to be caught in a cozy moment. We act like the person asking is the fortunate one.

I pull up my latest post instead, and check for reader comments.

IF YOU LIVED HERE—NEW LISTING! 6BR/4.5BA WIDOW'S PEAK STUNNER

Overheard at the open house for this "historically significant" property today: "The problem with shopping for real estate around here is that your money goes so far. This house is gorgeous, but it's just so obvious, you know? It's like, hi, I'm the fanciest home in town. Who wants to invite that kind of scrutiny every weekend?"

How very, as the Heathers would say. My whole real-estate-as-atonement thing is starting to feel like a pretty thin excuse for bringing so many assholes to this town. Truth be told, I'm just the cidiot who got here first.

You know the funny thing about living upstate? No one who grew up around here calls it that, *upstate*. The Hudson Valley is upstate if you started out in the city, because everything is upstate from there. But the true locals, they say upstate is Buffalo, Ithaca, Syracuse. Upstate is Niagara Falls and the Dannemora prison and close enough to Canada to run across the border if it ever came to that.

It's kind of like how European explorers "discovered" Australia and dubbed it *Down Under*—a nickname Australians then embraced, despite knowing full well they weren't walking around upside down. It's the rest of the planet who, gravity be damned, still marvels at how the blood doesn't rush to Australians' heads when they get up in the morning.

No wonder we can't get along. The cidiots move in and we try to fix up this place to make it charming—to make it more "small town." We're outraged when CVS puts the local, family-owned pharmacy out of business, even though half of us still see doctors back in the city. And then we go ahead and call this place something new, like the entire river valley was just waiting for someone important to discover it.

Sorry for the downer post. I love this place, I really do, but sometimes it feels like it doesn't love me back.

xok

---

really_jen: *No need to apologize. Today you sounded a whole lot less like a realtor and a whole lot more like a human being.*

i_live_here: *Jen, I wish someone had told me they were two mutually exclusive concepts! xok*

ann-no-e: *Aw, you're way too self-aware to be a cidiot.*

While I'm typing another response, a text notification from Laura pops up, and I drop my phone with a start. She is listed in my contacts as *Laura (Maddy's mom)*, and I think about how, despite everything, this will always be true. I bend over double to retrieve my phone from the floor, and for an insane moment I consider crushing it beneath the gas pedal and throwing the SIM card out the window. I don't know how to talk to the woman who is still Maddy's mom. I don't know how to talk to the woman whose husband kissed me.

Kevin filled me in, she texts. *We're going with another realtor. Please remove your sign from our lawn at your earliest convenience.* The excessive formality of Laura's message, *at your earliest convenience*, tells me what she really means: *You kissed my husband.*

I wonder when he told her. Maybe he drove straight home that afternoon and confessed immediately. Did he even try to tell her that I'm the one who stopped it? And if Laura knows, how long before she tells a friend? Once the word is out, it won't matter how long the kiss lasted, or how hard I shoved Kevin away. It will only matter that it happened. That I, the woman who got to keep her child, kissed the husband of a woman who did not. Who *wouldn't* share that story?

And then it will be too late to tell Ethan the truth, because nobody believes the woman who's backed into a corner. She's just trying to save her skin, everyone knows that.

At home, I sit in the driveway and re-read Laura's message for the hundredth time, trying to figure out how I'm supposed to respond. Finally, I get it: She wants nothing from me. She wants me to vanish from her life. Yes, she wants to pretend there was never a time when her husband kissed another woman, but more than that, she can't live in a world where her God spared one girl, but not theirs. I thumbs-up her request and power off my phone.

chapter twenty-seven **Indie**

It's way too hot in my room and I think the AC must be broken but when I hold my hands in front of the vent, I feel cold air on my fingertips. So why does the rest of my body feel so warm? I open a window but it's hotter outside; I lie down to feel the cool hardwood floor against my cheek, but that doesn't work either. I sit up and my throat feels tight, like I drank hot cocoa too quickly and everything burns. When I open my mouth to cool my throat, the air doesn't go anywhere, it just swirls around my teeth like mouthwash. My breaths get shorter and faster and it feels like someone else is controlling me remotely, speeding up my body into tiny, ineffectual acts, as if I suddenly had the lungs of a mouse. I don't know how long I can survive with such tiny lungs. I put a hand on my heart to see if it's still beating, but my fingers are tingling and I can't feel a thing. I lie down again because I'm dizzy, like I might throw up, and if I'm on the floor I won't have so far to fall when I stop breathing. I try breathing through my nose but that doesn't work either, the air just gets trapped in my nostril hair. I hear myself whimper before I realize why: *I'm dying*. I remember Maddy's dad telling me that when patients say they have a feeling of impending doom, EMTs listen, because the patients are often right. I try to focus on the words, *impending doom*, but my vision goes black at the edges. I am terrified now and it is too much and I thought I would be okay with dying, I thought I didn't believe it was real, but now I am looking down into a bottomless pit of black and I don't want to fall in. I don't want to fall in. I don't want to—

"Indie!" Dad is gripping my arms, forcing me to look at him.

I open my mouth to tell him I'm dying but no words come out. I put my hands to my throat, hoping he gets it. I want to tell him I'm sorry, it happened so suddenly, I tried to stop it. Maybe if I can get one more breath, I can tell him.

"Look at me," he says. "I need you to look at me."

His face swims before me.

"Breathe in," he says. "While I count. I need you to breathe in slowly and listen to me count, can you do that?"

I shake my head *no no no* because he doesn't understand, I've already tried that, and there's no breath left, it won't work.

"Indie!" Dad squeezes my upper arms. "You're having a panic attack, do you hear me? You're not dying, I promise you. We just need to breathe together and you'll be okay."

I shake my head again because he doesn't know about the impending sense of doom, Maddy's dad didn't tell him, and now he'll never know that I saw death coming and I was so, so scared.

Dad puts his arms around me and pulls me in.

"Shhhhhh," he says. "Shhhhhh. It's okay, sweetheart, it's okay, I can feel your heartbeat, you're still here. It's a panic attack, do you hear me? It's a panic attack, and we can make it stop."

I can't talk but I squeeze him back. I'm counting on him to understand what this means: *Make it stop.*

"I'm going to start counting," Dad says slowly, softly. He pulls away from me. "Don't worry about breathing. Just watch me while I count. One, two, three, four. One, two, three, four."

He counts over and over and I stare at him, my eyes wide with fear. How many seconds do I have left to live?

"Watch me breathe," Dad says, like it's nothing to pull air into his lungs. "Watch how the air fills my lungs, count in your head while I do it. In for four, hold for four, out for four."

I blink my eyes four times instead of counting and that feels good because I can make it happen, I can make it stop.

"Good," Dad says. "Keep counting, and then we'll do it together. In, two, three, four; hold, two, three, four; out, two, three, four; hold, two, three, four. It's called box breathing. Can you picture the box? Let's go around the four sides together."

He keeps counting to four and I keep gasping for air but then I notice that my breaths are getting a little longer and I can feel my lungs inflate and they are expanding now to human size.

"Keep going," Dad says. "You keep breathing and I'll keep counting. I'm not going anywhere."

I don't know how long we sit and breathe together, but at some point I realize I can talk again.

"I didn't die," I say, my voice quavering.

"No," Dad says, and he smiles. "You didn't die. You're okay. It was a panic attack."

"I thought I was going to die and I was so scared," I say.

"That's what it feels like," Dad says. "It feels real, and that's scary. Panic attacks are real."

"That's not what I mean," I say. "Why was I so scared of dying? Why did my brain let me down like that?"

I hiccup a fast breath and Dad holds up a finger to me, starts counting again. *In*, two, three, four. *Hold*, two, three, four.

"Your brain didn't let you down," Dad says, once I'm breathing normally again. "Your body convinced your brain you were dying, and your brain is hard-wired to avoid death. Your brain did exactly what it was supposed to do."

"You're not listening," I say. "My brain made me feel like there was a *me* that was dying, and I know there's no *me*, there's only a brain. There's only particles. Why did it do that?"

Dad pulls me into a hug again.

"I used to have panic attacks, too," he says. "Eventually I learned to see them coming and now, mostly, I can ward them off."

"It's a stupid trick," I say. "My brain tricked me into being scared. I'm not afraid of dying. My brain knows that."

"Shhhhhh," Dad says, stroking my hair. "It's okay. Don't try to talk. Don't worry about your brain, just focus on your body. Feel the breath going in and out."

I feel my lungs constrict again and this time I'm mad. All those things I said to Maddy's mom, and yet here I am in my room, having a stupid fake-dying panic attack because I'm afraid of death. What a hypocrite I am. What a coward.

"Shhhhhh," Dad says again, although I didn't say anything out loud. He rubs my back, then he lets go and faces me, the two of us cross-legged on the floor.

"We're going to try something," he says. "It's called the three-three-three rule."

"I didn't see the stream," I tell him. "I didn't see my reflection. I was looking for the stream of consciousness, but I didn't see any whirlpool. I looked, but all I saw was a black pit."

"The three-three-three rule will help," Dad says. "I promise you. This is how I ward off the beast."

"The beast?" I say eagerly. Maybe he is listening after all. I want to hear about the beast.

"The panic attacks," he says. "That's what I used to call them."

I shake my head because he doesn't see. I'm not afraid of panic attacks. I'm afraid of *dying*, and I don't know how to fix that.

"First," Dad says. "You name three things you see. Then three sounds you hear, and finally, you move three parts of your body. So, let's start with what you can see. Tell me three things."

"Do you believe there's a *you* behind your eyes, looking out into the world and seeing things?" I say. "Most people do. Scientists did this study where they asked people to tell them where they thought the self was. And that's what they all said: Right behind the eyes. How dumb is that?"

"Three things," Dad says firmly. "Tell me three things you can see."

I see nothing, and so I say nothing. There is no *me* to notice anything.

"I see something beginning with a B," Dad says, like we're playing "I Spy" on a road trip.

Every muscle in my body aches like I ran a marathon, and suddenly I am so, so tired.

"Just try it, Indie," Dad says. "Please."

"I see a bed," I say.

Later, when Mom gets home, she finds Dad sitting on my floor, reading something on his iPad, and me, on my bed, listening to a podcast.

"This is cozy," she says, and her voice seems way too loud for the space. *Inside voice, Mom*, I think. "Does anyone need anything?"

"We're good," Dad says.

He looks so smug, like he just cured me of everything while Mom was out at yoga. Like this is a contest, and he just lapped her. Her face falls, and she turns to leave.

"Would you mind making me some mint tea?" I call after her. "It helps me sleep."

Mom glances back and smiles so wide, I think she actually believes me.

chapter twenty-eight **Kate**

When Ethan gets back from his fifty-mile bike ride, I am waiting for him in the kitchen, like a fifties housewife who anticipates her husband's every need, who takes pride in doing this better than any other housewife on the block. I get ice from the freezer and hand him a huge glass of water. I am oddly touched when Ethan stands to drink the water; he knows I like him to shower before sitting on the furniture. ("Gross, Dad," Indie said once, when she saw Ethan on the couch, still in his bike shorts, checking his phone. "I *sit* there.")

"How was the ride?" I say.

"Hot," he says. "Good."

"Hey," I say, aiming for a casual, just-thought-of-this vibe. "Maybe we could go out to dinner tonight, just the two of us."

The idea of dining alone with Ethan terrifies me, which is exactly why I suggest it. If I sit across from him for an hour, surely he will see it in my face—and then I will have to tell him.

"What about Indie?" Ethan says. "I think it's better that we eat with her right now. If you don't feel like cooking, let's just get take-out."

"Right," I say. "Yeah, you're right."

I want to grab him by the shoulders and shake him, tell him, *Can't you see? I'm trying to confess!* Except this feels like further evidence of my wrongdoing. I'm a bad mother for even suggesting a date night, for not wanting to cook something nutritious and eat with our daughter. What would Ethan think if he knew the truth?

Because suddenly the truth feels glaringly obvious to me: I fucked up. Our marriage can't handle this right now. And our daughter—

I can't even think it, what any of this would do to Indie.

Ethan takes his phone out of the little zip pouch in the back of his cycling jersey and starts typing a text. Instead of reaching for my own phone, I force myself to really look at him. How did we end up here, across from each other in the kitchen but so far apart? I think about the first morning I rolled over in bed to see Ethan naked in daylight, the sun streaming through his apartment window and the two of us still near-strangers to each other. How I ran my fingers over his tattoos as if I were reading braille. How anything at all seemed possible.

Now, though, I see the top of his head, because I'm always looking at the top of his head these days. I see a cyclist who likes to educate passing motorists about road-sharing etiquette. I see a middle-aged man wearing padded Lycra bib shorts that present a topographical map of his crotch. ("You wear tights," I teased him once, quoting *The Breakfast Club*, and after quoting Emilio Estevez back at me, he told me enough about groin chafing and the pudendal nerve to ensure I would never make this joke again.)

"She wants Indian," Ethan says, still not looking up from his phone. "I'll call it in."

"Thank you," I say reflexively, because the good wife enjoys her husband's company but does not demand it.

Back in high school, I was taught that being a good wife began years before I even met my future husband, because a good wife saved herself for this theoretical man. (Conveniently, Jesus—and, I suppose, my future husband—was rumored to turn a blind eye to hand jobs.) The youth pastor at my church referred to the state of marriage as being "under the dome," and I always pictured a Greco-Roman structure, and me standing beneath it in a virginal white gown. In these fantasies, my future husband was usually serenading me with a heartfelt cover of "More Than Words" by

Extreme—the same song the dreamy boys liked to strum in the high school courtyard at lunch. For my actual wedding, Ethan suggested we write our own vows, but I said this felt corny, that I was afraid of being judged by my eye-rolling future self. It was the worst kind of writer's block, I told him. So we recited traditional vows—to have and to hold, in sickness and in health—but without all the God bits.

Here's the problem with losing your religion: The wrong things linger. You let go of heaven and hell, but you're left with a vague sense that you have some kind of special protection. I was raised to believe that the sanctity of the dome would protect me from all manner of secular misfortune—unwanted pregnancy, STDs, heartbreak, a bad reputation, marital dissatisfaction, infidelity. I was so sure none of this would befall me that I tuned out every sex-ed lecture in health class. I actually left my flour baby in my high school locker over the weekend, something only the stoners and jocks did.

Even after I married a heathen, barefoot on a beach in Cape May, I had faith in the dome, as if marriage were this preexisting structure you could just move into, like a hermit crab in an abandoned shell. I didn't know you were supposed to build the structure yourself, not until it was too late. No one told me how you clear the ground, how you collect the lumber, how you gather your friends and family around and how, together, you raise the barn.

chapter twenty-nine ❦ Indie

Mom adopted a puppy. Go ahead and call me a conspiracy theorist, but it seems my school counselor is violating that whole confidentiality thing she made such a big deal about. Next time I'm going to tell Mrs. G it's axolotls that make me happy. Or maybe narwhals.

Bringing another sentient being into the house seems like it belongs in the *group decision* category, but apparently Mom knows better. Buddy is a five-month-old shepherd beagle mix, and he came fully house-trained, Mom bragged, like she scored a winning lottery ticket.

Last night I heard her say to Dad, "I just don't get it. For *years* she begged us for a puppy."

By this logic, her next attempt to fix me will be a Barbie Dreamhouse.

Ten more days until school starts up again, although this is just a way to count time. It's not like school will be an improvement. Maddy and I used to love reading those *Would You Rather?* books out loud to each other. Would you rather sweat maple syrup or cry melted cheese? (Both, we agreed, because we were eleven at the time.) Would you rather eat a bowl of moldy strawberries, or drink a glass of expired, chunky milk? (Me: strawberries. Maddy: chunky milk. Her answer still blows my mind. Who picks chunky milk?) Would you rather be trapped in a domestic Cold War with two parents who think they know what's best for you, or stuck in a school with four hundred people who think they knew Maddy, who think they *miss* her? Or, more likely, four hundred people who hung out at the pool every day this summer and forgot Maddy even existed.

I would prefer not to, I think. Final answer. And now, at last, I understand Bartleby the Scrivener. Mrs. Cincotta would be so proud.

chapter thirty — Kate

Sara and I are eating lunch at our desks, mason jar salads from the new juice bar across the street. Salad in a jar! No wonder people hate liberals so much.

"How's the new puppy?" Sara says, between bites.

"Good," I say. "I think Ethan's coming around to him."

This is a slight exaggeration. Ethan is tolerating Buddy.

"I can't believe he finally agreed to a dog," Sara says. "Tim's holding firm."

"I kind of surprised him," I say.

"Bold," Sara says, raising her eyebrows. I know she will tell this story to her husband later tonight, an anecdote to shine a flattering light on their own marriage. I want to tell her, our family is malfunctioning, these are desperate times—it's just that Ethan doesn't see it yet.

"He said it's a trial period," I say. "So, you know, as long as Buddy doesn't poop in the house."

After Ethan got done yelling at me for going behind his back, I tried to explain to him: A dog is something real, something physical, something to anchor Indie to this world. A living, breathing, pooping creature. Buddy *needs* us, and Indie needs that. "Dog poop?" Ethan said in response. "That's your solution?"

I don't tell him that I am shoring up our family's defenses, even though the enemy is already inside. Also, if I'd been harboring any doubt about how Ethan might react to me *going behind his back*, now I know for sure. And that was over a *puppy*. A really cute puppy, too.

"I saw the news," Sara says. "About a hearing date for the driver. How's Indie?"

"She wants space," I say, which is true, but it's also another way of saying that I don't know.

I am standing in Indie's doorway, my toes not quite touching the line where the hallway meets her room. I feel like a superstitious kid, *step on a crack, break your mother's back*. If I don't actually enter her room, maybe she won't ask me to give her space.

"Want to go shopping for a back-to-school outfit?" I call out. "You must have grown an inch this summer."

This is something Indie and I do together every August. Maybe, I think, a tradition will carry her through to the next moment, even if it feels empty and rote.

"Clothes shopping?" Indie says. She has her back to me and is looking out the window.

"I know it's last minute," I say. "But the stores are open till ten tonight, I just checked."

Indie turns to face me.

"No," she says. "I don't want *new clothes*."

It's not sarcasm exactly, it's something worse. It's Indie alone in a place I can't reach, like she's up on the roof and everything I yell to her sounds the same: *Come down*.

Ethan lifts his head when I enter the kitchen.

"I think we're past clothes shopping as a cure-all," he says.

"I'm not trying to fix her," I say. "But thanks for shooting down my idea, *goalie*."

Except, he's right. I would do anything to lessen Indie's pain. I would drive to the mall the night before school starts, but also, I would cut off my right hand.

Here's what Ethan doesn't see: Every item of clothing Indie owns is something she wore when Maddy was alive. Everything has Maddy's seal of approval, because Indie would FaceTime her best friend from the fitting room. Maddy probably borrowed half the clothes, too.

The night before school each fall, Indie and Maddy would text each other photos of their first-day outfits. Indie would stand on her bed to get a bird's eye shot: The clothes and accessories, even the shoes, laid out on her bedroom floor in the shape of a human, like the person wearing the outfit had been called to God in the Rapture. Ethan never understood this ritual. "It's not your fault," he said to Indie last year. "You're just a victim of a capitalist society. Even in the Great Depression, kids begged their parents for new clothes. They actually wrote to Eleanor Roosevelt and told her how embarrassing it was to go to school without nice things." Indie nodded politely and then returned to her phone. "It's got nothing to do with capitalism," I told Ethan later that night. "It's about who she and Maddy are going to be this year."

On my way to bed, I notice Indie's door is ajar, and I tiptoe across the hallway, pausing at each floorboard creak. Through the two-inch gap, I see her, and I gasp.

Indie's room used to be papered with mini to-do lists on colorful Post-It notes, lined up across her desk and dotted among the posters on the walls, fluttering like butterflies whenever a breeze came through the window. Some of the lists were trivial—her morning skincare routine, room decor ideas—and others were endearingly deep: ways to help the planet; tips to thrive in college (*#3: Don't drink alcohol*); piano concertos to learn before she's twenty. They're all gone now.

I watch Indie move onto her artwork next, placing each drawing in the recycling bin beneath her desk. She's not crying, although this doesn't surprise me; I haven't seen her cry since the morning of Maddy's funeral. But she doesn't look angry or manic either. She is calm and methodical, the way Ethan looks when he's pulling weeds in the yard. She's actually *recycling* the things she removes. This is why I tiptoe away. Tonight, at least, she knows what she needs.

Indie was a preschool Picasso. Every day she came home with an armful of art. I went through the stack at the end of each week and divided the pictures into three piles: hang on the fridge; save in the cardboard storage box in her closet; stash at the bottom of the recycling bin. As I sorted, I would remind myself that I could choose to be both like and unlike my mother, that I could be unsentimental about Indie's fair-to-middling works of art without rationing my affection for her. Sometimes, though, after Indie was asleep for the night, I would feel a pang of remorse and rescue her paintings from the recycling bin, smoothing them out on the kitchen island before adding them to the storage box. Ethan caught me once and asked what I was doing. I didn't say what I was thinking, which was, *What if she dies tomorrow? I would want everything she'd ever touched.* Instead I told him, "She mentioned this one when I tucked her in, so I thought I should hang it up." He rested his chin on my head as he examined the painting. "Trees or lollipops?" Ethan asked. "I think it's us," I said. "She's in her abstract period."

In grief, though, would I really want more *things*? To witness Indie's sterile bedroom walls, empty of everything that stood for anything, the answer, for her at least, is a firm no. We are told to let go of anything that does not "spark joy," but what vacation trinket or item of clothing could possibly spark joy for my daughter right now?

Those cardboard storage boxes full of Indie's artwork and report cards are now stashed at the back of her closet. I'm saving them for when she ages into wistfulness. I bought a new box when she started middle school, but it's still almost empty. I always loved the manga sketches Indie and Maddy worked on after school, lying on their stomachs on the bedroom floor, leaning on old picture books and watching drawing tutorials on YouTube. But she never let me have any of that artwork for the box. What if the drawings Indie ripped from her sketchbook never get replaced? The absence of new things is too much to bear.

chapter thirty-one ❦ **Indie**

Tomorrow is my first day of high school. If I were a normal teenager writing in a journal or posting online, that sentence would get at least two exclamation points. Tomorrow is my first day of high school!! I get to dissect a frog in science class this year!! Should I wear the faux vintage NASA hoodie or the faux vintage Friends hoodie?!

Here is all the proof I need that the idea of a continuous "me" is just an illusion: I used to care about this stuff. I actually stressed over which clubs to join, and whether I had a shot at being president of any of them, because I knew that college admissions officers preferred students with depth rather than breadth. If there was a real me who existed behind my eyes, an unchanging core or soul-self, then I would recognize that girl who used to give a shit. But she is a stranger to me.

A year ago today, this girl called Indie was using her mom's vintage label maker to organize her binders. She had new purple Vans and a matching purple streak in her hair. She was *pumped* about starting eighth grade. She liked school. She liked making the honor roll. She understood that art and music were rewarding hobbies but a risky career choice, and she already knew which colleges had the best public policy programs.

And here is how I spend my last night of summer break *this* year: I strip my walls and bulletin board of everything a girl named Indie once considered worth saving. The miniature Polaroids, the "Sailor Moon" poster, the county fair ride tickets, the ramen noodles line drawing Maddy made me, the honor roll certificates, the Post-It notes. I keep going until my walls are bare.

When I am done, I stand at my window and look into the yard, past the chicken coop and the decrepit treehouse and Dad's vegetable garden. There is one tree that always turns red early, and I stare at its leaves until the word *tree* floats away from me and I think only *red*. I wonder what it feels like to be the color red. I move my eyes to the sky. It is indigo blue and so am I. I am blue and I am red and I am out there, I am everywhere, and I turn quickly to look for myself, to catch myself missing, to prove there is nothing there. I am so close and then—

"Indie! Can you let Buddy out to pee before you go to bed?"

I am that girl again, and she has a dog. And tomorrow is my first day of high school. Period.

chapter thirty-two ❦ **Kate**

My alarm goes off at six because it's the first day of school, and while there's nothing for me to do this morning—Indie has been fixing her own breakfast and packing a lunch since sixth grade—I want to watch her get on the bus. I want to take her back-to-school photo.

I hear Ethan downstairs, making breakfast. He'll be out the door in five minutes so he has time in his classroom before the students show up. Every first day of school since we moved here, I have joined him in the kitchen, and it is always bittersweet: On the one hand, my husband will no longer be around all day. On the other hand, my husband will no longer be around all day. Ethan would tell you that my resentment regarding his ten-week summer break gradually builds to a peak in mid-August, at which point I forget there was ever a time when he set an alarm to wake in the morning. And perhaps he's right. But, also: I used to miss him those first weeks of September. I missed making a pot of coffee for two. I missed looking out the kitchen window and seeing him tend to his raised beds. Ethan's teacher friends, many of whom are married to other teachers, call ours a "mixed marriage."

Today, though, I sit in bed and wait until I hear Ethan leave.

I pull on a sweatshirt and sweatpants. I hear Indie showering, and as I pass her room, I push the door open a few inches. Back in sixth grade, Indie chose camo jeggings for her back-to-school outfit, and Ethan dad-joked that her legs had disappeared, that she was just a torso suspended in the room. As I stare at the empty spot on her floor where her clothes should be laid out, I understand: She wants to disappear, head to toe. She doesn't want to play dress-up; she wants to slip under the door like Flat Stanley.

Indie passes through the kitchen without looking at me, and when I offer her eggs, she shakes her head *no* without slowing down. I take a photo as she climbs onto the bus, but she does not turn her head to look and I do not check my phone to see how it turned out. I have this absurd fear that if I did, I would see only a bus.

chapter thirty-three ❦ **Indie**

I stand for the Pledge of Allegiance, because what do I care? A bunch of dumb teenagers mumble some words, or they don't, and the Earth still turns on its axis. I can't change a thing.

chapter thirty-four ❦ Kate

Did u hear about a lockdown? Indie texts me. *They nvr schedule drills 1st day.*

Hold on, I text back, my fingers shaking as I type. *Let me find out. Can I call you? Where are you?*

DON'T CALL, she texts. *I'm hiding in the bathroom.*

I check my email, I check my voicemail, I check the school website, nothing. *Shit.* I call the school and get a busy signal. A *busy signal*, are you fucking kidding me?

What does Dad say?

Nothing.

Ethan always texts Indie to let her know what's going on. Teachers aren't supposed to have access to this information, but somehow the gym teacher finds out every time a drill is planned, and he gives Ethan a heads up. "The patriarchy at work," Indie said once, because the principal is male, too. The gym teacher made Ethan swear not to tell Indie in advance, so instead Ethan texts her right when the siren first sounds: *Only a drill.* I text Ethan now but he doesn't respond. I turn on his iPad to see if he has the gym teacher's number saved, then realize I've forgotten the guy's name. Ethan is always saying how terrible I am at remembering the names of his friends, but he has so many.

You sure you have cell service in there? I text Indie, only realizing how dumb this sounds as I click Send. *Sorry*, I add. *Stupid question. Maybe Dad doesn't have service?*

Are you ok? I ask.

I'm crouching on the toilet seat. I think this might be real.

I love you, I type, and then I delete it, because that's what you say when you think someone might be about to die. *Hang in there*, I type instead. *I'm going to find out what's going on. Don't move.*

I love you, Indie texts, and my heart stops. I actually feel it sputter and then restart in my chest, like an old car engine that might not make it home.

I call Ethan and then hang up quickly, because what if he's hiding, too? I call the school but the line is still busy. Fuck it, I think, and I text every mom I've ever met, from La Leche League and Gymboree all the way through middle school soccer. Everyone except Laura.

It's ok, I text Indie. *It's going to be ok. You're going to be ok.*

What did you find out?

Nothing yet, I type. *But I think that's good, I think we'd know by now if it was real.*

I don't believe this for a second.

And then one of the moms texts me what she learned from the wife of the school resource officer: It was a false alarm. She adds: *Sorry, who is this? New phone!* [Five winking emojis.] What looked like a credible threat turned out to be a hacked social media account and some dumb ninth-grade boys quoting a *John Wick* movie. I'm about to call Indie when my phone rings. It's her.

"Mom?" Indie says, and her voice sounds tiny and far away, like she accidentally butt-dialed me.

"It was a false alarm!" I call out. "It's okay, everything's okay, you're safe."

"I know," she says, and her voice is still so small. "They just announced it, I have to get back to class, I just wanted you to know."

"I love you," I say, but she's already ended the call.

Even before this summer, before she stopped talking much at all, Indie and I rarely talked on the phone, because that's for old people, she told me. She would message me instead, and her text voice was always big and loose and *ttyl* and *yaaaa*. But today on the phone, Indie sounded five again, the age she was the first time she ever called me. That was back in kindergarten, and the school nurse put her on the line so she could tell me what was wrong. (I guess to call Indie's bluff?) At first I thought the school nurse had made a mistake, because the girl on the phone didn't sound like my daughter. But then, how would I have known what her phone voice sounded like? The only other times in her short life she'd really needed me, I had been within shouting distance.

Apparently you need to be older than five to have the school nurse take you at your word when your stomach hurts, although five is plenty old enough to practice lockdown drills at school, according to the state of New York. And fourteen is when you get off the bus at the end of your first day of high school and tell your mom, "Sometimes I wish we'd just have a shooting in our school and get it over with."

chapter thirty-five **Indie**

Today was my first day of high school! I hid in the bathroom! I thought I was going to die! Like, *literally* die! I wonder if Asher thinks my hair looks cute?

chapter thirty-six ✔ Kate

I make Indie an after-school snack (salted cucumber slices) and I empty her lunchbox, something I haven't done in years. We sit in the kitchen together, Indie on her phone and me eating the leftovers from her lunch. I say nothing, because I want to give her space. She's always been so good at telling me what kind of mother she needs me to be, if I just stop talking and listen for long enough. I accidentally drop a fork and flinch, as if a loud noise might scare her away.

"Sorry," I whisper.

Who knew that parenthood could feel so much like trying to soothe a feral cat? I bite my lip and wait.

Finally, eventually, I break the silence in the room.

"Want to talk about it?"

"No," Indie replies, her voice flat and calm. "It was just a drill, no big deal."

And just like that, she is once again the fourteen-year-old who needs space more than she needs me.

IF YOU LIVED HERE—NEW LISTING! 4BR/2.5BA MODERN FARMHOUSE

Earlier this week, my newest clients sat on the front porch of this white on white farmhouse, gazing out at the front yard and trying to dream up a life for themselves. I waited for them to ask me about local schools, property taxes, sidewalk culture, farm-to-table restaurants. Or maybe they were going to grill me about the celebrities who own the old-fashioned candy store in town. But the woman had noticed a lawn sign in the neighbors' yard: REPEAL THE SAFE ACT. She pulled out her phone and googled the phrase, which is totally something I would do. "Welp," she said to her husband, titling the phone in his direction. "The neighbors are gun nuts." They both turned to me then, her expression anxious and his accusatory, as if I might be concealing a handgun in my *New Yorker* tote bag. He said, "What can you tell us about this town's gun culture?" She said, "Do a lot of people hunt around here?" Really, though, they wanted me to answer an impossible question: Does the next school shooter live in this town?

We left the city soon after 9/11, and I wasn't even pregnant yet. We just knew we couldn't raise a family there. Remember how all those people thought the South Tower was safe? They didn't leave the building when the North Tower was hit. Back then, I couldn't shake the thought: What if we were the South Tower? People would say, *two buildings came down, why would you stay in the city*?

So we moved to the country, where the tallest building around was the fire station. We got chickens. We felt safe.

And then in kindergarten, my daughter told us about her first lockdown drill. It was in case a wild animal got into the building, she said, which made sense to her. She remembered the time a bat got into our house. I remembered the South Tower, except tell me where in this country is any safer? And it's not like Canada wants us.

So I cuddled my child and I cut the crusts off her whole grain bread. I taught her how to recognize poison ivy in the yard and how to find ticks on her body. I thought maybe there was more I should do; I've heard about liberal moms who ask, before each new playdate, *Do you have guns in the house, and if so, are they locked away?* Maybe we should do that, too, I told my husband, but neither of us ever did. It just seemed rude.

Anyway, this is how I answered my clients today (because I choose hope over despair, and also, *ahem*, I'm a realtor): The most recent school board election was decided by seventeen votes. Seventeen! Imagine living in a place where your vote matters that much. This is the kind of place where voting happens on a human scale—where you've probably had dinner with at least one of the candidates. Now picture your house in this place. What signs are on *your* lawn? Because this is how we keep our children safe—not by moving to Canada, but one lawn at a time. One family at a time. I'll say it again: Won't you be my neighbor?

xok

---

mazel-tough: *So HAVE you met the celebs who own the old-fashioned candy store in town??*

i_live_here: *A realtor never tells. xok*

mazel-tough: *I thought your whole deal was being the realtor who tells all?!*

i_live_here: *Good point. But I figure you guys come here for my take on the everyday and the ordinary. There's a million other places where you can read about celebrities who are Just Like Us, if that's your thing. xok*

go-ask-your-dad: *Translation: She hasn't met them.*

i_live_here: *Okay, fine, you got me. xok*

ann-no-e: *Raising kids in this country means living in a state of denial, no matter what state you call home. "You're right, it's totally normal that Bed, Bath, and Beyond sells bullet-proof backpacks in their back-to-school aisle."*

i_live_here: *OMG I just googled, and you're right, Ann: Not just bullet-proof backpacks, but PINK bullet-proof backpacks. As my daughter would say, I just can't with this country sometimes. xok*

ann-no-e: *Maybe Australia will take us?*

really_jen: *Lawn signs keep us safe, really? In my experience, lawn signs divide a town. I prefer to keep my children safe by getting to know my neighbors.*

go-ask-your-dad: *I wish being a good neighbor was enough, but unfortunately I think we need the bullet-proof backpacks, too.*

i_live_here: *Jen, if you lived here, I would totally bake you an apple pie, no matter what your lawn sign said. xok*

chapter thirty-seven **Indie**

"Anyone home?" Dad calls out as he opens the front door.

"Just me," I reply from my room. There's no way he could hear me, but I don't feel like raising my voice.

He says something else, but there are too many words to make it upstairs in the right order.

"Can't hear you," I reply, still not getting off my bed, still not raising my voice.

I listen as Dad climbs the stairs. Usually he takes them two at a time, like he's in a race, but today I hear him step heavily on each one. He pushes open my bedroom door, knocking gently as he does. I don't bother pointing out that this is not how knocking is meant to work.

"Hey, beautiful," he says from the doorway. "Rough first day. You okay?"

I nod and turn on my phone. I swipe my finger to seem busy, to pretend I'm catching up on text messages—*so many text messages to respond to*—although Dad must know I'm faking. Who would text me?

I see him take in my bare walls, the blank spaces where my posters used to hang—twenty-four-by-thirty-six-inch rectangles of paint that never faded in the sun. Like ghosts.

"Minimalist," he says, nodding. "Nice."

I nod again, because, sure, why not? I picture a photo spread in one of the interior design magazines in Mom's office. I am a single plant on a white table in a white room. I am learning to appreciate the absence of things.

"Today sucked balls, huh?" he says.

"Pretty much."

Dad seems to decide this is an invitation to enter my room all the way. He looks around and picks my fuzzy desk chair. The chair spins as he sits, which makes him look ridiculous, like a little kid.

"Fuck the NRA," Dad says.

Officially, we don't use the f-bomb in our house, but my parents make an exception for the gun lobby. Even then, *I* never say the word in front of my parents—it's too weird. Mom and Dad find this "cute." Whatever. Maddy and I used to swear all the time, I just don't feel the need to do it around my *parents*.

"Eff Keanu Reeves for making all those dumbass hitman movies," I say, not because I really care, but because it's what I would have said last year. "And eff the bros who quote them, too."

"Yeah," Dad says, smiling. "Can't disagree with you there. If it helps, those bros will grow up soon, I promise. It's like they crawl out of the bog in eleventh grade."

I can't believe he thinks it was the *bros* who were the worst part of my day.

"Why didn't you text me?" I say.

"I didn't know what was going on," Dad says. "They never have drills the first day back."

"Exactly."

"What do you mean?"

"You thought it was real and you didn't text me."

"I'm so sorry," he says. "It was a total shit show today."

"You didn't answer my question."

"Sweetheart," he says. "I had thirty freaked out kids in the room, they all ran in from the hallway and I don't even know their names yet. I was texting with the other teachers, trying to figure out what was going on. I thought if I texted you before I had an answer, I'd only make things worse."

"I was trapped in a bathroom stall waiting for some maniac to walk in and shoot me," I say. "How much worse could it get? Also, you didn't text Mom, either."

Twenty-five minutes isn't objectively a long time. Dad can easily spend twenty-five minutes in the bathroom doing a crossword on his phone (I know: *ew*). Twenty-five minutes is approximately the length of my bus ride to school, and a couple of minutes longer than an episode of *Friends*. But twenty-five minutes is a long time to spend waiting to be gunned down. Call this episode, "The One with the School Shooting." Twenty-five minutes is enough time for panic to turn to quiet dread. It's enough time to check if anyone's posting about what's happening (of course they are). It's enough time to think about your best friend, and feel both gratitude and envy that she never saw death coming. It's enough time to text each of your parents, and then to text your mom again because (a) she actually responds and (b) she's your *mom*. It's enough time to then put away your phone and close your eyes and slow your breaths and stretch out your arms until each palm is flat against the sides of the stall as you remember that none of this means anything.

chapter thirty-eight ❦ **Kate**

A long-ago temporary friend I made through a breastfeeding support group once said to me, "Isn't this the greatest feeling in the world?" We were nursing our babies side by side, like obedient cows on a dairy farm. I made a *hmm* sound as I moved my newborn daughter from my left breast to the right, steeling myself for the searing pain that always came when she first clamped down on my nipple. "It's like my entire body is being flooded with this love drug," the woman continued. "You know? Like, a *tsunami*."

I didn't know, and it made me wonder what I was getting wrong. Usually I scrolled through my phone while nursing, but only when no one was watching.

I assumed I would get the hang of things, and eventually I did find a way to nurse without pain. But for my daughter's entire life, I have returned to this question: What am I getting wrong? Every day, she is a pop quiz without an answer key.

I never saw Ethan searching for the instruction manual. We moved upstate and, *bam*, he was a small-town history teacher. Our daughter was born and, *bam*, he was a father. This looked less like instinct than pure logic: He was a father; therefore, anything he did was something a father would do. Logically speaking, I am a mother. *Etymologically* speaking, I am no more and no less a mother than any other woman who takes the name Mom.

So why do I feel like this is all an act? As if any moment now, someone will walk on stage to reveal me for who I really am.

There is no such thing as quantity in love
my mother said, correcting me.
No such thing as "much" love.

I loved this poem once. I even wrote it out by hand and kept it in my nightstand drawer. Julie Cadwallader Staub's words—*I love you, she said. That's sufficient*—reminded me of the way my own mother spoke, and reading it felt like a warm bath. Some days it helped me detect the love in my mom's terse manner, in the economy of her affection; other days, the poem could quiet my mom's voice in my head, the one pointing out all the ways *I* was falling short as a mother.

It's a crock of shit, though. I understand that now. There's nothing *sufficient* about maternal love. When Indie pushes me away and asks for more space, I sometimes find myself doubled over, as if in physical pain, but even this amount of love is not enough to keep her safe.

Sure, I believe in the kind of love that can be neither calibrated nor offered on a conditional basis. But I also believe in equality and kindness and feminism and all the other words on my lawn sign; unconditional love is just another abstract concept to add to the list. A really *nice* concept—definitely the nicest one on the list—but an abstraction, nonetheless. When your child is drowning in grief, does she need an inspirational lawn sign, or does she need someone to tow her to shore?

In the abstract: I love Indie. In the concrete: I kissed her dead best friend's dad. In the abstract: Home is where the heart is. In the concrete: My body tenses with every alert from my phone or Ethan's, because I am certain that my marriage—Indie's home—is on the line.

chapter thirty-nine **Indie**

Sometimes I miss middle school. Back then we were all raw and unassembled, though I didn't see this at the time. It was like we were made of Lego bricks that could combine to become anything, and we were too busy mocking up prototypes of ourselves to hide this process. We were so *visible* to each other, if only we'd known to look.

One time in eighth grade, Zeke threw a pool party and announced he was skipping his ADHD meds for the occasion. I didn't go to the party because I wasn't invited, but everyone talked about it at school the next day—how Zeke was so fun without his meds. "It totally made the party," one of the Minkles said, and just like that, Zeke became someone new. A few weeks later, Hunter showed up at school with an unflattering center part—"Is there any other kind?" Maddy mused out loud—and by the end of the day not a single girl had a crush on him anymore. By the end of the week, Hunter was walking into town alone after school.

But something happened as we faced down eighth-grade graduation. We figured out how to piece ourselves together into these legible human beings. We each became a single version of ourselves, one that made sense to our classmates. We started saying, "Oh yeah, that tracks."

Maddy and I went through this process together, trying out identities until we found something that fit us both. Ultimately, we settled on a nonspeaking role for ourselves: We would enter high school as the emo girls in black eyeliner who drew manga characters on our binders and wore fishnet tights under ripped jeans. We even started a Manga Club so we could eat lunch in the library, and we hand-made just one small flyer, ensuring that only the two of us ever showed up. The middle and high schools share the same library, which meant we would start ninth grade knowing exactly where to go. "We *totally* understood the assignment," Maddy joked.

I'd actually been looking forward to bumping into my dad in high school. He's not so bad, I thought. For a dad. Our entire friendship, Maddy's dad had been the star of the show—literally the head of every parade—and secretly I wanted our friends, including Maddy most of all, to see *my* dad like that.

But when I showed up for ninth grade this year, it hit me: Maddy was my only friend. *She* had other friends, from church and 4H, and when we saw them around school, they would say hi to us both. Because Maddy and I shared everything, I'd never thought too deeply about whose friends they were. But when I pass these girls in the hallway now, they smile at me sadly then look away quickly, like the only thing we have in common is a dead friend. (They're right about that, by the way.) *Everyone* in the school leaves me alone, actually—even the teachers don't know what to say to me. It's easier just to pretend I'm not here, I guess.

So now I eat my lunch in a bathroom stall, which is gross, yes, but I don't touch anything, and it's better than eating alone in the library. And it's a whole lot better than pretending I care about a bunch of normal people doing normal stuff in the high school cafeteria. After eating half a sandwich, I pace the hallways until the period is over. I have a carefully planned loop that avoids Dad's classroom, plus anywhere else he might eat lunch, because I doubt he would approve of my "minimalist" approach to high school.

It's not just that I miss Maddy, although I do—it's that I am no longer that version of me. The girl who drew manga with Maddy is a memory, and I am atomized.

"What's up," Asher says, sliding into the seat next to me on the school bus ride home.

There's no question in his voice, so I figure an answer is not required of me. Also, I can't remember what I'm supposed to say back.

I know that smartphones are this supposed scourge on society. Our computer science teacher makes us read articles about it all the time: Smartphones are turning us into illiterate cyberbullies; we'll end up with permanent nerve damage from text neck; our entire generation suffers from confirmation bias because we get our news from social media bubbles. But man, have cellphones improved the school bus experience. The moment middle school hit and most of us got our first phone: serenity. I could actually meditate on this bus if I wanted to.

Which is why it's weird that Asher is sitting next to me this afternoon. There are enough seats that every student can have their own double, and most of the time, that's what we do. We listen to music, we do our homework, we go on our phones. Occasionally, someone might lean across the aisle, holding out a phone, to say, "Bruh, check this out." (And contrary to what old people think, "this" is much more likely to be an animal doing something funny than a person doing something naked.) No one is throwing food or punches like they do in those eighties movies Mom makes me watch. I guarantee school bus drivers consider the invention of the smartphone to be right up there with the fork and knife in terms of its civilizing influence.

"You're not drawing," Asher says.

I look up at him but don't say anything. He pulls a stainless steel bento box from his backpack and starts eating leftover edamame from his lunch. Of course he has a bento box.

"You always used to draw on the bus," he says, between bites. "Those anime pictures."

"Manga," I correct him, on autopilot. Nobody ever gets this right. "Anime is on TV."

"Yeah," Asher says. "Manga, duh. That's what I meant."

He looks at me like it's my turn to speak, but this doesn't feel like a conversation, so I go back to gazing out the window.

"Ohhhh," he says after a beat, drawing out the word. "Riiiight."

I turn back to him, a what-the-fuck look on my face.

"Maddy," he says knowingly, like this is a trivia contest and her name is the answer to everything. "You and Maddy always drew together, right?"

I don't know how to respond to this. My brain is screaming *NONE OF YOUR FUCKING BUSINESS* but my heart aches because I miss sketching with my best friend. Mom thinks it's strange that I never kept a diary, but that's just because she doesn't know how to read my drawings. Maddy knew how.

"You doing okay?" Asher says.

Apparently Asher wants to be my emotional support dog. Awesome.

"You mean, now that my manga-drawing best friend is dead?" I say. "You're wondering how it feels to be in a club of one, is that it?"

Next he'll want to know if it's true that Maddy was my girlfriend. That's what the bros used to say at lunch. It was easier for them to call us lesbians than to believe we just didn't find them funny. Straight girls have long hair and giggle at boys' jokes—everyone knows that.

"Oh, shit," Asher says. "No, I mean, you weren't in the cafeteria at lunch today."

I wasn't in the cafeteria today because I'm never in the cafeteria, but I guess it's nice that I was eventually missed. Here is evidence that I am not completely dead inside: Something tiny lights up in me at this development, just for a second, and then it blinks off again. *Asher noticed I wasn't there.* It's like a push notification from my former life.

"I figured it was because of what everyone was saying," Asher continues. "That why you skipped lunch?"

"What was everyone saying?" I ask him.

"Oh, shit," Asher says again, his eyes bugging out a little.

"WHAT WERE THEY SAYING?" I watch him shift uncomfortably at the volume of my voice.

"It was mostly just Violet," Asher says.

"Okay," I say slowly. "What was mostly-just-Violet saying in the cafeteria?"

Violet Mills, OG Minkle, queen bee of the popular kids' lunch table since elementary school. Daughter of Mrs. Mills, Class Mom from kindergarten through fifth grade (which must be a school record), and top of the text chain when it comes to local gossip. Mrs. Mills delivers homemade cookies to the lunch ladies at Christmas, because lunch ladies know everything. "She acts like she's visiting the poor," Mom said once. "It's straight out of a Jane Austen novel." I would have suspected Mom of exaggerating, except Maddy's aunt is a lunch lady, and she shared the snickerdoodles with me and Maddy last year. They were really good.

"Violet said that your mom—" Asher glances across the aisle and then back at me. He slumps down in his seat like he's hiding from someone, though it's my eye contact he appears to be avoiding. "She said, uh." He swallows again. "You really didn't hear?"

"Obviously not," I say.

"Maybe you should just talk to your mom," Asher says.

"*You* sat next to *me*, remember?" I say. "Use your words."

"Sorry," Asher mumbles. "It's just—she said—she heard that your mom, you know, hooked up with Maddy's dad or something. I guess Maddy's mom posted a comment on your mom's thing last night? Your mom deleted it but Violet's mom took a screenshot. Or someone did."

There is a siren going off in my brain and I hear the word in my head, *EMERGENCY*, over and over, in that loud robot voice that comes out of our smoke alarm whenever Mom uses the broiler. I look around the bus for a lever to pull or a button to press to make it all stop. If I had one of those key chains with a panic button I would squeeze it right now; I would blow a rape whistle until the sound drowned out all the gossip in the world.

The bus pulls up outside Asher's house and I take a deep breath as I stare at a tree in his front yard. It's no help. The leaves are plain crayon green. Not a swanky Crayola shade like Fern or Mountain Meadow, just one of those generic green crayons that comes free with the kids' menu. This is not a color to lose myself in.

"I didn't mean to tell you," Asher stammers. "That wasn't my plan, really. I just wanted to make sure you were okay. After everything, you know? It sucks."

I don't turn to face him, but I am aware of him standing, then looping his backpack over one shoulder.

"Stay in your lane, dude."

It takes a lot for parents to become headline news in the school cafeteria. The last time it happened was back in sixth grade, when one of the Mackenzies had to get a restraining order against her own dad. *Because of his drinking* is what everyone said, though I realize now it must have been more than that. Everyone made a big deal about the fact that Mackenzie had to go somewhere on Valentine's Day to get the restraining order; this detail was shared with an air of concern for Mackenzie. We all claimed to "feel so bad" for her. That was our cover for spreading the news.

How am I going to remain invisible if everyone feels so bad for me? Then a second possibility enters my brain, and I can't tell if this is better or worse: What if they *don't* feel bad for me? What if they just feel bad for the dead girl?

I find Mom sitting on her bed, knees up to her chest, wide-eyed and jittery like this is *A Nightmare on Elm Street* and she's the final girl, terrified of falling asleep. *Nine, ten, never sleep again.* Her phone is next to her on the bed, face down.

"Is it true?" I say. "Did you and Maddy's dad—"

I feel myself gag. I can't say it.

"No," Mom says, and it's like her whole body is in a spasm now. "No, no, no, of course it's not true. Oh baby, I'm so sorry." She opens her arms wide like she expects me to go rushing in for a hug. "It's an ugly rumor, that's all it is. I am so, so sorry. Come here."

"THEN WHY IS EVERYONE SAYING IT?" I yell.

"People love to gossip," she says, her arms still waiting for me. She's trembling, like it hurts to hold them out. "You know that."

"Maddy's mom wouldn't lie," I say. "You must have done something to make her say that."

"Grief makes people do crazy things," Mom says, except she's not quite looking at me, she's looking over my shoulder, like Freddie Krueger is behind me in the hallway. I actually turn my head to check, because apparently I'm trapped in the horror movie inside her head.

"I don't believe you," I say. "You're lying to me."

Mom takes a deep breath and finally makes eye contact.

"Kevin kissed me," she half-whispers, like it doesn't count at that volume. Like I might only half-hear. "That's all that happened, I swear to you. He was so sad and confused and he didn't know what he was doing. It lasted a couple of seconds, that's it. He felt awful after, we both did. And I'm the one who stopped it. I stopped him as soon as, as soon as—"

I step into the bedroom and look around wildly. It isn't until my hand lands on a vase that I realize I'm looking for something to throw. It's a clay coil pot I made at a pottery camp one summer, a murky shade of blue because everything I made that summer turned out murky blue. Mom ducks her head a little, like I'm going to throw the vase at her. Like she's the victim here. I open my hand into a flat palm and watch the vase tumble to the floor. A small piece chips off the rim as the vase rolls under the bed. I use my arm to swipe all the framed photos off the dresser, and they clatter to the floor. I don't understand how everything is broken and yet nothing breaks. I am just making a mess, like an angry toddler.

"Indie," Mom says. "I swear that's the whole story: A kiss that lasted a few seconds. But I know you have questions, and I will tell you anything you want to know. What do you want to know?"

And then I find the words.

"NOTHING!" I scream. "I WANT TO KNOW NOTHING!"

I spin around in the bedroom, feeling possessed, and suddenly I *am* the supernatural serial killer. I am the monster, the mummified terror, the poltergeist, the walking dead. I see objects go flying across the room—my mom's jewelry box, the books from her nightstand, a mason jar half full of water, a wooden backscratcher. I keep spinning, and I think I must have telekinetic powers, because still the objects fly.

"INDIE!"

She is screaming my name but I do not stop because I am possessed. I am the stuff of nightmares and I wonder why I do not see blood and gore.

"INDIA!"

I stop spinning and I am dizzy now; I stumble and bump into the edge of the bed. Mom steps forward to catch me but I turn away and run for the door, leaning forward as I stagger across the hallway, the house still spinning around me. I slam my bedroom door behind me and push my desk against it because I am not allowed a lock. I don't know why I bother. Mom knocks once, calls my name, and leaves.

I sit on my bed, holding my phone. I click the screen on and stare at my five unanswered texts to Dad. When I first texted him, the three dots popped up to show he was typing, but only for a second and then nothing. I call the school and enter the extension for his classroom, but it just rings and rings.

It's better this way, to sit waiting. In the quiet, I can pretend I am five again and my dad is all-powerful, able to explain away the cruelty of the world. I want to hear Dad say, *It's just a drill, stay calm, it will all be over soon*. If he doesn't pick up, I don't have to hear him tell me this is the real deal.

chapter forty ⸙ Kate

It's possible Laura thought she was being cryptic. It's possible she was drunk. It's possible she wanted consolation more than revenge. But either way, I get it, because: Why should her family have all the pain?

I sit on my bed, refreshing the feed on my phone, watching my subscriber count go up. Who knew that getting canceled would feel so much like going viral? I force myself to read every comment, because this hurts less than waiting for Ethan's call.

scary-mommy: *This is the same woman who complained about the school cafeteria selling chocolate milk. Chocolate milk!! Yeah, you're right, chocolate milk is the real villain in this town, THAT'S what's hurting our children. /sarcasm*

mama_needs_wine: *So much for not connecting with the locals. I think that's what's called an over-correction?*

glue-gun-mom: *GO BACK TO THE CITY*

mom4liberty: *It's not enough to take over our schools, now you want to sleep with our husbands too?!*

mommylikeswine: *WHORE*

really_jen: *What happened?*

ann-no-e: *No idea, Jen. Who are all these new people??*

boy-momma: *WHORE*

really_jen: *Will someone please tell me what I missed?*

butterfly-kisses: *WHORE*

chapter forty-one ❦ **Indie**

My parents are fighting in the kitchen while I hide in my closet, the podcast turned so high, my ears hurt. But it doesn't help. It's like the house itself is vibrating with Dad's rage.

Is Maddy's house still quiet? I try to picture her parents arguing on their side of town, but it's literally impossible—I can't make my brain imagine them talking about this. That's how unthinkable it is, what Mom did.

I pull out my earbuds, ashamed. If Maddy's mom had kissed my dad, if I were dead and my friend were still here, Maddy wouldn't hide in a foxhole. Maddy would listen. She would demand answers. And so I force myself out of my bedroom. I sit on the bottom stair, just outside the closed kitchen door, and I listen to the unthinkable.

Which is how I find out this wasn't the first time Mom cheated on Dad.

It happened back when they were dating, I learn. Mom was drunk that time and—*ew*, just *ew*. Just *no*. I do not want to know any of this, but I am frozen in place, learning way too much about Drunk Mom. That time didn't count because they weren't married yet, I guess. Or maybe because Drunk Mom. And this time doesn't count because? Because everyone's sad, she seems to be saying. Because Mom's still sad about Grandma. Because of Maddy.

"It was just a kiss," Mom yells. "And *he* kissed *me*."

I'm trying to remember the last time I saw my parents kiss. I wonder if Dad is thinking the same thing.

"So why didn't you tell me when it happened?"

It's a pretty good question.

"You know why," Mom says. "*This* is why. I knew you wouldn't believe me."

Fair point, I think. I should be in the kitchen scoring this match for them. I curl my fingers into my hands like a kid about to start counting.

"Well, you were right about that," Dad says.

"It just happened," Mom says. "Kevin didn't mean it. It didn't mean anything."

"It just *happened*?" Dad says. "Bullshit. These things don't just happen, Kate. People don't just bump into each other at the post office and start sucking face. You *stalked* this man at church. You even tried to use our daughter as a cover story."

Who am I kidding, there's no contest here.

The landline rings and I flinch. The landline *never* rings. The phone is in the entryway at the bottom of the stairs, within arm's reach, and I pick it up—it's muscle memory; I am ten again and Maddy is calling to ask if I'm free for a playdate. But it isn't Maddy on the phone, it's her mom, and she wants to speak to Dad.

I look up and both my parents are staring at me from the kitchen doorway.

"What is it, Bean?" Mom says.

I stare back. *Bean*?

"It's Maddy's mom," I say eventually.

Mom blanches, and I think she might actually pass out.

"It's for you," I say quickly, handing the phone to Dad.

Mom tells me to go upstairs, but I refuse. Standing side by side, she and I watch Dad's face turn white, then really, really red. He's nodding into the phone but he's staring at Mom. He isn't saying much besides *yes* and *no* and *I see* and *I understand* and *of course* and *I'm so sorry.* And then he hangs up the phone, replacing the handset delicately, like it might explode. As if it's the phone itself that holds the bad things.

"What did she say?" Mom says, putting a hand on his arm. "Did she tell you how it happened, did she say it was me who stopped it?"

Dad shrugs out of her grip and crosses the room for his car keys. His hands are shaking so hard, the keys jangle when he picks them up, and when he tries to put them in his pocket he misses and they land on the floor. As he reaches the back door, he turns around and looks at Mom one more time. There are tears in his eyes.

"The truth matters," Mom announces to the room, like someone asked her to give a little speech. "And the truth is that he kissed me, and I stopped it."

"Can you for once not make this about you?" Dad says, and then he walks out.

I turn to face Mom, and she hesitates for a second before following Dad out the door. It's like she forgot that's what you're supposed to do.

"I'm so sorry," Mom says as she walks back into the kitchen. She opens her arms again and moves toward me for a hug. She looks more like a walking mummy than a mom. "I'm so sorry this is happening."

I duck out of her reach and open the fridge. I lean my head in and feel the cold air surround me.

"It was one kiss!" Mom insists, her voice so high it hurts my ears. "And *he* kissed *me*! It was two seconds, and I stopped it, I stopped him. That's it! That's the truth. I'm sorry I didn't tell you sooner. But, please, you have to believe me, Indie, you know everything now."

"Chill, Mom," I say into the fridge. "You already told me all this."

The details don't matter, Mom's wrong about that. The difference between one kiss and all the other things I don't even want to name—although no one else in town seems to have a problem naming them—it's all greater than zero. It all makes me want to puke. No difference between one bucket of vomit or a whole bathtub full.

"I'm sorry," she says again. "You've been through so much already, and now this? Jesus, I can't even imagine, I—"

I wonder how long I'd have to stand here, in front of the open fridge, before Mom would interrupt her own apology tour to remind me how much cold air I'm letting out.

"I'll find a way to fix this, I promise," Mom says. "I'll find a way to make it up to you."

I spin around to face her.

"You'll *make it up to me*?" I say. "What were you thinking, Mom? A big ice cream sundae with all my favorite toppings? Or, wait, no, I've got it! How about we go shopping together, and you can buy me a cute new outfit! Is that what you had in mind?"

"I'm sorry," Mom says. She's full-on sobbing now, and it's disgusting. "I'm so, so sorry. If I could take it back, I would. If I could go back in time, I would fix everything, I would change everything, I would do it all differently."

She is a spinning top of feelings, a whirlpool of words, and she is going to suck me in. She is Charybdis, I think, the giantess from Greek mythology who takes the form of a huge mouth in the ocean, sucking in water and debris three times a day. Thank you, sixth grade ELA unit on Percy Jackson.

"Going back in time wouldn't change a thing," I say. "This moment has always existed, and so have all the moments before and after it. You were always going to turn out to be a shitty mom."

chapter forty-two ❦ **Kate**

The local bridge spanning the Hudson River has a sign that reads: YOU ARE NOT ALONE. HELP IS HERE. There is a phone, too, connected to a twenty-four hour hotline. And what I used to think every time I passed this sign on my way to Target was not how true the message was, but rather how it must *not* be true for so many people, to necessitate a similar sign on every bridge over the Hudson.

I have never understood the impulse to jump—not even close—but I can't stop thinking about that phone. Because what I do understand today is the loneliness of having no one to call. *My mom*, I think. *I want to talk to my mom.* Now that she's gone, it's easier to imagine her picking up the phone and actually hearing me. It's easier to imagine her saying the right thing.

What would happen if I crossed the bridge halfway and picked up? Is it against the rules to call if you just want to talk? I would tell the person on the other end of the line, *The sign says that help is here. Could you clarify what kind of help?* In my fantasy, this person has an advanced degree in finding hope in unlikely places, like a search and rescue dog exploring the rubble of a collapsed building.

I don't do it, though, because what if the hotline is local? What if the person who picks up the phone has already heard the news? It's Kevin who shows up whenever someone jumps from the bridge, the lights and sirens a mere gesture, because no one survives the drop. Who would take my side over his?

chapter forty-three **Indie**

That first night Dad walked out with his car keys, he was gone less than an hour. I guess that's how long it took him to come up with some sick burns.

"You wanna know the worst part?" Dad yells one night.

Up in my room, I steel myself to hear this, what Dad considers *the worst part.*

"What really killed Laura is that Kevin cried," Dad says. "He's never cried in front of her, not once since Maddy died, did you know that? And yet he cried with you. How did *that* happen?"

Dad was wrong, though: That wasn't the worst part. The worst part is after my parents stop fighting about the Chief and start saying all the other mean things they've been saving up for years. They go low and then they go lower. "You're about as self-aware as a celery stalk," Dad says one night, which kind of makes me want to tell him about panpsychism. "You're just like your mom," he says another night, which is shockingly uninspired, even for him. Really, Dad? It's like he's just goading Mom into saying that her mother never liked him anyway, which of course she does because, you know: *parents*. Unoriginal. It makes me nostalgic for the days when they only half-listened to each other.

Still, though, Dad doesn't leave, and it doesn't take me long to figure out why.

"Why are you still here?" Mom says one night, and I can tell from her voice that she's crying. She's always crying these days. "No one's making you stay."

I creep to the top of the stairs so I don't miss his response.

"You know why I'm still here," Dad says, his voice eerily calm and soft. "You know I'd never do that to her."

Of course. He's sucking it up for my sake. Not that he asked my opinion on the matter. Dad is so sure he knows what's best for me, as if a shitty, falling-apart marriage would convince me the world is still running according to plan.

Most days I'm glad Maddy is not here for this. She'll never have to wonder what our parents talked about, or which room they kissed in, or why her dad cried in front of my mom but not hers. But other days I hate Maddy for leaving me, for being dead when I need a friend. On these days I fight with her ghost, and it doesn't matter that I don't believe in spirits or souls—I just want her to feel this, too. I tell Maddy it's her fault, that none of this would have happened if she'd just jumped into the bush when I screamed. I tell Maddy it's her dad's fault for kissing my mom. And when I really want to hurt her feelings, I tell her that none of this matters anyway, because even if she'd survived, we'd have gone our separate ways after high school. My parents used to agree on everything that matters, and even *they* couldn't stick it out. No way would Maddy and I have gone the distance.

chapter forty-four Kate

"It's good you're not fighting so much anymore," Sara says. "Right?"

She's standing in front of her desk, shoving papers into a bright yellow leather tote, on her way out to meet with clients.

"I don't know," I say. "I think maybe he's just checked out. It's not like we resolved anything, you know?"

"But he's still here," Sara says, her smile hopeful. "*That's* good, right?"

She wants this to be over, I can tell. She didn't sign on for anything deeper than an office friendship. We're colleagues who make disdainful bets on whether or not a house will have pimento cheese in the fridge or monogrammed hand towels in the guest bathroom.

"I don't know," I say again. "I don't even know that I want him to stay, if it's going to be like this."

Sara picks up her coffee cup, one of those travel mugs with a wood grain finish, and looks at the time on her cellphone. She leans forward and squeezes my shoulder with a hand.

"Talk later, okay?"

I once heard someone say that divorce in a small town happens like that old Hemingway quote: slowly at first, then all at once. I think what that person actually meant is that it's always happening, but suddenly it's happening to you.

I've never told Sara—I've never told anyone; who would I tell?—how Ethan and I became ordinary to each other. Or how this, the process of becoming ordinary in each other's eyes, *did* happen slowly at first, then all at once. Ordinary is hard to fight about, though. It's a smooth rock face with no handholds. It's the day-in, day-out, and who's to say anyone else has it better?

There are countless small ways Ethan and I wore each other down, the *drip drip drip* of a marriage eroded by water, but I wasn't paying attention; I didn't realize this is what we were doing until it was too late. Sure, we scroll through our devices in bed at night, and we reach for them first thing in the morning. He forgets to clean up his toenail clippings, and I leave hair in the shower drain. I sleep in moisturizing aloe socks, and he taps his smart watch into sleep mode when he turns off his nightstand light, meaning his watch knows before I do that we aren't having sex. But show me a couple that doesn't fall into habits like these.

The key, I think, is that we stopped expecting to learn anything new about each other.

There was a boy I dated the summer between high school and college. He was the new pastor's son and he was funny, and he knew how to make one dish, spaghetti carbonara, which was one more dish than anyone else our age. He cooked it for me, late at night while his parents were sleeping, and we talked about everything—school, friends, family, God, what we wanted to be when we grew up. Also, we made out. A lot. We did pretty much everything it's possible to do on a couch, fully clothed, when you're half expecting his dad (your pastor) to walk in at any moment. For a couple of weeks I thought I'd met my future husband. And then, about a month in, lying on his parents' couch with my head in his lap and an empty pasta bowl on my stomach, I said, "There's so much more I want to know about you." He was silent for a moment and then he said, "What do you mean?" I wasn't sure exactly what I meant, just that I felt like I was falling in love and I wanted to know everything about him; I wanted to rush through every detail but also take my time and savor each moment—I wanted it all at once but I wanted it to last forever, too. "I feel like we're just starting to get to know each other," I said. "You know?" He ruffled my hair with his hand like I was a cute kid, although we were the same age. "Nope," he said cheerfully. "You pretty much know me."

That conversation hurt more than the inevitable back-to-school breakup in the fall, because that was the moment I realized I'd made him up. He was a preacher's son, and everyone knows that means complications and hidden depths. But this son of a preacher man meant what he said—I did know him. I still see him online sometimes, which is how I know that he became a pastor, just like he said he would. I realize social media isn't the most reliable tool for reporting on other people's level of satisfaction in life, but in his case, I genuinely believe the sunny status updates.

I would think of this preacher's son a few years later, when I took up online dating. Over and over, I fell in love with guys' online personas, only to meet them for a drink and feel nothing. One time I emailed with a guy for months before we met, because he was on assignment in Paris. Paris! How could I resist? He said he'd bring me a scarf! When we finally met up, at a restaurant in the East Village, I knew before I'd even crossed the room to his table that he wasn't the guy I'd been picturing in my head. I'd made him up, too.

And so imagine my delight when I found myself on a blind date with a schoolteacher who was secretly brilliant, who didn't go to Paris on assignment, who didn't feel the need to advertise himself to the world, but who surprised me each day with what he saw in the world—and what he saw in me. *Over here!* I wanted to shout to every man who'd ever let me down. *This is what hidden depths looks like.*

The morning after our wedding, I woke to the oddly pleasant sensation of being hungover in the most comfortable hotel bed in the history of down. I read Robert Browning's poem "Now" to my brand-new husband, because I finally understood it—how you *make perfect the present.* How ideal love cannot exist in everyday life, but it can exist in a moment that feels perfect. I'd never read this poem out loud before, and as I spoke, and felt the rhythm of each line, I understood it even more:

Thought and feeling and soul and sense—
Merged in a moment which gives me at last
You around me for once, you beneath me, above me—
Me—sure that despite of time future, time past,—
This tick of our life-time's one moment you love me!

That morning in our hotel bed, I thought that marriage was defined by such moments, and that a successful marriage meant learning to bide your time between them. Eventually, though, I discovered it was the in-between that was truly ours—the secret downtime of a marriage. The long car rides bingeing true crime podcasts. Ethan chopping onions for a breakfast scramble while I read out clues from the Sunday crossword. Assembling IKEA furniture together while we listen to albums from our vinyl collection (Fleetwood Mac's *Rumors* for me and the Beach Boys' *Pet Sounds* for him).

We all become ordinary to each other in the end, but this doesn't have to destroy a marriage. A stable marriage depends on ordinariness, in fact, and even if it feels like a grind sometimes, it's *your* grind. You are two human beings who leave toothpaste splatter on the bathroom mirror (or leave passive-aggressive Post-It notes about the toothpaste splatter). You tell each other the same stories over and over again, and, on a good day, you pretend you've never heard this one before, or that it gets better with each telling. The ordinariness is the reward you earned when you chose each other: When you chose a lifetime of being rooted in place by habit and time, by the imprint each of your bodies made on your side of the mattress. Tell me there's not something beautiful in that.

I don't know when we stopped seeing the beauty.

I do know that hitting bottom felt like an arrival at first, as if we had always known this was the point of a marriage: to plumb each other's depths. To know each other completely—or, at least, to think we did. But then, at some point, this felt like being stuck at the bottom of a well. Worse, like being stuck at the bottom of a well with someone whose cellphone keeps beeping with text alerts that crack him up, though he never explains why. And when you ask this man at the bottom of the well if he has any ideas on how the two of you might get out of there, he looks irritated, like you just interrupted him in the middle of something. "Don't get mad at me for ignoring you," he says. "You're the one who started a conversation while I was reading a text."

Except, he's always reading a text.

IF YOU LIVED HERE—NEW LISTING! RESTORATION-WORTHY BARN AND 5 ACRES OF OPEN MEADOW AND WOODLAND

You don't have to stick around here for long to know how much I love a rustic barn, especially in fall. I mean, just look at this beauty! In all the years I've lived upstate, there's only one barn I've driven by without pulling over to photograph it, and it's the one twenty miles north of us that features a certain president's name painted in six-foot-high letters. (It *would* make for an excellent picture, but, as my husband pointed out, "They have guns, and you have bumper stickers.") My teenage daughter groans dramatically from the back seat whenever a barn comes into view. You wouldn't *believe* how hard she has it. Unless you have a teenager yourself, in which case, you already know: Moms are the *worst*. Here are the top ten ways my daughter has found fault with me lately (not including the barn thing, which barely scrapes the top hundred).

Emma Tourtelot

1. Why do you open your mouth like that when you're listening to me? [Demonstrates, in case the scathing review of my facial expression was too cryptic.]
2. Is that supposed to be funny? [Looking over my shoulder while I text a colleague. Meanwhile, I'm not even allowed to glance at her lock screen.]
3. Boundaries, Mom.
4. Ew, what kind of music is this? [Turns off car stereo.] Stop asking me to pick a song, you're just trying to find out what I listen to.
5. [When I offer to read a book from her summer reading list.] You're not in high school anymore, stop trying to piggyback on my life. Don't you have a book club or something?
6. Why are you yelling? [Me, confused: *That's* yelling?]
7. I can't believe you're being so calm right now. Why can't you just yell like a normal mom?
8. Dad's right.
9. [Me: What is it about me that you find so annoying?] Oh my god, why would you even *ask* me that?
10. Me, over text: I love you. My daughter: [thumbs-up]

xok

---

ann-no-e: *My kid told me I was being "hyper" when I laughed at something on my phone the other day. What the hell, he's twelve and already he knows how to neg? What kind of boyfriend is he going to turn out to be?*

go-ask-your-dad: *Thank you, I feel seen. Apparently I sneeze in a weird way and it's super embarrassing when I do it around her friends.*

mazel-tough: *ME.*

f-bomb-mom: *OMG at least half of these happened to me and that's just counting this week!!*

[DELETED POST: **mom4liberty:** *I'd like to hear the top 10 things your daughter said to you after you slept with her dead best friend's dad.*]

[DELETED POST: **butterfly-kisses:** *hell yeah I believe how hard your daughter has it.*]

[DELETED POST: **glue-gun-mom:** *Your husband's right. We have guns. Just sayin'.*]

[DELETED POST: **boy-momma:** *WHORE*]

really_jen: *Really, are we all that predictable? I have a teenager and I don't relate to ANY of these "mom" jokes. Maybe you all need to stop rolling your eyes so hard and start seeing your kids as individuals instead of funny memes. #NotAllTeens #NotAllMoms*

i_live_here: *Jen, I think my daughter would love you. The rest of you: Thanks for reminding me that it's not just my teenager who has a black belt in undermining. xok*

chapter forty-five Indie

They've stopped screaming at each other, but it turns out the silence is worse. My parents have always fought in front of me—they claimed it was a life skill they were passing on, to let me witness both the argument and the apology—but now they drift around each other like mismatched roommates. I know they're seeing a counselor once a week, so I guess they talk then. I think that's the rule in couples therapy? And maybe they whisper-fight in their bedroom at night. Mostly, though, I see them each communicate with their own devices. It's like the most depressing Apple commercial in the world.

Dad occasionally laughs out loud when he gets a funny text from a friend, and the sound is comforting but strange, like hearing a snippet of English in a foreign country. Mom looks put out when this happens—she gets this prickly *is-there-something-you'd-like-to-share-with-the-class* look on her face—but then again, she's always done that. Dad's friends love to send him dumb videos. A chimp throwing poop at an old lady in a zoo. A man—millions of them—getting kicked in the nuts. It's like, who's the real teenager in this house?

According to Dad, Mom doesn't think it's funny to laugh at other people's misfortune, which means she basically misses the entire point of the internet. (Has she checked her comments section lately?) Really, though, I think she was just done asking both of us, *What's so funny?* Because Maddy used to send me videos, too. Every day brought a new round of viral videos that made

Dad and me laugh—harder than we ever laughed at anything Mom said.

Ever since he found out about the Chief, Dad has been going on more walks than usual, sometimes twice in a day, but he never takes Buddy with him. This move is both juvenile and brilliant, and I wish I'd thought of it first.

"I see what you're doing," I say to him one evening as he sits in the mudroom, lacing up his sneakers. "Going on all these walks."

"Your powers of deduction are brilliant, Nancy Drew," Dad says. "Yes, I'm going on another walk."

"You know what I mean."

Dad doesn't smile, except maybe in his eyes a little.

"Want to come?" Dad says. "I saw a bald eagle yesterday. I'm going to look for the nest."

That's when I realize he has a pair of binoculars around his neck.

"You are *such* a dork," I say, but I don't really mean it.

I mean, I do—he's a big fucking dork. But I'm glad he has something to look for on his walks. Something to look forward to.

"Nah," I say. "I'm good, thanks. Maybe another day."

I think he walks not because he wants to leave, but because it helps him stay. Like, it makes his world feel a little roomier.

I watch for Dad's return from my bedroom window. I'd like to see an aerial map of my parents' daily walks—Mom with the dog, and Dad without. I picture them like ghosts in a Pac-Man game, Blinky and Pinky, moving left, right, up, down, speeding up, slowing down, bumping into walls and looping back on themselves, but always, somehow, just missing each other.

"Indie!" Mom says as I walk into the kitchen. She always ambushes me when I'm looking for a snack. "Buddy and I just got back from the vet. He was *such* a good boy"—here comes the baby talk—"weren't you, Buddy Boo-Boo?"

I back away from her and make my way toward the fridge, moving sideways so I can keep her in my sights. If I turn my back, she might sneak up behind me for a hug.

"He could use a walk," she says, bending over to clip a leash onto Buddy's collar. As Mom leans in close, the dog licks the tip of her nose. "Want to take him around the block? It's beautiful out. I don't have to come with you. I mean, unless you want me to."

Buddy sits obediently, his whole body wiggling in expectation as he stares at Mom, not me. The dog gets it; he treats me like a piece of furniture. I wish Mom would do the same. She thinks I hate her, but as always, she misses the point. I don't feel *anything* toward her. Sometimes when I'm home now, I forget she's even in the room.

I grab a yogurt from the fridge because it's the only snack I can see that requires neither chopping nor reheating, and I can't stay in this kitchen a minute longer. If I hang around, Mom will start crying again, and I don't know what to do with that. How long before she accepts that I have nothing left to say to her?

Only when I get back to my bedroom do I realize I forgot to grab a spoon. I scan my room for an alternate yogurt-eating utensil. Nothing. Whatever, I think, and pour the yogurt down my throat, like I'm some dudebro in the school cafeteria. Then I sit cross-legged on my bed and close my eyes, palms up. Maybe today will be the day I finally break through.

I read online that if I keep practicing, if I meditate every day, eventually I will unlock a kind of awareness, and then I will know for sure that the self is an illusion. After that, it will be an understanding I can tap into at any time, the experts promise me. They tell me that when I get to this stage, when I embody the universe's point of view, I will experience firsthand how pain and suffering feel no different from joy. I will know that feelings are simply sensations, in the way that extreme heat and cold are sometimes indistinguishable on the skin. Or the way that even professional chefs fail the blind taste tests on Gordon Ramsey's *Hell's Kitchen*. (Apparently everything tastes a little bit like a boiled potato if you can't see what you're eating.)

The experts tell me to sit, to still my thoughts, to slow my breathing. They tell me to let go of this idea I am so attached to, of a present-tense me in the world. They say that meditation is like rubbing two sticks together to make fire, and the moment you take a break or get distracted, the sticks go cold again and you have to start over.

And so I sit in my room, eyes closed, trying to unthink myself. I sit cross-legged for hours, until my legs tingle and go numb, until a hundred itches on my body come and go, because I am committed to the task at hand, and also—what else do I have to do? I tell myself that I am not a person who chooses to think thoughts, I am just a vessel, and these things—thoughts, feelings, memories—should flow through me without making any stops along the way. I am Tom Hanks in *Castaway* and I rub two sticks together until my hands are raw and bleeding.

But every time I open my eyes, I am still trapped in this house with my mom, who faithfully returns from her walks every day, just like Dad does, even when I fantasize that she won't. I'm not just trapped in this house, either—I'm trapped with this idea of me. There is a place, or a reality, where none of this means anything, I'm sure of it. But no matter how long I sit, how little I speak, how deeply I breathe, or how much I read about what it means to lack a self, I am still here, and Mom is still there, and Maddy is still gone.

chapter forty-six ❦ Kate

The tub of eggshells and vegetable peelings that we save for the compost is overflowing and attracting fruit flies, and I take this to mean it's my turn to empty it. Perhaps this is how Ethan intends to punish me: prosaically, in small and mundane measures, for as long as we both shall live. I walk barefoot across our yard, the lawn damp and freshly mown and the grass clippings clinging to my feet. Behind me, I hear the back door swing open with a force that can only mean Buddy threw his full body weight at it, and before I can fully process this thought, he is running directly into the back of my knees, knocking me to the ground and spilling the entire contents of the compost tub. I lie in the grass, the wind knocked out of me, and then Buddy licks my face as if he had nothing to do with any of it. As if he just showed up to check if I was okay.

I turn my head and see a banana peel next to me in the grass, like the aftermath of a vaudeville pratfall. It would be a funny story if I had anyone to tell. I imagine Ethan and Indie's blank expressions, and me, up on stage, doing my bit and bombing. "You had to be there," I whisper to myself.

Back in the kitchen, I sit gingerly, wincing at my bruised tailbone. I pick up my phone because—why, exactly? To post something wry about the banana peel? I throw my phone across the kitchen island, disgusted with myself, then pick it up again and delete every social media app I've ever joined. It's not enough, though. If I had a hair shirt, I would walk through the center of town wearing it, so everyone would know: *I see it too.* I see what you see, and I don't like me either.

And then I realize what I've got to do. I open my laptop and I delete *If You Lived Here.* Every post, every comment, every follower, every like—I delete the entire story of my made-up life. In less than ten minutes, it's official: I am no longer the person with the enviable upstate dwelling; the one who posts photos of Christmas tree farms and drive-in movie theaters; the one who only gets stuck in traffic when a tractor is up ahead; the one with the kitchen island that looks big as a continent when I frame it just so. I am no longer the person anyone wants to be.

chapter forty-seven **Indie**

Okay, fine, I admit it: the puppy is adorable. It's not like I'm some heartless android. And when Mom and Dad are out—when I'm the only available human in the house—Buddy stops treating me like furniture and instead becomes a bottomless pit of need. He stares at me from across the room, his eyes saying *love me love me love me*. Or, maybe it's more like *feed me feed me feed me*. Who knows what it feels like to be a dog? Buddy knows, I guess.

If I ignore Buddy, he stays where he is across the room, practically quivering with unmet need. It reminds me of STEM class and all the different kinds of energy an object can possess. This puppy on the other side of the room is pure potential energy. But if I tilt my head a few degrees in either direction, in acknowledgment of the indisputable fact that, *yeah, you're adorable*, he is in my lap. That's how fast it is: I am never aware of him running toward me. Instead, in an instant, he is on me, his warm weight holding me in place.

But then Buddy hears a car pull into the driveway and he is downstairs again, in the kitchen, waiting for Mom to walk in the door like he never abandoned his post. If it wasn't for the dog hair on my sweatpants, I would think I'd imagined the whole thing. *I get it*, I think, as if the universe can hear me, and I suppose this is how people pray. *Nothing lasts forever. Thanks for the reminder.*

I click on my phone to see if The Guy posted a new video today. This is what I call him in my head, *The Guy*, because he doesn't use his given name online, and he has no particular *nom de guerre* either (hat tip to Madame Wheeler's French class). He claims he will answer to whatever honorific or title we are each comfortable using, depending on our individual backgrounds and cultural traditions. Guru, Swami, Healer, Teacher, Reverend, Pastor, Sensei, Ninja. His handle is @insert_title_here.

Some of his fans try to sleuth out his real name—they trade guesses in the comments section—but I'm good sticking with *The Guy*. Like he could be anyone; he's just the messenger. If I was a fucking cheeseball, I would say Maddy sent him my way to comfort me. But this has nothing to do with comfort.

There's no new post, so I rewatch The Guy's last video, so many times that certain words he uses a lot—*thoughts*, *self*, *attachment*—do that thing where they go from familiar to foreign and back again. I adjust the settings and play the video at half speed, then double speed, then with the sound off, captions on.

And then I do exactly what The Guy says.

I try to imagine myself without a body. I want to feel nothing, think nothing, need nothing, be nothing. I take a finger and draw a thought bubble above my head like The Guy does, I see it hover above the cartoon panel that contains my body, and then I watch it float away. The sky is filled with my thought bubbles, all the way to the horizon. They are pretty as Chinese lanterns, glowing in the night sky. My body has no fixed border, I see it now: "I" do not stop at the outer layer of my skin, and the world does not begin there either. We are one and the same. And suddenly, or maybe it isn't suddenly, maybe it's hours later, or maybe it's both, because time becomes irrelevant: I feel it. An energy that begins in my stomach and rolls through my body, straightening my spine like I'm being pulled to the ceiling by a string. I open my eyes and I know—with a deep certainty I hadn't realized was possible—I *know* that everything I can see and everything I can't see, all of it exists in one space. It's as if the whole world has emptied into my cartoon panel. I understand that all points in time and space are the same, that time has no tense, that objects have no fixed coordinates. Subject becomes object, object becomes subject, and all of it is built from the same blocks: particles, atoms, molecules. I am empty, I am light and nothingness. I am no longer a fragment of the universe, I *am* the universe. And this feeling, it feels like love—an impersonal, absolute love that is almost unbearable in its perfection. *Goddamn*, it's beautiful. I am struck down with awe and wonder, and I want to be in this moment forever.

And then the feeling evaporates and I am back in my room and I feel myself choking, like I'm gasping for air. Like I'd been breathing underwater, like I *was* the water, until I remembered I had a body that needed air. A body that aches with sadness—a body that is so, so heavy, and too much in this world.

I look up and Mom is at the door, she has opened it just a crack and she's watching me. Her face is red and puffy, like someone punched her. I stare at her face for a few more seconds before I register that she's been crying, and must have been crying for a long time. My brain is sluggish, and I imagine literal gears clunking into place as I put together the pieces: red and puffy equals crying. Crying equals sad. She asks if she can make me a grilled cheese and I shake my head no and crawl into bed, still in my pajamas from the night before.

chapter forty-eight ❦ **Kate**

There's a white noise machine in the marriage counselor's waiting room, the same kind we once kept next to Indie's crib to help her sleep. The sound, like a hair dryer on the lowest setting, is not calming to me. It makes me think of sore breasts and an inconsolable baby and that one endless night when she woke right after I'd pumped myself empty and refused to take the bottle. I should have put the white noise machine next to my own pillow instead, so that I could sleep through the crying and Ethan would be the one to wake. My husband, who would sit bolt upright in bed, alert, at the sound of a twig snapping in the yard, yet could snore softly, a fairytale slumber, through our daughter's screams.

I never did this, though, because secretly I loved our separate roles—my husband alert to intruders, and me alert to the human needs inside our house. To this day, my sleep is punctuated by the sounds from Indie's room—as she closes the drapes, blows her nose, tosses the throw pillows to the floor.

Ethan sits across from me now, grading quizzes. He always brings work to these sessions, I guess to remind me that he's doing me a favor, squeezing me in like this.

"How's Indie doing at school?" I say.

"Hmm?" he says, not looking up.

"Do you ever see her in the hallway?" I say. "Does she walk to class with anyone?"

"We're on different floors," he says, his voice neutral, as if he'd found himself next to me at a dreary office party. He keeps right on marking up the paper with red ink.

Ethan told me we couldn't afford this therapist, and he was right. It turns out couples therapy isn't covered by his health insurance plan, as if it were some kind of cosmetic procedure. But I'm not asking for a *pretty* marriage—I just want something we can live with. I told Ethan I would find the money, and I did, although I don't tell him how and he doesn't ask, because nothing about me interests him right now. I sold a ring and necklace that were gifts from Ethan's mom, not out of spite, but because I'd rather give Indie a family than a family heirloom. No doubt the jeweler gouged me—I chose a store in Poughkeepsie, to be discreet—but I couldn't afford to wait: I'm paying two hundred dollars an hour so Ethan will listen to me. Or, do I pay the fee so he'll talk? Some days I think I would pay two hundred dollars a word just to hear him say something nice again.

"Oh," I say loudly, as if I just remembered something important that needs his attention. "Is there anything in particular you want to talk about today? I just wondered if we should have a game plan for the session. You know, to get the most out of our money."

"Let's just wait," he says, motioning with his head toward the therapist's door, "until we're in there."

And that's when I know our marriage is over. *In there* is the only place where he still considers me part of the equation. In there, he will go through the motions and later say that he tried his best, because he is a man who plays by the rules. We will each recite lines for the therapist—*You're not listening* and *You're not trying* and *You always* and *You never*—because this is an unoriginal situation and in there, nobody gets to be a maverick. The therapist will observe criticism, contempt, defensiveness, stonewalling—the four horsemen of the apocalypse she has been trained to look out for. She won't say it, but I will see it in her eyes: We are in the end times of a marriage. And Ethan will endure this for weeks or months or years or however long it takes until he decides that *now* is when the good dad gets to leave.

Out here, though, we are already just two strangers in a waiting room, drinking crappy free coffee and watching the clock.

chapter forty-nine ❦ **Indie**

The last time Maddy and I ever ate lunch in the school cafeteria, we watched this nerdy Gamers Guild kid ask Asher to open his ketchup packet. "I touched the grilled cheese and now my hands are all greasy," the kid said, his shoulders hunched forward as if he were wearing a heavy backpack. Asher was so surprised by the request that he took the packet and ripped it open without a word. "*Dude*," one of Asher's soccer buddies said. "What even is that? Does he think you're his mommy?" Everyone at the table snickered.

What I mean to say is, the school cafeteria sucks, and not just for the kids who play Magic: The Gathering. It's a Minkle world, and the rest of us are just NPCs—that's what Maddy used to say. NPCs, the non-player characters controlled by a video game's artificial intelligence system. Meanwhile, the popular kids get to be the player characters, the only ones with a controller to choose their own actions. They're easy to spot, these player characters—fit and confident, effortless hair, charisma radiating from their perfect pores. They even *smell* good.

As for the NPCs: too quiet, too loud, too dumb, too smart? Total NPC! Feminist, gay, goth, emo, woke, weird, ordinary, clumsy, boring, fat, scrawny, BO, eczema, wrong phone, no phone, wrong parents, no parents: NPC central.

Those were the days.

Now I hide in the school bathroom with my phone, because it's the only place where I still feel like an NPC. The Minkles don't get it, though—we're *all* non-player characters, every last one of us. No one gets to control their own avatar, no matter how good they smell.

The Guy says that I have to give up anything I'm too attached to. *Easy*, I think, as I slide the bolt on the bathroom door. I could give two shits about any of this.

chapter fifty ✎ Kate

It begins with pasta, because I married a man who is serious as cancer about not eating carbs.

"You made spaghetti carbonara?" Ethan says, peering into the pan like he's the health inspector.

"Indie loves it," I say.

This is true, but also: whenever I've made carbonara in the past, I've always cooked zoodles on the side for me and Ethan.

"I'll just make something else," Ethan says, opening the fridge in a huff.

"Super helpful," I say, stirring the sauce so aggressively I splash my shirt. "Can you at least set the table first?"

I'm embarrassed to be doubling down on something as petty as carbs. This is not the hill I want to die on.

"Jesus Christ," Ethan says. "I'm just trying not to have a heart attack before I'm fifty. I was under the impression you were on board with that goal."

It didn't used to matter to me that I couldn't distinguish Ethan's desires from my own. I thought that was marriage: a melding of two souls. You eat cauliflower rice, I eat cauliflower rice.

"I'm always on board," I say. "And honestly, it's kind of exhausting."

"What are you even talking about?" Ethan says.

I could tell him I'm talking about cauliflower rice, and perhaps I am, but I've been on board with everything for so long, even *I'm* not sure whether or not I actually like veggie noodles.

Either way, now that I've said these words out loud, they feel true in a way that has nothing to do with carbs.

"You have this idea of what it means for someone to have your back," I say. "And I'm tired of always falling short."

Ethan closes the fridge door with his foot, a jar of kimchi in one hand and a carton of eggs in the other.

"Well, I *do* expect you not to kiss other guys," he says. "But that's a pretty low bar, wouldn't you say?"

I close my eyes in a pathetic attempt to protect myself. I see years of arguments ahead of us, every single one of them coming back to this.

"Admit it," I say, my eyes still closed. "I was disappointing you long before that."

"You're not disappointing *me*," Ethan says blithely. "But I do think you should try to get a handle on your mom stuff, for our daughter's sake."

"My *mom stuff*?" I yell. My stomach hurts and I feel a sudden desire to curl up on the floor in a ball. "She fucking *died*, Ethan, and I'm really sad. Every day, I wake up and I still feel sad. But nobody's allowed to be sad around here because nobody suffered as much as you did, and look how *fine* you're doing."

"So you threw yourself at *Kevin*?" Ethan says, then he shudders like he tasted something unpleasant. "You needed a shoulder to cry on, and you picked him? I thought you'd have a little more class than that, Kate. The man lost his *child*. And you didn't even like your mom."

I let out a single sob, like a gasp for air, and I see it in Ethan's eyes, how much he hates it when I cry. It's always been like this: My tears harden him. And then I can't control it any longer, I start to full-on ugly cry. I cry because Ethan is right: She was a shitty mom. But I cry, too, because she was the only mom I had. Ethan turns his back and begins to prepare his gut-biome-friendly meal.

"I'm sure that must be cathartic for you," he says eventually, when I am quiet again. "But do you ever wonder if maybe that's why our daughter never cries?"

More tears spring to my eyes and I wipe them away quickly, guiltily. Not my turn, I think. I remember the plumber, how it was his turn, that afternoon in the kitchen. But since when do we have to *take turns*? Fuck Ethan for parceling out his comfort like this, as if I were a pet he was training with treats. I take a deep breath to steady myself.

"You want to know why she doesn't cry?" I say. "She's not sad, Ethan, and that terrifies me, because she should be really, really sad right now. But she's totally disconnected—she can't feel a thing. You ever wonder who taught her *that*?"

Ethan crosses his arms and looks at me blankly, like he genuinely doesn't know.

"I'm talking about your brother," I say, my voice a little softer now, because maybe he doesn't.

"Yes," Ethan says, his voice thick with sarcasm. "I got that part."

"You have to let her feel something," I say. "Even if it hurts you to see it. Even if it hurts you to remember."

Ethan links his hands behind his head and takes a deep breath, and for a second I think he might actually cry.

"I don't think I love you anymore," he says.

I am so shocked, I almost ask him to repeat himself, thinking I must have misheard.

"I don't believe you," I stammer. "This is just what you do around death. You disconnect."

"Okay," Ethan says coolly. "I guess you know better."

And then, calm as anything, he picks up the jar of kimchi, selects a fork from the cutlery drawer, and walks out of the kitchen.

I turn off the stove, nauseated. The smell of bacon suddenly seems inappropriately festive, like someone telling a knock-knock joke in the middle of a eulogy. I dump the creamy sauce in the trash and text Ethan. *Heading out to yoga. When you've finished feeding your microbiome, please make dinner for your daughter.*

chapter fifty-one **Indie**

"Want to head into town for dinner, just the two of us?" Dad says. "I don't feel like cooking."

Dad *always* feels like cooking, especially when it involves something from his vegetable garden.

"I don't feel like eating," I say.

"Dinner is not optional," Dad says. "We've been through this."

"Do I get to pick the place?"

"Sure," Dad says. "Wherever you want."

Apparently someone has abducted my opinionated foodie father and replaced him with the shrug emoji. I don't let the opportunity go to waste.

"The diner, then," I say.

"The diner it is," Dad says airily, as if he hadn't spent the past decade grumbling about its sugary salad dressings and burnt coffee.

As soon as we walk into The Village Diner, I realize my mistake. This is the locals' place. The Chief used to treat me and Maddy to milkshakes here whenever we had something to celebrate, and even when we didn't. It looks like an old railroad dining car, and it's the last holdout in a town that's gone apeshit for turmeric lattes and smoothie bowls. Maddy's dad used to roll his eyes whenever a new restaurant opened in town, pointing out that no one *he* knew could afford twenty-eight dollars for a beet burger—and they wouldn't eat it if they could.

I walk toward a booth in the back of the diner. Dad catches the waitress's eye and orders a light beer before he's even in his seat.

"So," I say, once we're seated. "How's *your* fall semester going?"

Dad loves summer break. He loves hiking in the Catskills, he loves his vegetable garden, and he really loves pickling shit. Back-to-school is always a cold plunge for him, although Mom rolls her eyes at this, like Dad is a little kid who wants five-day weekends and candy for breakfast.

"Same old, same old," he says.

Not really, I want to say. When I got off the school bus today, I noticed he'd let his hot peppers wither and die.

"Are they all talking about it?" I say. "Your teacher friends, I mean."

Dad swallows loudly. Did he really think we were just going to do small talk?

"My *friends* aren't," he says eventually. "I can't say for sure about the rest of them."

"That's good you've got friends," I say, and I mean it. He needs his friends.

Dad opens the oversized menu and starts to page through it, though we both know exactly what he's going to order. I think maybe he's trying not to cry.

"Sorry," I say, although I'm not sure what I'm apologizing for. I don't think I can handle seeing Dad cry right now, especially not in public.

Three guys walk in, each wearing a fire department tee and a pager on his belt, and I watch Dad stiffen as they sit at the counter right next to our booth. Could this town be any smaller?

When the waitress comes to take our order, I ask for a veggie burger, no cheese. Dad looks at me quizzically.

"What, no patty melt?" he says. "I'm not sure I can handle any more change right now."

It's true that we've both been ordering patty melts at diners since I turned twelve and officially graduated from kids' menus across the planet. I cried that day and told my parents I felt like I was growing up too fast, because only the kids' meals came with free ice cream. Dad suggested I try a patty melt, and when I admitted it was amazing, he told me that not everything about growing up would be a disappointment.

"I'm vegan," I tell Dad firmly now.

"Since when?"

"Since today."

"Okay then," Dad says.

I stare at him, waiting for more. Dad is always up for a debate. A few months ago, this conversation would have taken up the entire meal. The old Dad would have asked *why* I wanted to give up animal products, and he wouldn't have dropped the matter until I'd changed my mind—or changed his. If he was feeling generous, he would've let me pull out my phone to google supporting evidence.

"That's it?" I say now.

"You sound pretty resolved," Dad says. His eyes flit over to the firefighters and back to me. "What am I supposed to do, force-feed you a patty melt? God knows where this place gets the beef from, anyway."

"It's not about the cows crying," I tell him, although if it was, that would totally be on him. I can't believe my parents told me about weaning season when I was *five*. But I don't want Dad to think this is a sentimental decision, like I'm going to get one of those buttons for my backpack that says, *Animals are my friends, and I don't eat my friends*. "It's not about the cows at all, actually."

If Dad asks—if he really wants to know—I will tell him how The Guy had a full-body, spontaneous awakening after switching to a raw food diet when he was in college. The Guy eats everything now—he especially digs bacon, he says—because he doesn't need the push anymore. He can reach that state of mind anytime he wants. But for beginners, he recommends letting go of *anything* that comforts you, including food. Just until you understand that you don't need it, he says.

"Vegan, huh," Dad says, like he only half-believes me.

We sit in silence for a while, each of us contemplating the paper placemats in front of us. They're crammed with badly designed ads for local businesses: auto body shops, landscapers, doggie day spas, and a "sealcoating" company, whatever the hell that is. Eventually, Dad flips his placemat to its blank side, grabs one of the broken crayons from the Dixie cup next to the salt and pepper shakers, and draws a tic-tac-toe grid. He hands the crayon to me to go first.

"I need to tell you something," he says when I hand him the crayon for his turn.

I take a deep breath. This is how he leaves, I think. Not on foot during one of his daily walks, but right here, in the middle of the diner: a place where I can't cry and beg him to stay.

"Can we finish the game first?" I say.

The waitress arrives with our food and Dad leans back in his cracked pleather seat to give her space. When she walks away, he reaches for the Tabasco and douses his patty melt. Dad doesn't "do bread," unless we're in a place where he's too embarrassed to admit this to the waitstaff. The diner is one of those places.

"Want some?" he says when he catches me staring at him. He holds out the bottle of hot sauce. "I think your meal could use it."

I look down at my desiccated veggie burger. I'm sure there are restaurants where being a vegan doesn't feel like a sacrifice, but this is not one of those places.

"No thanks," I say, because the point isn't to enjoy the meal. So why would I try to fix it? I pick up my burger. "You can go ahead and say it now."

chapter fifty-two **Kate**

I sit at the kitchen island, staring at the text from Ethan: *Crashing at Caruso's tonight. Need to cool off. Already told Indie.*

Pete Caruso, the gym teacher. That's why I couldn't remember his name during the lockdown at school, because he and Ethan always call each other by their last names. God, my husband can be such a penis sometimes. My heart contracts at the thought that I may never get to tease Ethan about this again. Like slipping on a banana peel, it's only funny if he's here.

I call Ethan over and over, but he doesn't pick up. If I really believed that he needed to "cool off," I could convince myself he'd be back by morning. But he was cool as a fucking cucumber when he walked out of our kitchen.

Please don't do this, I text him. *Please come home.*

Of all the ways I could fail Indie, this is the worst.

I stare at my phone. I pick it up, remember I deleted everything, and put it down again. I look around the kitchen for something we need. Coffee filters, I think, the pour-over kind we can only get online. I order them. I wait.

The kitchen island is the first thing I loved about this house. Our one-bedroom apartment in Brooklyn had a galley kitchen, which meant Ethan and I had to turn our bodies sideways to pass each other. It was a kitchen meant for taking shifts, as if we lived and worked on a submarine. When the realtor showed us this house, I got goosebumps when I walked into the kitchen, because I could finally see around the bend. I saw myself sitting at the kitchen island writing a book review for the local arts magazine while Ethan cooked dinner, NPR playing in the background. I saw the *New York Times* spread across the surface, our coffee mugs leaving brown rings on whatever section we were reading. I saw us drinking wine here, sometimes just the two of us, sometimes with friends. I saw a selection of local cheeses on a piece of slate, each one labeled in chalk. I saw us lighting candles during power outages, or just because it was the weekend.

No wonder I ended up in real estate. I could sell myself swampland in Florida.

The funny thing is, I was right. Everything happened exactly as I'd imagined. (Or almost exactly: I hadn't imagined a local arts magazine could pay so little. Twenty-five dollars for a book review!) At first it felt magical, and then it just felt like ours, as if we deserved this new life because we'd made the right choices. *Make good choices*, that's what grown-ups tell kids. Ethan loved his job at the local high school, after almost a decade of teaching in the city, managing the anxieties and ambitions of Park Slope parents. Meanwhile, I thought I might write a novel, perhaps a feminist take on the legend of Sleepy Hollow—a town that turned out to be less than an hour from our new home. We were trying to have a baby, but at that point, the "trying" just involved a lot of missionary position. It had not yet occurred to us how hard it could be to get knocked up. My biggest concern back then was how long it would take to feel like we belonged in our town; I took for granted that I belonged with my husband, and he with me. I wish I had remembered to treasure that feeling I got when we closed the door against the world and it was just the two of us.

I read Ethan a Joy Harjo poem one morning as we sat, drinking coffee:

> *Perhaps the world will end at the kitchen table, while we are laughing and crying, eating of the last sweet bite.*

I thought my husband would always be there, sitting across from me at the kitchen island. It felt like the place where we would weather any storm. The stop sign at the corner of our street, one block down, is our actual family meeting spot, in case of a house fire or other emergency, but secretly, I always pictured the three of us finding each other here, the kitchen island still standing even if the whole town burned to the ground.

chapter fifty-three **Indie**

It's been a week, and Dad is still "crashing" in the gym teacher's guest room-slash-home gym. Gross-slash-sad. I guess Mom can't move out because she has no friends or something—not after what happened with the Chief. And I'm just a kid with a boo-boo, so I'm supposed to suck it up and stay with Mom and the dog and a coop full of chickens. I mean, it's not as if I can crash with Dad at Mr. Caruso's house. The gym teacher basically just graduated college—he's not even married yet. It's so weird that he hangs out with Dad.

Dad calls me daily, but all he wants to talk about is my schedule—how are my classes, who's my favorite teacher, how's the workload, what's my GPA. When I ask him about his day or his feelings, he tells me not to stress about him, he's fine. Like I should just finish my fish sticks and not worry about Grown-up Things.

This is the same guy, by the way, who told me—when I was in *elementary school*—that if you study world history for long enough, it's hard not to believe that life is nasty, brutish, and short. "We're doomed," he often announces, after catching up on the day's headlines. On a particularly bad news day, he might add: "The system is broken. Late-stage capitalism failed us. Globalism doesn't work. This brief experiment is almost over." And by "brief experiment," he means our entire civilization. Dad has always prided himself on his ability to stare down the cold, hard facts of life, barbarian-style. And *now* he decides I can't handle the truth?

So, yeah, fuck him, too.

chapter fifty-four ✓ Kate

For years, Indie filled the crevices of my days and nights; later, *If You Lived Here* did the same. Now, I have no posts to write, no readers to respond to, and a daughter who pulls out her phone and puts in her earbuds when she sees me coming. Indie is my own personal cold front.

Which is to say, I have become a sucker for 3 a.m. impulse purchases. The packages on my front porch feel almost like company, as if a neighbor stopped by and just missed me. A weighted blanket for the couch; a variety pack of herbal tea in a bamboo storage chest; a donut-shaped dog bed meant to lower canine anxiety; a self-help book containing far too many exclamation points. Things a friend might send me for comfort if she were too far away to stop in for tea.

The self-help book exhorts me to throw myself into my work. Except, mine is a word-of-mouth business, and word-of-mouth is not being kind to me right now. *Word-of-mouth referrals provide clients with a certain level of trust,* my real estate manual says. My real estate manual doesn't have nearly enough exclamation points. *Girl,* my self-help book says, *don't listen to the haters!* As if I had a choice in the matter.

I get up. I wash my face. I go to work.

The three of us once tried to come up with a slogan for our small town. Indie read something online about funny town slogans—San Andreas, California: *It's not our fault*—and she thought our town deserved to go viral, too. I think of this now as I sit in my office, reading an email from clients who no longer want me to sell their house, and I come up with a slogan: *Where bad news travels fast*. (The official slogan of Whittemore, Iowa, is *Cares more, shares more*, which is a polite way of saying the same thing.) It shouldn't surprise me, how easily a rumor becomes a cold, hard fact—at least half the people in this town don't believe in climate change or the peaceful transfer of power, either. But that doesn't make it hurt any less, now that I am the thing people no longer believe in.

Sara fills me in on the local gossip each morning. "Better to hear it from me," she says. "Right? So we can laugh about it together? Because you know I don't believe a word of it." According to the latest word-of-mouth news, I cheated on my husband because I am lonely and have no friends. A slightly conflicting report claims that, while it is true that I have no *female* friends, it was only a matter of time before I cheated on my husband, because at community gatherings, I talk exclusively to men. It's like being Yelped in real life, except there's no moderator, so the reviewers can say whatever the hell they want.

Ethan still hasn't called. It's been eight days. I checked his closet this morning, and nothing is missing. Is he buying new underwear at the overpriced men's store in town? Is he borrowing the gym teacher's shiny polo shirts? The only thing he took was his bike. I ask Sara if she knows anything, and she gives me a sad look, like I don't get it.

"Hey," she says. "My neighbor's hosting a Norwex party on Friday, wanna come? We can drink wine and buy shit we don't need. Or you can be my designated sober friend."

Sara and I once joked that this is the closest we ever get to a walk of shame these days: Waking up hungover after a friend's pyramid-scheme party and remembering that we bought five hundred scented tea lights we don't need. In the city, we mused, everyone has a therapist; upstate, everyone has their own multi-level marketing gig. "I mean, *tea lights!*" Sara said once, cracking up. "It's like, the nineties called, and they want their ambiance back."

"I can't make it," I say now, because there is no way Sara's neighbors want me at their Norwex party, and I'm sure she knows this. I force a smile. "You're on your own, sorry!"

"Okay, fine," Sara says, and smiles back, like we're doing a bit, which I guess we are. "But if I come home with any more microfiber cloths in fun colors, it's on you."

And then I go home and I drink elderberry tea and I pretend that any day now, Ethan will walk in the kitchen and laugh at me, because I always used to say that herbal tea tastes like dirty dish water. I was right, I will tell him. It does.

chapter fifty-five ❦ **Indie**

Every day, I sit in my room for hours, eyes closed, palms to the ceiling. I tell Mom not to disturb me, that I am doing my homework, although I haven't turned in an assignment in weeks. If she asked me point blank, I would tell her the truth: This is more important. But my mom believes my story about homework, because she believes in the story of a girl named Indie—the one who would disappear into her room for hours without being asked and come out with straight As every time.

I am trying to get back to that place I discovered in my head, or just outside my head—the empty cartoon panel that contains the world. Can I even call it a place? More like a state of wonder. I have that feeling of a word on the tip of my tongue, and I know what the word means, I know what it describes, I even have a sense of how many letters it contains. I am 100 percent sure the word exists, if only I could summon it again. That's how I feel *all the time*, except it's not a word I'm reaching for, it's the nature of reality, and it's *right there*, just out of my mind's reach.

The brief bliss I experienced that one day was more real than anything I've ever known. So, while I may *feel* stuck here now, a person in the present tense, I finally know for sure that this present-tense me is just an illusion. The past and the future are no less real than the present, because everything is always happening at the same time: Life with a best friend called Maddy *and* life without her; life with a set of parents under one roof *and* life without them. What makes a good or bad memory any more true, any more palpable, than a hope or a fear for the future? *Nothing*, The Guy promises. They're all just images projected onto the same screen. Now the only thing left for me to figure out is how to dispel this illusion of time. This illusion of me.

chapter fifty-six ✐ Kate

Ethan grew a beard. Sara tells me this is big news in town, bigger even than the fact that he's crashing with the gym teacher. I'm not sure which is the more public display of separation. Ethan once grew a mustache for "Movember," claiming his students dared him to grow it, although I think he actually believed a mustache might suit him. Now, he needs no excuse to try something new.

Also trending on Main Street, according to Sara: Ethan has a new weekday morning routine. He can be found reading the news on his phone at All That Java, drinking single-origin pour-over—seven dollars a cup!—before heading to the high school. I guess he decided to up his weekly coffee allowance.

I don't need Sara to tell me how local women are reacting to Ethan's real-life status update. A potentially single man in this town radiates a kind of energy that makes married women feel desirable. The idea that this man might be looking at them—might have been looking at them all along, in fact, if he was that unhappy in his marriage—fills them with a sense of possibility. It's a middle-aged woman's consolation prize for being invisible. It can be any man, really, not just someone who turns out to look surprisingly good in a beard. (And screw him for that serendipity.)

A potentially single woman, meanwhile, is the human equivalent of a McDonald's franchise opening up across from the town's historic inn. It's like one rogue woman has the potential to bring down this entire operation—the happy marriages, the excellent school system, the olive oil store, the whole nine yards.

It happened overnight. Women who barely know my name give me side-eye at the grocery store, like I showed up at the PTSA bake sale wearing a crop top and no bra. The ones who know me a little now avoid me completely. There is no way to convince them I'm not interested in their soft-bellied husbands, their men who wear khakis with flip-flops to dine out on a warm summer's evening. Even if I hadn't kissed someone else's husband, they would not believe me. Just the fact of me, a separated woman, brings down the tone of the neighborhood.

Ethan once told me about the *time to depart* law in Ancient Rome: No Roman citizen who'd been sentenced to death could be arrested until he'd been given time to depart. To choose exile, the Romans assumed, was a fate worse than death. That's what this town feels like right now—everyone looking at me like it's time to go.

Which is why I'm so surprised to get a text from a woman named Heather, asking if I want to meet in town for a glass of wine. I have her number saved in my phone from back when our daughters took a Music Together class, but we never met for a glass of wine—or anything, really—before. I don't respond immediately, in part because, what if she meant to text a different Kate? A minute later she texts again: *Sorry if this is out of the blue, I just thought you could use a friend.* My eyes fill with tears and I text her back: *I'd love to.*

A glass of wine turns into two and then three, and Heather drunkenly flirts with the young bartender so he'll charge us for a bottle instead. He is kind enough to pretend that this is why he agrees, and not simply because it's restaurant policy.

"It's okay," she says to me as she pours another glass from our second bottle. "We have Uber now! This town finally made it to the big time!"

Heather moved up from the city, too, but our lives were so different there, she may as well be from Ohio. She used to work on Wall Street and her husband was a surgeon somewhere on the Upper East Side. He's still a surgeon, of course. They moved upstate for his job, and she gave up her career to raise their three kids and "sit on the board of any nonprofit who'll have me," she says, rolling her eyes at herself.

Heather complains about the long shifts her husband works, on top of the hours he spends playing golf or drinking beer at the club after eighteen holes. Then she leans in close and tells me about the time her husband commented on how surprising it was, that not only her feet, but also her back, seemed to spread a little after she had kids.

"That's how he put it," Heather says, "That it was *surprising*. Like, he wasn't calling me fat, because everyone knows that's rude, he was just pointing out something quirky. My fucking *back*!" Wine sloshes out of her glass as she says this. "I kill myself at Pilates so I'll have the same abs as I did when he met me, and he thinks my *back* is too wide."

I sit and nod and make conciliatory noises, because I realize now this is why I am here: Heather assumes I give a shit about the many ways her own tedious husband has disappointed her. And then she brightens suddenly and says, "But tell me about *you*! How are *you* doing?"

Was it worth it, is what she wants to know. Or should she suck it up and stay with her doctor husband in their doctor house, with its immaculate, sweeping, doctor lawn. I am not the fun new friend, though, and I do not have a fun new life, and by the end of the evening I can tell Heather understands that I merely exchanged one dead end for another. I want to tell her that Ethan is just taking some space, that he'll be home soon, once he's "cooled off," but I can't bear to see the disbelieving pity in her eyes.

Heather returns to her husband (of course she does), and I know for sure she will never reach out to me again; she will never even acknowledge me in public, because it's easier to pretend she never told me any of it. And I am not her friend, I never was. I am a virtual reality ride at the county fair: Step right up and find out how much it sucks to be the other woman!

In this small town, I do not get to be an individual case, and the details about what actually happened are not important. It matters to *me* that Kevin never tried to clear my name, but it wouldn't matter to anyone else. I am an everywoman, the Other Woman. I am their dad's mistress or their frosty stepmonster. I am the cute babysitter. I am the woman their grad school boyfriend married, right after saying he wasn't ready to settle down. I am the mysterious "errand" their husband runs late at night. I am the unknown number.

A man gets to take on many roles: son, brother, drinking buddy, husband, father, firefighter, social studies teacher. He may turn out to be a "good man" or a "bad guy," a "good father" or a "deadbeat dad"—but these labels are always based on what he does in his own life. How he treats *his* family, *his* friends, *his* wife. He is never the Other Man. A woman, meanwhile, is held to a different standard. She is judged on how her behavior impacts not just her own family, but everyone else, too. She is the caretaker of all the feelings.

chapter fifty-seven **Indie**

What everyone in town thinks about my mother, according to the internet: The dress she wore to the funeral "wasn't right." She's elitist. She's a greedy realtor who single-handedly raised house prices in the area, and now only rich city people can move in. She was all over him at the funeral. She actually thinks she's good at yoga, LOL. She tells small children that heaven isn't real. She never volunteers her time at school. She once had an abortion because she wanted an only child. She thinks she's better than you. She doesn't belong here.

What no one says about my mother, but everyone is thinking: It should have been her. She should have been the one to lose a child.

What I think about my mother: nothing.

In French class, Madame Wheeler asks us to describe our bedrooms.

"*J'ai un bureau noir*," she suggests, as an example. "*J'ai une chaise noire.*"

Someone in the back of the room says *racist* into their hand, like a cough, and a bunch of people snicker.

"Oh my god," I groan, and I'm as shocked as anyone when I realize I just said this out loud. "You seriously don't even know how racism works."

"*Anaïs*," Madame Wheeler says firmly, which is the dumb French name she picked for me. "*En français, s'il vous plaît.*"

For the record, Madame Wheeler grew up in Poughkeepsie, though she says she visited the Eiffel Tower once when she was in college.

"Why?" I say. The gossip grapevine has stripped me of my invisibility shield at school, and I have nothing left to lose. Zero fucks left to give. "Give me one good reason why I should learn to speak French. You really think it matters if an adjective agrees with its noun? All these stupid rules, people just made them up, do you even realize that? It's all fake. School is just one giant Ponzi scheme. So, no, I won't fucking speak *en français*."

If I were any other kid, someone whose dad is a doctor or a lawyer, I'd be sent to the principal's office, and I wouldn't have to face my parents until the end of the day, or whenever they were able to get away from work. Instead, Madame Wheeler makes a call to the front office and asks one of the floating subs to cover Dad's class. Which is how I find myself in the guidance office conference room waiting for Dad less than two minutes after dropping the f-bomb.

"What the hell, Indie?" Dad says as he opens the door.

I look behind him, but my French teacher is not with him.

"I know, right?" I say. "Madame Wheeler is *so* sensitive!"

Like I said, literally no fucks. My fucks have left the building.

"You're failing French," he says, taking a seat across from me. Dad is suddenly calm, like he's my guidance counselor or something. "And apparently you're phoning it in for every other teacher, too."

Have you heard the urban legend that says if your college roommate commits suicide, you get straight As that semester? Well, I'm here to report that if you lose a friend at the end of middle school, the best you can hope for is a bunch of sympathy Cs from your ninth-grade teachers.

"*La connasse*," I say, scrolling through an English-to-French dictionary on my phone.

"What are you talking about?" Dad says.

"It's French for *motherfucker,*" I say, showing him my phone. "*Le connard, la connasse.*"

Dad reaches over to take the phone from my hand.

"Consider your phone gone," he says, putting it in his pocket.

"Okay Pol Pot," I say.

Dad taught me never to use Hitler as an example of anything. He says it demonstrates sloppy thinking.

"This is not happening," he says.

"We finally agree on something," I say. "None of this is happening. I'm not even sure space-time is happening."

Dad exhales aggressively, like an angry sigh. I've seen him do this with Mom before, but never with me.

"Enough with all the space-time crap," he says. "I thought we moved on from that over the summer."

"You want me to *move on*?" I say. "You're acting like this is some dumb TikTok trend. There's no *self*, do you realize that? So how do you propose I *move on*, exactly? You want me to pretend like I give a shit?"

"YES!" he yells. "You think the rest of us aren't pretending half the time? You've got responsibilities now. To your teachers, obviously. But more importantly, to yourself."

I think I preferred him icy-calm.

Dad comes around to my side of the room and stands in front of my chair, one hand gripping each of the armrests. I am distracted by his new facial hair. He looks like someone else's dad. His hair is brown, but his beard is flecked with gray. It's like we're in a time travel movie and I'm meeting Future Dad. Future Dad is older, but I am frozen in time. I should ask him what it's like in the future. Are there jetpacks and flying cars? And what about the polar bears, did we save the polar bears?

"I know Maddy's gone," Dad says. "And it's awful, it's so, so awful. You were in shock this summer, you were raw, we all were. But you don't get to throw in the towel."

I guess he's been talking this whole time and I only asked him about the polar bears in my head. I picture the Rewind icon on my podcasts. I select Skip Ahead instead.

"You don't need to like school," Dad is saying now. "I don't *expect* you to like it right now, but you've got to start going through the paces. You've got to do your homework and study for tests. I need you to face reality. I need you *here*."

His eyes have filled with tears and he's a little out of breath from his speech. For a weird moment I think about clapping.

"I *am* facing reality," I say. "That's what I'm trying to tell you. I'm facing reality, and there's nothing there. This conference room is not real. This school, this town, this whole world, it's not *reality*. None of it is real."

Dad raps his knuckles hard on the shiny oval table. He bends forward until he's at eye level with me.

"Did you hear that?" he says. "Sounds pretty real to me."

I shrug. He'll never get it. It's like trying to explain the risks of artificial intelligence to someone who thinks we can just unplug the robots when they turn on us.

Besides, I don't need him to get it anymore, because I've finally found someone who does. Someone who sees through the bullshit. Someone who doesn't fall for the grand illusion that most humans—my parents included—are living under. Someone who can help me. And this Guy, he says that the main thing holding me back is when I try to bring along all the people in my life who don't see things like I do.

"You think you don't care right now," Dad continues, because apparently he doesn't need me to participate in this conversation. He's in full-on TED Talk mode. "But sometime soon, maybe next week or next month or next year, you're going to remember how badly you wanted to get into Princeton. What are you going to tell the admissions committee then—that you can't submit your transcript because back in ninth grade you decided GPAs weren't real?

The rest of the world will keep on existing and getting straight As, whether or not you believe in any of it. Just like the sun will keep rising and setting at the horizon, no matter what the Flat Earth Society says."

I stare at my father. He's only inches from my face, and I can see the individual bristles in his beard, but he seems a million miles away. Distance is a funny thing, I think: Too close and someone could be a complete stranger. It's like those photos of objects magnified a thousand times and you have to guess what you're looking at. I start composing a message in my head. I want to tell The Guy about the microscope thing. I think he'd like it. Maybe he'd even use it in one of his videos.

"I don't want you to turn to me a year from now and ask why I didn't stop you from ruining your life," Dad says, and then he finally pauses to take a breath, like he just remembered how a conversation works.

"*Princeton*?" I say. "I tell you the whole world is a collaborative fiction, and you want to discuss the Ivy League?"

I wonder if Dad remembers that he's the one who taught me that phrase, *collaborative fiction*. Except he didn't go far enough. He was only talking about political systems and national borders.

"I'm keeping your phone," he says, straightening his body so he's standing upright again. "I have to get back to class, but this conversation isn't over."

He leaves me alone in the room and I sit at the table, unsure what to do next. Isn't he supposed to transfer me into the care of another responsible adult before returning to his class?

I lean forward and look at my reflection. This glossy oval table was once a beautiful tree that soared into the sky, and now it's here, suffering the indignity of countless dumbass guidance meetings about "potential" and "achievement" and "goals." I have no idea what kind of tree it used to be, and this seems like such a slight. Once it had a species and a genus and blossoms and leaves.

It had seasons. Now it's just "wood." How can my dad possibly think this table proves the concept of permanence? Did we not read *The Giving Tree* together, over and over, until the pages were soft as an old t-shirt?

I look up at the clock. Apparently no one is coming back for me. I rap my knuckles hard on the table, once, twice, then a third time for luck. "Bye, Tree," I say. "So long, sucker."

chapter fifty-eight ❦ Kate

"We need to talk about Indie," Ethan says, as soon as I pick up my phone.

"Hi," I say into my headset.

It's the first time Ethan has called since moving into the gym teacher's guest room two weeks ago. This seems like more than enough time to "cool off," which makes me wonder if Caruso knows something I don't. Are they *roommates* now?

Ethan makes an odd noise that is maybe a half-hearted apology for not calling sooner? It's hard to tell.

"Yeah," I say. "I heard from the school, too."

"I didn't *hear* from the school," Ethan snaps. "I was *there*. I *work* there, remember?"

"Tell me what happened," I say, like he's a toddler having a little tantrum. "Do you know what set her off?"

"She needs to get her act together," Ethan says. "I realize she's still grieving, but she doesn't get to be an asshole. She can't treat teachers like that."

"What if she can't get her act together?" I say. "I know it feels to you like it's past time, but sometimes your deadlines are a little unrealistic."

"Are you kidding me right now?" Ethan says. "This is not about your mom, Kate. Not everything is about your mom."

I press my lips together so I won't cry. I remind myself that I am not special. Millions of estranged couples on this planet co-parent their children. This we can handle: There's a template for it, and lawyers, too. There's a warehouse of self-help books and an entire neighborhood of the internet devoted to the topic. I tell myself: *You are blessed*. You still have a daughter to argue about.

"Did you talk to Indie?" I say, calm as anything. *Act as if*, the self-help books tell me. And so I do. I act as if I am not a wrecked wife. I act as if I am simply a concerned mother. "How did she seem?"

"Like she doesn't care about anything," Ethan says. "Like she's not really there."

I nod and then remember he can't see me. I pause before responding, because I don't want to say, *I told you so*. I will not stoop that low, but it would be nice to hear him say it on my behalf.

"She's Alvy Singer," I say. "The universe is expanding and she doesn't want to do her homework, she doesn't see the point."

"The *point*," Ethan says, "is that she's in high school now. Everything she does counts—it's her permanent record. We can't let her screw this up."

Despite everything, that *we* goes straight to my heart.

"I know," I say softly. "So how do we get her to see that it matters?"

We've faced parenting challenges before, but never have we tried to make a compelling case for the real world. To prove to Indie that despite the expansion of the universe, the impending death of all starlight, the eventual collapse of space-time, and the distinct possibility that humans will destroy Earth trillions of years before any of this happens anyway—that despite all this, there's still a way for her years on this planet to count for something. And *then*, how do we convince Indie that her GPA has anything to do with any of it?

"I'm keeping her phone," Ethan says. "And she does her homework with me. She comes to my classroom at the end of the day and you pick her up after work. That's the plan."

I stare at my phone's screen, like there will be something there to explain Ethan's willful denial. *Your daughter's grief is expanding with the universe*, I want to tell him. *Her grief is so immense, she's lost the ability to believe in anything. Do you remember what that feels like?*

Then I accidentally hit the speakerphone button and can't figure out how to turn it off.

"Got it," I say loudly, because I still don't quite trust speakerphone. *Old person*, Indie would say. "And lights out by eleven."

chapter fifty-nine ✒ **Indie**

The police found the drunk driver twenty minutes after she killed Maddy. She was parked sideways in her driveway, slumped over her steering wheel. She'd hit a neighbor's mailbox as she pulled in. A different neighbor called the police because we live in a small town and that's what neighbors do—they look out for each other. Or at least each other's mailboxes.

Today, that woman was sentenced. She got four years, plus her driver's license revoked. This does not feel like news, or new pain. It's just the same old pain in a different form. Maddy's death makes no sense to me, so why should I expect the woman's punishment to make any sense? Four years is not enough, everyone says. No shit. But this implies there is an upper limit, a number of years that *would* be enough.

This is why Maddy's family believes in God, I guess. Because life on Earth is arbitrary. Pain, suffering, joy, delight—it's all random. But an afterlife for your lost daughter, and an eternity in hell for the woman who killed her? Now *that's* starting to feel a little more fair.

Back in fourth grade, a new girl, a Jehovah's Witness, arrived at our school. This was my introduction to the many things God (at least, her version of him) frowned upon: Halloween parades, Valentine's Day candy hearts, chapter books about talking animals, Mother's Day craft activities, *birthdays*. That last one blew my mind. And the thing was, this girl loved cupcakes. So she came up with a work-around: Every time one of us brought in birthday cupcakes to share, the teacher would save one for later in the day, at which point she would leave it on the girl's desk without a word. A "just because" cupcake was apparently okay, and at the time I thought this was a genius hack. When I told my parents, though, my dad said it seemed to him that any religion with such an obvious loophole was essentially meaningless.

"What's a loophole?" I asked him.

"It's a weakness in a system," he said. "People exploit loopholes when they have no inner sense of right or wrong."

"Jesus, Ethan," Mom said. "We're talking about a little kid here. A kid and a *cupcake*."

"A loophole also used to mean an arrow slit in a castle," Dad said, like he didn't even hear Mom. "An archer could shoot through it with almost no risk of getting shot back at. It was basically a medieval drone attack."

Welcome to my childhood, where magical thinking went to die. Our house was barren land for any kind of belief. When I started middle school, Dad increased the scope of his nihilism lecture series, informing me that all religions, from Anglicanism to Zoroastrianism, are just a way to deal with the terror of death. There is no belief system my father cannot puncture, and no opportunity for a history lecture that passes him by.

So maybe he shouldn't be all that surprised to find himself crashing with the gym teacher. Couples always brag about finding "The One," as if they were fated to find each other. Talk about magical thinking. It's no more rational than believing in angels, when you think about it. Basically, marriage is just one more item on the long list of things my dad no longer believes in. I'm wondering whether his end goal is to believe in nothing. If that's true, then we're not so far apart. Except he'd probably say that believing in nothing is like drinking alcohol or smoking pot—benign when he does it, but dangerous for my "developing brain."

"Indie," Dad says. He raps on my open notebook with his pen. "Focus."

It was his idea to come to All That Java after school. A "study group," he said—homework for me, grading essays for him. I think maybe he just needs a break from the gym teacher's bro jokes. Dad ordered me a hot chocolate with whipped cream on top like I'm five or something.

Maddy and I had planned for this to be our hangout spot in high school. By ninth grade, we figured, we'd be mature enough to like coffee. We were going to ease into the idea by eating coffee ice cream the summer before.

No feeling is final. That's what The Guy said in his latest video. It's from a Rilke poem.

Let everything happen to you: beauty and terror.
Just keep going. No feeling is final.

I watched the video on one of the computers in the school library, then asked the librarian to help me find a book of Rilke's poetry. Carrying the book around in my backpack makes me feel connected to The Guy, imagining him with the same tattered paperback in his back pocket. It feels like a promise from him to me: No feeling is final.

I pick up a pencil and wait for Dad to go back to his own work, then I start writing tiny numbers on the page, zero to nine and back to zero again, like my own version of box breathing. *Just keep going.* A ten-sided shape is called a decagon, I recall. *See,* I want to tell Dad. *I'm doing math.*

chapter sixty **Kate**

I get into my car and a light on the dashboard indicates that I am supposed to do something, but I am not sure what that thing is, or how urgently I am supposed to do it. I dig out the manual from the glove compartment. *Check engine*, that's what the light means. Check it for what, though?

Every day I discover some new household task that was Ethan's responsibility. I am sure the Instant Pot cannot be that complicated, but I never learned how to use it myself, and the thought of googling the instructions is overwhelming. If it were just the Instant Pot, then, fine. But it's also how to check the salt in the water softener; how to clear the gutters; how to use the broiler; how to turn off the smoke alarm without ripping it from the ceiling every time I use the broiler; how to extract the heart from an artichoke.

I know: *artichokes*. But it's not the artichokes I miss—okay, fine, I'll miss the artichokes eventually—it's the shared repository of knowledge and skills. It's the prerogative to be competent in some matters and inept in others. It's having someone else play good cop or bad cop; someone with a full spool when you're at the end of your rope. I remember reading this somewhere, how divorce feels a lot like a death—or maybe it was that divorce feels a lot like dementia? Because there are things you forget, things you lose, things you no longer know how to do, and it's too late—or you're too old or too sad—to get those things back.

I reach over my shoulder for the seatbelt and feel a constriction in my chest. My hands shake as I buckle in. Too much caffeine, I think, although I've barely sipped from my travel mug. I feel Ethan's absence on a cellular level, a state of being as deep and old as the human race. My mate has left me, and a prehistoric alarm system is going off in my body, a rush of cortisol meant to warn me: You are alone in the wilderness.

After I married a schoolteacher, my magazine editor friends in New York seemed confused. "You can do that in the city?" one of them said, like this was a quaint, Midwestern, 1950s career choice. Who did they think taught all the children? It was something I adored about Ethan back then, how little he cared that he was the only schoolteacher at all the publishing parties I took him to. He didn't even mind when people he talked to at these events failed to hide their surprise at how well-read he was, at how he was often the smartest person in the room. And then we moved to the country and I tried and failed to become a freelance writer while raising a baby, and then I tried and failed to get a job at a local newspaper while raising a toddler, until I finally had to admit: Ethan was as at home here as he'd been everywhere else his entire life, and I was just another cidiot with no relevant skills.

The peppy self-help author tells me that old habits and new responsibilities will save me. *Girl, remember what you used to love to do! Girl, find something else to take care of!* Not necessarily a puppy, she clarifies—an orchid will do.

But I am struggling to recall what habits I had before I met Ethan. Because once we got married, he became my old habit. Even the time I spent apart from him was steeped in an awareness that it was time apart from *him.* I do not know how to spend time away from him without thinking of it in this way.

As for those "new responsibilities," from the Instant Pot to the ride-on mower? I'm still waiting for that moment when mastering a household appliance helps me face down the abyss.

chapter sixty-one ✎ **Indie**

"Indie!" Mom shouts from the kitchen. "Indie, are you here?"

I am in the upstairs bathroom, examining my reflection in the mirror. Right before Dad took my phone, I DM-ed The Guy a question about visualization. He'd posted a video suggesting that we imagine a chainsaw cutting off our limbs, one at a time. *Have you ever seen a chainsaw in action?* I wrote to The Guy. *It's hella loud and smells like gasoline. Not exactly a peaceful "letting go" of the tree.* I know this because my dad uses a chainsaw to trim the trees in our yard, and when he cuts into a limb, wood chips go flying and his arms tremble with exertion. *I tried your exercise,* I told The Guy. *But I kept picturing fragments of bone being tossed into the air like microwave popcorn. Tbh, this made me feel pretty attached to my own body.*

I snuck onto my mom's laptop last night while she was sleeping. The Guy wrote back: *New video up today!*

Which is how I ended up in the bathroom after school today, my dad's hair clippers in hand. "Attachments are the cause of suffering," The Guy says in the new video. "Don't just *visualize* letting go. You've got to fucking *do* something. You've got to actually let go." He looked directly at the camera and my heart sped up; it was like he made the video just for me. "Dump your boyfriend. Leave your job. Shave your fucking head if it's your physical appearance you're so attached to."

As I watch my hair fall to the tiled bathroom floor, I give a name to each clump: *vanity, personality, ego, identity.* I am no longer the girl with the cute pixie cut. I watch more hair fall and I think: *pain, suffering*. I think: *Maddy*. I think: *Indie*.

When I am done, my hands get that itchy feeling of wanting to take a selfie. To send The Guy a photo and tell him: *I fucking did something*. Then I remember Dad still has my phone.

Good, I think. I don't need anything, not even a smartphone. (Although, social media does offer daily proof that the self is a sham.) I walk back across the hallway to my bedroom, the floorboards creaking beneath my feet.

"Indie?" Mom says. "Is that you?"

I pull on a hoodie and sit, cross-legged, on my bed. I wait.

"Indie!" Mom calls again. "I know you can hear me!"

"WHAT?"

The word echoes strangely in my newly empty room, and I barely recognize the voice as my own. When I got home this afternoon, I emptied my room of everything I could carry, filling trash bags with clothes, shoes, pillows, blankets, books, photographs, art supplies, an old skateboard, my alarm clock, even a few cactus plants that, it turns out, *can* be killed if you ignore them for long enough. As I raced against the clock—I'd scheduled a Salvation Army pickup and wanted the stuff gone before Mom got home from work—I imagined I was destroying evidence at a crime scene. I carried all my furniture down to the sidewalk: a bookshelf, a nightstand, a desk, a beanbag, even the faux fur spinning desk chair that I'd once loved. *Especially* that, because it was the most damning evidence of my attachment to this world. There is no way my dad could mistake my efforts for minimalism this time. Because I looked up the word *minimalism*, and it's all about framing what's left, to create a "feeling" or "experience" in a room. Last time I cleaned house, I just stripped the walls. This time around, I made sure: Nothing is left. Nothing that would create any kind of feeling. There is no experience of being in this room.

"INDIA!" Mom yells. "Will you please come down to the kitchen so I don't have to yell at you?"

"Is that a promise?" I shout back.

Mom is silent for a moment, apparently confused by my response.

"Is *what* a promise?" Mom says eventually. "Please just get down here so we can have a conversation like normal human beings."

"IF I COME TO THE KITCHEN," I yell, "DO YOU PROMISE NOT TO YELL AT ME?"

Mom is silent again.

"OR JUST TEXT ME!" I add. "Oh, wait, that's right. Dad took my phone."

I hear her stomping up the stairs. She is not a large person; it must take focus and determination to make that much noise.

Buddy comes trotting into my bedroom ahead of Mom and I help him onto my lap. I know Mom intends to make a dramatic entrance, and she will not enjoy being upstaged by the dog in this way.

"You told me you were going for a bike ride with your dad," she says as she crosses the hallway, a little out of breath. "And you told him you were going to a yoga class with me."

"Yep," I say, as she enters my room. "Sounds about right."

It's so easy to lie to your parents when they're basically not speaking to each other.

"So you lied to us both," Mom says, but there's not much conviction in her voice. She's too distracted by my immaculate room: the stripped bed, the missing bookshelf, the empty closet. I even donated the hangers.

I see your decluttering fixation, America, and I raise you. Behold my scorched-earth policy: I don't need *anything*.

"What did you do?" she says. "Where's all your furniture? Where's your stuff? Where are your clothes?"

She narrows her eyes and scans my room like it's an *I Spy* book.

"Where are your throw pillows?" she says.

I mean: Who really needs *throw pillows*? I point to my ears and make a *can't-hear-you* face, though I'm not wearing my earbuds—I no longer own any—and I know she can see this. I rub Buddy's belly and nod my head rhythmically, just to mess with her.

Mom is staring at me now, trying to figure me out. She does this all the time lately, but she has no idea she's looking into blank space. I am not a thing for her to figure out; I am not who she thinks she sees. I am a space for the world.

She frowns and steps toward me, pushes the hood off my head.

"Jesus fucking Christ," she says. "What did you do to yourself?"

"Dad left his clippers behind," I say. "I gave myself a haircut."

"That's not a *haircut*," she says. "You shaved your fucking head!"

"Oops," I say and shrug.

"OOPS?" she yells. Buddy jumps off my lap and cowers in the corner of the room, where my desk used to sit. "That's all you've got to say for yourself? What the *fuck*, Indie?"

Mom never uses the F-word.

"Jeez, Mom," I say. "Will you stop yelling? It's freaking Buddy out."

Mom steps away from me and sinks to the floor. She leans against my bedroom wall and pulls her knees up to her chest. I hear her inhale deeply, and her breath is shuddery.

"Fuck," she says. "Your dad should be here for this. *Fuck*."

Seriously, like, *never*.

"I guess you should have thought of that before you messed with someone else's husband."

I wait for Mom to drop another f-bomb, but she just presses her forehead to her knees. Has she given up already? She used to be a much hardier opponent than this.

"So," I say eventually.

Mom doesn't lift her head. Her hair is frizzy at the nape of her neck, the hair she can't see in the mirror. These flyaways suddenly fill me with sadness. How many hours of her life has she wasted, how many dollars has she thrown at "miracle" hair-smoothing balms, in a losing battle with her frizzy mane? My whole life, she's told me how grateful I should be that I inherited Dad's hair and not hers.

"It's just hair, you know," I say gently. "A bunch of dead cells. Hair grows, we cut it, it grows again. Like weeds. Think of it this way: You don't have to worry about me getting head lice anymore."

Mom finally lifts her head and looks at me. I wonder if she's remembering all the times she combed through my hair, looking for nits. How, every time she did this, she would say, "I do not envy Maddy's mom right now." Maddy with her thick, curly hair, impervious to combs. Maddy and I spent our lives head to head—lying on my bed drawing, sprawled on the couch doing homework, huddled over my phone or hers—and so whenever Mom spotted lice in my hair, she'd buy enough medicated shampoo for two.

"Help me understand," Mom says, and her voice is kind, like she really means it this time. "I want to understand."

I think, what can it hurt, to try one more time. Maybe it would even help her. And now that Dad's not around to lecture us both—about how the Stoics approached misfortune, or how sugar increases anxiety, or whatever else he just learned on a podcast—maybe she'll actually hear me.

I take a deep breath and try to remember how I used to think about the world, back when I still believed in free will, and the concept of a self, and the importance of an Ivy League education. Where should I start? The Guy likes to compare life to a role-playing video game, and Mom once told me she played Mario as a kid. She also played Minecraft with me a handful of times, which I'm sure was some parenting advice she'd read online, about bonding with me in my "natural environment." So maybe the RPG thing will help her, too.

"Look out the window," I begin. "You see a tree, and you assume it's 'real,' that it exists outside of your experience of it, right? But what if it just renders for you when you look, like you're in a video game?"

Mom nods and smiles like I'm a little kid at a talent show. Like this is some lame magic trick she can see right through, a fake plastic thumb or a "disappearing" ball in a vase.

"You need to actually look," I say, pointing to the window. Mom moves her gaze dutifully, but I can tell she's not really seeing.

"It's like, the only thing we can be certain of is our conscious experience," I say. "There's literally no way to tell if anything else is real. I can *remember* a tree, I can *imagine* a tree, or I can look out the window and I can *see* a tree, and they all appear in my consciousness in the same way. It's all just me being aware of a tree. So what's the difference, really? The trees are all made of consciousness. There are quantum physicists who understand it way more than I do, but that's the basic idea. Does that make sense?"

"BUDDY!" Mom yells suddenly, jumping to her feet.

The dog is still in the corner, but now he's squinting. Mom calls it his apology look.

"Tell me that's not real," Mom says, except she sounds like a cartoon character, because she's holding her nose. She pulls a Kleenex out of her pocket and picks up the impressively large and mercifully solid poop. How is it that moms always have Kleenex on hand?

"You honestly think that's a 'rendering' of a dog poop?" Mom adds, still holding her nose. "Because it smells pretty fucking real to me."

"What the eff, Buddy?" I say. "I thought you were house-trained."

I look at Mom to see if she noticed my eff-word. One of us has to be the grown-up around here.

"He's just marking that spot as his territory," Mom says. "In case you don't invite him back to your room anytime soon."

This is how Mom communicates her hurt feelings these days: by assigning them to the dog.

"I don't own the room," I say, but Mom isn't listening. She's already across the hall, depositing Buddy's poop in the toilet and washing her hands. I raise my voice: "I don't own anything."

"Oh my god, Indie," Mom calls out. "Oh my god."

I picture her shuffling through the clumps of my hair on the bathroom floor, the fine strands clinging to her feet like metal filings in one of those Mr. Doodle Face games. Then I remember that I already swept up all my hair and put it in the trash can—because, yeah, I shaved my head and gave away all my belongings, but I'm not a *dick*. Still, though, the bathroom won't be Mom-clean. She's like a forensic scientist.

I rub a hand over my scalp. It feels good, like fine-grain sandpaper, but it doesn't feel like *my* head anymore. Mom must see this, how easy it is to dismantle the idea of me.

"Where were we?" Mom walks back into my room wielding a bottle of Febreze and a paper towel. She's been gone long enough that I know she finished cleaning up my hair, too. I can see a few strands stuck to her knees. "Go ahead," she says as she sprays and wipes my floor clean. "I can listen while I clean up."

"No," I say. "You can't."

I wait until she's done and my room smells like fruity chemicals instead of dog poop.

"Take a seat," I say, which she doesn't find as funny as I do. There are no seats.

She sits on the floor.

"Close your eyes," I say, and she does.

It was perhaps a bit ambitious to introduce Mom to the concept that everything she believes to be real is a hallucination—that what she thinks of as "reality" is just a shared delusion. I decide to try a gentler approach.

"Think about the molecules that make up people and mountains and everything on Earth," I say. "Think about how those molecules came from the stars, billions of years ago."

Mom presses her lips together, and I can tell she's not thinking about stars.

"*Mom*," I say. "The stars. Can you picture them?"

"I'm trying," she says. "It's just—your beautiful hair."

"It's only stuff," I say. "Everything is stuff. We tell stories about the stuff we own to make it seem special, but it's really not. I just have less stuff now, that's all."

"You're *bald*," she says, opening one eye to peek at me. "You look like you're going through chemo."

"So stop looking," I say. "Just *listen*. Think about how we're made up of those ancient molecules. Breathe in through your nose, out through your mouth, and think about how every human in the history of this planet breathed those same molecules. Try to feel it in your bones, how everything is connected, how it's all just one thing. Breathe the molecules in, breathe them out."

Mom closes her eyes and breathes fast and loud, like she's practicing for childbirth.

"What are you *doing*?" I say. "I thought you did yoga? Just breathe normally, Mom."

"But what are people going to say about your hair?" Mom says, her eyes still closed. "I just don't understand why you would—"

"You're sweating what people will *say*? Are you for real right now? Do you have any idea what people are saying about *you*?" Mom opens her eyes and looks at me, her expression a combination of hurt and fear. "You know no one blames the Chief, right? They all just feel sorry for him."

"Oh god," she says, and she squeezes her eyes shut tight again, like she has a migraine. "You're so right. They'll blame me for your hair, too."

"You don't get it," I say. "Who *cares* what they think? I don't care about any of it. The Minkles and their lame Minkle moms and everyone else in this stupid small town whispering behind their hands—they're just dust devils whirling across the desert."

We learned about these storms in sixth grade science. When Maddy and I studied for the quiz together, we compared each type of storm to someone in our grade, to help us remember its attributes. I can't remember who we assigned to the dust devil, but it was definitely one of the Minkles.

"All that drama, it's just hot air and dust," I say. "The storm dies and it becomes part of the desert again."

Mom opens her eyes again, and this time she looks stunned.

"Who said that?"

"Um, me," I say. "I just said it. Like, five seconds ago. Is it so hard to believe I could come up with it myself?"

"I didn't mean it like that," Mom says. "I just—it's lovely. The way you think."

Mom used to read poetry in bed at night. But when I glanced in her room the other day, I noticed a ton of self-help books stacked on the nightstand and spread across Dad's side of the bed. Every single cover featured a photo of the author smiling and shaking out her beachy waves. I guess people like getting advice from women with good hair?

"You've just been reading too much trash lately," I say. "That crap lowers your standards, you know that, right?"

Mom smiles.

"Busted," she says. "Don't tell Dad about my tragic nightstand, or he'll never come home."

She grimaces at her own dumb joke, but I can tell she's scared herself, as if just saying something out loud could make it true. Maddy's dad was superstitious like this. If anyone commented on how long it had been since there was a house fire or car accident in town, he'd gruffly tell them to stop talking. And not in a jokey, knock-on-wood way. He genuinely believed that idle talk could cause houses to burn or cars to collide. All the firefighters did.

"I need you to know," Mom says. "This isn't your problem to fix. This is my work. You need to let me fix it."

Her *work*. I picture my mom building a wall of self-help manuals, stacking them high, assembling a shiny new house out of these bossy, glossy books.

"You don't need to fix anything," I say. "I'm showing you how meaningless everything is when you look closely enough, when you see the particles. It's all just dust and air. Can't you see?"

"I'm sorry," Mom says, tilting her head back. "I'm just really distracted right now. I'm trying to figure out why you'd give away all your clothes. Am I supposed to just replace everything?"

"You don't get it," I say. "I don't need any of that stuff."

"No," she says huffily. "*You* don't get it. You're a privileged white kid who's never had to worry where your next meal is coming from. You think some girl living in a shack in Mumbai would say she has too much stuff? This whole 'protest' of yours—do you have any idea how *lucky* you are?"

"Because of the throw pillows?" I say. "Or because it wasn't me who got hit by the car?"

"Oh god, Indie," Mom says. "No, I would never—that's not what I meant. Not at all."

I don't believe her.

"Also," I say, "white people didn't come up with the idea of giving away their stuff. You do realize the concept dates back a little earlier than the invention of The Container Store, right?"

Mom laughs at this, and I feel the moment slipping through my fingers. Why is it so hard for parents to believe their kids know something they don't?

"Yes, I believe the Buddha and Jesus were both early adopters of the minimalist movement," Mom says. "Look, I get it—this past year made you realize how unimportant our possessions are. I can respect that, I really can. But, sweetie, all this *nothing is real* stuff"—she gestures toward me like she's throwing a frisbee in my direction—"it's a little woo-woo for me."

"It's not *woo-woo*," I snap. "Yoga is woo-woo. Self-help is woo-woo. And so are all those weird teas you bought at the health food store—woo-woo central. *This* is just the way things are."

Mom still has that stupid smile on her face.

"You're not *listening* to me," I say. She's not talking, but there's absolutely nothing quiet about the way she's sitting there. I can hear her thoughts, and it's like a classroom of little kids all raising their hands at once. "Will you just close your eyes and stop talking for five minutes?"

"Fine," Mom says, and she does.

"Okay," I say, but I don't feel like the universe anymore. I feel like a moody teenager.

"Pretend you're an astronaut," I say.

"Got it," Mom says. "I'm Sally Ride."

"Oh my god," I say. "Seriously, Mom? Were you like this in school? Just *listen*."

She nods and does that dorky mom thing where she pretends to lock her lips and throw away the key.

"You can see Earth from your spaceship," I continue. "You know that photo of the Earthrise? Look at Planet Earth, it's blue-green and it's spinning through space like any other planet. See how we're not at the center of anything? We're all just hurtling through space."

The space thing feels a little stoner to me, but I'm grasping for anything that will help Mom let go of this idea that she matters to the planet. To any planet.

"From the spaceship, you can't see cities or buildings or harbors or ships," I tell her. "You can't see anything man-made. You can't see humans. You can't see anything that hasn't always been there."

Mom nods. She opens her mouth to say something but I shush her.

"Now turn away from the planet," I say. "And look out into space. If you never looked back again, you wouldn't know if Earth was still there. You wouldn't know if I was still there."

"I'd know," she says.

"Imagine me gone," I say, ignoring her interruption. "Imagine you gone. Imagine it all gone, everything except the blankness of space."

"No," she says, her eyes flying open. "I can't do that."

"Can't or won't?"

"Both," Mom says. "I can't, I won't, ever imagine you gone."

"You went to *church*," I say. "Why won't you try this?"

I already know the answer, though. She went to church for the Chief.

Mom takes a deep breath.

"Why don't you just tell me about the empty room," she says, looking around.

"I already told you," I say. "I had too much stuff. Everyone has too much stuff. This whole planet is suffocating under a giant pile of useless stuff. Earth wasn't designed to be a life-support system for humans, you know that, right? We're all just creatures in the slime."

Mom suddenly jumps to her feet and sprints toward my closet. She peers inside to the right, to the little nook where I used to store my snow pants in summer and my bathing suits in winter.

"WHERE ARE THE BOXES?" she says, spinning around to face me.

This is classic Mom. I shave my head and give away all my possessions, but what she really cares about is that I threw out my preschool artwork and my grade school projects on the Titanic and Ancient Egypt and the Native Americans.

"Gone," I say.

Gone like the Titanic, gone like Ancient Egypt, gone like the Iroquois longhouses.

"No," Mom says. "You wouldn't do that. Where did you hide them?"

"Trash pickup already happened," I say. "It's Tuesday, remember? You're too late."

"Who told you to do this?" she says after a long silence. "Did you join a cult?"

I can't help it then, I laugh out loud. The idea of The Guy spreading doomsday prophecies or asking us to commit mass suicide—Mom is so far off the mark.

"Where would I go to join a cult in this town?" I say. "The farmer's market? I don't even drive."

I wait for her to make the very valid point that a modern-day guru could just as easily recruit acolytes online, but she doesn't. As an only child, I'm used to my parents being all up in my shit. Did they really confiscate my phone but not bother to check my browser history?

"I know it would be very convenient for you," I continue. "If there was a guru you could blame."

This isn't technically a lie. He's not a *guru*-guru. It's not like he lives in an ashram or anything.

"Nothing about this is convenient," she says. "I'm just trying to understand."

"You mentioned that," I say. "But I really don't see you trying that hard."

Mom puts her face in her hands and massages her forehead, like I'm some exasperating toddler.

"I'm going downstairs to call your father," she says, standing up. "And then we can talk."

"Great," I say, giving her a cheery thumbs-up. "Can't wait!"
Mom turns back to face me, one arm on the doorframe.
"I just don't know what you want from me," she says.
"Nothing," I say. "I want nothing."

chapter sixty-two ❦ **Kate**

"Maybe this could be a good thing," Sara says to me, like there's an obvious life hack I'm missing. "If you and Ethan separate, you'll get so much time off."

As if my entire life were just a job I do to get by.

"All those things you've been wanting to do for years," Sara says. "Writing a novel or whatever. Taking *If You Lived Here* to the next level. Becoming a yoga instructor. You'll have the time. Who gets that?"

There was a period of my life, during Indie's infancy, when a weekend off would have sounded like bliss. Like a "good thing," sure, why not? I used to fantasize about contracting a highly contagious but not fatal illness that would require me to spend a few nights—okay, the original fantasy was two weeks—in the hospital, so Indie would be forced to take a bottle from Ethan, and maybe even learn how to sleep through the night. But now that Indie barely acknowledges me, a weekend off is simply an opportunity to imagine how much better Ethan is handling things.

"No one gets that," I say dutifully.

How many times over the years did I tell myself to cherish the moments when my daughter needed me most? I cannot count the nights I lay in bed, regret coursing through me for the tiny, missed moments that day. *Tomorrow*, I would swear. Tomorrow I will sit and play with her instead of tidying the room around her.

I remember an afternoon when Indie asked me to sled with her in the backyard, and I said she'd have just as much fun without me. I said this not because it was true, although perhaps it was, but because I'd been craving some alone time. *If You Lived Here* was just starting to gain traction, and I wanted to reply to my reader comments. When Indie came inside an hour later, cheeks red and eyes shining, I made her hot cocoa and silently vowed to join her the next time it snowed.

I'm not sure I ever did.

And then one day I woke to a daughter who would excuse herself from the dinner table or family movie night because "Maddy really needs me right now." One time after she said this, I found Indie in her room, playing Minecraft on her iPad.

"I thought you said Maddy really needed you?"

"She does need me," Indie said, using her new, you-couldn't-possibly-understand voice. "She's super bored right now, so I joined her Realm."

I think of the hours I spent chatting back and forth with my readers while Indie played chess on her phone in the next room. The field trips I didn't chaperone, the books I insisted she read herself ("so you'll learn new words"), the kid's birthday party invite that said, *feel free to drop off or stay*, and how greedily I claimed the afternoon to myself. The way I could only truly listen to Indie tell me about her day when I was simultaneously unloading the dishwasher or folding laundry. All the parenting moments I treated like hours to slog through, as if I were punching a time card.

And then I think of Laura, and how no one told her how much time she had left. No one told her what percentage of the whole each snowy day represented. If we knew these percentages, if every moment were presented to us as a fraction of the whole, would we do anything differently? It's a cheap question, of course, because a good mother shouldn't need to calculate the odds in order to pay attention to her child. *Pay attention*, we tell children in school, as if it were as basic a skill as holding a pencil or cutting with scissors. As if the adults on this planet were any kind of experts at all.

"I secretly love the weeks when Tim's out of town," Sara says. "You could have cereal for dinner, that's what I do. It takes thirty seconds to pour a bowl, and then I have the whole evening to myself."

I smile and nod.

"I mean it," Sara says. "This could be good for you."

Sara's husband retired early from the finance world and now he gets paid stupid money to attend occasional board meetings in various cities across the country. He has thick salt-and-pepper hair that he pomades into Patrick Dempsey waves. Their sons are both in college (Cornell and Vanderbilt), and neither child suffered more than a grazed knee in childhood, so far as I know. *That's* what a good thing looks like, I want to say.

"Lucky me," I say instead.

"Yeah," Sara says. "Lucky bitch!"

We both smile like this isn't the saddest conversation in the world. It occurs to me then that Sara's husband makes his own keto ketchup, and they both put coconut oil in their coffee. There is no way they even keep cereal in the house. ("The cardboard box has more nutrition in it," Ethan told Indie once, when she asked how come she couldn't have Frosted Flakes for breakfast like Maddy and her sisters did.) Is this how Sara means to help me, by pretending she's the kind of woman who self-comforts with Cinnamon Toast Crunch?

"Indie and I had a huge fight last night," I blurt out, because I want her to know the truth. "She shaved her head and gave away all her possessions. That's how she put it, her *possessions*. I guess she's into this whole ascetic non-possession thing, although I'm not quite sure where the sacrifice is when you live with your parents and they pay for everything. So I told her she's a privileged white kid."

I watch Sara force a neutral expression onto her face, and I see the hesitation. Maybe I'm a bad mother, she's thinking. Maybe I should get *all* the weekends off.

"Wait," Sara says, confused. "Did you say she shaved her head?"

"I mean, she buzzed it," I clarify, as if this made me a better mother. "She used Ethan's clippers."

I gave up a beloved possession once, in high school—my only Benetton sweater, purchased with my babysitting savings—but this had nothing to do with asceticism. Two girls had smirked as they passed me in the hallway that day, and the only reasonable explanation I could come up with was my outfit. Was the sweater too big? Too green? Benetton had always seemed like a sure thing to me. I left it in my locker that day, then dumped it in the school's lost and found at the end of the year.

I would never be able to explain this feeling to Indie, because she exists on a higher plane. She knows the things we desire will fail to comfort us, and she knows this is especially true of the things we hold the closest. Even if I'd rescued every drawing she made, every scrap of paper she daubed with finger paint, this fact would not change: Opening these boxes and remembering how she used to be would break my heart.

"Is Indie okay?" Sara says, and I can't tell if there is genuine care in her question, or if this a prompt, reminding me how to be a good mother. Good mothers don't care about *stuff*. "I mean, I know she's not, obviously. But this sounds like—"

Sara pauses, as if she's looking for the right word, or considering whether or not to say the word she's thinking of. I wish she'd say something, though, because I want to know: What is it that my daughter is doing? What *does* it sound like?

"I think I just wanted her to be a normal kid for one night," I say eventually, when it becomes clear Sara is not going to find the word. "I wanted us to have a normal fight, you know? I wanted to be one of those parents who tells their kid she's lucky to have a roof over her head. I wanted to say this and not have it be about Maddy."

"Lucky to have broccoli on her plate," Sara says wryly. "Been there."

I used to daydream about what I would give for one more day when Indie really needed me. I'm talking deep need: tears streaming down her face, arms reaching up to me, heart broken at the unfairness of the world. What would I allow my daughter to suffer in order for me to experience that need again?

But now I know: It couldn't possibly be worth it. Because when your child is fourteen, heartbreak does not look like arms reaching for you, begging to be held. It looks like a turned back, a slammed door, and you, on the other side, begging to be let in. Should a good mother shoulder her way into that room? My own mother would have said yes, I think, but then again, she loved the feeling of being necessary, so long as it was on her terms. And perhaps *this* is what it means to be a mother: to force yourself to stand down when your child cannot bear the idea of needing you. To just stop knocking. To sit at the kitchen island and wait for your daughter to need you again.

Tomorrow, I tell myself. Tomorrow, tomorrow, tomorrow.

"Are you free tonight?" Sara says. She's looking at her phone now, typing a text while she talks. "I'm playing pickleball later if you want to join. There's a group of us and we rotate in."

I stretch my eyes wide so I won't cry and then open a browser on my desktop and pretend to read an email. *Pickleball?* I think. I tell you my daughter shaved her head and you want me to play pickleball?

"Maybe another time," I say. "But thanks for the offer."

chapter sixty-three ❦ Indie

A week from Friday will be my fifteenth birthday, a.k.a. another excuse for capitalists to sell dumb shit. Heart-shaped locket necklaces and Mylar balloons that end up in the Great Pacific Garbage Patch, where they look just like delicious jellyfish to the poor sea creatures who ingest them. How many sea turtles have to die so the youth of America can celebrate another year on this planet?

A fifteen-year-old in New York State can't drive, can't vote, can't consent to sex, can't drop out of school, can't emancipate herself. A fifteen-year-old can't even buy her own ticket to an R-rated movie. What a sham. Still, my parents won't stop asking how I want to celebrate. They've always been big on birthdays. Dad says it's because birthdays are one of the few holidays that celebrate something that actually happened. You know, with evidence. But if you ask me, birthdays are just one more way we try to trick ourselves into thinking our lives have meaning. Squirrels don't throw birthday parties, even bonobos don't blow out candles on a cake, so we must be special. Right? Wrong. Six months ago today, Maddy was killed on her fourteenth birthday. How "festive" is that? Bet you can't find a Mylar balloon that says "Happy Hit-and-Run Half-Birthday!"

Maddy and I always celebrated each other's half-birthdays with half-cupcakes from the French bakery in town. We'd end up with a whole cupcake each—we just liked the ritual of halving the cupcakes and sharing them. Mom said this sounded like a flimsy excuse to eat cake, but what makes a half-birthday any more random than a birthday?

When I come downstairs to pack a lunch before school, both my parents are waiting for me in the kitchen.

"What is this?" I say, hovering in the doorway. "A family reunion? You should've told me, I'd have brought chips and dip."

"Mom wants to talk about your birthday," Dad says.

He reaches down to rub Buddy's head, though we both know he's not that into "Mom's dog," which is what he called Buddy even before he moved out. I know what's really going on: Ever since I shaved my head, he's had trouble making eye contact with me.

"*We* want to talk about your birthday," Mom says. "It's less than two weeks away."

"I'm aware of that," I say. "Thank you."

"Take a seat, kiddo," Dad says, and smiles. "Please?"

Buddy starts whining at his feet, and apparently Dad's interest in the dog has already peaked, because he crosses the room to open the back door and let Buddy out.

"Oh my god," I say, mock-palming my forehead. "This isn't a reunion, it's an intervention!"

I don't sit down because then I'll be trapped. I know how an intervention works. "I'm right, aren't I?" I say. "It's a birthday intervention?"

Dad looks at Mom meaningfully, and I think he genuinely believes I won't notice. It's one of those looks that could mean, *I told you so,* or maybe, *We told each other so*. Either way, why? It's like adults find talking to kids so dull that they have to layer a silent conversation on top, just to keep things interesting.

"I'm literally *right here*, Dad," I say. "I can see you."

"I know you think you don't deserve another birthday," Mom says. "But Maddy would want you to celebrate."

I'm glad I'm still standing. It's easier to count my breaths here in the doorway. I can fill my lungs. I turn away from my parents to look out the kitchen window and I see Buddy literally *frolicking* in the yard. It's like he's auditioning for a dog food commercial.

"I realize you gave birth to me," I say, keeping my gaze on Buddy. "So if you really feel the need to celebrate, then go right ahead. Just don't expect me to show up."

"I know Maddy," Mom says. "She would have wanted you to celebrate, even if she couldn't be here."

"Stop making this about Maddy," I say. "I just don't believe in birthdays. What's the big deal? You guys don't believe in Easter. Same thing."

Dad used to call Easter the "Zombie Jesus holiday," and Mom would always add that this was a private family joke, and I shouldn't share it with anyone else. The only major commercial holiday Dad really approves of is Halloween. He used to dress up every year to take me trick-or-treating, even though I told him none of the other adults dressed up, and none of the kids knew who Ruth Bader Ginsburg was anyway.

"Maddy loved birthdays," Mom says now, apparently suffering a sudden attack of selective hearing. "Remember those purple velvet cupcakes she made you last year? What did she call them again?"

Maddy called them *gothcakes*, and I'm sure Mom remembers this. It's that lame thing parents do to little kids, where they try to trick them out of a bad mood by getting them to talk. They pretend they can't remember something and they need the child's help jogging their memory, or they say something blatantly false that requires an immediate correction. *Cats go woof and pigs go moo! You're too young to have real feelings that people take seriously!*

"You don't know what Maddy would have wanted," I say. "You didn't even like her."

"What are you talking about?" Mom says. "I *loved* Maddy! We all did."

"You thought she was small-town," I say.

This was a guess, but I can tell by Mom's frozen expression that I've hit on something. It feels good, or at least, it feels like *something*, so I press harder.

"Funny," I add. "That didn't stop you from going after her dad."

"Indie," Dad says, before Mom can say something gross about how it wasn't even a tongue kiss. "Let's not go there today, okay, kiddo?"

What's up with all this *kiddo* shit today? That's what the elementary school principal used to call everyone in the hallway, because he could never remember any of our names.

Dad rubs his face irritably, like his beard is an itchy sweater on a hot day.

"I don't know where this is coming from," Mom says, her voice breaking.

Great, here come the tears.

"I *loved* Maddy," Mom says. "She was part of our family."

"She *had* a family," I say. "She was your charity project."

I'm on a roll now. I can't stop.

"You were so proud that time you introduced her to kohlrabi, remember? *Kohlrabi*. Like that made you a better person."

"Stop," Mom sobs. "Please. I just want to throw you a birthday party."

"Only so you can write about it online," I say. "Can't you just, like, post a photo of some apple cider donuts instead?"

Dad laughs at this, but it's a joyless sound, like a cross between a belch and a sneeze. Mom glares at him, and—no joke—he says, "Excuse me." Are these people for real?

Ha. Of course they're not for real. Check me out with the existential pun.

"Do you think Maddy would understand what you're going through right now?" Dad says, I guess to prove he's one of the adults in the room, despite the laugh-burp. "What if you imagined telling her how you feel? Can you imagine what she'd say back?"

"You're still here?" I say to him.

I turn to Mom.

"You didn't even like her *name*," I say, and I hate that my voice quavers.

"You can change your name," Mom says. "I don't care. You think I'd love you any less if you were Kaylee or Kylie or Krista or whoever you want to be?"

"OH MY GOD MOM," I say. "Do you even hear yourself? No wonder everyone in this town hates you. I'll tell you what my birthday wish is. I want to get on a plane and fly around the planet in reverse. I want to cross time zones so fast the day never comes."

"Indie," Dad says softly, and he tries to reach for my hand. I yank it away like we're playing slapjack. He never could beat me at that game.

"I know you think I'm not old enough to mean what I say, or to know my own mind. So let me be 100 percent clear: This is not teen code for *please just throw me a surprise party*. And I don't secretly need a hug, either. I don't secretly wish for anything. Are we clear?"

Later that night, Mom crawls into my bed and curls her body behind me. This is how we used to make up after a fight: She would stroke my hair while we talked, or, if I was still mad, I would fake sleep and she would lie there, breathing softly, until I fell asleep for real. Either way, we would be friends again by breakfast.

Now, she puts a hand on my shaved head and pats it awkwardly, then stops. I hear her take an unsteady breath, and maybe she's crying, or maybe she's about to say something.

"Can you please just leave?" I say, and she does.

chapter sixty-four ❦ **Kate**

As the supermarket cashier scans my groceries, she tosses them carelessly into the bagging area, the heavy bottle of detergent crushing the avocados and peaches that tumble toward me like bowling balls. She glances up at me as she does this, as if she's daring me to even consider being irritated at something as petty as bruised fruit. It's hard to believe there was a time when my greatest concern in this grocery store was being judged for the contents of my cart, for being known as the woman who spent four dollars on a single, organic avocado.

Everyone loves Kevin and Laura in this town. Everyone loves Ethan, too, because he's their kids' favorite teacher—even the kids who only like gym. The last time Ethan chaperoned prom, students posted videos of him dancing to "Ice Ice Baby." *Oh shit*, one kid wrote, *Mr. C has moves*. And every Friday, Ethan hangs out at "teachers' happy hour": two-for-one beer and wings from 3 to 5 p.m. at the place where everybody knows your name.

Who would believe the woman who screwed with two of this town's most beloved men? I never stood a chance.

This is nothing, I want to tell the cashier. I am the mother of a fourteen-year-old girl who has said everything you've posted online and worse; if you want to hurt me, you've got to come at me a whole lot harder. Except, it doesn't work like that. My daughter has not given me thick skin, she has flayed me.

"I'm sure you were just imagining it," Sara says when I call from the car to tell her about the cashier.

Only then does it occur to me that Sara and I never talk on the phone unless it's about work. To her credit, she acts like this is totally normal.

"Yeah," I say. "You're probably right. I'm just imagining it."

"I don't think the women who work at Tops can even afford to live here anymore."

Something else they can blame me for, I think.

I lug the groceries in from the car. Ethan hasn't been home in weeks, but I continue to feel aggrieved at being stuck with this task. I shop and he unloads—that was always our deal.

"Indie!" I yell up the stairs. "Want to go to Lenahan and Lopez for dinner?"

Lenahan and Lopez is the local Irish-Mexican family restaurant, serving both corned beef and burritos, plus chicken Alfredo, because every restaurant in town seems to serve chicken Alfredo. "It's like a joke with a built-in punchline," Ethan said when Lenahan and Lopez first opened. We assumed the restaurant would be closed within months, which shows exactly how little we understood this town.

I am about to climb the stairs when Indie finally replies.

"I'm not hungry," she says firmly, like she can sense my foot on the bottom step. "And I'm vegan, remember?"

I make myself a bowl of Grape-Nuts for dinner and open a bottle of room-temperature sauvignon blanc. I don't bother with ice. I google myself to see if anyone's talking about the dissolution of *If You Lived Here*, but of course they're not. The internet at large has already moved on. And those people I thought of as my "friends"? I don't even know their real names. I refill my glass and pull up the local parenting group, which is surprisingly easy, given that I could swear I'd deleted my account. I skim posts about secondhand furniture for sale, the drama at the recent school board meeting, and other women's daughters dressed up for the homecoming dance. I even read the posts about which late-season apples are still available at the pick-your-own orchard, despite the recent "heavy picking volume" (the implication being, of course, that cidiots ransacked the place). If there's a better way to assault oneself fully, mind, body, and soul, I do not know it. I open a second bottle and keep scrolling.

At midnight I knock gently on Indie's door and whisper goodnight. She does not reply and I do not open the door, because I am too drunk to pretend I'm not. Indie used to take all school seriously, even health class, and after making a Google slideshow about alcohol back in seventh grade, she concluded that anything more than a glass at a time was "problem drinking." I do not want to be her problem right now.

I wake at 3 a.m., parched and confused and fully clothed. I stumble downstairs to let Buddy out to pee, and that's when I realize why he woke me: the sounds of distress coming from the chicken coop. The coop I forgot to close before I went to bed drunk, because closing the coop was always Ethan's job.

I read somewhere that foxes engage in "surplus killing" when they hunt, and I know we have foxes in the neighborhood because we see the kits appear every spring. One magical year, three fox kits ambled onto our front porch as Indie and I watched through the transom window, hands on our faces in silent wonder. But I'd never really thought about what surplus killing would look like in practice. What it looks like is this: Three chicken carcasses in the coop, and a trail of bloody feathers and chicken parts leading out of the yard and into the dense wooded area across the street. It looks like a *Law and Order* crime scene.

As I step into the backyard, I reach for Buddy, but he is no longer by my side. He is next to the coop, nose in the grass, chicken blood and feathers around his mouth.

"BUDDY!" I scream, but he can't hear me, because he is not my pet in this moment, and he does not answer to humans.

The guy at the pet supplies store warned me not to feed Buddy any chicken-flavored dog food, so I bought only salmon and beef. He said this would help Buddy think of the chickens as his pack, rather than his dinner. I guess that plan works until it doesn't.

I hear a noise behind me and turn to see a bleary-eyed Indie standing in the open kitchen doorway. As she steps onto the back porch, the motion-sensor security light turns on, and her shaved head glints like a beacon in the night. We make eye contact, and she shrugs.

"Nature's only cruel when you pick a side," she says.

In a moment she is gone again, and I am left standing under the too-bright light, like a vanquished loser in an Elizabethan tragedy. *All my pretty ones? Did you say all? O hell-kite! All? What, all my pretty chickens and their dam at one fell swoop?*

The rumor mill is right: I am unfit. I can't even take care of a few dumb birds.

chapter sixty-five **Indie**

I find Mom in the kitchen, her eyes wild and her hair wilder. I'm guessing she's been up since the chicken massacre. Buddy is snoring in his doggy bed like a hungover bro the morning after a frat party.

"You're not going to school today," Mom says.

"What are you talking about?"

"You didn't eat dinner last night," she says. "And you need to help me clean up the coop. You're not going anywhere."

"You're not making any sense," I say. "Those things don't even go together. Why don't you go back to bed? Also, you can't stop me from going to school. That's against the law."

Mom's trying to make coffee but she can't seem to get the grinder to turn on. She stares at the whole beans in the plastic hopper like she can will them into a latte.

"You can't leave," she says, still eyeing the grinder. "You need to stay here with me until I know you're okay."

There's a box of Grape-Nuts on the table, so I pour some into a bowl. I make a big show of slicing a banana on top.

"Most important meal of the day!" I say, and give her a fake cereal-commercial smile. I lean against the counter and eat my breakfast standing up.

"I'm scared," she says. "I'm scared how this ends."

"I'm eating *Grape-Nuts*," I say. "It's hardly Froot Loops. I think I'll be okay."

She abandons the coffee station and turns on the kettle instead.

"I don't think this is an herbal tea kind of day," I say.

"I used to believe in heaven," Mom says, and now she is literally watching the pot boil. "I thought it was an actual place, although I kept changing my mind about what it looked like there. Kind of like rearranging the furniture in my bedroom, you know? One time, I decided that everyone in heaven was on horseback."

"The *National Velvet* years?" I say, and Mom turns to me, smiling a little.

"It was a place I could go to in my head," she says. "A made-up place I could decorate any way I liked. A place where nothing else mattered. Not acne, not mean girls, not death, not even my mom."

"That's nice for you," I say. "But I'm not you. I don't believe in anything."

"But you *do*," she says.

"I believe in *nothing*," I say. "You're the one who believed in a place made of cotton candy."

"You made up a place where no one exists," Mom says. "Because it's easier for you to imagine the loss of eight billion strangers than it is for you to believe that Maddy is gone. What terrifies me is that I think you're trying to find this place you made up."

"I DIDN'T MAKE ANYTHING UP!" I yell. "I figured out that nothing is real. Just because you don't get it doesn't make it any less true." I point to my head and tap hard with my index finger. "There's no one in here. YOU made ME up. You're the one inventing everything."

"I found a place," Mom says, so quietly it's like she's talking to herself. She's back to watching the kettle. "It's less than an hour away. I watched a video tour this morning and it looks amazing. You'll get to spend time in nature, take care of the animals, do yoga. You can draw there, too. It would only be for a few weeks—"

"What the *fuck*, Mom?" I yell. "You're seriously going to lock me up right now? What the fuck, what the fuck, what the FUCK?"

On the last *fuck*, I throw my cereal bowl into the sink from halfway across the room and it breaks apart, splashing leftover milk all over the countertop and cabinets.

I turn around to see what Mom will say about the broken bowl and all the *fucks*, and she is suddenly *right there*, standing in front of me, her toes almost touching mine. I see her raise her hand, and it feels like slow motion, the way she lifts it toward my face, and I have time to think two things at once as I watch her hand move through the air: The first thing is, *This is what it feels like to be a fly, to watch everything happen so slowly it's like you can predict the future*. The second thing is: *She's going to slap me.*

Except, she doesn't slap me. She cups her hand around my cheek instead.

"It's not that kind of place," she says softly. "It's more like a retreat. And they can help you. I'm trying, Indie, but I don't know what to do anymore. And I can't stand to see you like this."

"So you want to send me away?" I say, stepping away from her hand. "*That's* your solution? If this is you trying to help, then I need you to stop. I need you to stop trying to be my mom."

I hear the lumbering engine of the school bus as it rounds the corner of our street, the ancient squeak of brakes as it pulls up outside our house. I grab my backpack and sprint for the door.

chapter sixty-six Kate

"Please tell me you didn't try to have our daughter committed this morning," Ethan says the moment I pick up.

"It was just a *suggestion*," I say. "I was never going to force her to do anything."

"Bullshit," Ethan says. "Also, did it not at any point occur to you that maybe you should consult me before having our daughter locked up? Jesus Christ, Kate. What were you thinking?"

"I didn't even contact this place yet," I say. "Of course you were going to be part of the conversation."

Ethan makes a crazy sound, like he's trying to lift a heavy piece of furniture.

"Indie is *terrified*," he says. "Do you realize that? She doesn't want to go home in case there's a white van waiting for her in the driveway."

"It's not what you think," I say. "They do yoga there, they have therapy lambs. It's hardly *One Flew Over the Cuckoo's Nest*."

"Well, that's a big fucking relief," Ethan hisses, and I wonder if he's hiding in the supply closet at school so no one can hear him. "I'm so glad to hear that you ruled out electroshock therapy for our fourteen-year-old daughter who is just horrifically fucking *sad*."

I glance at the clock on the microwave. Homeroom is almost over; his students will be walking in any moment.

"*Ethan*," I say firmly. "I think she's having a psychotic break. She's lost touch with reality, and I don't know why you can't see that. Will you please just check out the website? I'm sending you the link now. I think Indie will agree to go if *you* tell her it's okay. She trusts you on this stuff."

"She trusts me because I'm not trying to have her committed," Ethan says.

"You don't—"

"I have to go," he says, his voice neutral now, and I can hear students in the background. "Indie's having dinner with me tonight."

"But I already prepped something in the slow cooker," I say pathetically, as if butter chicken meant a thing in a world where my teenage daughter ran away from me this morning. Not that it matters either way; Ethan has already hung up.

A few seconds later, my phone chirps merrily.

You ever try anything like this again, Ethan texts. *I will fight you for full custody.*

I click my phone off and stare out the kitchen window at the feathers strewn across the yard. Ethan has finally found the right time: *Now* is when the good dad gets to leave.

Ethan drops Indie home at ten that night. He texts me from the car: *She's coming inside to sleep, but she doesn't want to talk.*

Indie walks into the kitchen, drops a tiny wooden spoon and plastic tub into the trash, and leaves the room without a word. When I hear her bedroom door close above me, I cross the kitchen and step on the trash can pedal to confirm what I already know: Ethan, the good dad, took his daughter out for an ice cream sundae.

I wake in the morning to the sound of the school bus pulling away, but I sprint downstairs anyway, as if it would mean something to Indie that I tried to catch her. I stare at my phone dumbly. The alarm is vibrating the phone in my hand. It's been trilling for an hour, and I slept through the whole thing, my body claiming its sleep debt after the bloodletting in our coop. As if this were any kind of excuse. A good mother wouldn't need an alarm on a morning like this, and she certainly wouldn't sleep right through it.

chapter sixty-seven **Indie**

I find a seat on the bus. Hands on my knees, I breathe. In, hold it, out, hold it. Repeat. Again. And again. I keep going until I feel calm. *Fucking do something*, I think, and then I have to start my slow breathing all over again.

It doesn't matter what they say about me at school. "I" am just a story they tell each other, and they can tell it however the fuck they want. It's still fiction. These storytellers are boys who call each other *retard* when no adults are listening; who know the number sixty-nine is funny but don't know why; who think bike helmets and diet soda are *gay*. They are girls who hug every single time they pass each other in the hallway, as if forty years had passed and not forty minutes; who worry about seeming *basic* and dream of becoming internet-famous; who let the boys decide who's prettiest and what's cool. All of them, the boys and the girls and the teachers alike, the lunch ladies, too, and my own parents most of all, they are drowning in the rushing river of their own thoughts.

"Asher," I say, leaning forward in my seat and tapping him on the shoulder.

He pulls out his earbuds and turns around to face me.

"Can I borrow your phone for a second?" I say. "My parents confiscated mine."

Instead of handing me his phone over the back of the seat, Asher stands and relocates to the seat next to mine, holding up both hands in apology as the school bus driver yells something unintelligible in our direction.

"Here you go," he says as he takes a seat. "All yours."

"Thanks."

I scooch closer to the window. I'm not used to someone else's body being near mine. In the hallways at school I have learned to shrink into the wall so no one brushes my shoulder or bumps my backpack. When I do this, it's easy to remember that my physicality is just an illusion: Look how they fail to notice me when I'm not in their way.

"Is it because of your hair?" Asher says.

"Huh?" I type something into his phone.

"Is that why they took your phone?"

"Hmm," I say distractedly. "Kinda."

I can sense his eyes on the phone's screen, although he's pretending not to look at what I'm doing. Fair enough, I suppose. His phone.

"I like your hair," Asher says. "Or, you know, your head. You look like Charlize Theron in *Mad Max*."

"My parents freaked," I say. "My dad said I looked like an extra in a Holocaust movie."

Asher laughs, and I feel suddenly, oddly, protective of my dad. I don't know why I let that slip. Actually, I do know. Asher compared me to Charlize Theron, and my brain short-circuited.

"Don't tell anyone I said that. He was really upset about my hair, that's all. He's not someone who makes Holocaust jokes or anything. He's super, you know, evolved."

"It's cool," Asher says. "I know who your dad is. He's cool."

"Yeah, well, he likes to think so."

He didn't try to have me committed, I think. So there's that.

"What about your mom?"

For one brief, idiotic moment I consider telling Asher what my mom tried to do, and then I remember: We aren't friends. It's been so long since I shared something personal with anyone, I've forgotten how this works.

"Hard pass," I say.

"Sorry," Asher says, and I think maybe he's blushing. "I forgot, I'm such an asshole. We can talk about something else. Or not."

My breath catches, and I know why. I'm getting that familiar feeling of wanting a good moment to last forever, but also wanting it to end quickly so I can text Maddy and tell her that it happened. This is magical thinking, I remind myself: There is no such thing as a moment in time.

"Sure," I say. "We can talk about something else."

"Can we talk about the guy you just looked up?"

"He's a meditation expert," I say. "Like, a meditation guru, I guess. He's really good."

"Okay," Asher says. "And you had a meditation emergency this morning, that's why you needed my phone?"

"Have you met my life?" I say. "I'm kind of in emergency mode right now."

"He doesn't look like a guru," Asher says, leaning in to look at the phone. "He looks more like a tech bro. And he's smoking a cigar!"

Okay, so here's the thing: I tried the Burmese monks in robes and the yogi influencers in Lululemon; I tried the poet-philosophers and the astrophysicist-philosophers and the podcasters in button-down shirts who brandish their advanced degrees like a bishop's crook—but none of them has the answers I'm looking for. So why *not* a guy in Jordans who likes expensive cigars? Who's to say one is closer to spiritual awakening than the other? I'm not looking for a messiah. I don't believe in that crap. The Guy is *human*, and most humans suck. He just happens to be the one human on this planet who gets it.

"What do you think gurus are supposed to look like?" I say to Asher.

"Not like this," Asher says. "I mean, he's wearing a backwards baseball cap. Also, check out his watch."

He reaches over to his phone that I am still holding and zooms in on a photo. *Maddy*, I think, before I can stop myself. *You should have seen me and Asher on the bus this morning! He did that cute half-smile thing, and then his hand totally brushed against mine.*

"That's a $30,000 diving watch."

"How can you tell?" I say. "Are you an Elon Musk fanboy or something?"

"My dad's kind of a tech bro," Asher says, grimacing. "He's always showing me pictures of the next watch he wants to buy. I don't get the watch thing. He has a phone, you know?"

I float above myself and look down and I see a girl in a body, and she is *flirting* with a boy. I think, *there is more than one way to be trapped on the ocean floor*. There is kelp around your ankles, but also there is your brain's ability to hallucinate, to see a merman swimming by. *Follow me*, the merman says. *And we'll live at the bottom of the ocean, happily ever after.*

Mom made me and Maddy watch the movie *Splash* one summer as part of her eighties film curriculum. Maddy loved the idea that a mermaid invented her name, Madison, while clothes shopping in Manhattan. I was the only one who found the ending a little creepy.

"What is this guy, twenty-two?" Asher swipes through a few more photos while I sit, frozen in place. I stare at my hand and wonder if I'm holding the phone in a weird way. Asher is so close, I'm sure he can hear my heart beating, rabbit-fast, like it's about to break a rib. "He obviously goes to the gym, like, a lot."

"He's twenty-five," I say. "And I think he just does a lot of yoga."

Asher laughs again, and I realize I've found the secret to talking to cute guys: Investigate the nature of consciousness and reject the idea of objective reality. I wonder if *Teen Vogue* would be interested in an article on the topic. "How to Stop Believing in a Dualistic Universe and Win Over the Guy of Your Dreams in 10 Easy Steps!"

“Trust me,” Asher says. “I’m a guy. That dude lifts weights.”

“Fine,” I say. “He’s a dude who likes to meditate *and* lift weights.”

“And he *really* likes to take selfies with hotties,” Asher says, swiping through more photos.

I give Asher a look.

“I was being ironic,” he says. “I meant, ‘hotties’ in air quotes.”

“You forgot the air quotes.”

“If I used actual air quotes, you’d never talk to me again.”

I look out the bus window to hide my smile. I wonder if a school bus driver has ever taken a wrong turn and driven all the way to Canada by mistake.

“For real,” Asher says. “What’s your deal with this guy? Do you have a crush on him or something?”

“No! God, no. I’m not a groupie. Ew.”

I’m suddenly embarrassed by The Guy’s piercing blue eyes and his blond hair that’s just the right amount of messy.

“So, what then?”

“Here,” I say, taking over the phone again. “I’ll show you.”

I scroll through the videos in The Guy’s feed, trying to find the perfect one. I skip past “Letting Go of Attachments,” because I don’t think Asher is ready for the *fuck your relationships* mantra. Also, he probably thinks gurus shouldn’t swear. Ditto the video where The Guy mentions the asteroid NASA is supposedly covering up because it’s a secret hideout for alien spies. At this point, I’ve gotten used to wading through The Guy’s nutty conspiracy theories to get to the good stuff, but I don’t trust Asher to do the same. Not after the fake moon landing shit he pulled last year. Finally, I click on a recent upload, a video where The Guy lays into scientists who miss the whole point of consciousness.

Asher hands one earbud to me so we can listen together. I don’t tell him I could quote this video verbatim because *holy shit we are sharing earbuds.*

"If perception is *dependent* on consciousness," The Guy intones, "then how can any scientific instrument possibly allow us to *observe* consciousness? We have no proof that this external world of objects and instruments actually exists. So the scientists are the ones with blind faith, if you ask me."

I turn to Asher to watch his reaction. He's doing that squinty nod thing I recognize from school, when he hasn't done the assigned reading but doesn't want the teacher to know.

"It gets better," I say, suddenly aware of how much lingo The Guy is throwing around. The awareness of awareness, the noetic quality of an experience, non-dual states, equanimity, centerless vision, cellular transformation, self-actualization, transcendence. So much for me being Charlize Theron in *Mad Max.* It's a whole lot easier to seem like a badass when you keep your mouth shut.

And then the bus is pulling into school and Asher is tugging his backpack on and I feel the moment slipping away.

"He's speaking in the city tonight," I say to the back of Asher's head. I am behind him in the center aisle of the bus, and I can see his phone in his hand; he's already swiped back to Spotify. "Near Union Square."

"Cool." Asher turns his head to throw this response over his shoulder. "I used to live in the city."

And then he disappears into the mass of bodies exiting the bus and I am alone with my lame response: *I know. You said.*

chapter sixty-eight **Kate**

It's been twenty-four hours since I heard Indie's voice. I close my eyes and press my fingertips into my eyelids, trying to erase the image of her stunned face: *You want to send me away?* But instead her face multiplies and I see her at fourteen and then ten and seven and five years old, ever smaller versions of Indie nestled inside each other like Russian dolls. I see the tiniest Indie doll, so small she is made of solid wood, her painted face the picture of fear.

I remember, suddenly, a day when I picked up Indie from kindergarten, how I crouched down to her level to ask what happened, because her eyes were full of tears. She looked at me for a second, as if trying to decide how to explain life to this lumbering, peanut-brained dinosaur in front of her.

"These are just tears that are left over," she said eventually. "From other crying."

It was the first time in my life I'd shown up too late to comfort her. Someone else got there first, or perhaps no one got there at all, but either way, the hurt was no longer mine to fix.

chapter sixty-nine **Indie**

I pause outside the entrance to the high school. My face feels warm and I can tell my neck is splotchy and red. My scalp itches, and then it occurs to me that maybe my scalp is red, too. Back when I had hair, I never had to consider whether or not a scalp could blush.

It's as if my body knows before I do how this day will go: Asher in the cafeteria grabbing breakfast, telling all his friends how the freak with a shaved head has a guru. Asher texting his friends links to the guru's videos during class, and me surrounded by dumbass boys, all snickering inside their hoodies as they watch their phones under their desks. My brain, thin-sliced and mounted on slides for the entire school to inspect.

And then I remember: I don't believe in school. I don't believe in popular kids, or unpopular kids, or any differences between the two. I don't believe in dumbass boys, and I definitely don't believe in dumbass boys who are secretly into the weird girl, like some lame teen rom-com. And this thing that's happening to my neck and spreading across my face right now? The average humans in this school would guess that I'm embarrassed about something, possibly related to a crush. The science nerds might infer that a sudden rush of adrenaline has expanded the capillaries that carry blood to the surface of my skin. But I can't see it. I can't see my face. I am a girl without a head.

I loop my backpack over both shoulders and turn away from the school. I hear the first bell ring behind me. Five more minutes and I will officially be late.

Route 9 is a twenty-minute walk from here, and then the train station is a straight shot south. Ten miles, I recall, which means I can probably make it in three hours. If I keep a decent pace, I can catch a train before fifth period is over. Fifth period is Algebra. If x equals the amount of money that was in my savings account, the one I emptied last week, and y equals the "suggested donation" at The Guy's event, will I have enough money left over for a train ticket and a pretzel from a street vendor if I'm hungry? I pull up the hood of my sweatshirt and start walking.

It's not like I want to pray at The Guy's feet or kiss his ring or anything. He's not into that stuff, anyway. It's just—rubbing two sticks together isn't working, and I need him to tell me why. I sit and I stay and I breathe and I visualize and I even chant a mantra under my breath, but none of it works. I shaved my head; I gave up animal products and gave away my possessions; I tried sleeping on the hardwood floor in my bedroom and I tried sleeping sitting up; I didn't even put up a fight when Dad impounded my phone. No matter what I do or how much I give up, I can't ever find my way back to the state of bliss I experienced that single day, when I realized that I *was* the universe. Call it an awakening, call it enlightenment, call it nirvana, call it walking on fucking sunshine. If *you* knew a place like that existed—and I use the word *place* loosely, like, well, a placeholder, although Mom will never understand this—wouldn't you do everything in your power to find your way back?

chapter seventy ❦ Kate

I remember climbing into bed next to Indie after my mom died. I stroked her hair and felt each of her sobs against my chest, as if we shared one double-sized heart that was breaking. And I remember, too, how she told me an hour later, "I'm really hungry." She was too young to feel guilty about this feeling, the way that grief can coexist with a sudden craving for a PB&J.

I flash to Indie even younger, when she used to channel Big Bird to help her voice the thoughts that confused or upset her. Sometimes she even gave him time-outs. "Big Bird told me fish sticks have dead fish in them," she whispered to me once, glancing nervously at the diner waitress taking our order. "He said dead fish tastes good." Indie was an animal lover who favored the fish sticks on kids' menus, and I watched her work through this conflict rather adorably. "What do you like better," Indie asked me ten minutes later, as she dipped fish sticks into tartar sauce. "Watching animals play, or eating them?" There was an admirable bluntness to the way she talked through her concerns, ultimately owning every thought she'd once assigned to Big Bird. "I eat animals but I love them too!" she announced to new friends she made at preschool.

Only in hindsight can I fully appreciate the way Indie was able to hold onto two conflicting beliefs at once. "Whenever I eat meat, I feel sad the animal had to die," she shared from the back seat of the car, on our way home from the supermarket one afternoon. And then, as we passed the dairy farm half a mile from our house: "Oh, look! Cows! I feel good that they're still alive!" It never occurred to her that she had to choose one position or the other. She seemed to accept that this was what life entailed: eating animals and feeling sad about it.

Now, though, she does not accept this about life. She wants a single, coherent credo that compels everything else to make sense. Death can't be both meaningless and heartrending. It can't be random if it also feels so deeply, personally, uniquely like her own pain. But because the universe won't pick just one thing, she is doing that herself. Death is meaningless, period. Death is random, period.

She thinks she has found an overarching principle, a way of looking at the world that answers all her questions—or, more precisely, that makes her questions irrelevant. It is a solution in the way that a house fire cures a termite problem, or a tornado clears out clutter. And yet, part of me still listens in wonder, just as I did when she was small enough to blame Big Bird for her darkest thoughts. Once again, I find myself stunned at this child's ability to interrogate the universe—life, death, and everything in between.

Not a child, I remind myself. Not anymore.

Still, though, she is *my* child. And in the moment when I should have held her close, I tried to send her away. As if *she* were the one who needed to come to her senses, when really, hers is the most rational response to the understanding she received far too early: that death can touch the things we love.

Have you heard the one about the optimist who jumps off a hundred-story building? As she passes the tenth floor, she says to herself, "Well, so far, so good." This is parenthood, I think. We were flying, Indie and I, feeling the breeze in our hair. I didn't see the ground rushing toward us until it was too late. And now I'm trying to build a parachute as we fall at a hundred miles an hour. Except my daughter no longer trusts me to help her. And why should she? I have no parachute. In the world she is building for herself, in the story she is telling, she feels no pain. How dare I try to take that from her, when I have nothing to offer in return.

chapter seventy-one ✎ Indie

I'm on Route 9 now, a place meant for cars and the people who drive them. If I zoom out, it could be one of those dystopian movies where I'm the last pedestrian on Earth. Route 9 is lined with auto dealers and Dunkin' Donuts franchises and a confusingly high number of Jo-Ann Fabrics stores. I feel doll-sized as I hike south, dwarfed by the scale of this highway. If I stepped on a drain, I might slip right in.

An empty school bus rumbles by and I stick out my thumb for a ride, only because I know the driver would never stop. I may be skipping school to meet a guru in the city, but I'm not rebel enough to *hitchhike*. Or maybe it's that old people tricked my generation into believing that hitchhiking is not just unsafe, it's also pretty lame. Lame like tie-dye shirts. Lame like white people wearing South American ponchos and buckskin vests.

I think that's what I like about The Guy, actually: He's not playing dress-up. He doesn't do healing crystals or Tibetan singing bowls or lotus position, and he never ends his talks with *namaste*. The Guy isn't a meditation try-hard, either. He doesn't believe in devoting hours a day, year upon year, to a continuous mindfulness practice. He doesn't believe in rubbing two sticks together. Enlightenment, he says, is our natural state, which means it's really only a single thought away. When we work up a sweat like we're in training, we're doing it wrong. It's like a dog trying to learn how to play fetch so he can understand what it feels like to be a dog. *He's a dog.*

I'm starting to wish the school bus had stopped for me. My feet hurt and I'm thirsty and I'm so over breathing in car exhaust. I've hiked miles up and down mountains with Dad—he's determined to join the ranks of the Catskill 3500 Club, and every summer he makes me hike at least one of the thirty-three peaks—but on asphalt, the miles feel different. The club gives you a patch if you climb every peak in a single year, and a special patch if you scale them in winter. Dad's all about the patch. I'm wondering what kind of patch I get for hiking past thirty-three Jo-Ann Fabrics stores in a single day.

I keep walking, though, and here's why: Enlightenment may be a single thought away, but that's like saying skydiving is a single step out of a plane. I need someone to push me into free fall.

chapter seventy-two ❦ **Kate**

I change into shorts and sneakers and leave the house at a sprint. I haven't jogged in years, and within a block I have a side stitch, but I keep running. I run until my legs are splattered with mud and my throat burns; I don't turn back until I feel like I can't possibly run another step, and only then do I notice Buddy behind me. He must have let himself out. I run the route home even faster, as if I could leave the world behind, but still I see Indie's face. Now, though, when I picture my daughter, her eyes are full of tears, from all the times she cried and I wasn't there.

chapter seventy-three ❦ Indie

The train carriage is quiet; I missed the morning commuters. My fellow passengers are a random assortment of people heading to the city on their own schedule: doctor's appointment, shopping with friends, museum excursion, cult gathering. No one is wearing a suit.

Mom loves to tell the story of the first time I visited Wall Street. We took the train down to see the Statue of Liberty, and afterwards we walked to the Financial District for a deli lunch. I was maybe five, and I couldn't stop staring at the line of men waiting to order a sandwich. "Why are they all dressed the same?" I asked my parents. "Are they wearing a uniform?" I'd never seen a bunch of dudes in suits before. Mom smoothed my hair out of my face and called me Country Frog. I think she meant this as a term of endearment—it was from her favorite picture book she read to me—although she always seemed a little disappointed that I didn't like the city more. Look at me now, Mom! Go, Country Frog, go!

I look out the train window at the Hudson River rolling by. One of the many analogies I learned this year—meditation gurus *love* analogies—involves a window. It goes like this: Standing at a window, you can admire the world beyond, or you can adjust your focus to examine your own reflection in the glass instead. In the same way, understanding the true nature of reality is just a matter of how you look. You don't need to stand at a window for twelve hours, waiting for the glass to offer up your reflection—you just need to change your focus. I soften my gaze until I see myself in the window, and I flinch; I look *nothing* like Charlize Theron.

The train pulls into the city just as seventh period is beginning. Lunch period. My stomach rumbles right on schedule, even without hearing the bell, and I realize I forgot to pack a lunch. I do, however, have a change of clothes for gym, so that's helpful. I stashed my binders behind a guardrail on the side of Route 9, half an hour into my hike south. My shoulders are still mad at me for taking that long to dump the *seven* binders my teachers insist I carry to and from school each day.

I have hours to kill and no money for a MetroCard, so I decide to walk. I step onto the street and try to figure out which way is south. For some reason, I just thought I'd *know*. At home, I can always point out north or south because I always know where the Hudson River is in relation to me. But here in the city, I have no lodestar. Mom says New York got a lot harder to navigate after the Twin Towers fell, although it seems to me it would be hard not to notice a hole in the sky where a pair of 110-story buildings used to be. Also, there's the Freedom Tower now. I guess Mom doesn't count anything that was built after she and Dad left the city.

I'm finding it difficult to concentrate when my backpack keeps getting jostled by strangers and the smell of roasted nuts is *everywhere*. I swear I can see the smell waves wafting through the air toward me, like in those old-fashioned black-and-white cartoons. Who eats roasted nuts anyway?

When I was still young enough to attend the county fair with my parents each August, before Maddy and I went just the two of us, Mom would use a Sharpie to write her cellphone number on my arm. She had me memorize the number, too, just in case the Sharpie sweated off. As we walked from our car to the fairgrounds, she would drill me on our family safety routine: "What do you do if you get separated from us?" Like a tiny soldier in basic training, I would reply, "Find another mommy and ask her to call you." Once, I asked why I couldn't find another *daddy*, and she informed me that mommies are more helpful.

It occurs to me now that this safety drill must have killed her a little. How many protest marches, how many feminist tees and bumper stickers, how many arguments with her own mother about what it means to be a wife—all thrown out the window every August so she could teach me how to avoid county fair creeps. But she did it to keep me safe.

I swivel my gaze, looking for someone to ask for directions. I don't want to bother anyone with a stroller today, so I wait until I spot a middle-aged woman with a dorky mom haircut—it's all flippy and poufy on top, like Hillary Clinton's 'do.

"No thanks," the woman says brusquely, quickening her pace as I step toward her. I didn't even open my mouth.

No thanks?

I want to call after her, "Do you even have kids?"

I see a younger woman lumbering up the stairs of the station, a collapsed stroller under her arm and a toddler balanced on one hip, plus another kid tugging on her hand. *Find a mommy*, I think, as I approach her. I ask which way is south and she points with her chin, because her arms are full. I thank her and walk in that direction. Yeah, moms are more helpful. I'm a block away before it occurs to me that I should have offered to help her with the stroller.

When I reach Union Square I slow to catch my breath. There is space here, and open sky. I walk the perimeter slowly but not too slowly, over and over again, like I have somewhere to be, just not yet. Which is true, but it's also true that I am a fourteen-year-old girl whose parents have no idea where she is. I feel like I'm back in school, doing laps in the hallway to avoid being identified as a loser who has no one to eat lunch with. I stop into a deli and count out the last of my change for a large coffee to go, then I add cream and four sugars, because sugar is free and coffee is gross and the vegan thing didn't really pan out. Now I'm officially broke.

(Except for the cash for tonight's event, which is bundled in my pocket, held together by one of Mom's elastic hair ties.) I sip the coffee slowly as I walk, doing another loop. The caffeine kicks in and I start to feel a little less like a lunchtime loser, and a little more like Madonna in *Desperately Seeking Susan*. I lift my chin, grateful to be tall for my age.

Eventually I take a seat on the wide steps at the south end of Union Square. I flip my backpack around so I can hug it to my chest, then I trace each button with my fingers, trying to guess which one I'm feeling by its size and location.

I glance around like I'm waiting for a friend. I see styles of hair and clothing I don't even have names for. Our small town may be divided, but pretty much every kid in my grade wears the same sneakers, no matter who their parents voted for. Here, though, people even have their own *walks*. I guess that happens when you don't have a car? No one is staring at my shaved head, either, maybe because no one knows *why* I'm bald. Could be cancer, could be punk rock, could be none of their fucking business. How nice, to grow up in a place like this. Anyone can be invisible here. I pull the book of Rilke's poetry out of my backpack, because that seems like something a local would do. None of the poems make sense to me, though.

I look across the street at a huge LED display. It's a clock that goes in both directions, I remember Mom telling me. I squint at the numbers until I see what she means, and that's when I realize: It's showtime.

chapter seventy-four ❦ **Kate**

I shower after my run and miss a call from the school. There's a voicemail, which means it can't have been Indie calling because she doesn't believe in voicemail, but maybe it's Ethan. I dry my hands on a towel, the rest of my body dripping all over the bathroom floor, and press the speakerphone button.

> *Hello, this is a message from the attendance office at Rivertown High School, calling to inform you that your student, India Campbell, was marked absent today. Please contact the attendance office to clear the absence, or send a signed note upon your child's return to school.*

I text Ethan: *Did you see Indie today?*

n, he replies. *teaching can't talk.*

She's not in school, I write back, but he doesn't respond.

I text Indie: *Where are you?*

I text again: *???????*

And again: *Please answer me you're not in trouble I just need to know you're safe.*

My thumbs hover over my phone as I search for the words that will bring her back to me, and then I remember:

Duck. Dad took your phone.

FUCK

I pull up to the school, my hair still wet from the shower. I park in the fire lane in front of the building, leave the engine running, and sprint inside. I don't understand why Ethan isn't in the lobby waiting for me.

"Can you page Ethan?" I ask the secretary, startling her.

She looks at me like I'm a small child who forgot to say please.

"Mr. Campbell," I add, but she doesn't reach for the phone. "Social studies teacher. He didn't answer my call, I think he's teaching, he's my husband, it's an emergency, can you reach him?"

I am breathless from delivering this litany of information, and finally she picks up the phone. A minute later Ethan is in the lobby, and he is staring at my bare legs because somehow, despite the shower, they are still splattered with mud.

"She's gone," I say. "She's not here."

He looks confused and I shake my phone at him like this explains everything.

"There was a voicemail from the school," I say. "You didn't get it?"

"I was teaching," he says. "A voicemail?" Ethan adds, like someone faxed him from the nineties, and maybe Indie's right, maybe no one listens to voicemail anymore.

"She cut school," I say. "We need to find her."

A siren blasts right over my head—part klaxon horn, part emergency broadcast alert—and my arms fly up in shock. Ethan doesn't even flinch.

"End of the period," he says coolly, as if it were some kind of weakness, the way I cowered. I've always had an exaggerated startle response, and there was a time when Ethan found this endearing. "Indie wouldn't cut school," he adds. "What did *you* do?"

I blanch.

"Nothing," I say. "I didn't even see her this morning. I was in the bathroom when the bus pulled up."

"You didn't *see* her? You just let her leave?"

I open my mouth to say something but the siren goes off again and this time my shoulders jerk dramatically. I can't believe students are assaulted by this noise nine periods a day. Whatever happened to old-fashioned bells?

"Late bell," Ethan says. He pulls out his phone to check the time, although I'm pretty sure that's what the bell is for. "I have to get to class, but I have a prep right after and I'll find her then. I'm sure her friends know where she is."

He turns and leaves before I think to ask him, *What friends? She doesn't have any friends.*

chapter seventy-five **Indie**

I take an elevator to the fourth floor, heart pounding and hands shaking. It's becoming increasingly difficult to act casual. There are four other people in the elevator, but I am staring at the floor and see only their shoes. All of them are wearing high-top sneakers, and my five-year-old self wants to know, "Are they wearing a uniform?" Still, I am happy to be wearing my own high-top checkered Vans.

The elevator opens directly into a massive open space with crazy-high ceilings, exposed brick walls painted white, and floor-to-ceiling windows. Mom would flip over this place, the way the entire room is flooded with natural light. It reminds me of Tom Hanks' apartment in *Big*—you know, that eighties movie where a twelve-year-old boy has sex with a fully grown woman and *no one thinks it's weird.*

Two women in their twenties are sitting at a folding table, and they smile at us as we exit the elevator. Big, bright, kindergarten teacher smiles that reach their eyes, like we were the exact people they were hoping to see.

"Welcome to The Gathering," one of them says. She's blond and Disney Princess–pretty, her hair piled in a messy bun on top of her head.

"You can sign in here," the other woman says. She's Black and even prettier, and I find myself staring at the spiral curls that fall to her shoulders.

I move to the back of the group so I can watch what happens. The sign-in table is empty except for two iPads with those credit card swiper thingies attached. I watch the other attendees hand over a credit card and use a finger to sign their name on the screen. For some reason I'd been expecting a clipboard and tip jar.

When it's my turn, I step forward nervously, crumpled bills in hand. My cash—five hundred dollars, the remainder of my life savings—seems dirty and out of place here.

"Um," I say, holding out the money. "Is this okay?"

Both women are wearing plain black tees and black leggings; they don't even have pockets. Where will they put my money?

"Sure!" Messy Bun says cheerfully, smoothing the bills and tucking them under her iPad. She doesn't count the money. "Just enter your email address here."

"I like your hair," she says.

I instinctively run a hand over my scalp. It feels softer today, less like sandpaper.

"Yeah," the other woman says, looking up from her iPad. "And cute backpack!"

Only then do I realize I'm still carrying my backpack in front. If this were high school, I'd be able to tell whether these women were messing with me, but here, I have no idea. It's like my signals are being jammed.

I step into the room. One half of the space is filled with a few hundred folding chairs, all facing a small, low stage. On the stage is a dark brown leather armchair and a side table holding a green banker's lamp and a glass of whiskey. I recognize the setup from The Guy's videos. The chair and lamp look so out of place in this room of pale wood and exposed brick, it's like they're props for a play. Or one of those pranks where people take all the furniture out of a room and set it up somewhere funny, like a front yard or a bathroom.

The other half of the room is completely empty of furniture, except for what looks like a DJ booth in the corner. I'm guessing this is usually a wedding venue, and I half-expect someone to start passing hors d'oeuvres. Bacon-wrapped scallops, maybe.

I've never seen so many attractive people in one room—it's like I've stepped into the TV show version of this event, and all the civilians have been replaced by celebrities. A bunch of people are milling around in the open space, while others have found a place to sit. Some of them are removing their shoes and socks. It seems as if the people standing came with a friend, while those in chairs came solo. Everyone is glancing around but pretending not to. I take a seat in the back row, because I'm fourteen and that's what teenagers do. I untie my sneakers and retie them, undecided on whether or not to remove them. What if the people without shoes got it wrong?

After a few awkward minutes of trying not to stare at people, I notice that a woman who also picked the back row has her eyes closed, and this feels like the best gift ever. I'm allowed to close my eyes! No one will think that's weird!

I close my eyes, slow my breath, and feel almost calm for the first time in days. I am starting to make sense here.

chapter seventy-six ❦ Kate

A recent post in one of the local parenting groups raised the alarm about kids cutting school to eat garlic knots at Village Pizza. The mom who posted this seemed to think it was one of those online challenges, although it sounded like old-school truancy to me. I check Village Pizza, but of course Indie is not carb-loading with her imaginary friends, nor is she vaping in the restaurant's bathroom (also "trending," according to a different parenting post). The place is empty except for a woman cutting up a slice of pizza into square inches while a toddler plays on her phone. Indie is not swinging listlessly at the town playground, she's not playing video games at the comic book shop, and she's not loitering in the CVS parking lot, either, which means I've exhausted the list of places where the concerned moms of Rivertown think kids go to misbehave. I drive home; Indie is not there either. I call the school and leave a message for the principal and then I call the police and ask them to send someone over and only then do I allow the words to form: *Indie is missing.*

After the police officer leaves, I stand in Indie's room, stripped bare of everything she ever owned. It's as if she were never here. As if we never had a daughter. Is this what she wanted me to see?

Bile rises in my throat and I run to the bathroom and dry heave into the toilet. I sink to the bathroom floor and pull my knees to my chest and press my forehead to my knees, and when I scream, the sound that comes out of my mouth is like glass shattering and maybe I made that happen, maybe mirror shards fly through the air, but my eyes are closed now and I see nothing.

I press my phone between my hands and sob. *Indie*, I say, *Indie*, *Indie*, *Indie*. I chant her name over and over like an incantation. And then, miraculously, the phone rings; I feel it vibrate all the way up to my elbows.

"Indie!" I sob into the phone.

"Mrs. Campbell?"

"Yes," I say, and this person is not Indie and he sounds too young to be the principal or a police officer or anyone else who should be helping me find my daughter.

"This is Asher Davenport," he says.

"Asher from the city?" I say dumbly.

"Um," he says. "Asher from the bus. I think I may know where Indie is."

I leave three notes in the kitchen for Indie—on the fridge, on the microwave, on the island. I leave notes in the dining room, in her bedroom, and on the TV, plus one on the back door and one on the front porch, because what if a note floats out the window, or what if she walks past the first three notes and thinks no one cares that she left? I get in my car, cursing the near-empty tank. I run back inside, leave one more note on the piano that Indie hasn't played since before Maddy died, and another stuck to the bathroom mirror. I text Ethan and he doesn't respond so I call him but he doesn't pick up and what the fuck is he doing because our daughter is *missing*. I can't wait, I can't be still, I have to start moving toward Indie, even if it's just a teenager's hunch, even if she's not there, because she has to be *somewhere*.

I start driving south, my stomach roiling with dread. Indie is not a city kid. I never taught her to be street-smart. She knows how to spot an animal with rabies and how to wash the slugs off homegrown lettuce, but she doesn't know how to make herself invisible on the subway, or how to stride briskly on an empty block. She doesn't even know to fear the empty block.

I remember snuggling up in bed with Indie to read her favorite picture book, *City Dog, Country Frog.* It was the frog my daughter always identified with, the creature who had never known a world without ponds, and this surprised me the first time she said it. But why *wouldn't* she feel at home in the place where she was born? In the book, Country Frog dies when the seasons change. The life cycle of a frog does not make him a good long-term friend, and City Dog has to start over with Country Chipmunk as his new best friend. How easily Indie accepted this back then—the way life forces us to swap out one friend for another. This is the same girl who no longer wants to call any place home, neither country nor city, because she and Maddy lived in a place of their own invention and now Maddy is not here and Indie is a citizen of nowhere.

Also, I can't believe I read that book to a *child.*

An hour later, Ethan finally calls me back.

"I can't find her," he says, his voice serrated with fear. "No one knows where she is."

"I know," I say. "Where the hell have you been?"

"I had to pick up my car," he says. "I rode my bike to school this morning."

I picture him standing in the gym teacher's house, sweaty and confused. I picture him in Lycra, because of course he would have taken the time to change.

"Jesus Christ," I say. "Our daughter is missing. You do realize that, right?"

"I'm calling the police," he says.

"I already talked to them," I say. "But you should call too. They need more details."

The police officer—barely out of his teens, his neck still inflamed with acne—wanted to know what she was wearing, and I had to tell him, I don't know, I didn't see her, I was sleeping. I had to tell him, here's a photo, but she doesn't have hair like that anymore. She doesn't have hair.

"Are they looking for her?" Ethan says. "What did they say?"

"I'm on the Taconic," I blurt out. "Asher thinks she might be in the city."

"*Asher*?" Ethan snaps. "Where does he live? I want to talk to him."

"He already told me everything he knows," I say. "You should call the police."

"She's in the *city*?"

"I don't know," I say, and the truth of this statement shoots through my body like white-hot pain. "Asher said she mentioned some event. I'm going to look there first."

"Indie ran away," Ethan says slowly, like he's finally putting it all together. "She ran away from *you*."

The road curves suddenly and I squeeze the steering wheel, holding my breath as the car hugs the guardrail. My hands ache. As the road straightens again, I feel myself exhale, and I stretch my fingers into starfish. *If I'd sent her away*, I want to say, *at least we'd know where she was right now*. Except, we both got it wrong, the good dad *and* the bad mom. Indie didn't leave us this morning, she's been slowly disappearing for months, and we didn't see it until she was gone. She could be locked up right now, a therapy lamb in her lap, and still we wouldn't reach her.

"I've got to go," I say. "This fucking road."

chapter seventy-seven ❦ Indie

I hear the hum of conversation around me halt suddenly, as if the crowd were being conducted like an orchestra.

"Welcome, fellow nomads."

My eyes snap open. I'd know that voice anywhere. The Guy likes to call people nomads because the self is fluid; it has no fixed abode.

He smiles out into the audience, which is now full. He says nothing else. He keeps smiling, making eye contact with every single person in the room as he does so. I blush when he gets to me because—and perhaps I failed to mention this—he's fucking gorgeous. The haters in the comments say he wears tinted contacts, but whatever. Is it so hard to believe someone is just that much better looking than you? I mean, you've heard of Timothée Chalamet, right? The Guy is wearing a fitted black tee and black cargo pants with lots of pockets, and his feet are bare, which makes me feel like we're in his house. I realize I'm staring at his feet, and I blush again.

After what feels like eight hours but is probably more like eight minutes, based on the videos I've watched, he says, "Sit in the silence. Get comfortable with the silence."

He smiles again. More silence. I don't know how he holds that smile for so long without it turning into the Joker's grin. When I watched his YouTube videos, I didn't always sit in the silence. Usually I skipped ahead.

Finally, he speaks again. Around the fifteen-minute mark, I'd guess. I feel the room collectively exhale.

"I am not your guru," The Guy says. "I am not your friend. I am not your therapist. I am not your healer. I am not here to make you feel good. I am not 'nice.' I am no one, and I am tethered to nothing. You. Don't. Need. Me."

Everyone nods, making those annoying murmuring sounds grown-ups use when they want people to know that they're intelligent and perceptive and they know exactly what the speaker is talking about. Except I think we all just shelled out five hundred bucks to be here because we *do* need a guru.

"You don't need an ashram," he continues. "You don't need to sit on your ass and meditate for twelve hours. You don't need a fucking *sage*. Everything you need is within your reach. You are already enlightened. You are already free. Your mind is a prison, but there's no lock and no key. The door is open. It always was. You're asleep, but you don't know you're dreaming. Tonight, you will wake the fuck up and walk through that door."

More murmuring. I get it, people. You've watched his videos. Me too. Now can we all please just listen to the one person in the room who knows what the fuck is up.

"It's time," he says, and Jesus Christ how is he still smiling? "It's time to walk through that door. But I'm not going to take you through some lame guided meditation. We're not going to sit on our asses and feel our bodies get soft. We have this space. Let's use it!"

The Guy asks us to remove our shoes and socks: "Shoes? Where we're going, we don't need shoes."

Did he just make a *Back to the Future* joke? I hear a few people chuckle to themselves. I guess he did.

I realize I'm still wearing my backpack, except now the only thing it contains is my change of clothes for gym. I shrug it off and place it under my chair, along with my sneakers and socks.

"Thank you," he says, once we are all barefoot. I was expecting a bad smell, but I get nothing. High ceilings, I guess. Or else people in the city just don't have toe cheese.

"We're going to dance together," he continues. "It's called ecstatic dance, and the rules are simple: No shoes, no booze, no schmooze." The Guy pauses for laughter; clearly he's done this before. "Laughter is encouraged, though. Just let your body move with the music. Feel how your body is not *you*. When our bodies move in sync, our minds can connect to a single, cosmic consciousness."

He pauses to let that sink in.

"My friend Harry"—at this, The Guy points over to the DJ booth—"will be our tour guide."

On cue, Harry presses a button, and the room fills with the sound of a pan flute, which I recognize because a Peruvian pan flute band visits the county fair every August. I believe this is what's known as "world music."

"For the next three hours," The Guy continues. "Harry is going to take us on a journey."

Three hours of world music? Oh hell no.

"Touching is optional," he says. "If someone approaches you and you'd rather dance alone, just put your hands in the prayer position at your heart."

I suddenly wish I was still wearing my backpack in front. I feel naked without it.

"Make your way over to the dance floor in your own time," he says. "Let's get connected."

Everyone stands, and so I do too. I've come this far; I'm not giving up now.

I look around and realize there is no one even close to my age here. They all look like people with jobs and apartments and stainless steel cookware. People who pay their own utility bills and choose their own bedtime. Nobody else cut school to be here. One woman about my mom's age catches my eye and smiles. She has dark shoulder-length hair with a white streak in front, like Rogue from the X-Men.

"You okay, honey?"

Honey? She's acting like I'm a toddler who got lost in the supermarket. I nod without smiling and walk toward the dance floor before she can ask if I need help finding my mommy.

People begin to sway to the ambient music. Maybe they imagine they're reeds in the wind, but they look more like those inflatable air dancers outside car dealerships. I passed a bunch this morning. It's hard to believe that was the same day. I feel lightheaded and overheated, like I might pass out. Breakfast was a really long time ago, and I have a sudden craving for a cheese stick, although Mom hasn't bought those for years. It's so loud in here. I don't see The Guy anywhere. Is this when he goes on break?

I move to a corner of the room, where I won't be mistaken for a willing dance partner. I shift my body a little, side to side, because I don't want to look like a party pooper, either. I feel like Dustin Hoffman learning dance moves in *Rain Man*.

All around me people are in motion, heads tipped back, arms out, and they're smiling smiling smiling. If I didn't know better, I'd think they were all on Ecstasy or mushrooms. Maybe they are. At some point, the music picks up and it has a driving beat now and the bass drops are insane. I guess this is world music meets electronic dance? I can still hear pan flute in there. The people start bouncing and bopping, shaking their hair out like this is a shampoo commercial. I see a woman doing Bollywood dance moves, a man attempting to breakdance, and one dude combining tai chi with the Running Man. I'm impressed by his dance-like-no-one is-watching mindset. He looks like he's trying to get dog shit off his feet.

I want to feel it, I really do. I try moving my body more. I roll my shoulders. I shake my arms like I'm air-drying my hands when the girls' bathroom is out of paper towels. I even try the shampoo commercial head shake, but it doesn't work with a shaved head;

instead, I feel my brain bouncing around inside my skull, like I shook something loose. The music rises and falls and then rises again, peaks and plateaus of sound, over and over. He wasn't kidding about this being a journey. The room feels suddenly more crowded, like everyone here spawned a twin. What if the crowd keeps spawning until we are all jammed up against each other and no one can breathe? My chest feels tight, like my body already knows what's about to happen.

If Maddy were here, she would tell me to chill out. She would remind me that I always feel this way in big crowds. She would tell me that the only thing this dance party is missing is Patrick Dempsey in *Can't Buy Me Love* doing his African anteater dance ritual.

If Maddy were here she'd dance with me. She would spin me around and twirl her hands in the air and try out a new move she'd seen online. She would laugh at the adventure of it all—at grown-ups trying to dance, at barefoot men with hairy toes.

If Maddy were here. If Maddy were here. If Maddy were here.

I back into my corner again, stiff arms at my sides. It's even louder now, and I wonder how much longer this can possibly last. It feels like it's been hours already. The dancers are blissed out and sweaty, the women knotting their shirts into crop tops like this is *Flashdance.* They look so at home here, like they belong—in this room, on this planet, and to each other, even. If I'd wanted to feel like a wallflower, I could have just stayed home and gone to the fall dance.

Two people in front of me start doing this thing where they dance in sync without touching, mirroring each other's moves like two stoned mime artists. Mom's right; this is some woo-woo shit. Still, I'm mesmerized. It's impossible to tell who is following whom in the couple, and there's something magical about this, like they're attached by invisible fishing wire.

I feel someone nudge my shoulder, and when I turn to look, *holy fucking shitballs it's him.* The Guy is standing next to me, leaning his shoulder into mine as he scans the dance floor. I feel my entire body blush instantaneously, head to toe. Weirdly, he looks freshly showered, and that's when I realize I'm full-on staring at him again, except now it's a little more obvious and I am beyond mortified. I suddenly have no idea what to do with my body, and before I realize it, my arms are crossed over my chest.

Great. Now I'm not just a wallflower, I'm also an uptight priss.

"Hey," he says softly, nudging me again, his eyes still focused on the crowd. I guess he's allowed to break his own no-talking rule. "Nobody puts Baby in a corner."

What the actual fuck? Is this real life?

I look out at the dance floor to see if anyone else has noticed The Guy's sudden appearance at my side. A few people sneak glances in my direction, while pretending to be immersed in the ambient sound. Okay, so he's really standing here, next to me. But did he really just quote Patrick Swayze? Also, am *I* supposed to break the rules now and say something back? I have no idea how this works. And even if I knew, what the hell do you say to a guru who smells like guy shampoo and quotes *Dirty Dancing* at you?

He leans his head into mine.

"I want to show you something," he says. "Follow me."

I follow him. It's not a decision I make; there is no list of pros and cons, there is only that invisible fishing line, tugging me along. I feel like the girl pulled up on stage at a rock concert.

We climb a set of stairs near the entrance, and suddenly we're in a loft area, looking down on the dance floor. How did I not notice this before? It's like a magic treehouse. I see a kitchenette and a door that I assume leads to a bathroom. This must be where he disappeared to while we all danced. I follow him over to the railing and look down. I feel the music slow again, like we're in a plane preparing to land. I wonder if my ears will pop. Up here, I am at eye level with the pendant lights that hang from the ceiling, and that's when I realize the sun had gone down while we danced.

Watching the bodies from above is like looking into a kaleidoscope, and I wonder if this is what he wanted me to see. Up here, it is so much more obvious how the parts make a whole. And it's so beautiful. I couldn't figure out how to be a jewel in the kaleidoscope, so he showed me the viewfinder instead.

"You see it now, right?" The Guy says. "You just needed the bird's-eye view, I could tell."

I have a million questions about what I'm doing up here in the loft—*Does he know I'm the one who messaged him? Is that why he came looking for me?*—but they are all drowned out by this goofy cheerleader in my head who is doing backflips and high kicks and yelling HE! PICKED! ME!

"Most people just need the music," he continues. "They go on the journey with Harry, and that's all it takes. But you're different."

"Maybe it's the pan flute," I say.

He laughs loudly, then shakes his head like he feels bad for doing this.

"I hate the fucking pan flute," he says. "But it works. I think it makes people stop caring about how they look, you know? Because nobody looks cool dancing to the pan flute."

I lean over the balcony for a better look.

"Good point," I say.

He doesn't say anything else, and I start to panic that I've squandered my moment. Was that it? Is he going to send me back to the dance floor and pick a different, prettier girl who knows exactly what to say?

"So, you like eighties movies?" I blurt out.

Real smooth, Indie.

The Guy nods, thoughtfully, like I actually said something deep and interesting.

"I like *all* movies," he says. "I like storytelling. It reminds me how most people view their lives. Everyone thinks they're their own *plot line*, right? They think there's a beginning, a middle, and an end. They want to tell their story, and they want someone to listen to it. Watching movies keeps me tethered to humans, to what makes them tick. Also"—and at this he turns to me and smiles—"eighties movies are the most fun to quote."

"My mom says the same thing," I say. "I mean, about quoting eighties movies, not all the other stuff you said."

My *mom*? Jesus Christ, I'm a loser. I should just throw my dork-ass self over the railing and end this torture for both of us right now.

He steps away from the railing and takes a seat on the couch. It's brown leather, a matching set with the armchair on stage. He places a palm on the cushion next to him—not patting it like a creepy uncle, just holding his hand there like he's saving me a seat on the bus.

"Sit," he says, and then pauses. "If you like."

I hesitate a second because here is a man on a couch and we are alone and I hear a voice in the distance saying, *Don't*. But then I realize: That voice is far away because it comes from my other life. The story I've been telling myself with a made-up plot line. The story no one wants to hear.

So I sit on the couch, facing forward, my hands clasped awkwardly in my lap like we're passengers on that imaginary bus. Out of the corner of my eye, I see him turn his body toward me, and so I do the same, sliding back a little as I do. He moves back, too, and leans against the armrest behind him. He meets my eyes and smiles but says nothing. I feel my panic dissolve. We have all the time in the world.

We sit in the silence together, and holy fuck, it's intense. There's nowhere else to look. He smiles and he waits and suddenly I can read his mind, and he's telling me: *It's okay. Ask your question*. And so I do.

"Why can't I feel it?" I say. "When I look down at the dancing, I can see what's happening, but I'm not part of it. What am I doing wrong?"

"Let me guess," he says. "Straight-A student, right?"

"Yeah," I say with a smile, then roll my eyes so he doesn't think I'm bragging.

And maybe *this* is why he picked me, because he could tell. Because world music doesn't work on the smart kids.

"They always struggle with this," The Guy says. "The jocks get it much faster, because they're used to feeling things in their bodies. The straight-A types don't know how to stop trying."

Even at a meditation dance party, apparently, the gym rats are outshining me. Also, he basically just called me a try-hard. What the fuck?

I open my mouth to respond but I have nothing. I am the loser at the lunch table, and now I get it: He pulled me off the dance floor because I was a buzzkill. I crashed his cool dance party and now he's going to send me home.

The Guy looks at me and it's like he's taken a knife and split me open. I can feel him seeing me, reading me. He nods slightly, like someone is talking to him through a hidden earpiece.

"What are you holding onto?" he says eventually, and his eyes are so kind now. "Something is holding you back."

I dig my fingernails into my palms. If I cry now, I will never stop.

"I had a friend," I choke out. "A best friend. How do I let her go?"

He leans forward and rubs my upper arm, just for a second, but I can feel the heat and the pressure of his hand even after he is sitting back against the armrest again. It feels like he just branded me with a hot iron, giving my arm a permanent memory of his touch.

"You have to stop giving her meaning," he says. "You're holding onto her because you attached meaning to your friendship with her."

I stare at him. I think maybe he misunderstood my question. Does he think I'm here because I got *dumped* by a BFF? I'm simultaneously mortified and annoyed.

"Think about it this way," he continues. "You probably took a subway to get here, right?"

I nod like I take the subway to work every day, because what does the truth matter so long as I can picture a subway car in my mind?

"Close your eyes," he says, and I do. "Picture the subway car you sat in today, except now, it's filled with an entirely different group of people. Does this make you sad?"

I shake my head *no*, my eyes still closed.

"How many strangers did you see on that train today? People you know you'll never see again, but this doesn't bother you because you've given them no meaning. You do this hundreds of times a day—you leave people behind without a second thought, because you attach no meaning to any of them."

This reminds me of a line in a poem Mom once read to me:

Lose something every day. Accept the fluster
of lost door keys, the hour badly spent.
The art of losing isn't hard to master.

"She died," I say flatly, opening my eyes. "I was there."

"I know," he says. "That's the story of your life. It's a sad story, but it's still just a story."

Sad like *Terms of Endearment*, I think. Sad like *Beaches*.

"A sad story," I repeat.

I look down at my hands in my lap. Can't he see that I need more help? I need him to push me out of the plane.

"May I hug you?" he says. "You look like you could use a hug."

I nod mutely, and he puts his arms around me.

"You are liberated," he says softly, and he's so close now, he's like a voice inside my head. "Everyone you've ever met, your family, your friends, even your *best* friend, they're strangers on a train. You can walk right past them. You can get off at the next stop and leave them all behind." I force myself to picture Maddy on the train, the last time we came to the city together. I picture myself getting off one stop early. "When you do this, you'll be free of everything—you'll be free of pain and suffering, and you'll be freed from happiness, too. No more trying to resist bad feelings, and no more chasing after good ones, either. All your feelings will pass over you like weather. Look up and watch the weather go by; it's all the same to you."

His chest presses against me, his hand rubs my back, his knee nudges mine. He is right: Comfort and grief feel the same. Being free feels the same as being trapped. Fear and longing feel the same. Panic and desire feel the same. I feel everything, and I feel nothing.

"Good weather, bad weather—it doesn't bother you," he whispers into my ear, and I feel my entire body break out in goosebumps. "Winter is coming, but you don't give a fuck, because it's just weather, and you? You. Are. Not. Playing."

If Maddy were here—

He pulls me in closer, tighter, one hand on my back and now, one hand on my knee.

"You walked out that prison door," he says. "I can feel it. You woke up."

It's so hard to think in words with his mouth on my ear but something is nagging at me and then I realize what it is: *I know that speech*. I've heard him use that *Game of Thrones* line in his videos. The subway thing, too—he has a whole bit he does about strangers on a train. He's not talking to me; he doesn't even know my name, he's just quoting himself and I am a warm body on his couch. I am not the girl up on stage; I'm the backstage groupie. I'm a dumb kid with a crush on a guru and he has his hand on my knee. He's not the boy on the bus—he *is* the creepy uncle and I am just another easy mark.

I push myself out of his embrace and find myself standing at the balcony again, breathing hard. My hands shake and my throat is dry and I have no idea what to do next. This was the plan, to make it to the city, to meet this man; *he* was supposed to show me the way out. Instead I'm trapped in a blind alley. I try to focus on the dancers but my vision blurs with tears and all I see is bodies in motion. *Call for help*, I think, but nothing happens. It's like the time I half-woke from a nightmare and felt my body pinned to the bed, my mouth flapping like a guppy. And then I sense The Guy rising from the couch and moving toward me and suddenly my legs take over and I am running down the stairs and into the elevator and across the street and it is not until I am sitting on the steps of Union Square again that I realize I left my backpack behind and I am barefoot.

chapter seventy-eight ❦ Kate

I am doing eighty-five on the Taconic, blowing past all the cross streets that make this parkway feel like a practical joke. It's hard to believe that locals are expected to just *cross* the Taconic, like a game of *Frogger*. But I can't slow for them, not today. If I get pulled over I will tell the police my daughter is missing and they will have to escort me to my destination like they do for women in labor. I don't care if it's the last day of the month and they have a quota of speeding tickets to meet. Since the moment I birthed this child, I will tell them, I have existed in reaction to her.

No one stops me, though, maybe because I'm a middle-aged white lady in a Subaru Impreza, or maybe because the universe owes me one. More likely, it's just dumb luck. The same dumb luck that spared my daughter when a car swerved into one girl and missed the other. The same dumb luck that could just as easily spare someone else's child the next time around.

She's not here, Ethan texts me from the house.

Not here, he texts me from Maddy's house, from her grave, from her roadside memorial.

Where else should we look? Ethan texts.

We? I think.

I picture those scenes in network shows, hundreds of concerned citizens fanning out across a field, flashlights in hand, yelling the missing girl's name.

I've got Buddy, Ethan says. *And I grabbed Indie's phone, in case she tries to call it. Does she even know our numbers?*

She knows mine, I text back, not to one-up him, but because it's true, and maybe it will comfort Ethan to hear this. I made Indie memorize my number when she was five, back when the worst I could imagine is that we'd get separated at Target.

I remember a day when Ethan imagined the worst. He was holding newborn Indie, looking down at her sleeping face, and he murmured, softly so as not to wake her, "I just realized that she's never going away. And right after that I had another thought: What if she goes away?"

Over the years we learned to suppress our worst fears in order to raise a daughter who had none, but now, my brain spits them back out like dark fortunes. Horrific images pop up over and over, glimpses so vivid they feel like memories.

What if I'm too late? What if the worst has already happened?

I tell Ethan that I'm going to call Indie's phone and leave a voicemail, because if she dials in from another phone, I want her to hear my voice. I think that's still a thing, calling to check your voicemail? It's a long shot, I realize. But it also feels a little like talking to her. Transmission is a thing, too, and maybe the universe will know that I am trying to reach her.

chapter seventy-nine ❦ Indie

I wrap my arms around my knees. The only true thing The Guy said tonight is that I don't need him.

I am no more conscious than the step I am sitting on, or the WALK/DON'T WALK sign across the street. I don't need anyone to tell me this, I just need to try harder. I need to rub two sticks together until my flesh shreds into ribbons, right here, right now.

There is an LED clock on the building across the street and there is something which is aware of this clock. There is the cold and the hunger and the feeling of a tag in a shirt, irritating the skin at the back of a neck. There is something that is aware of this neck. There are drunk women, their arms around each other, weaving down the sidewalk. There is a siren in the distance and there is music drifting from a restaurant with outdoor seating. There is the feeling of asphalt. There is the East River to the left, the Hudson to the right. There is the wide open sky, black and empty of stars.

And then there is a screech of brakes and I am back on that country road again, the fireflies in the trees and Maddy's body crumpled before me. I am holding her hand and begging her not to die and I am trying to remember what to do. Do I pump her chest? Breathe into her mouth? There is blood, so much blood, and maybe I'm supposed to stop the blood first, but I can't tell where it's coming from, and so all I do is clutch her hand and scream her name. If there is no past and no present, then this moment will always exist and I will always be here, on the side of the road, fumbling with my phone, dialing 911, telling them—

I suddenly remember the song we were singing. I remember how Maddy used to say, "This song gets me all up in my feelings." I remember, I remember, I remember.

I remember the comic book store that's a block and a half from here. I remember the hours Maddy and I spent there, while Mom patiently browsed the aisles of the Strand bookstore, two doors down. Maddy and I pooled our babysitting money and built a manga collection between us, because why would we need doubles of anything? I remember how we ate hot dogs from a street vendor for dinner because it was almost time for our train and Mom didn't complain, even though she'd wanted to take us to her favorite noodle restaurant. I remember this super-tall guy playing clarinet on the subway platform; it was hilariously screechy, but Mom wouldn't let us take a video on our phones in case he wasn't in on the joke.

Worst of all, I remember me. I remember that I am a fourteen-year-old who skipped school today. I am a ninth-grade student who is failing the marking period. I am hungry and thirsty and tired. I have to pee. I *really* have to pee. I am a girl who has no one to eat lunch with. I am a loser who has no plans for my birthday. I am an idiot who just emptied my savings account for a world music dance party hosted by a perv. The idiot who bought a one-way train ticket because if I'd bought a return, I wouldn't have had five hundred dollars for the event, and I didn't understand what "suggested donation" meant. I am so real, it hurts.

There is no dream to wake up from. There is no open door. There is no shortcut, because there is nowhere else to go. There is no *story* of me, there is only me. Me without Maddy.

Actually, yes, there is a story, but it's the oldest story in the book. It's about a stupid girl who thinks she's something because an older guy notices her. It's about a girl who thinks her grief makes her special. A girl who thinks the world is happening only to her.

The last time Maddy and I came to the city together, it was for a women's march. We took the train down with Mom, and we were so proud of our hand-lettered sign: GRAB 'EM BY THE PATRIARCHY.

That day, it felt like Maddy and I could do anything we set our hearts on. We could make the world take girls seriously, we could clear the ocean of trash and curb population growth, we could stop all the hate and end all the violence. *We* were the weather. We were winter, and we could cool the entire planet if we wanted to.

Talk about delusions of grandeur. Nobody gets to control the weather or be the weather or act like the weather doesn't affect them. Winter comes and the sky turns pale and it snows. You wear heavy boots and a puffer jacket. You shovel the driveway and you hope for no school. It's not snowing tonight, but it's dark and cold now and my feet are bare and I am freezing my fucking ass off.

chapter eighty ❦ Kate

Fuck this city's parking rules. Fuck everyone who is hogging a parking space who doesn't really need it. Fuck the traffic and the honking and the pedestrians who cross when I have the green light. Fuck every person in the city who is not Indie.

I'm sorry, Ethan texts me as I pull into a parking garage. *I thought I could find her.*

"Hey Siri," I yell into my phone as I run down the sidewalk. "Send a message to Ethan."

I'm here, I tell him.

Bring her home, Ethan says.

chapter eighty-one ❦ Indie

I want my mom.

chapter eighty-two ❦ **Kate**

I'm on my way don't move I will find you.

chapter eighty-three **Indie**

Across the street, an old woman is pushing one of those folding shopping carts you see only in places where people don't have cars. Except her cart isn't full of groceries; it seems to be stuffed to the brim with her worldly possessions. *Street nana*, Mom would say. Everyone just walks by this old woman like it's the most normal thing in the world. What kind of place is this? I squeeze my eyes shut and when I open them again, the old woman is gone and in her place there's a woman who looks like my mom and I am sure I must have dreamed her into existence but suddenly she is running across the street against the light because she sees me.

And then she is there, bent over me, her arms around me, her body blocking out the world, as if someone exploded a building and she is shielding me from its blast.

"It's okay," she says. "It's okay, it's okay, it's okay."

I want to tell her it isn't okay because Maddy is really gone, she really died, and I am really here and everything is real. Everything is too real. The cold is real and my body is real and everyone has a beginning and a middle and an end. Maddy had an end. I want to tell Mom I'm sad because she's dead. But I can't talk, I can't breathe, it's happening again, my lungs are shrinking and I'm gasping for air. I think of a cardboard box and I can't remember what I'm supposed to do next, but Mom knows and she is counting slowly, she is telling me to look at her, she is telling me to breathe with her, to follow her count. *In-two-three-four, hold-two-three-four*. Dad must have told her, too.

As my breathing slows and my lungs fill again, I realize it doesn't matter what I say, because my mom already knows. She has always known it was real. I don't need to tell her anything. I think about how my first word was *mama,* but before that, before there were words, there were feelings, and the feeling of her came before everything, and that feeling was *safe.*

And for the first time since the morning of Maddy's funeral, I cry.

"Did he hurt you?" Mom is saying now. "Tell me he didn't hurt you!" She squeezes my arms a little like she's trying to make sure I'm real. "Swear to me," Mom whispers. "Swear to me he didn't hurt you!"

And I shake my head *no no no* because that's not what hurts.

"Oh, Indie," she says, and she pulls me close again.

Mom calls Dad to tell him she found me. She presses the speakerphone button and motions me closer. I stare at the screen and watch the seconds tick up. "You there, sweetie?" Dad says. I nod my head and then shake it, pushing the phone toward Mom's ear. I don't know how to explain myself to him, I don't have any words. When she hangs up, we get burritos to go from Dos Toros and start our drive home, the heat cranked high and the radio low. Mom's the only person I know who subscribes to Spotify for the uninterrupted classical music. It's the one genre we agree on, so Mom always plays it when I'm in the car. I recognize a Haydn piano concerto and turn the volume up a notch.

"How did you find me?" I say eventually. "How did you know?"

"Asher called," Mom says.

"*Asher* called *you*?"

"He found my number on some old class list," Mom says. "He was worried when he didn't see you on the bus home. I met Brandon, by the way."

"Brandon?" I say, but I'm still thinking about Asher.

"The guru," Mom says, and I can tell it pains her to use this word. "*Insert Title Here*. The barefoot douchebag."

I swallow hard and look out the window.

"He told you his name?"

"I asked," Mom said.

"And he just told you?"

"I was in Mama Bear mode," Mom says. "I might have kicked him."

"You *kicked* him?" I say, turning to look at her.

"Just a little," Mom says, and she shrugs and smiles. "In the shin. I think I stepped on his bare toes, too. I wasn't feeling very reasonable when I showed up. I'd had hours in the car to get worked up, and then he fed me some bullshit line about how he had to *respect the privacy of all attendees*. I lost it."

"Good," I say. "I'm glad you kicked him."

"Me too."

I look out the window again and take a deep breath.

"What else did he tell you?" I say.

"He said you ran out halfway through the event. He gave me your backpack."

"That's it?"

I can't look at her.

"As soon as I knew you weren't there, I ran out to the street and sprinted north," Mom says. "Thank god I didn't pick south."

"He didn't say anything else?"

"The rest is your story," she says. "Tell me when you're ready."

My *story*. The Guy said my whole life was a story, but he didn't want to hear it.

We fall quiet for a while, and it's good quiet. It's library-during-lunch-period quiet. I watch the mile markers on the side of the Taconic, guiding us home.

"Why didn't Dad come?" I say eventually. "Is it because he's still mad at you?"

"Oh, god no, Indie," she says. "No," she says again, more firmly this time. "He stayed in case Asher was wrong. We should tell him we're on the road now." She presses a button on the steering wheel. "*Call Ethan*," she tells the car.

"Cancel!" I shout, and then I smile a little. I'm always telling Mom not to yell at Siri.

"Just text him," I say to Mom in my regular voice. "Please?"

Dad will want a play-by-play, I'm sure of it. He'll want to know who The Guy is and where he posts online and what exactly he said to make me go there. He'll want to know what The Guy *did*.

"He's been driving around town looking for you," Mom says. "He and Buddy. The police found Buddy on Route 9 a few hours ago. I guess our pup was out there looking for you, too."

"The *police*?" I put my face in my hands. "So everyone knows?"

"We thought you might—" Mom's voice breaks.

We both sit in silence, giving space to the words she can't say.

"I never would have done that," I say eventually. "I swear. I didn't want to die. I don't want to die. I just—"

I look at Mom's hands, at ten and two, and then her face, so still, like she'd wait forever for me to finish my sentence.

"It hurts," I say, and now I'm crying again, deep noisy sobs. I bend forward and the seatbelt strains across my chest, so I duck out of the shoulder belt and fold into my knees, wrapping my arms around myself. "He was supposed to make it stop, but it hurts so much."

She says nothing for a few minutes, but I feel her steer the car into the slow lane, ease off the gas, and gently put her hand on my back.

"The hurt is Maddy," she says. "That's how you keep her. By remembering. That's how you keep all the days you had together."

I shake my head into my knees. I don't want to remember. I don't want to keep the days, I want to give them back. I feel the warmth of Mom's hand as my back rises and falls with sobs.

Eventually I sit upright again. For a brief moment, Mom takes her eyes off the road to look at me, but she doesn't say anything. It's dark, and the Taconic is slick with rain, reflecting the headlights of cars driving the other way.

At some point, Mom takes her phone from the cupholder and hands it to me.

"Asher asked me to let him know when I found you," she says. "But I think he'd rather hear from you."

I stare at the screen. It's been so long since I texted anyone besides my parents. I forgot what it feels like, to know someone is waiting to hear from me.

Hey, I text. *It's Indie on my mom's phone. I didn't join the tech bro cult!*

I delete the exclamation point, then add it back in, then delete it one more time. I add, then delete, an *eek* emoji.

Thanks for—

I pause. Thanks for telling my mom instead of your dumbass friends? Thanks for not staying in your lane?

Thanks for noticing, I type, and I add a Dwight *thank you* GIF.

Seconds after I hit Send, I see the three dots appear on his side of the screen. I glance at Mom to see if she's watching, but she is eyes-straight-ahead like it's her driving test.

I want to hear the story, Asher writes. *See you at lunch*?

The Guy was right, I guess: Everyone tells stories. It's how we make sense of the world. The Guy wanted me to un-tell myself, to unravel the yarn, but then what would be left? I remember the *Bodies* exhibit my parents took me to a few years back, all the internal organs and systems dissected and displayed. The circulatory system was so beautiful—a hundred thousand miles of arteries and veins, coral-red and branching like delicate seaweed. The muscular system, though, made me want to gag. It looked like human jerky. This, I think now, is what's left without a story:

blood, bone, muscle. Meat. Maddy deserves to be more than that, and maybe I do, too.

But when I try to imagine walking into the cafeteria to meet Asher, I see myself standing awkwardly as I scan the room, clutching my lunchbox to my chest like a comfort object. I see the Minkles following my gaze to spot who I'm looking for. I don't know where Asher sits this year, but it's probably at one of the big round tables with his soccer buddies. It's not like the school cafeteria has tables for two. (That's not a joke. Maddy and I checked.)

The Manga Club meets in the library, I text back. *New members welcome.*

I click off the screen so I don't have to see my message to Asher hanging out there like underwear on a clothesline. My head feels heavy now, my eyelids are drooping, and the next thing I know, Mom is nudging me awake.

"We're home," she whispers, and I hear the gentle clicking of the turn signal as she steers onto our street.

I look up, and there's my dad, sitting on our front porch, his arm slung around Buddy like they're two dudes sharing a beer. Dad is wearing ski mittens, a wool scarf, and his winter hat with the ear flaps. He looks ridiculous. I step out of the car and run into his arms and he doesn't have any questions, he doesn't ask me a thing, he just says, over and over, "You're home." There is wonder in his voice, as if he's saying something he can hardly believe, and I think maybe he sees it now, how easy it is to unbelieve what's right in front of you. "You're home," he says one more time, and I can't speak, not yet, but I think back at him: *So are you.*

chapter eighty-four ❦ **Kate**

"I saw Indie walking through town yesterday morning," Sara says. Her tone is grave and unsettled, as if she'd seen a ghost. "I'm so sorry. I should have told you, but I figured she had a dentist appointment or something. I figured you knew where she was."

The people of this town look at Indie and they see only what's missing. They see a girl who lost her best friend in an instant, and also a girl who lost herself by degrees, the color draining from her body like an old photograph left in the sun. They don't see how every day Indie builds upon herself, an epic novel spanning across the years. And they don't see how the tiny girl in the turquoise Bumbo chair is always there, no matter where you start reading.

"Hey," Sara says. She tilts her head a little and smiles. "Did I lose you?"

The kindness in this phrase, *Did I lose you?* The even kinder implication: *I'm still here*. Tears spring to my eyes and I smile back.

"We could have lost her," I say. "What if we never found her?"

And then my work friend Sara steps around her desk, crouches next to me, and puts her arms around me and my chair. My work friend who didn't know how to help except to invite me to play pickleball, because she is just another human who feels helpless in the face of grief. Who said the wrong words because she couldn't bear to say nothing. Not a work friend, I think. Just a friend.

"You're her mom," Sara says. "Of course you found her."

This is not true. There is nothing supernatural about a mother's love—we can't really lift cars or see through buildings or track down missing children through instinct alone—but sometimes just believing in this is enough.

I remember the way Indie used to comfort herself when she fell from the monkey bars or scraped her knees on the asphalt learning to skateboard. By the time Ethan or I reached her, she would already be chanting under her breath, in a heartbreaking imitation of parents across the planet, *It's okay it's okay it's okay.* As if the words themselves could banish the pain. She hadn't yet learned that parents say this even when it's not okay. That what parents really mean is, *I'm here I'm here I'm here.* But Indie has seen behind the curtain now, and she knows that some things are not okay. Some things will never be okay. And all I can say is that I'm here.

One day soon I will tell Sara how the girl in the turquoise Bumbo is who I picture when I remind Indie to look both ways before crossing the road, when I warn her not to dive in the shallow end, when I ask her to call if she's running late. This girl, I will say, is who I answer to every time Indie stumbles and I don't catch her, every time she cries and I'm not there. Every time she hurts and I make it *worse.* This tiny girl who looks across the kitchen island at me, her perfect rosebud mouth an oval of dismay, as if to ask: *How could you?*

How could we, indeed? We leap off the hundred-story building and we pray—or something like prayer.

chapter eighty-five **Indie**

"So," Asher says, taking a seat across from me in the library. "How does this work?"

"You mean, like, coming back to school?" I say. "Mrs. G checks on me every few periods, to make sure I'm not planning any more unauthorized field trips, then I meet up with her during study hall. I'm guessing I'm the first ex-cult member she's had to deprogram."

Asher laughs and then glances over at the librarian.

"I meant the secret Manga Club," he whispers. "But I'm glad Mrs. G's looking out for you."

"Oh," I say, blushing. Actually, I think I've been in a permanent blush since Asher texted me about lunch. "It's not really a club. It's more like an agreement. The librarian pretends not to notice we're eating, and we keep our voices down and don't leave any crumbs."

"It's totally a secret club!" Asher says. "You think she'd do this for anyone else?"

The librarian has a super long gray ponytail and the widest, flattest butt I've ever seen. Every single day she wears the same purple fleece vest. But she fills the shelves with the kinds of books that get banned south of the Mason-Dixon Line (and north of it, too, lately). Critical race theory is the least of it, although she has plenty of that, too. Shelves and shelves of steamy paranormal sex, romantic suicide pacts, queer manifestos, plus a whole series of nonfiction how-to books called *Cool Careers Without College*.

These books actually claim you can have a fulfilling and successful life without going to college! I *know*.

"Maybe not," I say, shrugging. "But we're the only ones who asked."

We. For years, Maddy and I thought of ourselves as first-person plural. It's the way we approached the world.

Asher unpacks his bento box and glances around the room, checking out the book displays and posters. He walks over to the manga shelf and grabs the first volume of *Dragon Ball Z*. It's a kind gesture, like he wants to make the silence feel normal. He opens the book the American way and looks confused.

"Other end," I say. "It's Japanese. You read from the back."

"I totally knew that."

He reads for a couple of minutes while he eats, which is exactly what Maddy and I used to do. Read, talk, eat, repeat. I don't remember us ever deciding it was time to talk, or time to read. It just somehow worked out. I've seen the Minkles at lunch: If there's even a micro-second of downtime, someone will sing-song, "*Awk-ward si-lence!*" And then everyone giggles in relief and starts talking again.

"Were you running away?" Asher says eventually, not looking up from his book.

"No," I say. "I don't think so."

He nods and reads another page.

"Is that what everyone's saying?" I ask. "That I ran away?"

Mom told me there were MISSING flyers all over town yesterday, but I didn't see any when we drove to school this morning. I guess everyone knows I was already found.

"People were freaking out," he says. "But they just wanted to help find you. They were scared, that's all."

I bang my forehead on the table and groan.

"So I went viral?" I say, my head still down.

"Wouldn't it be worse if you hadn't?" Asher says.

Would you rather, I think. I have no idea.

"I watched some more of that guy's videos last night," he says. "Have you seen the one where he shows you how to text yourself?"

I shake my head, mute, trying not to give myself away. Asher pulls his laptop out of his backpack.

"Here," he says, and moves his chair to my side of the table, so close our arms are touching. "I'll show you."

He opens the messaging app and puts his own name in the To: field. He types *hi* and hits Send.

"Now watch what happens when I start typing another message," he says.

I watch as the three dots appear on the opposite side of the window.

"Pretty cool, right?" Asher says. "It's like, for a second, my brain thinks there's another me out there somewhere, texting me back, and then I realize, wait, that's just me!"

I don't tell him I saw the video weeks ago. I don't tell him how the text bubble thing blew up my world. How, when I saw those three dots, I understood that I was everywhere and nowhere at once. How the dots felt like the closest I would ever come to a visual representation of cosmic consciousness.

"Totally!" I say. "So cool."

Is this what it's like to be a human in the world? Is this what it's like to have someone to talk to? I am trying to remember.

"Do you think I'm crazy?" I ask him.

"No way," Asher says. He taps his screen. "*This* guy's crazy. You're just weird."

The Guy—Brandon, I correct myself—likes to quote Stephen Hawking when he's defending himself: *The thing about smart people is that they seem like crazy people to dumb people.*

"Weird," I repeat.

"Weird is good," Asher says. "Everyone in this school is way too normal."

"So I'm not normal?"

"Nope." Asher smiles like this is the best kind of classified information, like he's the first kid in school to find out we're dismissing early for snow. "Not even close."

chapter eighty-six ❦ Kate

My phone dings with a text from Ethan. It's 6 a.m., which means he's sitting in a coffee shop on the other side of town, the first customer of the day. I'm in the kitchen by six every morning, and sometimes Indie will eat breakfast with me. Mostly, though, I text with Ethan.

Check this out, he writes.

It's a link to download an app called Universe Splitter.

It's $1.99, I text back.

It's a quantum decision maker, Ethan says. *You can literally hack the multiverse. Total bargain! Thought you might want to write about it.*

I'm a realtor, I say.

Not buying it, Ethan texts back. *No offense, but for a realtor, you suck at the hard sell.*

So I download the app, which presents me with two text boxes, labeled: IN ONE UNIVERSE, I WILL NOW . . . and, IN THE OTHER UNIVERSE, I WILL NOW. . . . Two roads, I think. A yellow wood. The FAQ tells me to fill the text boxes with two choices. The well-worn path vs. the road less traveled. The small town where everyone knows your business vs. the big city where no one cares. The imperfect spouse vs. this whole forsaken imperfect planet. According to the quantum physicists who created it—I'm picturing Doc Brown in *Back to the Future*—this app ensures you will regret nothing, because you can try everything in one universe or another. It seems like a make-believe toy to me—a pink plastic stove that can't bake a thing, or a kids' stethoscope that hears no heartbeat. If science really had made regret as redundant as CD binders, I think I'd have heard of it.

Another message from Ethan pops up on my screen: *Did you try it?*

Scrambled eggs, I type in one box. *Granola and yogurt*, I type in the other. Then I click a button labeled SPLIT UNIVERSE, which allegedly sends a message to some device in Switzerland, which then fires a single particle of light, a photon, at a mirror. According to quantum physics, the photon will go both left and right. It takes the road less traveled *and* the well-worn path. But in *this* universe, the machine sees it go only one way—left, maybe. And based on what the machine sees, the app will tell you which path to take. Here's the thing, the app warns me: *You have to do this.* You have to take the path the app chooses for you. Because in a parallel universe, the machine saw the photon go right. And in that universe, the app is telling you to do the exact opposite.

The app tells me to go for scrambled eggs, so I pour a bowl of granola.

It's bullshit, I tell Ethan.

I don't mean the science, although I suppose that could be bullshit, too. I don't actually know what a photon is (or what it means to go both ways), which makes the app feel a whole lot like faith—believing in something you can't fathom. What I mean is that perhaps there *is* a universe in which everything turns out differently. If there are infinite parallel worlds, then there's a world in which I marry the boy who makes spaghetti carbonara. There's a world in which I become a poet and never marry or have a child, and there's a world in which I admit to my husband that I was never much of a poet but I do, it turns out, have a knack for real estate. There's a world in which I accrue a million followers and monetize my brand. There's a world in which the paramedics arrived in time to save Ethan's brother. And there's a world in which my daughter and her best friend called me for a ride home that night, instead of walking along the county road. But, if there are infinite worlds to consider, then think of how many ways I lose my daughter, too. There's a world in which that drunk driver hit *her*.

I don't believe in a world without regret, because regret is baked into every decision we make. Like the photon in the mirror, regret goes both right and left. I can't fix the planet for my daughter, and I can't hack the multiverse, either. All I can do is help her brave this one universe we find ourselves in.

Total bullshit, Ethan texts back, and I can't tell if he's reading my mind or missing the entire point.

#noregrets, he texts a second later, and I smile.

Years ago, after Indie introduced Ethan to hashtags, he started appending them verbally to conversation—"hashtag blessed," he'd say, after complimenting dinner—and even more so after Indie warned him off the habit. When Indie asked if he really had to wear cycling shorts in public, Ethan responded, "Hashtag no filter." She groaned dramatically like this caused her actual physical pain. "You don't even know what *no filter* means," she said. "Can't you just tell dad jokes?" Ethan pointed out that this was, in fact, the very essence of a dad joke, but she'd already returned to her phone.

I remember a poem by Dorianne Laux. I text the first lines to Ethan: *Regret nothing. Not the cruel novels you read to the end just to find out who killed the cook. / Not the insipid movies that made you cry in the dark, in spite of your intelligence, your sophistication.*

I hit Send and text him again: *#yolo.*

Yours? Ethan writes back, and I love him for this.

Just the hashtag, I say. I send him a link to a reading of the poem on YouTube.

A minute later, my phone rings and I drop it on the table, startled. It's Ethan.

"No one died," he says, as soon as I pick up.

Our old joke, because we called each other so rarely: Open with the reassurance. Dispel the fear. *Indie's fine.*

"I mean," he says. "Too many people died."

"Your brother died," I say. "I'm sorry."

"Your mom died," he says. "I'm sorry."

We are silent then, listening to each other breathe, and it feels like being held close. It feels like being understood, and I think that perhaps marriage, too, is believing in something you can't fathom.

"When Luke died, my mom couldn't stop crying," Ethan says eventually. "I couldn't bear it, her sadness, because I couldn't help her. It was like a black hole, sucking me in every time I got close. That's why I went back to college. But I should have stayed."

I remember the plumber in our house, the one who lost his mother, and then I think of all the cab drivers and car mechanics and post office clerks Ethan has connected with over the years, and I see it now: This is *his* response to the truth that nothing lasts. If anyone can leave us at any time, what does it matter if the connection is for twenty minutes or twenty years? The point is to try.

"You were still a kid," I say to him. "*Her* kid. She shouldn't have let you go."

"I couldn't bear your sadness," Ethan says. "You reminded me of her. I should have stayed."

He's not talking about the gym teacher's guest room; I understand this. He means our bedroom in the middle of the night, and me crying in the dark, his back turned.

"I shouldn't have let you go," I say.

A life can be split in two, but that doesn't mean it's broken—only that there is a first half and a second half; what comes first, and what comes after.

We hang up and I press Play on Dorianne Laux's poem, the link I just sent Ethan. The recording is by an anonymous English stage actor whose voice is both warm and steeped in a quiet understanding of loss. I would listen to this man read the Cheesecake

Factory's twenty-one page menu, and even that, I bet, would break my heart. The poet's words wash over me like holy water as I close my eyes and silently mouth the final stanza. *Relax*, the poem bids me.

Don't bother remembering any of it.
Let's stop here, under the lit sign
on the corner, and watch all the people walk by.

It is still dark out and I imagine seeing this town from a thousand feet up, the light from our kitchen window and the sign above the coffee shop pulsing like signal fires. The shortest day of the year, I remember, which means the longest night is already behind us.

Have a good day, I text my husband. *More tomorrow.*

chapter eighty-seven Indie

I'm eating breakfast when Mom calls the school and tells the secretary I'm home sick. I give her a look. I don't *feel* sick.

"Um," I say. "I think your mind-reading skills are a little rusty."

"Happy Birthday!" Mom says. "You get a mental health day."

"That's nice," I say. "But it would've been a whole lot nicer if you'd let me sleep in."

"That's called *Saturday*," Mom says, actually rolling her eyes. "Where's the fun in that?"

She's wearing denim overalls and a bright green trucker cap. I guess she's not going into the office either.

"Did you mean to dress like one of the Mario Brothers today?" I say. "Or was that just a happy accident?"

My parents agreed not to secretly tell the waitstaff to bring me a cake with candles when the three of us go out to dinner tonight. In return, I agreed not to boycott the day entirely. I guess Mom is going to milk this birthday agreement for all it's worth. I don't put up a fight, though, because the principal always announces student birthdays right after the Pledge each morning. If I go to school, people will fake-smile at me all day. Let them stare at my empty chair instead.

Mom texts Dad to remind him I won't be at school, then tells me to text Asher, too. Because nothing would ruin a day of playing hooky quite like a police APB.

Happy Birthday is a shit song, Asher texts back. *Listen to this instead.*

It's a Spotify link to "Dear Prudence" and another link to a video essay explaining the song's backstory.

I don't need the second link, though. Dad told me years ago how John Lennon wrote the song for a girl he met at an ashram. It was Lennon's way of asking, *Are you okay in there?* For weeks, Prudence wouldn't leave her hut or stop meditating. "Not even to hang out with The Beatles!" Dad said, aghast, although that was the part of the story I always found most impressive.

Mom and I stop in town to pick up sandwiches and cupcakes, and she makes me duck out of sight in the car, like we're starring in a remake of *Thelma and Louise.* Buddy presses his nose to the window in the back seat and whines until Mom returns, as if he's all alone in the world. I'm not *that* good at hiding, so maybe Buddy is kind of dumb? Or just really into Mom.

I listen to the song on my phone and wonder if anyone ever asked Prudence what she learned in that hut. Or did they just want her to come out to play?

The coffee shop is just across the road, and for a second I think I see Dad sitting at a table in the window, but then I realize it's already second period and he'll be at school by now. I wonder how long it will be before I bump into Dad randomly in his new life. Just accidentally, in the supermarket or something, and not because it's his turn to see me. Until I do, it's almost possible to believe he's making it all up—the new morning routine, the new facial hair, the gym teacher's guest room-slash-home gym. Like this species of *Dad* is just a case of mistaken identity. Remember how brontosaurus used to be a type of dinosaur, and then it wasn't?

"Pick a hike," Mom says as we pull out of town. She reaches into the back seat and rubs Buddy's head. He is drooling and carsick but somehow still looks happy to be here. "Any hike."

When I was a kid, I always needed to know whether our family hike was going to be an up-and-down hike, a loop, or just a there-and-back hike. There-and-back hikes were the *worst*, as far as I was concerned. Every step you took was a step you knew you'd have to retrace in order to get back to the car. It wasn't that I hated hiking—I actually liked it, though I never admitted this to my parents—it was more the concept of walking without a destination and then deciding, at some random point in time, to turn back again. It made the whole thing feel a little pointless. I liked hikes with definition: You reached the top of the hill, and then you knew you were halfway done. It was, quite literally, all downhill from there. Or, you hiked a loop, and every step out was also a step home. There was something poetic about a loop.

For my birthday, I pick my favorite up-and-down hike. There's a mountain with a fire tower on top, so you get to scale a peak *and* climb a Rapunzel tower. It's like a multi-tiered wedding cake.

The hike begins with a gentle slope, but the path is narrow and overgrown, so we walk in single file—Buddy, then Mom, then me. We don't say much. It's shady and damp here and the ground is brown and pulpy with fallen leaves. We used to come here in spring, when the woods were lush and the path was lined with ferns, because Dad liked to forage for fiddleheads. He'd collect them in the deep pockets of his hiking shorts and later sauté them in olive oil and lemon juice and serve them over zoodles. They really do look like the scroll on the neck of a violin, except way smaller, and nuclear green. Mom joked that every fiddlehead dish was a trust fall, because there's only one type of fern that's safe to eat. Dad used an app on his phone to identify the right ferns, and I guess it worked, because we never got violently ill after eating them.

Mom pauses for a sip of water. Neither of us is carrying the hiking water bladder with attached straw that Dad got each of us for Christmas, because (a) they're the nerdy backpacker equivalent of those beer-can hats dudes wear at football games, and (b) water bottles work just fine. Dad always insists on using his, though, even if he's only strolling a few miles.

Some people get dads who sip Coors Lite from cans on their heads, and others are born into water-bladder-carrying, fiddle-head-foraging families. Go figure. It's your starting point, I guess. Your baseline for what's normal. Parents are the context for the big question of your life: Where do you go from here? It's a question Maddy never got to answer.

In a clearing at the base of the fire tower we find two picnic tables, so we take off our packs and sit at one of them, across from each other.

"Do you know," Mom says, as she unwraps the sandwiches and opens a bag of SunChips, "when you were really little, we stopped for a picnic lunch during a hike and you said, 'These chips taste so good, I wish I could just keep eating them and never die.'"

"That's pretty dark."

Buddy is sitting under the table between us. I put some Sun-Chips in my hand and offer them to him.

"I don't think so." Mom shakes her head. "You weren't afraid of dying. You were like this miniature Zen monk. You'd found a moment that was worth staying in forever, and you just wanted the world to work around that."

"So, more like a miniature tyrant, then?"

Mom always gets nostalgic on my birthday. She already retold my birth story over breakfast. Her favorite part is how the nurse gave Dad a cup of ice chips and a little plastic spoon and told him to feed them to Mom whenever she asked. Apparently it wasn't until many weeks later that Dad realized the nurse only did this to help him feel necessary.

"Even during childbirth," Mom said to me this morning, "women work together to make sure men don't feel incompetent."

Buddy barks softly in the direction of the path, like he's clear-ing his throat, and Mom and I both turn to look. It's three guys I don't recognize, maybe a year or two older than me, I'm guessing from the high school the next town over. Apparently it's a good day to play hooky. They're all wearing blue jeans, white tees, and work boots. "Farm boys," Maddy would say. Her cousins go to that high school, and she told me that's what they call themselves. "It's their way of embracing the hick thing," she explained.

The guys take the other picnic table and each of them looks in our direction and touches the brim of his baseball cap as he sits. Maddy's cousins do this, too. "Straight out of the Redneck Book of Manners," she said once, which I immediately understood to be a joke I could never make myself. Maddy was my conduit to another world.

One of the guys pulls out his phone and starts playing country music. It's a song called "Don't Go City on Me," which I know because Maddy used to sing it sometimes, when she thought I was turning into my mom. Like when I posted a picture of a cow in my feed, or when I packed LaCroix in my school lunch. It wasn't always this way with me and Maddy, but I remember now: Sometime during middle school, she started to point out how our families were different. Not all the time, and usually framed as a joke, but often enough for me to realize she noticed *everything*, and maybe always had. The seventeen-dollar price tag on the bag of paleo granola in our pantry. The look on my mom's face when Maddy said she drank SunnyD for breakfast every morning. The glossy alumni mailings from Princeton and Brown stuck to our fridge with a SUPPORT LOCAL BOOKSTORES magnet. The dinner parties my parents hosted that her family was never invited to. It was Maddy who informed me that my parents clearly had help buying our house.

"You must have rich grandparents," she said one afternoon. We were sitting on opposite ends of my porch, trying to toss popcorn into each other's mouths. "Teachers don't live in houses with wraparound porches."

It sounded like something her dad would say.

I never asked my parents if this was true, because they don't like to talk about money. I figured Maddy was probably right, though, because Dad's parents live in a huge house in Connecticut, and whenever we visit, there are always people hanging around, doing stuff for them.

When I was a kid, I thought Maddy's house was way nicer than ours, because they have a double garage, which meant their cars never got covered with snow in winter. When I asked my parents why *we* didn't have a two-car garage—or any kind of garage, for that matter—Dad said, "Because our house is old." I asked if we could maybe get a new house one day, and they both made that *hmmm* sound parents use when they don't want to answer a question. Or when they've moved on from the conversation and are checking something on their phone, only half-listening to you.

The guys are singing along. Of course they know every word. Mom catches my eye and smiles.

If I asked Mom to tell me the unvarnished truth, would she say that I was always going to lose Maddy, one way or another? Maybe. Mom can be a bitch like that sometimes.

She'd be wrong, though. Mom was so focused on how Maddy's family was different from ours, she completely missed what held Maddy and me together. Take a piece of paper and draw a line down the middle. In one column, put all the secrets Maddy and I shared, all the days we spent doing everything together, all the hours we spent doing nothing. In the other, put a fancy bag of granola from our pantry and the BLUE LIVES MATTER sign from Maddy's front yard. No contest. Even if you added in Mom's thing with the Chief, whatever that was—a grease stain across the entire sheet of paper—I'd bet on our friendship every time.

Except, there will never be anything new to add to the Maddy-and-me column. Draw a line under the list and put a bow on it. The second column, meanwhile, will grow with every milestone I celebrate without my friend. Mom told me that remembering is how I keep Maddy. What she meant was, remembering is how I trap her in time, like an amber-preserved mosquito. Remembering sucks.

"Is this too loud?" The dude with the phone is talking to us. "We can turn it down if you want."

"No, no, we like it," Mom says. "We were about to climb the fire tower anyway."

A sign at the entrance to the tower informs us that a dog once plunged to its death here.

"Jeez," I say, reading it. "Buzzkill."

Mom loops Buddy's leash around one of the legs of the picnic bench.

"Would you boys mind keeping an eye on our dog while we climb?" Mom calls out. "We'll be quick."

"You *boys*?" I mutter under my breath.

Mom winks at me like this is an in-joke. I'm dying.

As we climb the tower, the music from the guy's phone fades to a tinny high hat.

"I can't believe you called them *you boys*," I mumble to my mom's butt, because she's a few steps above me. "It sounded like you were flirting."

"Who says I wasn't?"

"Gross, Mom."

"I'm kidding," Mom says, and then, after a beat: "They're totally not my type."

I don't reply because there are a shit ton of steps to climb, and I'm already out of breath. Also, since when did Mom start making dad jokes?

The fire tower is rickety and sways in the wind. I can't believe Mom considers the *fiddleheads* the risky part of this hike. It's like we're scaling the Drop Tower ride at the county fair, the entire structure dependent on some rusty bolts and a dude who is high as fuck.

By the time we reach the top, I can't hear the music at all. We're above the tree line here, and the canopy of hemlock trees below us looks like a trampoline, as if I could leap off the tower and bounce right up again.

I look out at the Catskills and imagine I'm searching for wildfires. What a job description: Forest seeks person to watch over the world, to look for warning signs that something is going terribly wrong. Would the lookouts just yell FIRE super loudly if they spotted one?

Mom asks what I'm thinking.

"I'm wondering if anyone ever stopped a fire because they spotted it from here," I say. "Or did it just make people feel better, to know someone was watching over the forest?"

I'm also thinking of Maddy's dad, of how safe and cozy I always felt when I saw him driving the fire truck around town, especially when he waved to me. It made me feel special to know the Chief was looking out for me, but he probably makes everyone feel that way. Who looks out for him, though? Maybe that's what Mom was trying to do.

"How many generations came and went while the trees below us kept doing their tree thing?" Mom says. "And yet, some guys built this spindly tower to prove they were in charge of the forest. Like, *Hey, we've got this*! Uh, no you don't."

"I don't feel like I'm in charge up here," I say. "I feel pretty insignificant."

"That's because you're not a guy," Mom says. "Men climb to feel like they've conquered something. Women climb to get a little perspective."

"Is that what you think about Dad? You think that's why he's so into hiking?"

Mom reaches out a hand toward me, pauses in mid-air, and then smooths my brow. I think she meant to tuck my hair behind my ears; that's what she used to do when she was thinking of an answer. She forgot I have no hair, even though she was looking right at me.

"No, sweetie," she says. "Dad's not that kind of man. Lucky us."

We both turn to look out at the view again, and we're quiet for a few minutes.

"Last time I visited my mom's grave, I shooed away a squirrel," Mom says eventually, as if we'd just been talking about squirrels and graves and this isn't the most random thing in the world. "I didn't like how it sat there eating a nut, as if the gravestone was just another place to sit, no different from a rock or a tree. I was so *mad* at the squirrel." She laughs softly, shaking her head. "But I think I get it now," she continues, "what you were trying to explain to me the other day. How we're all made of the same molecules. The gravestone, the squirrel, my mom. I mean, by the end, my mom was barely a person anymore. Everything that made her *her* had disappeared. She could have been a squirrel. Or a tree. But I still loved her." She takes a shaky breath, like she's trying not to cry. "The world doesn't belong to us, you know? We belong to the world."

I turn to face her. She doesn't *look* any different. She looks like she's discussing where we should go for dinner tonight.

"But doesn't that *blow your mind*?" I say.

I think of Asher. Of how he thought the text bubble thing was *pretty cool*. If this is what it means to grow up, then I don't see the point.

"Do you remember the argument we had on the train that time?" Mom asks. "On our way back from the climate march in the city?"

I remember. I was confused that day, and also pissed off, because the adults seemed so calm. They carried signs about the rising seas and the warming planet, and they chanted slogans and demanded change, but no one was acting like the forest was on fire. They just sipped their cold brew coffee and took photos of their favorite signs to post online.

I nod.

"And do you remember what I said?"

I nod again. She told me, yes, we have to save the sea turtles and plant a billion trees and stop stripping the planet of its natural resources, but also, we have to buy groceries and make dinner and load the dishwasher. "We can't stop being human," she said that day. "We just have to be *better* humans." I told her that if this was adults trying their hardest, then humans were the endangered species. But, hey, let's drink more cold brew. It's everyone *else's* caffeine addiction that leads to massive deforestation in Brazil, right?

I remember, too, how quiet Maddy got on the train while I argued with Mom. She just stared out the window and acted like she wasn't with us.

"Maybe you're right," Mom says now, gesturing toward the trees. "Maybe none of this is real. But it's the one illusion we get, and sometimes it's really beautiful."

I turn my eyes to the horizon and try to remember what it felt like, to care so much about every tree. Mom takes my hand and rubs it along her arm.

"Feel that!" Mom says. "This view is literally giving me goosebumps. So, no, I don't think it's a waste of time to be a person in this world."

"Dad says chimps feel the same way about nature," I say.

"I'm sure he's right," Mom says and smiles. "So I guess it's not a waste of time to be a chimp, either."

She gives my hand a squeeze.

"I think you're trying really hard to find a way to stay in this world." She squeezes again, like she's sending a separate message to my body, this one in Morse code. "I just want you to know that I see this, and I'm sorry I didn't see it before."

The Guy says that the moment you start *trying* to do anything, you've already failed.

"You don't have to worry," I say, pulling my hand out of hers. "I'm giving up all that stuff. I got it all wrong."

Mom places a hand on my arm.

"Look at me," she says. "Please. I want you to hear this: *You* decide what to believe. Don't let anyone take that away from you.

Not me, not your dad, and certainly not some douchebag guru named Brandon."

The railing seems suddenly too low, and I feel dizzy.

"I miss her so much," I say, sinking into a squat.

I picture these words ringing out across the forest with no answer, like the saddest bird call in the world. *Endling*, I say to myself. Dad taught me the word; it means the last known individual of a species. When an endling dies, the species is extinct.

"I know you miss her," Mom says softly.

"I miss her every day that's she not here," I say. "Every time I wake up, it's one more day without her in it. It's another day when I don't see her. It's a day when we don't eat lunch together or walk into town after school. It's too many days. And now I'm fifteen and those days are turning into months, and then those months will turn into years. When will it stop?"

Mom crouches down next to me and puts an arm around my shoulders, pulling me into a hug. She says nothing, and I know why.

It will stop when I start to forget the details of Maddy. Her snort-laugh, her locker combination, her favorite quotes. Her devotion to cursive handwriting, years after our teachers stopped insisting on it. The way she doodled all over the covers of my composition notebooks, the way her curly hair tickled my neck when we watched ASMR videos together in the hammock. The way she'd text me on weekend mornings to wake me up, because she'd read online that getting up at the same time every day made you smarter and prettier. The way she made me feel like I belonged.

"Screw that guy," I say, and my eyes fill with tears. "He made me believe he could take Maddy away from me."

"He's an asshole with good hair and nice teeth," Mom says. "He thinks he deserves the things that come easily to him."

What is it with moms liking nice teeth?

"Guys like that rule the world," she continues. "But only if we let them."

"I get it." I wipe my eyes with the sleeve of my shirt. "No need to rub it in."

"That's not what I'm saying. Brandon's a privileged white guy who plundered three thousand years of Eastern traditions. He added a bunch of swear words and then took credit for the whole thing. Basically, he's Christoper Columbus in yoga pants. Look, there'll always be bad people who say true things. But there are good people, too. I bet you there's a kickass Buddhist nun somewhere out there who's a hundred years old and swims laps every day and speaks the same truths. Except she's not in it for the chicks."

I still can't believe his name is Brandon. I don't know what I was expecting, but not that. Also: Who still says *chicks*? Apparently my mom.

"Do you think the nun throws ecstatic dance parties?"

"Maybe not," Mom says. "But if she did, I would totally go."

I look down through the metal grating that makes up the tower floor.

"Did you bring a poem?" I say, poking my fingers through the grating.

"A poem, *moi*?" Mom says, hamming up the false modesty. Have I mentioned what a dork she is?

Mom used to write out her favorite poems on scrap paper and bring them along on our family hikes. She would read aloud to us when we stopped for a picnic lunch, although I suspect she was mostly reciting by heart. I often caught her looking off into the trees when she was supposedly "reading." Maybe she thought reciting a poem was too showy.

"I forgot to bring one," she says.

"Mom, I totally know you have them memorized."

She gives me one of those annoying mom looks, her eyes shiny and proud, like I just won a Nobel Prize or something. Why do moms do that?

"Don't make it weird," I say. "I just feel like hearing a poem."

She closes her eyes, like she's googling her brain.

"Mary Oliver seems right today," Mom says, as if she just thought of this, as if she didn't say, every single time we hiked, that Mary Oliver is the poet laureate of our nature walks. "*When I am among the trees, especially the willows and the honey locust—*"

Mom's phone chirps and she immediately whips it out of her pocket. I pull a face at her. She's the one who gets mad at me and Dad for checking our phones during family hikes.

"What?" Mom says, faux-innocent, opening her messages app. "It's your birthday, it could be for you."

She hands me the phone triumphantly. Her screen shows a text message from Dad, in all caps: *PLEASE SHOW THIS TO INDIE.*

"Huh," I say.

It's a panda pickup line meme: A photo of a panda chilling on a tree stump with a beer bottle photoshopped between its paws. In this version, the panda is quoting Joey from *Friends*: "How YOU doin'?"

"Huh," Mom repeats, and shrugs.

I'm about to hand the phone back to her when it rings loudly, vibrating in my hand. It's Dad.

"Hey," I say into the phone. "What's up with the panda?"

"You said no presents," Dad says. "So I got you a meme."

"A panda pickup line meme," I say. "A little weird."

"Is that a thing?" Dad says. "I had no idea. I just googled *funny panda meme.* I read an interesting article about pandas this morning, and I wanted to talk to you about it."

"Of course you did."

"Did you know that until the 1860s, a bunch of reputable scientists thought pandas were a myth? They publicly ridiculed people who believed in them."

"I did not know that, Dad. Thanks for the heads up."

"I can see how it happened," Dad says. "If you think about it, unicorns make a lot more sense than pandas."

"I guess they do."

"And it got me thinking. There's so much we know to be true today that would have sounded nuts a few hundred years ago, even to the smartest scientists in the world. Take quantum physics. That *still* sounds nuts to me. And you'd have to be a complete moron to think we're currently at the pinnacle of all human knowledge. Am I making sense?"

"Sort of," I say. "But we're at the *pinnacle* of the fire tower right now, so I should probably go. Can we talk later?"

"I'm almost done," Dad says. "What I'm trying to say is, there could be more pandas out there. Not actual pandas, but metaphorical pandas. Ideas that seem magical or crazy but that turn out to be true. What do I know? I'm just a high school social studies teacher. Anyway, that's all I wanted to say. Don't give up on the pandas."

"Got it," I say. "Save the pandas."

"See you at dinner?"

"Yeah," I say. "See you at dinner."

I hand the phone back to Mom. She gives me a questioning look and I smile.

"Just Dad being Dad," I say. "The panda was a metaphor."

She stands and puts her phone in her back pocket, then offers me a hand.

"Ready to return to solid ground?" Mom says.

I think of the first video I found on my own after Maddy died, the first link I couldn't send her because she was gone. We are all waves on the ocean, the monk said, and like waves we return to the ocean in the end. We are not separate from the body of water. If I crest high, if I crash to the shore, I am still ocean, down to the last drop. When I watched this video, I was so sure I was just salt water, I was so determined to *feel* this, I lost sight of the wave. The awesomeness of a wave and also the plain fact of it. She is ocean and I am wave and we are both water, but for now I am still rising and falling with the moon.

I take Mom's hand and let her pull me to my feet.

"Ready."

book club
discussion questions

1. Grief and Loss

How does Indie's experience of grief differ from that of the adults in the novel? What coping mechanisms do they each develop? Do any of these approaches feel "wrong" to you?

2. The Illusion of Control

"How does a parent fix the world?" Kate asks. The characters frequently confront the idea that life is chaotic and unpredictable. How do they each attempt to control or make sense of the things that happen to them? Does the novel offer any comfort?

3. Intergenerational Divides

Kate and Ethan struggle with how to support Indie in her grief. Kate and Ethan's relationships with their own mothers provide a contrasting perspective. What does the novel suggest about the limits and expectations of parenthood?

4. Living in the Digital Age

If You Lived Here is a curated version of Kate's life for the public. How does Kate's online persona affect her real-life relationships? How does the novel explore the tension between living authentically and performing for an audience? Does it offer any answers?

5. The Story of a Marriage

Early in the novel, Kate imagines telling her clients the ugly truth about their future together. Later, as her own marriage falls apart, she muses that "a stable marriage depends on ordinariness." Meanwhile, Indie describes her parents as "marching stiff as Lego people, not equipped to make a turn," and "like two customer service chatbots stuck in an infinite conversation loop." What do these moments tell us about Kate and Ethan's marriage? How does their marriage—and Kate's view of it—evolve?

6. The Nature of Belief

How do the characters grapple with different belief systems, particularly in the face of grief? How are these concepts—belief, faith, religion, spirituality, meaning—challenged and reimagined?

7. Consciousness and the Self

How does Indie's understanding of consciousness and the self impact her grieving process? How does her understanding of these issues evolve? Overall, would you say that her exploration of consciousness helped or harmed her?

8. Community vs. Isolation

This novel explores the complexities of small-town life, community, and belonging. In what ways do the characters experience isolation despite living in a tight-knit community? What role does class struggle play?

9. What About the Men?

Ethan often seems distant or detached from Kate and Indie's grief. Why is he unable to connect with them? And why does Kate find herself drawn to Kevin?

10. Dual Narrative

Indie and Kate's relationship is at the heart of this book. Why do you think the author used a dual narrative to tell their story? Is one of them a more reliable narrator than the other?

poetry credits

Maggie Smith's poem "Good Bones" is quoted in the epigraph, and also in Chapter 10, when Kate visits Ethan's mom's house. This poem is from *Good Bones: Poems*, copyright © 2017 by Maggie Smith. Reprinted with the permission of The Permissions Company, LLC, on behalf of Tupelo Press, tupelopress.org.

The Julie Cadwallader Staub poem that reminds Kate of her mother, quoted in Chapter 38, is "Remember" from *Wing Over Wing*. Copyright © 2019 by Julie Cadwallader Staub. Used by permission of Paraclete Press, paracletepress.com.

The Robert Browning poem, "Now," which Kate recites to Ethan the morning after their wedding, in Chapter 44, is from *Asolando: Fancies and Facts*, published by Smith, Elder & Co., 1890. It is in the public domain.

The Joy Harjo poem that Kate remembers in Chapter 52, as she sits at the kitchen island, is "Perhaps the World Ends Here" from *The Woman Who Fell From the Sky,* copyright © 1994 by Joy Harjo. Used by permission of W. W. Norton & Company, Inc., wwnorton.com.

The Rilke poem that Indie learns about from The Guy in Chapter 59 is "Gott spricht zu jedem . . . /God speaks to each of us . . . " from *Rilke's Book of Hours: Love Poems to God* by Rainer

Maria Rilke, translated by Anita Barrows and Joanna Macy, translation copyright © 1996 by Anita Barrows and Joanna Macy. Used by permission of Riverhead, an imprint of Penguin Publishing Group, a division of Penguin Random House LLC.

The poem Indie remembers her mom quoting in Chapter 77 is "One Art" by Elizabeth Bishop, from *The Complete Poems 1926–1979*. Copyright © 1979, 1983 by Alice Helen Methfessel. Used by permission of Farrar, Straus & Giroux, LLC, us.macmillan.com/fsg.

The Dorianne Laux poem that Kate texts Ethan in Chapter 86 is "Antilamentation" from *The Book of Men*. Copyright © 2011 by Dorianne Laux. Used by permission of W. W. Norton & Company, Inc., wwnorton.com.

The Mary Oliver poem that Kate recites in Chapter 87 is "When I Am Among the Trees." Reprinted by the permission of The Charlotte Sheedy Literary Agency as agent for the author. Copyright © 2006, 2010, 2017 by Mary Oliver with permission of Bill Reichblum.

further reading

I went down my own rabbit hole while researching Indie's discoveries about consciousness and the self. If you want to know more, I highly recommend *Conscious: A Brief Guide to the Fundamental Mystery of the Mind* by Annaka Harris. It is concise, clear, and engaging, and it has the most beautiful cover I've ever seen. I also listened to hundreds of hours of Sam Harris. Other great thinkers on the topic: Tara Brach, David Chalmers, Daniel Dennett, Thich Nhat Hanh, Dan Harris, and Alan Watts. Or you could just ask my husband, Rob Tourtelot, who actually walks the walk. None of them, for the record, has any designs on being a guru, and any misreading of their work is either mine or Indie's.

acknowledgments

Thank you to Caryn Karmatz Rudy, for having faith in this novel, and for helping me transform it into something I believed in, too. Brooke Warner and everyone at She Writes Press—you restored my faith in the publishing industry. Thank you to my early readers: Miriam Altshuler, Chloe and Megan Bunt, Lucy Barzun Donnelly, Josh Ferris, Avery Gilbert, Chris Jones, Nora Kindley, Lorelei Sharkey, and Nicole Tourtelot. Wyatt Kleitsch gifted me the Minkles, and always spilled the tea. Thank you to the Guiltiest Remnants, my Spice Girls, the Rhinecliff Menoposse, Amy Zemser, and Fauzia Burke. Thank you to my parents, who waited so patiently for me to write a book they didn't have to hide in polite company. My sisters, Becky and Hannah, are simply the best (better than all the rest). Everyone should be so lucky to grow up in a family like mine. Evie and Milo put up with my public displays of mom dancing, and they're also my first readers each morning. Thank you for appreciating my Post-It notes, especially on the days when I managed to write nothing else. And most of all to Rob, who said I could, and then made sure I did, and who read this novel first, last, and a hundred times in between, making it immeasurably better each time: Thank you for everything.

about the **author**

Photo credit: Cleo Sullivan

Emma Tourtelot is the co-author of eight nonfiction books about sex and relationships, and has penned regular columns for *New York*, *Glamour*, and *The Guardian*, among others. She was also the co-creator of Nerve Personals. After being a sex advice writer for almost two decades—as one half of Em & Lo—she is now a middle school librarian. This is her first novel. She lives in the Hudson Valley with her husband and two teenage children.

Connect with the author on
Instagram @emmatourtelot or at
www.emmatourtelot.com.

Looking for your next great read?

We can help!

Visit www.shewritespress.com/next-read
or scan the QR code below for a list
of our recommended titles.